The Great Dragoll War of Venosta
Book 2
A Novel by
Fred J. Hoyle Sr.

I0618776

ISBN-13: 978-578-56933-8

The Great Dragoll War of Venosta

Prologue

The blue dragons of Venosta won their battle with hunters from civilization. Fuzzy's childhood friends Cap and Jackson fought by their side throughout the warfare. The victory was emotionally costly for the young dragons, whose hopes and dreams were dashed at a time when they were maturing. Forced into a life-and-death encounter at their cavern, they saw members of their beloved den perish in front of them.

Their leaders, Fuzzy and Lester, have told the den that they must migrate to a new cavern in hopes of escaping further confrontations with man's civilization. This is the only way they can once again live like dragons.

Three dragons left before the battle began. They are making ready a new cavern far to the north. When they return the migration will begin.

The sun has set three times since the battle ended. Cap and Jackson are on their way home. Mason Smith, the man who assembled the hunters, waits in Water Town for the hunting party that will never return.

Chapter 1

The wilderness lies dark and peaceful tonight, except for the base of the plateau below. Lester is standing on the ledge in front of the entrance to his cavern with wind whipping across his brow. Fuzzy is in deep thought as he stands beside him.

"Why do you frown as you look down on our young ones celebrating our victory?" asks Lester.

"It troubles me that they don't respect the dead, or even feel the haunting of the men's spirits like you and I would. The younger dragons appear to regard the dead men as nothing more than pests needing to be rid from the wilderness."

"Fuzzy, you are very wise, but the battle has not been over long. I don't think this should bother you very much."

Fuzzy cocks his head slightly. "It bothers me a lot. Have they forgotten about the brave brothers Cap and Jackson, and how much they helped us? They risked their lives when they came to our den during battle. I'm afraid this generation will feel contempt for all humans and civilization. When we were their age, we just wanted to be left alone in our hiding places. The feeling of gratification they glean from winning this battle may end up making them aggressive, and they will thirst for this feeling again. Look at them."

Breathing rapidly with smiles on every young face, the youthful dragons chase each other sailing in and out between trees and landing on the men's wagons. Fuzzy drops his head, then looks into Lester's eyes.

"That is the look of euphoria," says Fuzzy.

"Don't worry, Fuzzy. We'll be gone soon."

Fuzzy looks back down on the younger dragons.

"No. Leaving will not end the way these young ones feel about mankind. I must talk to them this evening."

When the young dragons return to the entrance, Fuzzy is waiting for Lee and Kim.

"I would like to talk with you about the tragic turn of events that has interrupted your lives," he says.

"What's really on your mind, father?" replies Lee, cocking his head.

"The other young dragons look up to you and your sister and respect your judgment. It appears your friends like the fact that you two are fuzzy."

"Father, you have proven to the den that your appearance is the new look of leadership. The younger dragons accept it," replies Lee happily.

Fuzzy mulls over his son's words. "Then, as a proven leader, let me share some wisdom with you. As young, respected members of our den it's important that you show respect for the dead men. We at least owe that much to Cap and Jackson. It's not right to express joy in the hunter's deaths. The Creator of dragons and men alike takes no pleasure in seeing harm come to any of His creations, and I feel the other members of the den will respect you more if you show wisdom, self-control, and respect for all forms of life."

Lee squints as he looks Fuzzy in the eye. "I respect your opinion, father, but things changed when our den experienced the sorrow of needless death. We all saw mankind bring this upon us and themselves."

"Kim, do you feel the same as your brother?"

"I don't know. I need time to think," she replies with a slight grimace.

"Please promise me that revenge is not on your minds. Revenge will breed revenge. You can live in peace for a long time in our new home, if you just move on."

Lee and Kim bow in respect, but Fuzzy can tell they aren't convinced.

Fuzzy looks up and sees Nom peering at him. Nom instantly cuts his eyes away. He's standing close enough to hear everything, but he's not interested in talking about anything Fuzzy has to say. Fuzzy ponders his demeanor and feels the growing pain and hate in Nom's heart. He is the son of Leonard, and Fuzzy can tell he will never rest until he exacts revenge for his father's death.

<>

Cap and Jackson ride out of the wilderness and smile when unshaded sunlight warms their faces for the first time in days. They gallop along the last part of the trail as they head straight for the barn at their homestead. They tremble with excitement as they saddle fresh horses.

"I can't wait to hold Janice close and make her wonder if I'm ever going to let her go," says Cap, pulling his saddle strap tight.

Jackson hurries to finish saddling his horse and hops on. "I know mom and dad are worried sick, and they need to see us, but I can only give them a few moments. My heart is aching to hold Sandra again!"

They trot to the porch, dismount, and bound up the steps where they ring the porch bell. Inez comes running from inside. Her face bursts into a tearful smile and she embraces her boys.

"We are safe and all our families are safe again," says Jackson. She hugs them again. In the distance, Miles and Uncle Matt sound like a stampede as they run toward the house. They leap onto the porch and hug the boys as tears flow. The brothers soon pull back.

"We love and missed you terribly, but our hearts won't let us wait another second to find our brides! Please forgive us," says Cap.

Jackson hugs his mom quickly one more time and dashes off the porch. He takes one big hop and lands on his horse. Cap does the same and dust swirls as they tear into the trail.

At the Brittain farm, the cousins have no idea that their husbands are in full gallop toward them. Today is candle day and the cabin smells of honey. They pause to stand back and enjoy their handiwork. The candles are golden in color and are gathered in bunches. They gently lay them in baskets and head for the root cellar where they talk as they carefully place the candles on a shelf.

"I worry more every day," says Sandra wiping a tear that threatens to roll down her cheek.

Janice musters a smile. "Our husbands have not been gone long enough for us to start worrying." They lean toward each other and gently hug in the dim light as tears slide down their cheeks. Janice composes herself first, takes Sandra's hand and they quietly walk back to the kitchen. Homer is there to greet them with a playful bark when they enter, and then rambles back to his favorite spot next to the fire. But before he can settle, his head pops up and he springs to his feet. His claws spin on the wood floor as he darts toward the front door.

Janice raises her eyebrows. "I hear horses." Her heart leaps into her throat.

"Please let it be Cap and Jackson!" shouts Sandra as they run toward the door.

Homer is barking wildly, leaping up and down with tail wagging.

Sandra reaches the door, flings it open, and tears outside. She places a hand over her mouth and gasps. "It is them coming at a gallop!" She is bouncing excitedly as she bounds off the porch with Janice right behind her.

When the women are close, Cap and Jackson pull their horses' reigns abruptly and slide to the ground before they've stopped, almost tumbling. The couples collide in desperate hugs. They cling to each other, not wanting to let go.

"We need to tie our horses," whispers Cap.

Janice releases him and lets him tie the reins.

"I can't survive going through this ever again," says Janice, pulling two chairs close together so she and Cap can sit on the porch. Jackson and Sandra follow.

Buck catches a glimpse of the couples and rushes from his shop. He jumps up the porch stairs, and tears fill his eyes as he hugs Cap.

"Is it over?" he asks. The brothers' broad smiles give him the happy reply.

"I have worried as much about you as I would if it had been Janice and Sandra out there in the wilderness," he says tearfully.

"Wipe your happy tears away father," says Janice as she hands him her handkerchief.

Flavie is standing in the doorway, soaking in all the happiness of this beautiful moment, thankful her daughter's husband has returned from battle.

<>

With the new cavern ready, three young dragons are returning to inform their den that it is time to begin the migration. They are waking on the second morning of their return trip. The air is cool and crisp as the morning sun hangs below the horizon casting a pink glow in the eastern sky. They are happy and excited. Before the sun finishes its journey to the west, they will be back with their families.

Shim rises first. Vic and Tee are awake, but the grass pressed under them is warm and beacons them to linger. Yesterday they flew too long and too fast. The need to return to their loved ones overrode their self-control, and they were exhausted before the day was done.

"It is time to rise and fly my fellow den brothers," states Shim seeing that Vic and Tee are awake.

"I would like to take the lead today. We're too close now to be in a rush," says Vic.

Shim closes his eyes and smiles. "That sounds great to me. Today I am only interested in one thing: hugging my son."

Vic stretches his legs and wings, leans forward, and hops into the air. He spreads his wings wide while tucking his front legs tightly to his body. He sets a pace of one powerful flap every few seconds, and soon they are all in rhythm. The wilderness canopy drifts along below them. Shim is to the left behind Vic, and Tee is to the right making a V formation. Vic slowly swerves left, then right, and returns to the original path. Shim and Tee know that means: he sees the plateau ahead. A moment later, Vic slows to a hover and his wings flap nervously as he treads the air looking cautiously at the forest in front of the cavern entrance.

"Something is wrong." The dragons dive, darting toward the base of the plateau at full speed, they see a scary scene unfolding. Things that only could have come from civilization lay mangled in the weeds, and their imaginations explode. Their hearts race as they study the woods around the wreckage. They land and tremble as they examine the battleground.

"This is the work of men. But where are they?" Shim's eyes dart toward the surrounding woods. "I don't see any movement," he says.

"I fear the battle is over," replies Tee, with a long face. The stench of death wisps by in a gentle puff of wind and strikes fear in their hearts. There's no way of knowing if that smell is of men or dragons.

"We must be careful! Men may be hiding in the woods watching us or possibly waiting to ambush us in our cavern," says Vic.

"I will go to the entrance. You two find a safe place to hide and wait until I call for you," says Shim. He flaps furiously, anxiously peering around. He longs to hear a reassuring call or catch a glimpse of his den as he approaches the entrance. Shim and Tee hold their breath as he disappears over the ledge.

Fearful minutes gnaw at Vic and Tee's guts as the putrid stench of rotting flesh surrounds them and strange sounds in the forest become unnerving. Tee moves so close to Vic that they touch.

"Ureeeeee!" echoes from above.

"That sounds like Lester," says Vic taking a breath of relief.

Their fear fades as they ascend to the entrance. As their heads top the ledge, they see Shim and Lester standing together with the rest of the den quietly watching.

"What happened here? Is the battle won?" asks Vic, with piercing eyes.

"It is over for now," says Lester. "We rejoice to see you three are home! We have lost four wonderful dragons. Now that you are here, it is only right that the first thing we do is gather at the cremation pit and honor their sacrifice for our den."

The den quietly and solemnly walks to the ledge, and one by one they sail to the pit where they land and circle new ashes. Vic, Shim, and Tee stand tearfully next to Fuzzy and Lester. A breeze stirs the soot lying in a heap at the bottom of the pit. They experience their first taste of grief for their fallen brothers.

Lester's grief rekindles. "We humbly honor Auh! Leonard! Spar! Rah!" He speaks loudly and passionately and pauses after each name. Then he is quiet. After several moments of silence, the den ambles back to the cavern. Vic, Shim, and Tee stay. With their eyes closed they relive the good times they shared with their fallen friends. When a feeling of peace returns, they sail high above the pit and drift back to the entrance.

Fuzzy and Lester are waiting. The den stands nearby.

"Tell us about the battle," says Vic looking at Fuzzy.

The den moves in closer and Fuzzy tells the story as it will be passed on to future generations. It tells of the love, valor, and sacrifices that every dragon gave for the den. It ends with the sacrifice made by two young men and their idea that saved the dragons.

Fuzzy pauses to emphasize his resolve. "We owe our lives to these two men, and all of you must remember that neither they nor their families will ever be harmed by dragons."

Vic, Shim, and Tee are awash in happy and sad emotions as they head to their special places with their families.

<><>

Most of the dragons are settling in for the night as a cool breeze drifts into the cavern. The sun has diminished to a red glow behind the trees, and eleven young dragons have stolen away to the ghost camp.

Standing in front of a mangled crossbow, Gus and Nom draw the attention of the others. They are confident as they speak to eager ears filled with young and restless energy.

"We are all victims of the evil that mankind spreads in the name of civilization. Men come to the wilderness--our home--to take or do whatever they desire. It makes no difference to them if it's our lives or our hides. They do whatever they please for the excitement it gives them or for silver!" yells Gus.

He pauses and his audience eagerly awaits. Their anger and need for revenge grow as Nom quickly takes command. "Our fathers died needlessly! Look at man's evil creations all around us, that we have crushed. These things have no other purpose than to kill dragons. We must do everything in our power to stop mankind's advancement."

"Yaheeee, yaheee!" the group cheers wildly.

Gus steps back up and waits until the cheering stops. "We should not have to pick up our young and old and run to a new cavern. Man has no right to take this piece of wilderness and turn it into his civilization. If we do nothing, how long will it be before we look out from our new cavern and see another hunting party at its base? Are we always going to run away like cowards?"

The group cheers even louder as they are incited. The sound drifts in the heavy evening air rising over the ledge and into the cavern. Listening from above, Lester and Fuzzy look at each other with sad eyes.

"We have no choice but to try and stop this new trouble before they drag all of us into something even worse," says Fuzzy. They quietly move to the ledge and glide down to the camp undetected.

Lear, another of the young dragons speaks out. "I do not dispute what has been said, but we need time to heal our wounded hearts before we take action that we might regret later."

Victor pushes him to the side. "I respect Lear's opinion, but there is no doubt that mankind will take advantage of the time we take to let our hearts heal. They will be building weapons and preparing to return with an even bigger hunting party," he responds.

Gus's face turns red. "We must deliver some pain to their civilization! They deserve to suffer because of what they have done to us," he shouts out over the group.

Nom starts up again, "I say we attack Blade Town before we leave. It is small and close to the wilderness. With a surprise attack, there is little chance that any of us will be wounded."

Lee raises his wings to stop the ranting. "Look at us! We are too young for this. We must wait for our time to take control of the den. Until then we will study mankind to learn its weaknesses, and one day we will come back and take our cavern back."

Fuzzy's heart sinks. Hearing his son talk about waging war on humans sends chills down his spine.

Lester's face turns red and he rushes into the light. "Young fools! Have you gone mad?" he shouts.

"You can't just go on a killing spree. Remember the men who saved us? Some men are kind. If you kill one innocent man, we will lose the respect of the ones who trust us. They will regroup, unite, and build even more terrible machines of death."

Lee, Gus, and Nom say nothing. They lift into the air and disappear into the night. The others are quiet and slowly return to the cavern.

Lester and Fuzzy are left alone feeling a sadness caused by things over which they have no control.

Chapter 2

The sky is brightening even though the sun is still hidden below the horizon. The wilderness is already alive with the songs of birds greeting another day. The chill of the night is melting, and Lester tries to find a spot where the rays of sunlight can warm him. He shivers. They're not bright enough to be of any help. He turns and loudly calls, "Ureeeee!" It echoes down the passageways, and in a moment the den begins to file out.

Gus shuffles to Nom's side as they come out of the cavern. "I'm not going to follow leaders that run and hide much longer," he says.

"It bothers me, too, but we need time to figure out what to do. We do not have enough following from the others to do anything," replies Nom. "Time is on our side," replies Gus, nodding in Lee's direction.

The den gathers around Lester and Fuzzy.

"Fellow den members, it is a sad day. But a day on which we'll begin building a new future where we can all live in peace and prosperity. We must unite in the journey ahead as we travel to our new cavern," announces Lester.

Sadness creeps over the den. Lester waits for discussion. But no one speaks.

"Today we will prepare to leave. Tomorrow morning we will begin the journey to our new cavern."

"Wait, I wish to speak." The voice is that of Mona, Leonard's mate. She steps forward. "I have lived a good full life in this cavern. Like most of you, I would love to live out the rest of my life here. But we must be brave for our young ones, and I look forward to starting a new life in peace. Leonard loved and died for this den, and I know his spirit and all the spirits of our ancestors will go with us where ever we end up."

Nom comes forward as she speaks and stands next to his mother. He is calm and has an air of confidence as he speaks.

"I, too have enjoyed living in this cavern, and I vow to return one day to reclaim what is rightfully ours. The other young dragons and I will push back civilization and inflict pain on them much greater than what we have felt! The wilderness will be safe for us once again!"

Mona gasps. Fuzzy and Lester struggle to remain calm.

Lester raises his wings to demand quiet. He looks at Fuzzy. "Wise old friend; you always know what to say in a situation like this. Please speak to the young dragons."

Fuzzy feels emotions churning deep inside as he steps forward. He squints as he glares into the eyes of the young dragons one by one, penetrating their barrier.

"If revenge is what you bring back to spread from this cavern, revenge is what will surround you until you are sick of the word. The son or daughter of any man you kill will never rest until they kill you, and so on and so on, back and forth until no man or dragon is left. Only with the death of all of us or all men will the chain of revenge ever end!"

The young dragons say no more. Everyone is quiet.

"We close the entrance for good in the morning and depart for a new life," says Lester bowing solemnly to the den.

<>

The sun is barely above the horizon shining like a bright orange ball. Little dragons scamper after each other oblivious to the emotions festering in the adults around them. The den is placing the last stones that will seal the entrance. Those who are too old to carry stones wipe tears as they remember their past. The stronger ones labor away, their minds set on building a new future. For Lester, many sleepless nights have passed worrying about this day. He takes a deep breath and smiles when the last stone is in place. A cool breeze sweeps over the den as if attempting to blow away their anxiety.

Vic steps forward. "I will lead. Shim and Tee will be in the back watching for any trouble."

He looks to the beautiful blue sky and with powerful wings digs into the air. As he lifts off the ledge, the others follow. Most of them take a deep breath and gaze at the countryside, taking one last look at the view they have enjoyed all their lives, then lean forward and begin their journey.

The strongest dragons cling to youngsters nestled in their arms. The old dragons struggle to fly as fast as the rest of the den. They suffer even from the start and hope they can make it to the new cavern. Shim and Tee wait until the last of the den is well into flight before lifting into the air. Immediately they realize they will be flying much slower than they're accustomed. The slow progress of the den affirms their fears of how difficult the task ahead really is.

Gus and Nom stay close together.

"I have been watching the sky to the west and I feel energy in the air. A storm is brewing. This is not a good thing to be happening with all of us out here with no cavern for shelter," says Gus.

Two hours later, two of the oldest dragons are so far behind they have almost lost sight of their den mates. The den, in need of rest, descends and lands in a beautiful meadow near a stream.

Shim moves up to Seth and Lena, who are still in the air, but struggling to land. He looks into Seth's eyes. They are cloudy and full of pain. Seth takes a deep breath, stops flapping his wings, and spirals to the ground crashing with a bone crushing thud.

Lena lands, stumbling and disoriented. She doesn't respond when the other dragons try to comfort her. Her breathing grows jerky and deep. Her eyes turn glassy. The den fills with anguish as they watch her take her last breath.

"Wiiiiii!" wails the den in waves of sadness while Lester, Fuzzy, Vic, Shim, and Tee meet to decide what to do.

"We must do what we have never done before. We must render the bodies of these two beloved members of our den to dust out here far from our cremation pit."

The den hears their discussion and they quietly disappear into the woods to gather wood. Soon the mound is piled high and the bodies of Seth and Lena are placed with respect on top.

Lester spews the first flames. One by one, the den joins him until the fire roars and the burning wood crackles.

He slowly walks to Vic. "A storm is building in the west. We will have to find a place to protect our den."

"I will look for a safe place," replies Vic with tears still in his eyes.

Lester walks away, allowing Vic to take control. Vic wipes his eyes and begins the journey with a feeling of anxiousness.

The wind steadily picks up taking more of everyone's energy. Thunder faintly rumbles in the distance. Fear sweeps over the den as they watch the approaching storm. Fuzzy and Lester move up beside Vic. All three are searching for the best place to take shelter.

"I see a place!" shouts Vic. Seconds later, he points his head down and descends rapidly barely missing a stone ledge that stands high above a sheer rock wall that drops to a meadow situated on the banks of a river.

Once on the ground, the den feels a fleeting sense of security. The rocky cliff wall is blocking the wind, but the storm is almost on top of them.

Lester looks left and right, then calls Fuzzy. "Take half the den upstream. Look for the best place you can find. I'll take the rest downstream."

The den scurries aimlessly as clouds dash wildly across the sky. Twirling clouds dance as the meadow darkens. Gusts of wind furiously blow weeds and leaves over the cliff's edge. They spin and dart back and forth around the dragons, adding drama to their fear. Then thunder explodes, echoing up and down the river. Shards of lightning streak toward the earth while bursts of light dashes back and forth through the clouds, illuminating them as bright as midday.

Fuzzy takes control of the dragons near him. Sheets of rain begin to sweep over the cliff as Fuzzy tells several dragons to take shelter under a nearby rock outcropping. He leads the rest into a grove of cedar trees where they back as far as they can into the limbs.

Lester positions his group with their backs against the cliff. They watch as most of the rain blows over their heads. He takes his place among them.

The wind tears across the river turning its lazy, glassy smooth surface into white-topped waves that rise and dash to the banks as if trying to escape its fury. Thunderous booms roll and explode overhead, causing the den to flinch over and over. The sound is amplified by the shape of the river valley and echoes back and forth from one end to the other. The air turns cool and the dragons squeeze close together. The only dry place to be found is where they lean against each other.

Nature's fearful light show slowly turns to a drizzle over the meadow. Long after raindrops stop falling, tentacles of light race from cloud to cloud in the distant heavens, and a breeze sweeps across the wet dragons.

Fuzzy speaks compassionately. "It appears we will be cold tonight, but we are safe. Don't be tempted to wander off in search of a warmer spot. Stay where you are and huddle close to your neighbor." He lovingly slips a wing around Liz.

Later in the pitch dark of the moonless night, Liz nudges Fuzzy. "I see something moving along the river bank."

"Wolves, I suspect." He gazes into the darkness. "They're checking us out. As long as none of our young ones are where they can get close to them, we will be all right."

The wolves hover with their noses in the air. They gaze toward the den. Slowly the pack moves closer. Fuzzy signals Lester, and they step away from the den moving slowly toward the wolves.

The wolves pause, sniff the air, and move again. They inch closer and closer to Fuzzy and Lester, who wait fearlessly with their eyes fixed on the pack. They stand still; allowing the lead wolves to come so close that the den grows anxious. Without warning, they blast flames over the wolves' heads. Shrieks and ear shattering yelps erupt from the wolves as their fur blazes and melts away. They tumble and roll, pawing at their heads. Then with smoking fur, they dash back through their startled pack. The pack erupts into chaos as they scatter and dash out of sight. Sounds of their yipping fades into the night.

Fuzzy returns to Liz's side, but doesn't close his eyes again.

Hours later, he rubs his eyes as the meadow grows brighter. Sunlight glistens through millions of tiny drops of water, turning them into a foggy cloud. When the fog burns away, Fuzzy turns toward the sun and closes his eyes to absorb the long-awaited warmth.

When everyone is stirring, he calls out. "Let's catch some fish."

Several young dragons sail toward the river, and soon return with fish dangling from their claws.

Vic sits beside Fuzzy after eating his fill. He leans over to Fuzzy. "Thank you and Lester for leading us during the storm and protecting us from the wolves."

Fuzzy smiles. "You are welcome. When your friends are older they will be more interested in what is best for our den. Time will heal their pain."

Lester walks over. "Are we ready to go?"

Vic lifts off first and soon they're soaring above the cliff, headed north. The river disappears behind them.

Shim flies over to Tee and asks, "Have you noticed the younger dragons are grouping together, and staying close to Gus and Nom?"

"They're still rebellious about having to leave the old cavern. Soon they will be busy helping the den build a new life," replies Tee.

At midday, Vic spies a meadow and descends. He is pleased to find that the meadow is surrounded by berry bushes. Liz moves to Fuzzy's side, and they stroll through tall grass and bushes picking berries and are glad to share a moment of happiness.

The young dragons hop into the air and take off while the older dragons wait for updrafts and breezes to lift them. Soon they catch up and everyone is sailing together.

After flying a short time, Vic notices something strange up ahead. Fuzzy and Leonard see it too and move next to him.

"What do you think that could be?" asks Vic.

"It could be a dragon, but it doesn't appear to be moving, and it reflects sunlight now and then," replies Fuzzy.

"It may only be some kind of cloud. I will fly ahead and see what is going on," says Vic.

"I am going with you," says Fuzzy.

Vic takes off and Fuzzy loudly hails him, "Vic! Let me pass. You stay back in case this thing is not friendly. You can fly back to the den faster and defend them much better than I can."

Vic slows and Fuzzy moves ahead. He swallows hard as he approaches what begins to look like a silver dragon flapping gently, still suspended in one spot watching him approach.

"Wow," Fuzzy hears him say.

"What kind of dragon are you?" the silver dragon asks. He is bright-eyed and gazing at Fuzzy. "You are the most beautiful dragon I have ever seen. You are *just* a dragon, aren't you?"

Fuzzy shakes his head, "That is all I am. My den and I wish you no harm. We are migrating to a new cavern and wish to be friends with you."

Fuzzy wrinkles his brow as he studies the shiny silver dragon. "Oh, of course you don't have to worry about me, I'm the most peace-loving dragon you will ever meet. Too peaceful, according to my old den," replies the silver dragon.

Vic glides up beside Fuzzy and instantly he can tell that this dragon is no older than their rebellious young ones. The calm smile on the silver dragon's face reassures him that there is no danger.

"My name is Fuzzy and this is Vic. What would you like to be called?"

"Bird," replies the silver dragon.

The den catches up and hovers.

Bird studies the den and looks at Fuzzy. "It's midevening and soon darkness will fill the forest. Why don't you and your den follow me to my special place? A lake full of fish is nearby and all of you can find shelter. You will be more comfortable there than in the forest."

Fuzzy nods for Vic to decide. "We're going north. Is your place in that direction?"

Bird points ahead. "It's mostly north, and not far from here."

Vic smiles and nods in agreement.

Bird's eyes twinkle as he leads the way.

Gus and Nom are still staying close together. "This dragon is young like us. If I am right, this is going to be interesting," says Gus. Nom smiles.

Soon, a small lake comes into view. It is sky blue and sparkles in the sunlight. It is surrounded by green forest canopy, except for a jagged cliff rising on one side.

"My special place is inside a large cave beneath those cliffs," says Bird, looking back at Vic.

Vic smiles. "I have to admit this looks like the perfect place to spend the night."

"You will be pleased. There are several small caves along the shore, enough for the entire den to be out of the weather," says Bird happily.

As soon as the den lands, Fuzzy and Lester explore the cliffs and beach. "You truly are living out here all alone," states Fuzzy.

"I'm never bored out here. I really love being alone. I was never meant to be part of a den, but I'm pleased you have chosen to stay with me tonight.

"Is that a fire pit close to the cave entrance?" asks Lester.

"Yes. I know most dragons don't build fires, but it comes in handy for a lone dragon. It keeps wolves and prowling cats away. I don't build a fire if I am not in the mood. My cave has a high cliff inside. I just fly up there and nothing but bats can bother me."

A mischievous look crosses his face. "There are some lilies growing around the lake that may be of interest to some of your old creaky dragons who need to ease their pain, and to young dragons who just want to have some fun. You pull up the bulbs and place them around the fire and let them bake until they are soft and mushy. Eat one of them and nothing matters anymore, but you better be somewhere safe because you won't care if a predator eats you or not." He smiles a silly smile.

Several of the young dragons watch closely as Bird talks about the lilies. Being young and feeling stressed, they long for fun and adventure.

Gus, Nom, Leon, and Lear move away from the group to talk about things that are of interest to rebellious younger dragons. They can hardly wait to find mischief.

"I'm not leaving here without trying a mushy lily bulb," says Gus with a smirk. The other three are determined to not be outdone by Gus. It sounds like too much fun to miss.

The den is interested in deciding where they will spend the night, and they explore the cliffs. After everyone decides where they will retire, they return to hear Bird's story. Fuzzy and Liz sit close with Lester and Sada nearby.

"It feels strange sitting around a fire, but strange seems to be pretty normal for Bird, and he is very entertaining," says Fuzzy.

Bird walks up and plops down in a sandy spot.

"This is an amazing place, but how did you end up here? Don't you miss your den?" asks Fuzzy.

"My father was never happy as a member of our den. He left me and my mother to try his luck in a city called Dragonthal. While I was still very young my mother could tell I was a lot like him. She tried to change me but there is too much of my father in my spirit. I didn't know what I wanted, I just wanted something different."

"Dragonthal?" questions Fuzzy.

"If your old cavern lies south of here, I'm not surprised you have never heard of the glorious city. It is far north of here. Silver dragons with a yellow breast and trolls live there. Trolls are short, stubby creatures that walk on two hind legs. Their front legs aren't even legs. They hang by their sides and the trolls use them to carry things. especially weapons.

"Long ago, tall thin creatures that walked upright and carried things like the trolls began to move into this area. They had less hair than the trolls. The dragons and trolls call them 'scoundrels.' Scoundrels hunted any animal, even trolls and dragons. They used their hides for clothing and ate their meat. Dragons and trolls were abused until they could take no more. They formed an alliance. The combination was successful and for many years they waged war on the scoundrels. Finally they pushed them out of their world, and they have not been seen since. After the war, the dragons and trolls continued to work together to expand their way of life. After many years of working together a half-dragon, half-troll was born. He was called a 'dragoll.' He united and understood what dragons and trolls both wanted. He was a great king. Since his reign, all dragolls born in the city are taken to the king's cavern. The smartest and most cunning of them study in hopes of becoming king one day.

"I traveled to Dragonthal hoping to find my father, and maybe a place I belong, but it was not to be. They have too many rules. I left for the wilderness not caring if I lived or died. Many times, I almost perished. By luck, I found this place and I have been content ever since. If I am lonely or miss my old den, I just eat a mushy lily bulb and I don't care anymore."

Bird leans back, eyes twinkling. He feels their speechless intrigue with his dragon sense of communication, and it pleases him. "So why are you here beautiful dragon?" he asks Fuzzy.

Being called "beautiful dragon" annoys Fuzzy, but he pushes it aside.

"These scoundrels you speak of are called men, and they are not extinct. They're beginning to expand into the wilderness making it too dangerous for us to stay at our old cavern."

Gus abruptly interrupts. "I want to go to this dragon city."

"Who are you?" asks Bird, cutting his eyes toward Gus.

"I'm the son of a dragon that died at the hands of men while protecting our den. My name is Gus. I believe men *are* scoundrels."

Fuzzy interrupts. "We are a peaceful den and we don't want to lose more of our family fighting a losing battle with mankind."

"Wisdom, peace-lovers, youth, and hate--your den is in turmoil emotionally. I feel the lust for vengeance among some of you," says Bird, cocking his head, closing his eyes, and sniffing as if savoring the mix of dragon communication coming from the den.

"I will not talk of Dragonthal anymore tonight. But if the younger dragons continue to feel this way, I will share with them all I know about Dragonthal. However, they must return and spend some time with me if they wish to learn more."

Fuzzy shakes his head in disbelief. "We have a hard day ahead. It is time for us to say good night. Thank you for being so kind to us." The den departs for the places where they chose to spend the night.

As Gus walks next to Nom, he reveals a lily bulb hidden in his claws. Nom smiles slyly.

"I'm going to sneak back to the fire and let this bulb soften, then you and I will taste it later tonight."

The night is half spent when wild laughter echoes along the cliffs. The sounds of scuffling in the brush and running across the gravel of the beach wakes the den. Fuzzy and Lester reluctantly crawl out of their warm piles of grass and head in the direction of the chaos. Fuzzy cuts his eyes toward Lester in the faint light. They're both in disbelief. Gus and Nom are chasing each other like two infant dragons in play. They trip and fall, jump up and start running again. With silly grins they playfully throw sand at each other. Breathless with silly laughter, they fall in a heap and lay giggling. Their eyes are as big as walnuts, and they stumble as they jump up trying to run from the two older dragons. Fuzzy and Lester pursue them, catching up easily.

"Go back to bed! We are in no mood to be lectured to by two old fools," says Gus. He turns on Fuzzy, stopping inches from his face.

"What is wrong with you two? Don't you care that you're waking the entire den?"

"Sounds like you want to fight us young dragons. What about the men who killed our families?"

Lester rushes Gus aggressively; only to be pushed to the ground.

"Stop it right now!" commands Fuzzy, but Gus and Nom run away laughing.

Lear, Leon, Lee, and Pate land beside Fuzzy as he helps Lester to his feet.

"Leave them for now. We will round them up, and with a little persuasion they will soon be sleeping off whatever has gotten into them. Things will return to normal before long," says Lee.

When the rest of the young dragons catch up with Gus and Nom they put on big smiles. The inebriated dragons can hardly wait to share their joy with them. As soon as they step into the special place chosen by the young dragons, they stumble to the ground, and unable to stand again, they fall asleep.

The den is troubled and curious, but they are too tired to get involved. As soon as it's quiet, they fall asleep.

A beautiful morning greets the den. The sky is blue and an orange trail of sunlight dances across the lake's slick surface. Vic, Shim, Tee, Fuzzy, and Lester are already fishing for the den's breakfast. The conversation at the lake is about the excitement of the previous night. Fuzzy shushes them before the conversation turns judgmental.

"I am more concerned that Gus and Nom won't wake soon, and we need to continue on our way."

"I shook both of them and they didn't move," says Vic.

Everyone finishes eating and still no sign of Gus or Nom. Fuzzy grits his teeth, determined to be understanding as he marches to wake Gus and Nom. When he walks in where they are, they can hardly hold their heads up, and their eyes are swollen half shut. Gus is holding his head with both front paws. Nom's head hangs forward as if it is about to fall off.

"I can't stop spinning," whines Nom. Gus refuses to talk or move.

"We must move on. The den is waiting for you," says Fuzzy in a strong voice.

Bird walks up beside Fuzzy with two gourd cups. "Make them drink this mint leaf tea. It will stop their heads from spinning, but they will not feel very well until after midday."

Thirty minutes later, Fuzzy nods to Lester. "Ureeeeee!" he sings loudly, then faces Bird. "Thank you for sharing your special place with us."

"Please come back anytime." Bird watches as his new friends take to the air. Gus and Nom struggle to keep up as they climb into the sky.

The landscape is changing to beautiful mountains with green valleys zigzagging between them. Streams meander below, twinkling in the sunlight. The air is growing cooler as they sail along. The younger dragons look around in wonder at the beautiful new world unfolding beneath them.

At midday, Vic lands near a stream so clear they can see the snails sitting on white rounded pebbles on the bottom. The sound of water crashing and swirling through boulders and tumbling over little falls beacons the den to relax and drink their fill.

Gus and Nom catch Vic and Fuzzy's attention.

"How much water can those two hold? I will be surprised if they can still fly," says Vic.

Mona staggers toward Fuzzy as if to ask a question, but slumps to the ground and doesn't move.

Nom sighs and walks over. Before he reaches her a little flame belches from her mouth. He shrieks. "Mother don't leave me!" The words echo from the mountains surrounding the stream. He convulses, trying to weep and breathe. Slowly he falls to his knees.

"Wiiiiii!" sounds from every dragon as a wave of grief overtakes the den. Fuzzy's heart aches as he and Liz watch four strong dragons lift her body and lay it peacefully on top of a large, flat rock.

"We must return her body to the earth so her spirit can be at peace," says Fuzzy. He pulls her hatching stone from her claws and quietly hands it to Nom.

The den gathers wood, builds a mound head high, and lays Mona's body on top. As flames consume her Fuzzy speaks.

"Goodbye old friend. We are so close to our new cavern, and I wish you could have helped us start anew. Fly in peace with our ancestors and may your spirit be free."

Vic moves to Nom's side and with tears in his eyes he bows slightly. "I hope you will allow me to return to this place with you and we will build a stone remembrance to show where your mother's ashes are laid.

" Nom wipes a tear and doesn't reply.

After a short time, the den returns to flight, and in an hour the migration is over.

Chapter 3

Even though Mason never gave a second thought about how much suffering his hunting party was going to cause the dragons---or that some things in life are more important than earning silver---he is a deep man. He talked rough to his hunters and thought that they were indestructible. He now finds himself genuinely worrying about them. He is bored and trapped in his big barn waiting for them to return. Normally he would be scheming about ways to earn more silver, but depression dampens his will. He often goes outside hoping that this may be the moment that excitement is headed his way.

He listens and peers into the distance dreaming that he will see struggling dragons trying to resist his hunting party's commands. But Water Town is only busy with its normal day-to-day activity. He drops his head and thinks to himself.

"Surely soon, when I look out here, this town will be going wild as hideously ugly dragons with scaly sad faces are hauled down Main Street." He sighs in disgust and returns to the blacksmith shop where he used to work on new projects. Sleepy from boredom, he gives in to the call of his comfortable chair in his office and dozes off.

His thoughts drift and his mind's eye peers into endless purple darkness as blissful escape brings peace. His mind is captivated by a growing sound reminiscent of his traveling show. The purple opens to a stage where his men are surrounded by a rowdy group of spectators. He hears some talk of dragons. The growl of a vicious, infuriated creature sends chills down his spine and he tries to focus on the source, but he has never seen a dragon and his mind refuses to conjure an image. He twitches in disgust. The scene in his mind is so real that he fights to walk and move his arms to force his way through the crowd. With a jerk, he wakes, almost falling from his chair. His eyes slowly focus and he tries to catch his breath. He sighs sadly when he sees the inside of his office. He stands and rubs his eyes, then ambles into the barn and approaches the monstrous cage standing empty on the floor.

Jim, a man slightly taller than most, with grey hairs peeking out of his black beard, comes in and greets Mason.

"Don't worry; they will be back any day now," he says. He is Mason's lead blacksmith and a genius when it comes to building anything. He and Mason have worked together for a long time, and he is dressed as always in his work clothes with burns and stains all over them.

"I know," replies Mason for lack of a better response. He clinches his fist, and with the ball of his hand he hits one of the thick steel bars hard. "I really thought they would be back by now, especially with all the amazing equipment you built. We have never been as well prepared as this time."

A timid *tap, tap, tap* at the front door stops their conversation, and Mason walks over and flips the latch. The door squeaks as it opens to reveal a timid, well-dressed, middle-aged woman. She anxiously tries to smile.

Softly she speaks. "Mr. Smith?"

"Yes. Can I help you?"

"I am Virgil's mother, Ruby." A thought races through Mason's mind. "How could a man so consumed with the pursuit of fame and silver and willing to slaughter any creature in the wilderness have such a gentle mother?"

He swallows and thinks. "I'm glad to finally meet you. This is Jim. He built most of the equipment your son is using to capture a dragon."

"Have you heard from my son? It has been over three months. I didn't think he would be gone this long."

"Don't worry, Ruby. He is far out in the wilderness with the best group of hunters I have ever assembled. Everything will be fine. I expected this hunting trip to take a while," Mason manages to smile.

She gently bites her lip. "It's hard for a mother to have a son with such an adventurous spirit. I hope he will return soon and that you will be pleased with what he brings back." She turns, wiping tears.

Mason reaches for her elbow. "They will be back soon. I will send a messenger to you at the leather shop as soon as I hear anything."

"Thank you," she replies and walks away.

Mason looks at Jim and grits his teeth. "I hope I didn't lie."

Over the next few weeks, several women visit Mason asking about men they care for. And now another young lady cries as he speaks. Mason drops his head as she turns and slowly walks away, crying. Mason shuts the door and grief clinches his heart. He heads to Jim's forge where Jim is staying busy.

"Jim, it's time for us to find our men."

"I know," replies Jim, not looking up.

"Build something that six men can sleep in and feel safe. You and I will take four men with us out into the wilderness, and we will not rest until we find our friends.

<>

Jackson shivers, but he has never been so happy. He is on the roof of his and Sandra's new home. It's made up of two rooms connected to the larger Murray cabin. Soon, he and Sandra can enjoy being together in their own place. He is filled with contentment because one of the rooms will soon be a nursery for the child he already loves. Sandra's face has been radiant ever since she was sure that she carries a beautiful life-changing addition to their family.

Uncle Matt and Miles have gladly done most of the farm work since Jackson started building the addition. When the baby comes, they will help with everything. His face can hold no larger smile.

The bell on the porch rings and he realizes for the first time that he is starving. After ringing the bell, Sandra walks over and holds the bottom of the ladder for the man she loves more than ever.

"I love you," she whispers as Jackson steps to the ground. He catches her arm as she turns and pulls her back and hugs her. His eyes sparkle as he looks into her eyes, and then steals a kiss.

"The roof will be finished this evening and we can start moving in." They kiss again and then walk hand in hand to the kitchen. Inez has been tending to the soup all morning. She takes a ladle made from a small gourd and dips it into a big pottery bowl sitting on a rock in the middle of the fireplace.

"This will keep you warm while you finish up," she says.

Uncle Matt and Miles pull off their jackets, tossing them beside the door as they enter. "It sure is tough outside today. I bet it's really cold up there on the roof." says Miles pulling up to the table. He closes his eyes as he savors the mist swirling above his bowl of soup.

"It's no worse than being out in the field like you and Uncle Matt."

"I wonder if Cap has finished his addition at the Brittain's," says Uncle Matt.

"I am sure he is almost done too," replies Jackson.

"You boys are lucky to have such wonderful wives to give you children so soon," says Inez, smiling at Sandra.

"Sandra beams. Janice and I are the lucky ones. This family lives in such a beautiful place, and all of you are so loving and caring. Our children will grow up very happy."

"I'm glad both children will be born about the same time. They will play and fuss with each other and grow up to be best friends," says Inez.

After lunch Miles and Uncle Matt bundle up. Miles looks into Inez's eyes and steals a kiss, then thanks her for lunch. He and Matt trudge back to the field. Jackson returns to the roof.

Jackson has hardly begun working when the sound of horses clomping up the trail stops him. He moves from the back of the house, and when he tops the ridge he sees several men on horseback turning from the trail, and headed toward the house. Five of them are riding fine horses and one man is driving a cage wagon similar to the one Virgil's hunting party had taken into the wilderness.

"Greetings young man. My name is Mason Smith."

"Hello, my name is Jackson Murray. Glad to meet you."

"I'm searching for a hunting party that should have passed by here a few months ago. Did any of your family happen to see them?"

Jackson nods. "A large group of men with lots of equipment passed by, but they didn't stop. Is anything wrong?"

"I don't know. They should have been back by now, and I'm afraid something has happened."

Jackson feels sorrow and a mix of fear and worry as he tries to act as if he doesn't know anything more. He wipes a bead of sweat from his brow and speaks calmly, surprising himself.

"They looked like they could take care of themselves, but the wilderness can be unforgiving."

Mason looks up the trail toward the wilderness. Jackson points the way. "Stay on this trail. When it fades away, you will see where they hacked their way into the forest."

"Thank you, young man." says Mason. The men trot up the trail disappearing as the trail makes a gentle turn.

Jackson is still sweating, and he feels guilty. He worries about how he looked and what he said. He tries to tell himself to stop worrying. Days later he is still worrying.

<>

Mason smiles slightly when they find dry limbs that were hacked from trees lying about. They follow the trimmings, and after a brief time, brown crunchy leaves become a continuous cover along the trail's floor. Mason's thoughts drift.

"If only these leaves could talk," he thinks. He notices the wilderness is recovering as new light green leaves return to the trees that were stripped of their limbs.

"It took a lot of work to cut all this underbrush. The hunting party could still be out here chopping away," says Jim.

"No. It has been too long. Something has happened," replies Mason, his brow sagging. The horses trot along until Mason grows cautious. The search party slows as the vegetation grows thicker. The wilderness is intimidating. Its mysteriousness drifts around them like a green veil. Their imaginations make their skin crawl. Claws and hungry teeth could be hidden only inches away. A powerful predator could tear through, grab someone, and disappear in seconds. They grow quieter and the wilderness grows darker.

Suddenly a horrid *screech* rings out! A feathered creature zips out of nowhere with its claws lunging close to their heads. Terrified horses rear and scuffle at the instinctively frightening sound. The men gasp in fear struggling to hold their horses steady. They barely catch a glimpse of a large bird darting past.

Jim sighs. "He's warning us that we are too close to his nest." Several men grab bows, but the bird has disappeared. Mason takes a deep breath. "Calm down, men. In a few days you will feel more confident out here."

Mason looks ahead and sees a small stream crossing their path. "We have gone far enough today and darkness is falling. Tie the horses and gather wood. We will spend the night here."

Jim looks around and shivers. The canopy is so thick there will be no moon or stars tonight. "The darker it gets, the noisier the wilderness becomes," he whispers.

Mo, one of the more confident men, cuts his eyes toward Jim. He notices his wrinkled brow and how Mason keeps glancing around at every chirp and hoot.

"I don't think we have much to worry about. I have been in the wilderness many times, and this is the first time I have had a cage to sleep in. The only things we have to worry about tonight are snakes, rats, bats, bugs, or the paw of a large cat reaching through the bars and digging into one of us."

Jim smiles for the first time in a while. "Well, if that is all, I will sleep like a baby tonight." He rolls his eyes.

"Don't worry we will take turns guarding each other. The guard will take care of those things," says Cur.

"That's right, all the guard needs is a big stick. We should be fine unless a dragon comes by; and I don't think a guard will help much, if that happens," remarks Sul.

"I hope you don't think that is funny," says Dee who has been quietly listening.

"Build up the fire and let's climb into the cage. No one is to leave this cage to keep the fire going. I don't intend to lose any men out here," says Mason.

Morning arrives with a damp chill. Birds begin singing long before the sun's light penetrates the forest.

"Okay men it's time to get going," says Dee, the last guard.

Jim sits up and reaches for his saddle bag hanging from a hook in the ceiling. He passes around dried beef and apples and smiles as he watches the sleepy-looking group eating. "I slept pretty well in here last night. I forgot about all of Mo's varmints, and there probably isn't any such thing as dragons anyway," he says.

With a good night's sleep and the trail already cut out, the men keep their bows ready, but they are less intimidated than the day before and they enjoy their journey until it begins to drizzle. Mason hastily picks a place to stop for the night. A wall of rock stands along the left side of the trail.

"Pull the wagon close to the rock wall. That side will be safe and knock the wind off of us," says Mason.

"It's too wet to build a fire tonight, so we will have to eat left over beans," says Sul, joking.

"I don't care. Bears, wolves, and big cats don't come hunting scraps at night when you eat beans," replies Mo. Everyone rolls their eyes.

The wind puffs catching everyone by surprise as it knocks hats off and tosses leaves through the camp. Then a large rain drop hits the top of the wagon with a *pop*, then one on Mason's head.

"The bottom is about to fall out of these clouds. Head for the cage!" yells Mo. Everyone runs for the door, and before half of them are inside, water is pouring off the top of the cage. The horses are soaked in minutes.

"We need to cover the horses. They can't stand in rain like this all night," says Mason.

Dee and Mo pull their hats down as far as they can and crawl out. They struggle with tarps until only the horse's heads are left in the rain. They run back and jump in the cage.

"I'm about to freeze," says Dee.

"You two huddle in the middle of the cage. The rest of us will surround you," says Jim. They shiver for a few minutes and then they begin warming up.

It rains all night and finally turns into a drizzle at midday. Everyone is bored.

"Let's get out of here and try to make some kind of progress. The horses need to walk and warm up. We will all feel better after we walk a while," says Mason.

The group is quiet until they begin to warm up, and then they begin to talk like they normally do.

"I see a wagon up ahead," shouts Dee as he bumps his horse to a trot. When he gets close he turns and shouts back. "It's the heavy cage wagon."

They circle around the wagon. Mason rubs his chin as he studies. "They parked it here with purpose, and nothing looks out of order," he says. "At least we are on the right track," he tries to reassure himself, but fear clamps its claws into his gut--a horrid revelation could lie nearby.

"Pull our wagon beside this one. We will spend the night here. There is enough dry grass under the large wagon to start a fire."

The men are soon warming themselves by flames dancing under a pot of root tea.

Mason paces, occasionally stopping close to the fire to soak up its warmth. When he decides to sit, the men hush, and Mo cuts his eyes toward him.

"What's on your mind?" says Mo.

Mason takes a breath. "I don't want to scare you, but it's time to keep your bows by your side no matter what you are doing. Whatever is keeping our hunting party from returning could be watching us or waiting anywhere along the trail."

Mo stands first and one-by-one they all find their bows and return to the fire side. That night the guards are solemn as they carefully listen and watch the woods.

A peaceful night passes. The morning air is chilly and everyone wants the fire rekindled. While they rebuild the fire, Jim watches the horses as they snort and shake their heads, flipping their manes back and forth. They nervously peer into the forest ahead. He calls Mason.

"I don't know if we have a problem, but the horses know something we don't," he says.

The men pick up their bows. "Be prepared to defend yourselves," says Mason seriously.

A rustling noise comes from within the forest. "Something in the brush moves a little, then stops for a moment; then moves again," whispers Jim.

The sound grows louder and everyone fidgets with their arrows.

"Don't shoot. Wait until we can see it," instructs Jim.

The men pull their bowstrings back and hold.

Suddenly one of the horses snorts loudly. Several men flinch.

Another horse snorts loudly as the sound of crunching leaves is getting closer. The anticipation grows maddening.

"Don't waste your shot men, stay calm, and make it count," says Jim.

Suddenly a wild-eyed horse jumps out of the brush landing in front of them.

"Don't shoot! Slowly lower your bows. This is one of Cliff's horses," says Mason. There is a bridle in its mouth, but the reins are torn away.

With fearful eyes the thin shaky horse stands peering at them. Its mane and tail are full of sticks and twigs. It doesn't move as it studies them.

"Sul, your horse is the gentlest. Untie it and nudge it toward the stray horse. With a little luck, it will calm him," says Jim. Sul walks slowly to his horse and unties its reins. He makes a soft clicking sound and pats his horse on the rump. It walks toward the wild horse and they sniff each other for a moment. Jim nods when the two horses begin eating grass close together. Sul pours some grain in his hat and slowly walks toward the horses. He gently holds his hat out, and the famished animal dips its nose in and begins to chew. When the horse seems content to enjoy the taste of grain again, Sul reaches out and pats him gently while slipping the old bridal out of its mouth and inserting one with reins. The men want to cheer, but Jim puts his finger to his lips to shush them.

When the horse is tied up and has had a good drink, Mason smiles. "One step closer to finding our men," he says.

"This is not a good sign. I am sure you already know that," says Jim.

Mason sadly nods in agreement.

That night, weapons lay close to each man as they eat and sit by the campfire wondering what could have happened to their friends.

"If this horse made it out alive, then maybe some of the men are wandering around out here too," says one of the men.

"I want to think some of them are holding up out here waiting for us to rescue them." suggests another.

Mason looks at the men. "We are not a rescue party; we have only bows and arrows. They had two of the most powerful weapons ever made. I know all of you are grasping for a happy ending, and I hope one of your hopeful stories comes true. The answer is not far away."

Two days later at mid evening, a wisp of clouds dim the sun's rays. The forest is almost dark. Crickets and tree frogs begin to screech. The air is filled with a gentle breeze that is growing colder. Several men reach for their ponchos and slip them on. No one is carrying on a light-hearted conversation. Most everyone is quietly clomping along with their eyes on the forest.

"I feel as if many eyes are all around and watching us," says Jim.

"I feel something, too. Have you noticed that the frogs and crickets have hushed, and we haven't seen any wildlife in hours?" replies Mason.

Several men slow to a stop. With wrinkled foreheads they pull bandanas out and cover their noses. A hint of decay drifts and lingers.

"I think that putrid smell of death is growing stronger," says Mo.

"I have a bad feeling about this place," says Jim.

"The smell is definitely getting stronger. I wish the wind would pick up and blow some fresh air through here. All of us would feel better," replies Mason.

Mo is leading the group and stops suddenly in his tracks. As each man reaches his side, they stop and gaze in fearful awe. A newly-cut meadow with trees untouched lay decaying. Weeds and grass are reclaiming the area. Anguish sweeps through the men's minds as they realize that wagon tops are barely visible among the vegetation. They stand slightly taller than the weeds and are haphazardly scattered over the area.

The men move close to the first wagon and stare. Weeds and vines are crawling up its wheels trying to reach the top. A buzzard lazily sails out of the woods toward them. Mo sets an arrow and follows him. Then *zip* his arrow streaks through the air. The ugly, red-headed, long-necked creature flaps furiously barely escaping the arrow. It dives back into the forest.

"This is it. Set your arrows. We have no way of knowing what to expect. There could be something out here waiting to ambush us," says Mason, his heart drowning in fear and sadness.

It is deadly quiet. The men are too frightened to talk, and their imaginations run wild. A whiff of putrid decay drifts by, causing several to turn away and slide to the ground. They gag and heave until they can heave no more. Others wet their bandanas and cool their faces, and then hold their hands over their ears until the sick men stop gagging.

Slowly, Mason makes his horse walk ahead. Jim is close behind.

"This smell of rotting flesh is too much for me," says Dee. He trots back in the direction from which they came.

Sul watches him without judgment and rides toward the crumpled crossbows. He stops suddenly and stares. In front of him lies a decomposing horse that has been torn to pieces.

He turns his horse away, and suddenly he's holding on with all his might as it rears and jerks to the side. When he sees what spooked his horse, he gags. They had stepped into the remains of another horse. The smell overwhelms them as flies buzz into the air, and he trots away where he can breathe

"I have yet to see any human remains," says Mason.

Jim moves to a crossbow and studies the remains. He shudders to think that a crossbow so large that they had to be mounted on a wagon could be so completely destroyed. He looks toward the other crossbow and it is crushed too.

Mason rides up as Jim is pulling several large rocks off the crossbow wagon's floor. The same large rocks are lying all around, and most of the wagons have been hit by them also. Mason looks at him shaking his head. He dismounts and ties his horse to Virgil's cage wagon. The door is standing open, and it is one of the few pieces of equipment not damaged.

He moves to Jim's side. "There are too many large rocks lying around," says Mason. He pulls at one of the crossbows, and there mixed among the splinters of wood where the weapon is broken, lies a large rock. The seat and bow dangle over it as if hiding the culprit.

"It is obvious these poor men were bombarded with these stones from high in the sky," exclaims Mason sadly looking to the heavens.

"Most of their arrows have been shot away; some quivers are empty. They fought a hard battle" says Jim.

Sul is kicking grass and searching around, "Has anyone seen any signs of a rotting dragon yet?" he asks.

"Keep your mind on protecting us. There is a good chance something is still out there watching us," says Mason, as his demeanor sinks and anger makes his eyes twitch.

Mo stumbles across a mound of stones and rubs his chin. He smells the odor of death oozing through them.

"Mason!" he yells commandingly.

Everyone knows that this is something they must see.

"I don't like the looks of this pile of rocks. It looks like a burial site to me," says Mo.

Mason stands quietly. The stones don't look weathered and appear to have been placed with care. They form a perfect arch and the corners are squared off. He rubs his forehead as he tries to come up with any reason why this doesn't have to be a burial mound.

A breeze moves gently toward the men picking up the smell of death drifting out of the pile of rock, and it overwhelms them.

Everyone gags.

Mason stumbles to his horse and motions for everyone to ride down the trail. When his stomach settles, he wonders, "Did some creature bury their victims, or did some of the hunters bury their friends that died before them?" He takes a deep breath, "We're going back for a moment." He looks around and nods at Sul. "Hook your horse to Virgil's cage wagon. We will pull it back down the trail with us. We will feel safer with another wagon."

The men help Sul and no one talks as they leave. The only sound is the clomping of hooves and the wagon's squeaky wheels.

"If only this wagon could talk," thinks Mason. He rides quietly until he sees a safe place to spend the night.

"Build a good fire. We need the comfort it will give after what we have seen," he says meekly.

Mo steps beside Mason. "I don't know about the rest of you, but I want to get out of here and hurry back to Water Town," he says.

Mason speaks with an understanding tone. "We owe it to those men buried out there, and to everyone back home, to learn as much as we can about what did this to them. I think we will be safe here for one night."

Cur is quick to reply. "Those men were well prepared to fight, but it looks like they didn't stand a chance. We're sitting ducks out here with no more weapons than we have."

"There's not enough daylight left for us to start back now. Tomorrow we will try to gather enough parts to put one of the crossbows back together. Then we will have a fighting chance to make it home," replies Mason.

Everyone is emotionally tired and quiet.

That night, the men talk quietly about their friends lying under the rock mound. They agree that two guards are needed on a night like this, and they gladly work it out with plans of keeping the fire going all night.

Beckoned by morning light, the men are eager to start assembling a large crossbow. Jim chooses the parts to use and the men quickly pull them from the wreckage. Everyone is uneasy as they work and look often to reassure themselves that the guards stand ready, with bows in hand, scanning the sky and forest.

When the crossbow appears to be ready, Mo hops into its seat, turns the crank, sets an arrow and cocks the weapon. Aiming at one of the abandoned wagons, he pulls the trigger and the arrow destroys the side planks coming to a stop only after penetrating the opposite side.

Jim beams. "Now, the next thing is to gather as many arrows for this weapon as we can quickly find, and get out of here."

The men quickly search and in minutes they fill one quiver.

"Mason!" yells Sul as he drops to his knees.

Mason's heart sinks as he runs toward him. Sul doesn't move, his eyes are glued to the ground in front of him. Mason slides to a stop and sees two huge claws lying in the grass. He slowly picks one up, studying it intently as he brings it close to his face. It's a heavy, rock-hard, shiny, black weapon that curves slightly forming a crescent the size of a man's palm. Everyone surrounds him and stares.

"It looks like someone hacked these out of a monster's paw." Mason passes the claws to the men. They cringe when they touch them. The tip is as sharp as any of their flint knife blades.

"I have never seen a claw even half this size in all my days of hunting," states Mason.

"Can we go now?" asks Cur with wrinkles covering his face.

"Yes, we have gathered plenty of crossbow arrows, and Mo tells me the crossbow we assembled is as good as new," answers Mason.

"Mount up. We will keep the crossbow manned until we're home." He is still studying the claws as he walks to his horse. He can't stop wondering if they could have belonged to a dragon, and cringes at the thought of Cliff and his men being torn apart by a host of creatures armed with them.

<>

Several days later, the six men come out of the woods in view of the Murray farm. Dee is almost asleep in the saddle and sways back and forth as his horse tromps along. Mason, Jim, and Mo bounce along driving cage wagons. Behind them, looking threatening, is the large crossbow with Sul in the seat behind the weapon and Cur driving.

Sandra is in her little flower garden beside the house. The sound of squeaky wheels and horses cause her to stand and look up the trail. Fearful memories stir when she sees the wagons and crossbow. She slips behind the house before they notice her.

Once inside she whispers to Inez. "Follow me to the window." She points up the trail. "The men searching for the lost hunting party are returning, and they are bringing back several wagons and a large weapon. They all look tired and sad."

Inez touches her shoulder. "Move away from the window. We don't want to talk to them."

The men glance toward the house but, don't slow down and soon they're out of sight.

Inez rubs her forehead and closes her eyes. "I hope this is not the beginning of more trouble. Let's let the men work without worry until supper. Then we will tell them about the search party."

Miles, Matt, and Jackson are talking and occasionally laughing as they walk to the porch. They wash up and walk into the kitchen, still talking about a good day in the field. Miles notices Inez's eyes, and she is too interested in putting food on the table "What has happened?" he asks.

Inez carefully finishes setting a big bowl on the table, and Sandra moves next to Jackson. "The search party came back from the wilderness this evening. They brought back several wagons and a large crossbow. Only one of them was on horseback. They looked tired and solemn and did not stop to talk."

Jackson has his arm around Sandra's waist and pulls her close. "They found the remains of the hunting party, and I know how sad they feel right now. Unfortunately, others will soon come back starving for revenge. They won't know the dragons are gone, and they will search for them a long time," he says. The smile when he entered the house is gone as he takes his seat.

Miles takes a sip of tea. "Don't worry son. They will not bother us. No one will ever know about you and Cap."

Jackson sighs, "I hope you're right. Sandra and I will visit Cap and Janice tomorrow. They need to know what is going on." His head is spinning as he worries about the silver mine. Time is running out for them to cover it. Mason's men could stumble across the entrance next time.

After lunch the next day, Sandra and Jackson saddle up and head for the Brittain farm. Jackson rides closer than usual to Sandra. "I love being close to you even more than ever. I can feel the presence of our child when you are near me."

"I feel the need to be close to you too. It gives me a feeling of security. I already love this child who will carry some of you and me into the future."

They reach out and hold hands for a minute as they continue their journey. The turn off comes into sight.

"Cap and Janice will be surprised to see us. I hope they have time to stop what they are doing and enjoy our visit," says Sandra, wanting to talk about babies with Janice.

Jackson is happy, but there are decisions to be made and unfinished business in the wilderness for him and Cap to discuss.

Chapter 4

Two years have passed since the battle with the hunting party. The den has completed its cremation pit at the new cavern. It is the most important thing to them. Wood for the pit is stashed under an outcropping of rock close by. Fish are plentiful in the surrounding crystal-clear mountain streams and pools. The female dragons have cleared rambling paths to berry patches. Fruit and nut trees growing plush and green have been pruned by breaking off many lower limbs. Meadows of grass waving in the mountain breezes grow and ripen. The grass will be golden brown when it is time to furnish bedding for all the den's special places. Clear pools of water lie in several passages of the cavern. The den is content and happy with their new cavern, but time doesn't pass without cost.

Fuzzy and Lester are not yet too old to lead the den, and most dragon dens allow the old leaders to slowly and gracefully move aside. New leaders during this period rise among their peers. The old leaders accept new leadership as natures plan; however conflict does come into play among the younger dragons.

"Ureeeeeeeee," summons Lester. The members of the den amble out in small groups to hear what needs to be discussed. Gus, Nom, Lear and Leon are always together. Their minds were occupied as the den worked hard to prepare a place to live. Now they have time to think about revenge and lily bulbs.

Lester's face brightens and his eyes sparkle as he looks happily at the den.

"Fellow den members, we have worked hard to prepare for winter and I am proud of what we have accomplished. I am also glad to have the pleasure of sharing wonderful news that I have just received from Kim and Pate. They will soon need a pocket hewn in the stone wall near the entrance for their hatching stone! Hopefully we will soon have a new member born in this cavern." Kim leans against Pate and he sighs. Most of the den bows happily.

Gus smirks and looks toward his friends. "I had no idea Kim and Pate were interested in becoming mates. They are three years younger than me."

"You can forget about them and Lee joining our group now. Lee is just like his father, and now Kim and Pate will only be interested in starting a family. Fuzzy and all the other old dragons will be so happy," snorts Nom.

Fuzzy steps forward. "We will all have to work on the hatching stone pockets. It is time for our den to start growing again."

Everyone bows in agreement except the four dragons.

Fuzzy notices and raises his eyebrows. "Gus, are you and your friends not in agreement to work on the hatching stone pockets?"

"We are not sure this is where we want to raise our young and live out the rest of our days. We are curious about Dragonthal. There aren't enough females here for our generation to mate with, and this den needs new blood anyway."

Nom, Lear, and Leon slightly bow in agreement. "We're going to see Bird tomorrow. He can tell us how to find Dragonthal."

"You need to stop and think about this before you go. We are a small den and have barely settled in. This is where you belong, and who knows what kind of danger could be waiting there. Give this decision a week before you go," pleads Fuzzy.

"We will talk to Bird. He will know if going to Dragonthal is dangerous for the den. We will come back and tell you what he says before we leave for the city, but we are going to see Bird tomorrow," states Gus.

Later that evening, Lee, Kim, and Pate are sitting close together on pallets of grass in Fuzzy's special place. Liz pulls grass away from a pile of ten hatching stones. "I placed these in the sun today and they are warm." She hands a couple to each of them and the warmth makes them relax and sigh as they slide them under their wings. She then pulls out a gourd filled with dry figs and passes them around.

Liz notices Beada, Tee's daughter, nearby and realizes she seems to be near their passageway often. Liz smiles at her. Beada steps in looking shy, but with a big smile. "I brought your family a pouch of walnuts that I cracked for you." She hands them to Liz, but everyone sees that she is looking at Lee. Lee stands and bows to her and smiles. She turns and hurries away. Lee pauses and then sits back down.

Fuzzy and Liz's are cheerful. They are thankful that their children are happily spending time with them.

Fuzzy looks at Lee, "I am sad to hear that Gus and his friends want to leave. I hope your anger toward mankind is easing."

Feeling that Fuzzy has asked pleasantly he gladly comments. "I never felt as strongly as Gus and his friends. I still feel anger, but revenge is such a complicated thing. As you once said, some men are good. We witnessed that during the battle. With Kim starting a family, I am here to stay and don't want to do anything that would cause our den to suffer later."

Fuzzy smiles and wraps a wing around Liz. He bows to Lee to show appreciation for his wisdom.

That night while lying close to Liz, Fuzzy speaks softly. "I am troubled. I think I'm the only one who could talk the rebellious dragons out of leaving tomorrow, but I can't find the right words."

She snuggles close. "Let them go on their journey. They may find peace by having a little time away from the den. Gus and Nom lost their fathers in the battle. Only time can heal their pain. I think the best thing you can do is to wish them good luck and reassure them that the den is here for them.

Fuzzy smiles, "You are right my dear. They already have enough on their minds without the den adding more stress."

In the morning Gus and his friends are preparing to leave. Fuzzy approaches them. Before they have time to be defensive, Fuzzy bows and shares Liz's wisdom with them.

Gus's face brightens. He nods slightly as he looks toward his friends. "Thank you," he says. His friends smile and bow in respect.

The four rebellious dragons look happier than they have in a long time. That look pleases Fuzzy; even though he is sad to see them fly away.

<>

Happy to be flying together on a beautiful day with gentle breezes buoying them, the rebellious friends feel a freedom and peacefulness they have been yearning for. Soon they land at Bird's special place beside the lake.

"Ureeeeee," bellows Gus. His call echoes, and then it is quiet.

Several minutes pass without a sign of Bird.

"Leon, you and Lear search the other side of the lake. Nom and I will look in the caves," says Gus.

Lear and Leon enjoy their adventure exploring the shore. All they find is a path leading into the forest. As they amble onto the path, Bird appears. They gasp and smile. He has a plump apple in his mouth and two more in his claws. The corners of his mouth turn up when a broad smile erupts on his face, but his teeth remain clamped on the apple. He tosses an apple to Leon and then one to Lear. He then reaches for the apple in his teeth snapping off a big bite.

"Sorry I couldn't answer your call. I didn't want to drop such a beautiful piece of fruit. What brings you back to my place?"

"We have come to spend some time with you. Gus and Nom are here with us and are waiting near the cave. We want to hear more about Dragonthal."

Bird's eyes beam, and he snaps another bite, then talks as he chews. "Come, we will sit together and I will tell all of you a story that will amaze you. All of it is true I assure you."

Gus and Nom's faces light up seeing Bird who already has Lear and Leon laughing. Bird's eyes sparkle as he approaches, "I am pleased you returned to visit with me. If you spend the night, we will feast on fish from the lake and fresh red apples."

"We plan to spend the night," says Gus.

"Lear, you and Leon go back to the path and load up on apples, while Gus and Nom come with me to the lake," says Bird. With big smiles Gus and Nom splash around the lake catching fish with Bird. Even with fish dangling from each claw, Bird manages to pull a lily bulb growing along the shore as the three of them walk back to the fire-pit.

"Bird, don't place that bulb next to the fire tonight. We are serious about learning all we can about Dragonthal," says Gus.

"I respect your request. I will keep my head clear for the evening so I can give you all the details about a mysterious place. I really am glad you are here," replies Bird.

After eating their fill, Bird lights the fire and leans back in the sand. "This is a long story so get comfortable."

"The best way to understand Dragonthal is to start with a history lesson," he says. He can feel the anticipation of the four young dragons and he eagerly entertains his guests.

"This sacred story has been passed down from generation to generation of dragons and trolls for a very long time.

"There once was a time when trolls and dragons lived side-by-side, in caves and caverns far north of here. As you know, dragons are drawn to live under ground. When there were no longer enough caves or caverns to go around, the dragons forced the trolls to move out. The trolls began constructing crude rock huts, and soon they preferred living in huts. They discovered they could live anywhere they pleased, and they scattered throughout the woodlands. After that dragons and trolls learned to live in harmony. For a long time, they fished side-by-side along streams and lakes without interfering with each other. The dragons always caught fish easily and began to share them with the trolls. This changed everything. The trolls were better at gathering nuts, roots and other vegetables that dragons love. They would place them in baskets and take them to the dragon's caverns to thank them for the fish.

"Then, scoundrels, who you call men, began wandering through their woods. They looked similar to trolls, but traveled in packs and were very aggressive. They killed trolls and dragons to take their shelters or their hides. Many times, scoundrels would eat whatever they killed, but many times they would kill just for the thrill of the hunt."

Gus's eyes glare as he looks at Bird. "These creatures have not changed," he growls.

Bird stops and raises his eyes to Gus, nods and continues. "Their weapons were deadly, they reproduced rapidly, and after a few hundred years there were more scoundrels than trolls and dragons. The dragons and trolls would be wiped off the face of Venosta land if nothing changed.

"Then a strange thing happened. A male dragon and female troll fell in love. Her egg hatched, and a mythical-looking creature was born. It looked so strange that no one thought it would live, but its parents were determined and named him Alpha. Alpha not only lived, he thrived and grew to be very wise. His gift of being able to communicate with dragons and trolls inspired everyone. By the time Alpha was fifteen years old he was anointed as their king. From that moment on they worked together; they had a common enemy.

"In a few years, the offspring of dragons and trolls who grew up close to each other developed a new language that they both understood. The dragons sent messengers to other dens, and the trolls roamed Venosta telling their kin of the alliance. They all came together at a gigantic cavern where Dragonthal now stands. At the age of twenty, Alpha spoke to the gathering of dragons and trolls. He convinced them that joining together to fight the scoundrels was their only chance of survival. Everyone agreed to unite and fight, and soon a great army was assembled. Desperate to survive, they trained tirelessly and chose good leaders to command those who were ready and willing to fight.

"The trolls built crude bows and arrows. They carried short knives made of bone and made spears with bone tips. The dragon-troll army discovered that a troll riding on a dragon's back was a lethal tactic. They could shoot further aiming down than the scoundrels could shoot upward. The dragons learned to fly high enough to be safe. Scoundrels had few places to hide with trolls in the air looking down on them. Anytime scoundrels took refuge in caves or rock shelters, the trolls would dismount and fight hand-to-hand.

"Many dragons and trolls died in the war, but the scoundrel's numbers quickly dwindled. After the war, dragons and trolls had a common bond and continued to work together. As time passed, they built structures out of stone and wood that were almost as safe as caverns. Their quality of life improved, and both dragons and trolls grew in number."

"That's pretty amazing. Will it be safe for us to just fly there to see this city for ourselves?" asks Gus.

"You will be fine. The war has been over for hundreds of years, but everyone remembers the legend. Now only a few guards keep watch over the city from high places, but you will not look like a threat to them. I would like to go with you when you go. I could show you what I know when we get there," says Bird with a smile growing on his face.

"We will feel a lot more comfortable if you come along. We don't want to end up in trouble," says Gus.

"Oh, I can keep us out of trouble for a couple days," replies Bird.

The four blue dragons smile with him. "We will leave tomorrow. The journey is to the northwest and will take about three days."

"That means we will pass over our new cavern. We should spend the first night there," suggest Gus.

"Tomorrow it is," says Bird picking up the lily bulb.

"Let me show you how to enjoy one of these without becoming intoxicated." He holds the green bulb tightly and peels the dirty outer skin away. Then turning it upright, he digs a claw into the middle and pushes the core out; it falls to the ground.

"Now, after we roast this for a while, a pinch will give you a delicious night of sleep. If you ever want to lose your mind, eat a couple of the centers." He winks at them and smiles.

They all share one small taste of the bulb and continue talking for a while.

"I can hardly hold my eyes open," says Leon yawning. Gus, Nom, and Lear are nodding too.

"Bird ushers them toward the cave, "You will all be asleep in a few minutes."

They slowly amble into the cave and are asleep in moments. The next thing Gus and his friends hear is Bird's call. "Are you going to sleep all day?" he blurts.

"Is it time to get up already?" asks Nom.

"Yes, if you are going to arrive at your new den before nightfall," replies Bird. The four blue dragons look surprised. "The morning is half gone," assures Bird.

Gus stretches, "I feel really good after such a wonderful sleep. Let's catch some fish and head out."

Chapter 5

Physically and emotionally fatigued, Mason breathes a sigh of relief when the roof of his barn comes into view. Even though lots of people he passes are intrigued by the cage wagons and crossbow, he is too tired to respond to their questions. But their presence gives him a feeling of security that he has missed. Once the equipment is inside the barn, the men put the horses in their stalls and head for the door.

Mason calls for them to wait. "Before you go, I want to thank you for going with me. We have all been forever changed by the horrid sight we witnessed out there. I hope all of you will return in a few days and help me build new equipment. We will avenge the deaths of our friends. Go home, rest, and spend time with your families."

After the men leave, Mason slowly rides home. His body aches and his thoughts move slowly, but he ponders how to make the weapons stronger. After putting his horse away, he trudges to his porch. The moment he opens the door, he calls for his wife, Ella.

She hurries to him. "I have missed you," and kisses him lightly. Their children, Al and Alma, are close behind her. Alma is seven, and she hugs her father. Al is ten and mills around, glad he's home, but shows no affection.

After supper, Mason spends some time with Ella. He doesn't tell her about the horror he saw. There will be time for that when their children are not around. He sits close to her as Laya plays with a small loom, and soon she proudly shows them a wash cloth she has made. Al is busy making an arrow. He has mastered archery and is proud to be known for making some of the best arrows in town.

Too tired to talk long, Mason heads to his bedroom, where he flops into his waiting bed. It's warm, soft, clean-smelling covers feel wonderful, and he thinks slumber will carry him away. But sleep refuses to come and free his troubled mind.

Every time he closes his eyes his imagination comes alive and he sees the same scene. Rocks the size of the ones he saw strewn over the ghost camp begin falling from the sky like gigantic hailstones. They burst heads and crush bodies. Trying to clear his mind, he forces himself to think about his children, and he begins to drift away as a delightful spinning sensation soothes his body. His mind's eye comes into focus and he trembles in his sleep. A rock is crashing toward him. Before he can blink it smashes his head. He feels every crushing sensation the rock inflicts until it hits the ground. His spirit rises from his mutilated body and floats over the battleground where his men are being killed. He sees, hears, feels, and smells every sensation of the battle. Screams emanate from every direction, and the sounds of crashing rocks and splintering wood echoes in the field of death. Then he sees hysterical horses stampede across fallen men trampling them. His nightmare reaches a feverish pitch and his head roars. Mason leaps from his covers.

Ella rushes to his room and gasps. He's wild-eyed and drenched in sweat. She moves quickly to his side and speaks softly. His eyes slowly focus and he sobs as he sits on the side of his bed. "Can I make you some tea to help you relax? You need to rest," she says.

"Yes." he replies, rubbing his eyes.

As she prepares his drink, he shares his haunting dream with her. "I never saw what was dropping the rocks," he says, shaking his head. He sips the tea, and the warmth flows through his body causing him to finally relax. With drooping eyelids, he looks at Ella. "Let me sleep late tomorrow. I must have a clear mind to figure out how to never lose another man to these flying monsters."

"Don't blame yourself. No one had any idea what those men would be up against," she says softly.

Mason sinks into the covers and his mind slows. "Thank you," he says feeling as if he's pleasantly drifting away. He sleeps so soundly that he is free of grief and worry until he wakes at midday.

By evening Mason is in control of his grief. The pain lessens as grief changes into ambition for revenge.

Anxious to work on new equipment, Mason arrives at the barn early the next day to be alone and think before the men arrive. The barn door squeaks as he pushes it open. An eerie presence in the dimly lit room haunts its interior. There before him sets the dead men's weapons and wagons. He feels their presence, as if their ghosts are sitting in their seats watching him. A chill sweeps through his body, and he shivers.

He takes a deep breath and forces his mind to focus on the battered crossbow. He rubs his finger across its gashes trying to piece together its story.

The door swings open. "Good morning," says Jim, without a smile. Mo is by his side and waves.

Mason moves toward the equipment. "I know the first thing we need to do," he stops as the door swings open again. The last three men come in.

"Sorry, don't let us interrupt," says Dee.

Mason motions for them to come over. "As I was about to say, we should gather several stones the size of the ones we saw lying around the hunting party's camp site. We must figure out how to protect ourselves and our equipment when these horrid stones are dropped by creatures flying over our heads."

Jim creases his lips. "You mean creatures powerful enough to fly around carrying these heavy stones and armed with claws like we found?" Mason sighs. "Dragons," he states adamantly.

Jim nods solemnly, "I didn't believe there was such a thing when we started our search, but now I have little doubt."

"I can't wait to see what one of them looks like," says Mo.

Dee and Cur roll their eyes, "Don't wish for something that you will regret later."

Sul is wide-eyed and quiet as he walks close to the equipment and studies it for a moment. "I know the first step," he says. Mason gestures for him to continue. "Dee, Cur, and I will cut ten eight-inch thick logs five feet long. Jim, you and Mo, see if you can find a couple rocks the size Mason is talking about. Bring them back to the barn. We will meet you here with the logs in the morning."

"Is this for an experiment of some kind?" asks Jim.

"That's right. We must figure out how thick the logs we strap on the roofs of our wagons have to be to make them rock proof."

The next day, Sull, Dee, and Cur find Mason, Jim, and Mo waiting with several watermelon-sized rocks. "Now what do we do?" asks Jim before Sul can explain.

"You and Mo carry a couple of your rocks up on top of the roof and wait at the edge. When we are ready, you drop one of them on top of a box we are going to build out of these logs.

Mason watches as the experiment comes together.

Sul, Cur, and Dee finish lashing four of the logs across the top of a box they made with the other logs. They step back and admire their work for a second and then quickly walk thirty paces away. Sul looks up at Jim. "Let one go!" he yells.

The rock tumbles twice before it strikes the logs with a *thunk* and bounces off.

"The logs held!" cheers Sul.

The men on the ground run over to look. "There is only a little damage to the bark where the rock hit," cries Cur.

Mason is behind them and reaches out and rubs the gash in the logs. "Of course, the rocks will hit harder when dropped from much higher, but I think these logs will do the trick," he says.

"The next day when the men arrive, they are already talking about ideas. They tie their horses out front, and when they open the barn door, Mason is waiting for them.

"I hope you have some amazing ideas to share with me."

Dee can hardly wait to answer. "We start by building the lower frame and wheels just like the heavy cage wagon. We will need strong wheels. It is of no use to put a heavy log roof on a light wagon just to have them fall apart when the roof is taking a beating."

Jim closes his eyes, holds his chin in thought. "We will put a heavy beam upright on each corner of the wagon and two in the middle to support the heavy log roof. The roof will be hinged in the middle so either half can be lifted up when an archer needs to shoot or watch a dragon," explains Jim.

"This will be a fighting machine instead of a weapon for hunting," says Cur.

"That's what I want," says Mason with a wink.

A timid knock on the barn door turns their heads.

Jim walks over and pulls it open. A man and woman are standing in the doorway with long faces. They are well-dressed, but teary-eyed. The woman clutches a colorful handkerchief which she crumpled from wiping many of her tears. Mason recognizes her as Virgil's mom.

"Did you find any signs of our son?" she asks. Virgil's father places his arm around her waist.

Mason's excitement turns to sadness, and he lowers his head. "Come to my office and I will share all I know." He looks at the men. "Go outside and wait for a while."

As soon as Mason shuts the office door, the woman's tears begin to flow. "Virgil is dead, isn't he?" She manages to whisper.

Sorrow and guilt squeeze Mason's stomach. Seeing Virgil's mother wracked with pain strikes a nerve tearing away his composure, and he fights for words knowing that he must be honest without telling her all the gruesome details.

"We found the hunting party's equipment and it looked like a battlefield, but we did not find anyone."

The couple is quiet. They tremble as they weep together.

"I am very sorry. All of the men who went out there with your son meant a lot to me. They were my working family." Tears erupt, and he covers his eyes with his hand for a few moments.

Overwhelming grief prevent the couple from speaking. They nod goodbye and help each other out the door.

Mason sits in his office chair. His emotions are so painful that he is physically tired. He has no desire to work on anything for the rest of the day.

Chapter 6

As Jackson and Sandra's horses trot toward the Brittain farm, Jackson is so consumed by the possibilities the silver mine holds that he is shocked when their turn off appears. He raises his eyes. He can't remember one moment of the ride and forces himself to come back to reality. Janice runs out to greet them.

"What a wonderful surprise to see you," she says.

Jackson dismounts and hugs her. "Cap is in the shop helping my father," she says. She turns to Sandra and instantly they are lost in conversation about babies and head for the porch.

Jackson walks to the shop and opens the door. "Hello, Jackson," says Buck.

Cap's hammer rings two more times as he finishes the piece he is pounding on. He lays down the hammer and smiles at Jackson. "Is everything okay?"

"Everything is fine. Sandra and I just wanted to visit." Jackson shuffles awkwardly. Buck looks up. "You two go visit. I can finish this."

"Thanks, Buck." says Cap.

Once they're alone outside, Cap claps Jackson's shoulder. "You don't look very happy to see me," he says jokingly.

"Of course, I am glad to see you, but we do have a problem."

"The search party?" he asks.

"Yes and no." replies Jackson. "They came out of the wilderness yesterday and passed by the farm on their way home. They didn't stop, but I have a gut feeling that they will soon be back searching for more answers, and revenge. When they do, they will tromp all over the wilderness near Fuzzy's old cavern. It is time to decide what we are going to do with the silver mine."

Cap cuts his eyes toward the porch where Sandra and Janice are lost in conversation.

"We should discuss this with our wives."

They quietly walk toward the porch with guilty looks on their faces. Sandra and Janice stop talking and look them in the eyes. "What does this mean?" asks Sandra.

Cap sits and props his elbows on the arms of his chair, slides his hands together locking fingers. "Jackson and I made a discovery while traveling in the wilderness that we have kept secret. We waited until now to ask for your help in deciding what to do."

"Please tell us that this is not anything like last time we had a talk like this," says Janice, leaning back.

Sandra says nothing, but her smile softens.

"It's nothing like that. We discovered an abandoned silver mine in the wilderness, and it's obvious that it has been forgotten for a very long time. It was hidden deep in the forest until the ill-fated hunters cut a trail very close to it. Now it's less than a week's ride from here and close to a trail."

The women are quiet. "A little silver would come in handy with the babies on the way," says Sandra.

"I know, but it's not that simple. It won't look like the coins everyone is trading, and they will want to know where we found it. Our first thoughts were to cover the entrance and keep it hidden. If the people of Water Town ever find out silver is in the wilderness near here, they will destroy all its beauty and our way of life. I want our children to grow up beside the same peaceful countryside that Jackson and I love."

"I think we should wait a little while; this is a big decision," says Janice.

Cap nods. "I agree, but I'm afraid Mason will return soon, hunting dragons with a vengeance. If we don't hide the mine very soon, they will probably find it and trouble will start."

Janice looks at Sandra and they share a frown. "This means you will be in the wilderness again for weeks, doesn't it?" says Sandra.

"The trail is cut out now, and it won't take that long to get out there and do what we need to do," says Jackson sympathetically.

"Go cover it up. But I insist that Buck and Miles go with you. You will be safer with them along," says Janice firmly. She looks toward Sandra for her approval.

"Please go quickly and get it done. I don't want Jackson out in the wilderness around a bunch of hunters with bows and arrows. They may figure out what you're doing and kill both of you."

"I don't know if Buck and Miles can leave like that. They are old and have things they must do every day like taking care of this farm?" says Cap.

"They will be ready to leave before you. They are men who love to hunt and they still long for an adventure." replies Sandra.

Buck is excited when he learns about the unbelievable adventure, but is worried about Flavie. She assures him that she will be in a safer place than he will be. She agrees that Cap is right about the silver mine and that she and Janice can take care of each other.

In a couple days, Buck and Cap are at the Murray's spending the night so they can leave at daybreak.

Thank you for a wonderful supper," says Buck sitting on the porch talking with the Murrays.

Sandra is quiet and teary. She goes inside without an explanation.

Jackson looks at Inez. "I know this is going to be hard on Sandra. She needs me to be close now more than ever, but we have to do this and be back at the farm before the hunters return."

Sandra marches onto the porch, red ribbons in her hand. "I know you think the dragons are gone, but I am not taking any chances. I expect all of you to wear these from this minute on."

Miles smiles and ties one on his arm. Cap, Jackson, and Buck each take one and tie them on.

"Promise me you will seal the entrance and get out of the wilderness as fast as you possibly can," pleads Sandra.

Jackson walks over and hugs her. "I promise."

Buck takes a deep breath. "Well everyone, I am tired. I am going to my wagon. It took a lot of work today to get ready to leave. I will see you at daybreak."

Jackson takes Sandra's hand. "Good night Uncle Matt. You have the most important job of all, taking care of Sandra, mom, and Homer. Hearing his name Homer wags his tail.

"Just do what Sandra said and get back here ready to do some real work," he replies, pretending that he couldn't care less.

Cap stands. "Good night everyone. I am going out to the wagon too."

As Jackson closes the door to their bedroom, Sandra squeezes his hand and looks at him with sad eyes. "We're always going to have something to worry about, aren't we?"

He pulls her close in a hug. "I am going to do my best to make sure we don't."

<>

The men leave at first light. It's a cool morning and they are quiet as they listen to creaky wagons moaning as they sway and bounce up the trail. The horses' breath's freeze, making a misty fog that rises and melts away. The men are content to sit and daydream until they discover that the entrance to the wilderness is marked with brown foliage lying on the ground.

"The trail is cleared better than I remember," says Jackson to Miles who is sitting beside him in their wagon.

"If men keep using this trail, it's just a matter of time until they start settling out here," replies Miles.

Buck and Cap are in the lead wagon.

"I wish Janice could have come along. I love her more now than I ever thought possible. This child has made me see her and my mom and dad in a different way," says Cap.

"Trust me son. The more life you live together, the deeper your love will grow. You have just started that journey."

A stream comes into view at midday and they stop at the water's edge. They hop off the wagons and rest while the horses drink. Buck hands out jerky, and when the horses are satisfied, they resume their journey.

They ride with purpose the rest of the day. Everyone is growing hungry, and the sun is disappearing below the trees when Miles points to a pile of limbs cut from the trail.

"There's the wood we'll need for our campfire tonight." Everyone smiles as they stop.

Once the firewood is gathered and the fire is dancing, Jack pours beans, jerky, and onions into a copper pot. The men settle around the fire. "Buck, I am glad you and I are getting to go on this journey together. We work all the time and never have time to really get to know each other like we will out here," says Miles.

"I am looking forward to this trip too. For an old man this is the adventure of a lifetime," replies Buck.

Miles looks at his sons, "How much silver do you think is left in this old mine?"

"I have no idea, but I do know there are plenty of rotten bags filled with stones the size of walnuts lying around, and they look just like the one that the man in Water Town told me was silver." replies Cap.

"That's interesting," says Buck and he ponders a moment. "If all we have to do is just throw a bunch of silver ore on these wagons, then this is a whole different situation than I expected."

"We just want to close the entrance and leave the mine hidden. After everything we have been through out here, we want to keep our lives as simple as possible from now on," says Cap, glancing at Jackson.

Buck squints and looks toward Cap. "Let's think about this a little more. We could load up the silver that is ready to go and bury it at the farm. We can forget about it if we want to, but if there ever is a need, we can dig some up," he says.

"I don't know. The temptation will always be there," replies Cap.

"The temptation is sitting out here anyway. If you need it later, you won't have to ride out here to get it, and in the future, you may not have us to help you," says Buck.

Cap, Jackson, and Miles look into the fire thinking about Buck's idea.

Miles leans back. "The way I see it, the day you stumbled across the mine was the day you started having to resist the temptation to use it."

The brothers squirm. "I see your logic, but bringing it back will make it a little easier to give in to temptation. I see danger in making it easier. Easy silver could one day drive a wedge between our families," says Cap.

Everyone is quiet for a few minutes, and the pot smells wonderful as it bubbles. Steam swirls into the air and fades away above the fire.

"I think we should eat. I'm starving," says Jackson.

"Good idea. Then, we need to decide who is going to guard the camp first," says Cap."

Miles looks at Buck. "Why don't you take first watch. The boys can take their turn in the middle of the night, and I'll finish up and wake everyone in the morning." suggest Miles. They all agree and start dipping beans.

Sometime after midnight, the horses paw and snort restlessly, Jackson is on guard, and grows uneasy. He yells to Cap who reaches for his bow. "I need you to watch my back, something is spooking our horses," says Jackson.

Cap energetically hops to the ground and stands behind Jackson. "I don't see anything," says Cap.

It is eerily quiet for a moment. "I think I see two sets of eyes glimmering in the fire light just to my right." Jackson turns slightly with arrow pulled back. He sounds calm, but chills run up his spine.

"I have your back. Don't worry about this side." Cap whispers. "If you feel you have a good shot, take it. I will turn and cover you while you reset an arrow."

Jackson's eyes are fixed on one set of eyes that are slowly closing in. The orange glowing eyes never blink. Jackson shivers, he has to shoot soon, or he will be forced to shoot at a target streaking toward him. He cringes to think about what will happen if he misses. The orange eyes steadily continue straight for him. His hands sweat.

Suddenly, he hears an arrow *zing,* and instantly an ear shattering scream echoes through the woods. The scream of a night cat sends chills down the spines of every man.

Jackson flinches, losing his aim and fights to regain his senses. The big cat looks back at him. It squints, hisses loudly, and charges.

"Shoot!" screams Miles, sitting in the seat of their wagon with an empty bow.

Wounded and infuriated, the cat springs to a gallop. With his hands shaking Jackson fights to aim. The gallop turns to leaping and bounding, and there is no time. Jackson grits his teeth as he guesses when to let his arrow fly. He holds his breath as his fingers release the string. The arrow catches the beast in mid-air, and it falls like a rock near Jackson's feet. The shadows of the arrows protruding from the cat dance in the firelight. Two glowing eyes lay vertical, the cat's mouth opens and its tongue plops to the ground.

In the distance a second cat, whose eyes are all the men have seen, springs back into the underbrush thrashing noisily through the leaves and vines. A bloodcurdling scream emanates from deep in the underbrush. Moments later, another scream further away. Several more times the mourning cat screams. The screams grow faint.

Buck hops off his wagon. "I will stay up with Jackson until Miles takes his turn and I may stay up with him too. I can get along just fine with a couple hours of sleep in one night."

As day breaks, the silhouette of the big cat turns into a frightful sight as light grows brighter. Except for an arrow in its side and another under its throat, it looks like it could stand at any moment; its open eyes appear to follow anyone that walks near. The cat lays six feet from where Jackson stood.

Cap walks to the lifeless cat with his father. "I think we need two guards every night from now on," he says.

<>

Two days later, Buck and the Murray men come across the abandoned heavy cage wagon. It sits to the right side of the trail. It is solitary and ghostly in contrast to the wilderness greenery surrounding and overtaking it.

Buck is intrigued by the structure. "This took a lot of men a long time to build. These wheels are heavier than any I have ever seen. Whoever built this is capable of building almost anything."

"If we take this wagon with us, we won't have anything to worry about out here," says Jackson.

"This thing would slow us down," replies Cap.

Jackson rolls his eyes. "I was joking brother."

"Let's move on. We have half a day left," says Buck.

The next day, the trail turns slightly toward the plateau and the men begin to get glimpses of it looming ahead. Cap and Jackson slow down and study the forest to their left.

"I know we are getting close. The base of the plateau is a three-day walk from the mine," says Cap.

"Yeah, and that first day was a tough climb," says Jackson. They move up and stop where they can see the plateau through the tree limbs.

"I think if we were in the wilderness walking toward the plateau, we could be there in three days. We need to move into the woods. Let's spread out leaving a hundred feet between us and begin searching. The entrance isn't too far from the trail," says Cap.

The landscape is hilly and they all look the same. After hours of searching, Cap comes across the circle of rocks that he and his brother lay out in front of the mine.

"Over here!" he bellows.

Miles and Buck stop to look at the rock circle.

"Isn't our circle neat?" says Cap.

"Maybe it once was, but now it's a dead giveaway that something important is close by," states Miles.

Buck touches Miles shoulder. Look at this place. They walk up and poke their heads in. The mine is cold, dark, and intimidating. With wrinkled brows they look at Cap and Jackson. Cap smiles, "We will build a fire inside. In a while it will be warm and cozy. You will feel safer in there tonight than you have any other night out here."

They all gather wood and soon they have a fire burning outside. Cap takes a burning stick inside, and with its light he begins to place wood in the old circle of rocks. Before long the fire in the mine casts ample light in the chamber near the entrance. Buck and Miles come in and gaze at the place. Cap smiles as he watches them examine the walls. They carefully run their fingers across the little grooves in the wall where men from long ago had hewn at the silver bearing rock.

"I can build another fire deeper inside and you can see the whole place if you like."

"Maybe later, where are the rotten bags of silver ore," asks Miles.

"You're probably standing on some of them. They are lying all around the fire-pit.

Miles tries to pick up a bag, but it falls to pieces. He and Buck gaze at the floor. Little sparkles of orange twinkle around the chamber as they reflect the fire's flames.

"This place is covered with ore ready to just pick up." Miles and Buck shake their heads.

Buck looks toward Cap and Jackson. "This is too easy; I feel that sometime in the future you will regret leaving this laying here. Someday when you try to come back for it, there may be homesteaders out here watching every move you make."

Cap looks at Jackson and rubs his chin.

Miles clears his throat, "Think about it until after supper. Then whatever you decide will be all right with me."

Cap sighs. "Dad, you and Buck start supper. Jackson let's take a walk."

They don't go far until they sit on a large rock and talk. Miles can see them from the entrance and they are talking pleasantly. Miles and Buck lean back to relax and the brothers step inside.

Buck and Miles look to them for an answer. "Let's load it up. Like you both said, if we give in to temptation, we will come back out here later and haul it back anyway," says Cap.

"It's time to put the horses to work, we can eat when it's dark," says Buck.

They unhook the horses from the wagons and strap saddle bags on them. Then they head back to the mine. Jackson stops at the white stone circle. "You three start loading your saddle bags with ore. I am going to put these rocks into my saddlebags and take them out to the trail. I will place them so they won't be noticeable, but we can use them to find our way back if we ever need to.

They load the silver first and then begin closing the entrance. Its hard work but they are determined to get back home as quickly as they can. By nightfall the entrance is almost full. They leave enough room to crawl through and spend the night inside.

"We can tie the horses close to the entrance, but we will need to take turns watching them tonight," says Miles.

The next day begins with a quick breakfast. They are mindful that they have a cargo that no one needs to see, and they work hard to finish covering the entrance. Then they quickly harness the horses to the wagons.

Cap looks all around. "I feel uneasy like we stole something and we might get caught."

"No one alive knows about this ore. The only thing that makes me nervous is the thought of passing Mason or one of his men on the trail. He doesn't need to know that we have ever been out here," replies Jackson, as sweat drops from his brow.

"We will travel as fast as we can," says Buck.

"With a little luck we will be back at the farm in four days," says Miles.

They flip their reins and the horses tug until the wagons begin moving.

<>

Four days later, the Murray farm comes into view. "Now we need to get this ore buried," says Cap.

Buck smiles. "Don't worry we can unload the ore from our wagon into the Murray wagon. They can keep it shut up in their barn two or three days. We will all get together and bury it later. You and I need to hurry home to Janice and Inez."

<>

Two days later, Cap and Buck arrive at the Murray farm riding on horses with Janice and Flavie following in their wagon. Jackson comes running out and helps Janice step to the ground. "Thank you, Jackson," she says with a smile, while holding her bulging baby bump. She takes a deep breath and looks for Sandra. She and Flavie are nicely dressed. This visit is going to be all about babies.

Sandra comes to the porch wiping sweat, but her smile is radiant. Inez rings the bell so Matt and Miles will come to the porch. The cousins hug for a moment and take their seats as Flavie ambles up the steps with a basket of food to share with the Murrays.

Cap is talking to his brother when Miles comes around the house.

The men walk away from the women who are consumed in talk. The back yard is quiet and they resume being men on an adventure.

"I have been thinking about where we should hide our treasure," says Jackson.

Cap smirks, "Don't call it a treasure; that makes it sound tempting"

Miles clears his throat. "There is a large rock visible from here." He points toward it and everyone nods as they look.

"I suggest we bury it on its north side. We can easily keep an eye on it there. That rock will never be moved, so we will all know where to dig if the need arises."

Buck smiles and looks at the brothers.

"That sounds good to me," says Cap. He looks at Jackson.

"Let's do it," he says as he heads for the barn.

With shovels, plows and bare hands, the men dig until evening.

The next day as soon as there is enough light, they begin moving small loads of ore with the Brittain's wagon. By lunch they are leveling the spot where the ore is hidden.

After lunch, the men and women spend the evening sitting together. They talk about the two wonderful treasures that are about to be born.

Chapter 7

As they gaze out over the wilderness landscape, Fuzzy and Lester share a bond that has taken years of friendship to forge.

"Our den is settling in and I feel they are becoming endeared to this cavern. It is beginning to feel like home," says Fuzzy.

Lester hangs his head and Fuzzy feels his anguish. With watery eyes he shares with Fuzzy. "I wish I could be as fortunate as you. I know you are proud of Lee and Kim. They have chosen mates wisely. Soon they will have offspring and their respect and influence will increase."

Fuzzy's eyes turn kind. "I realize how lucky I am. At one time I thought Lee was hopelessly consumed with the need for revenge, but now he is content and in love. He and Beada are preparing a special place in the cavern to start a family. Take heart old friend, I believe time will bring Lear back to the den."

"I hope you are right. My heart aches when I think about the life that lies ahead for him." They are quiet until Fuzzy points to several dragons on the horizon.

A smile comes to Lester's face. "It's Lear and his friends."

"I count five dragons," says Fuzzy. He studies them a moment. "One of them is silver; that has to be Bird."

Lester wrinkles his lip. "I'm not sure that's good."

The dragons land with broad smiles and an air of confidence. They bow to Lester and Fuzzy.

"We wish to spend the night in the safety of your cavern. Are we welcome?" asks Gus.

"Of course, we're pleased that you are here, you will always be welcome," says Lester looking his son in the eyes.

Lear returns the look, showing little emotion.

"We are only here for the night," says Nom.

"We are on our way to Dragonthal. Bird is going to accompany us and show us around." states Gus.

"Join us tonight at our evening meal. We will feast on fish and apples," says Fuzzy. Lester's emotions stir deep inside, but he remembers what Liz told Fuzzy about letting them have a little time away from the den.

Later that evening, with full stomachs and possibly a taste of mushy lily bulb, they sit and talk. Bird is full of himself.

"Beautiful dragon, you should persuade your son of beautiful color to go with us. He would be the center of attraction in Dragonthal. The king would probably ask to see him."

"Lee speaks for himself; he has a mate now and soon an egg will be on the way." replies Fuzzy.

Leon wrinkles his lips. Is it my sister Beada?"

Fuzzy smiles with a nod.

"That means there is one less female in the den," complains Lear.

"Don't be concerned about mates now. We have a wonderful adventure ahead of us, and mates will only slow us down." says Gus, as Lear frowns.

Lester's demeanor wilts as he cuts his eyes toward Fuzzy.

Fuzzy tries to mellow their resolve, "Don't let the need for revenge keep any of you from living a rewarding life."

Bird lazily rolls his eyes. "You don't need a mate to live a rewarding life. Look at me."

Lester and Fuzzy are too kind to respond.

"We will leave at sunup. If all goes well, we will sleep in Dragonthal three nights from now," says Gus.

Lester and Lear lock eyes. "Come spend the night in my special place. You may be gone for some time after tonight," he pleads

"No thank you, father. You will not be able to resist trying to change my mind." He bows and leaves with the others.

Lester turns and walks into the cavern where his mate, Sada waits. Having heard everything, she leans her head on his shoulder for a second, and then they quietly amble to their special place.

Chapter 8

Buck, Flavie, and Aunt Mary's faces are bursting with smiles as Cap sits on the side of Janice's bed where she has just delivered a beautiful baby boy.

Cap leans next to her while looking at his son, "I never would have believed that I could love you more than I did, but I do. And I never thought I could love anyone else as much as I love you, but I already love this little boy the same." He wipes a happy tear.

Mary touches Buck's shoulder. "Ride to the Murrays and tell them about Cap and Janice's beautiful baby."

Buck rides along humming a tune and dreaming of the things he is going to teach his grandson.

In no time he is on the Murray's porch and surprised that no one has come out. He taps on the door and Homer barks. Miles opens it and at that moment Buck sees trouble on his face.

"Come in, Buck. Sandra is not feeling well. Actually, she hasn't felt well in several days."

Buck walks into her room where only one candle is burning. Jackson is close to her bed and too quiet.

"Hello Uncle Buck," sighs Sandra, trying to smile.

"How long have you been feeling like this?" he asks.

She looks down. "Several days."

Buck thinks a moment. "I'm going to get Mary right now. I want her to come help you. Janice doesn't need her now that she has given birth to a son."

Sandra smiles, "Is the baby okay?"

"Yes, they named him Ren. Try to rest and in a little while I will be back with Mary."

With a sense of urgency Buck mounts his horse and trots away. When he goes far enough that none of the Murrays will notice, he taps his horse to gallop. He dodges limbs and moves quickly until he is in his house.

Seeing Buck breathing fast and with a long face, Flavie wrinkles her brow. "Something is wrong," she gasps.

"Sandra looks bad, and she has been sick several days. I want to take Mary back right now," he says.

Mary grabs her coat. "Cap, saddle me a horse, and I will be ready to leave as soon as you reach the porch."

He runs to the barn, and when he returns, Mary hops on. She and Buck trot up the trail. They gallop gently until they are at the Murray house.

When they open the door, Inez tries to act casual, but wrinkles and her nervous speech tells Mary that she is scared.

Mary hugs her and she realizes the hug feels desperate. "Tell me what is going on," says Mary.

"We have done everything I can think of to make her feel comfortable, but she is miserable. She should have given birth weeks ago. Something is wrong." She tears up and tries to hide from Jackson. Mary takes her by the hand and leads her to the porch, where they sit.

Inez calms herself. "Sandra's pain increases every day. She must deliver soon or---."

Mary places her fingers over Inez's lips and shakes her head. "We will figure something out."

"But she hasn't even begun to show any signs that she is going to go into labor," sobs Inez.

Mary walks back into the house with thoughts racing through her head. She studies as Miles ambles to Sandra's side. Sandra lovingly looks up, grits her teeth and tries to smile for him

Mary begins gathering blankets, her bonnet and a bow. "Miles get your wagon. You must take me to Granny Da, she helped several women who couldn't go into labor long ago."

Miles heads for the barn asking no questions.

Jackson stands.

Mary looks him in the eye. "Stay close to Sandra. Don't leave for any reason. Your loving touch will give her the strength she will need until I return."

Miles is ready in moments and Mary hops in the wagon as soon as it is in front of the house. They are so nervous they ride without talking, and their insides tremble.

As they near Blade Town they begin to pass other wagons. It's hard for them to wave and act pleasant with all the heartache and anxiety they are enduring, but Miles waves time and again.

As sunlight fades, they see the blacksmith shop.

"Go straight to the house," says Mary. As soon as the wagon stops, Mary dashes toward the house and grabs a pot. She is in the garden in an instant.

"Miles!" she calls loudly. "Bring a shovel."

He turns the corner with a shovel in his hand.

"This is the plant we need." They dig up a spiny aloe plant and gently place it in the pot.

Hearing the commotion, Ed comes around the corner. "Is something wrong?" he asks without his usual smile.

"Yes. We must see Granny Da. I need her to tell me how to use this plant to make Sandra go into labor. She is running out of time." Ed staggers to sit on the rock in the garden; where he sobs. "Not my daughter," he barely utters.

"Mary's heart aches seeing his pain. She holds his hand as they quickly walk to Miles's wagon and climb into the back. Miles flips the reins and with a jerk they're on their way.

"Thank you, Miles, for helping Sandra and our family," says Ed.

Miles wipes trickling tears. "She is my daughter too," he says, barely able to talk.

They pull up to the porch at Fred's, and Mary dashes into the house. "Granny!" she calls. "Sandra needs our help. You told me long ago that the aloe plant in Sandra's garden can cause a woman to go into labor if something is wrong. Can you tell me what to do?"

Granny's eyes are piercing and teary as she is hit with her biggest fear. She takes a deep breath. "I learned long ago to overcome emotional sadness in time of need. When it's a matter of survival, you just get to doing what you have to do. I will cry later. Squeeze the juice out of an aloe blade. Choose one that is large, fresh, and healthy. Stir the juice in a half cup of honey. Make sure she drinks it all. If she spits some out, make more. This is a dangerous thing to do and will make her sicker than she has ever been."

Mary breaks down and sobs. Granny reaches out and takes her hand. "You have no choice but to be strong Mary. Do as I say. She and the baby will die if you hesitate. I must tell you she may die from this, but this is your only hope."

Granny staggers back to her bed and lies down. She places her feeble weathered hand across her forehead and cries.

The night is black. Miles and Mary sit in the wagon as Ed struggles to lead the horses back to his house.

When they reach their porch, Mary sighs, "Miles try to get some sleep. We will leave at first light."

<>

Jackson is sitting beside Sandra as he has all day. He lays his head on his arm that is stretched out holding her hand.

Inez walks to his side. "Son, you need to go eat something."

He slowly shakes his head. "I can't make myself eat feeling like this."

Inez starts to walk away when suddenly Homer scrambles toward the porch door and barks.

Matt hurries to see what he's barking at. His face brightens when he sees Mary climbing off the wagon. She dashes into the house. Ed is behind her carrying the plant.

"Go straight to the kitchen." She tells him as she walks over to Sandra's side. She smiles and lovingly slides her hand down Sandra's hair putting the strands back where they belong. She takes a deep breath, and heads to the kitchen to prepare the potion.

Ed and Mary quietly return. Mary is holding a brown cup with both hands. Inez and Miles step back and hold hands. Mary gently sits by Sandra's side and eases the cup close to Sandra's lips.

"You must drink Granny Da's medicine. She loves you very much and this will bring your baby into the world."

Sandra musters a smile, and drinks half, but then with a disgusted scowl she resists.

"Drink the rest for your granny, me, and our baby," says Jackson.

Sandra looks into his eyes for a second and then pulls the cup to her lips and finishes it.

"Let her rest for a moment," says Mary motioning for everyone except Jackson to come to the back porch. With the strength she saw in Granny, she speaks calmly. "The potion Sandra just drank will make her violently ill. She may not survive, but we have no choice."

Inez cries as Miles holds her.

"Something is happening!" yells Jackson.

Mary and Inez run inside to be met by the fearful sight of Sandra bouncing up and down while her arms and legs jerk aimlessly. Her eyes quiver wildly and look as if they will pop out.

Suddenly, green liquid gushes from her mouth soaking the entire bed and Jackson.

Furiously, Inez and Mary pull wet bedding out of the way as Jackson holds Sandra safely in bed.

Miles and Matt rush to them with wet towels. Ed is breathless as he looks at his little girl.

"She looks as if she's dying," he sobs.

"Have faith," says Mary.

Sandra stops flopping, gasps for air and tries to sit up.

Mary speaks softly to her as Jackson holds her back.

"I see the baby's head," gasps Inez. Sandra screams louder than any other time in her life and pushes the baby out.

Sandra loses consciousness and lies quivering. Her eyes don't focus or blink. Fear grips everyone like a vise. It's deathly quiet until suddenly the baby takes a deep breath and cries loudly. Sandra stops quivering and her eyes search for her baby. The baby cries again and when she sees it, peace fills her face as she sinks into a deep sleep.

Jackson doesn't ask if it is a girl or a boy. He can't take his eyes off Sandra.

Mary returns moments later with the sleeping child swaddled in her arms. "Jackson, you have a perfect baby girl."

Jackson lets go of Sandra's hand and stands. He looks at the face of the child and instantly falls in love. He reaches and touches her tiny hand. "I never knew what a precious gift a child is until now," he says.

<>

The next morning, soon after the sun is above the horizon, Jackson hears horses near the house and steps out on the porch. His brother and Janice are approaching in their wagon. In Janice's lap lying in a bundle is their newborn son, Ren.

"Is the baby here?" yells Janice.

Jackson smiles broadly. "She is! And Sandra is sleeping peacefully." He runs to the wagon to look at their son. Janice has him wrapped so neatly in a blanket that all he can see is the baby's face.

Janice hands the bundle to Cap and dashes into the house, only stopping when she reaches Sandra's bedside. Sandra is waking and looks toward her with weak eyes. A smile begins to spread across her face for the first time in weeks. Her cheeks fill with color, and the whole room brightens.

Cap walks up with Ren. Inez reaches for the baby and takes him in her arms. She pulls back the blanket and beams, "What a beautiful baby, so precious," she whispers. Cap smiles. "We were so worried about Sandra that we couldn't come see him, she says, as she sways the infant from side to side. She moves to Sandra's side and lowers him for Sandra to see. "This is Ren, your nephew," Sandra smiles.

"Where is my baby?" she asks.

"Your baby is beautiful too. Mary is bringing her in now." Mary gently caries the baby to Sandra and lays it in her arms. Sandra closes her eyes and leans her cheek against the child's face and sighs.

"We are waiting for you to name your beautiful daughter," says Mary.

"Renay, these cousins will play and discover the world together," she says in a whisper.

The family stands close; looking at the two wonderful gifts. Ren has curly blond hair and a button nose. His cheeks are full and he wiggles a lot. Renay has black hair and a tiny nose. She is thinner and is going back to sleep.

Later that day, the sound of wagon wheels and clomping hoofs on the trail catches Cap's attention. He and Jackson walk out to see who is coming. Fred and his wife wave in the distance. Fred calls out "Are Sandra and the baby OK?

Jackson's eyes beam. "They are both well!"

Fred wipes tears and takes a deep breath. He turns to look behind the seat and reaches to grasp a frail hand extending from the floor of the wagon. He lovingly squeezes it.

Cap and Jackson are beside the wagon before he turns back around. They look into the back of the wagon and are met with a tearful, wrinkly smile. Lively little Granny Da is nestled in a quilt and laying on a bed of straw.

Chapter 9

Excited by dreams of wonder and hope waiting to be discovered in Dragonthal, Gus and Nom wake early. They stretch and walk around bursting with energy. Gus stops and stares at their companions. They are curled up sound asleep with smiles on their faces. He puffs and shakes his head.

"Why don't you just wake them?" says Nom.

Gus looks at them again. "They look so peaceful, but we need to leave before the sun rises. We should avoid any fanfare from the den. Fuzzy and Lester won't be able to resist trying to change our minds again."

Bird stirs. Gus loudly clears his throat.

Bird rubs his eyes and stretches. Blinking, he looks at Gus and Nom. "Is it time to start our adventure," he yawns.

Nom walks over to Leon and Lear, extends his wing and lightly brushes it across their heads, and they stir. Bird smiles moments later when they sit up.

"A long day lies ahead of us, but it is going to be amazing. Let's leave now and find our breakfast before the other den members wake," says Nom.

Leon frowns and his head sinks slightly.

Gus looks him in the eye. "Are you not feeling well?"

"It's just that I thought I would say goodbye to my dad. It doesn't seem considerate to just leave. They will wonder why we didn't thank them for letting us stay here."

"I wish we could tell them we're thankful, but they would try to change our minds. There is too much opportunity and adventure just waiting for us to enjoy," replies Gus.

Nom cocks his head and interrupts. "I say we should waste no more time."

Bird stretches as he heads toward the entrance and then continues to the ledge. He sniffs the cool air that is blowing around the plateau. He looks to the sky where only a few stars are visible in the pink morning light. When he sees the others are behind him, he hops over the ledge and lets the current lift him high into the sky. The others follow. They soar and shiver until they warm from the labor of flight. Once they are comfortable, they dream of the beautiful city waiting for them.

<>

Lester has been awake for some time. He stares blankly as his mind races. He will only have seconds to plant a seed in his son's heart that he can only hope will grow. Sada quietly watches. She knows he is desperately trying to find the right words to say. She lays a wing over him and leans her head on his shoulder.

He sighs and turns to her. "I know you are worried too. It's taking our son a while to grow up and realize what is important. He is young and has seen things most young dragons never have to see. I know his wisdom will soon overpower his adventurous youth, and he will realize that the real joy of life can only be found when he is at peace with himself. When that day comes, he will return to help our den and make us proud of him."

Sada pulls back her wing. "I hope he will be safe until that time," she says. They rise and walk side-by-side to the entrance where the den has gathered to start the day. Lester sees Lee and Kim helping with the fish that have been caught for breakfast.

"Why can't Lear be more like them?" he thinks. Anger taunts him. If he loses his temper it will only fuel his son's rebellion. He looks into Sada's eyes for strength. They stroll toward the chamber where the rebellious dragons spent the night. When he looks inside and sees it empty, his heart breaks and tears flow.

<>

With a clear sky overhead, the sun's warmth bathes the optimistic dragons heading for Dragonthal. Bird's carefree lifestyle is contagious to his new friends and he enjoys being their leader. Gus and Nom gently flap their wings as they fly side-by-side behind him. Lear and Leon are content as they fly together.

Gus savors the moment. "If it weren't for our good fortune of meeting Bird, we would probably be on our way to surprise the men of Blade Town," he says.

Leon is next to him. "At the risk of sounding like Fuzzy, I think such an attack would only cause our den more pain." Gus looks at him and replies. "That is why we need to join a large army like the one at the dragon city."

Bird slows the pace at midday and begins a pleasant decent aiming for a lake ahead. The lake is small, but the water is dark purplish-blue. The trees surrounding the lake are some distance away because of a grey rock shelf that surrounds the water. The lake looks like a large pool with no beach. Everyone drinks their fill and leans back on the rocky ledge to rest. As they relax, the water begins to ripple. The ripple grows to a boil and fish begin jumping so wildly that they are sailing back and forth across the water. Being young and always hungry, they leap into the air. Their eyes sparkle as they fly among the school of excited fish, and they eat their fill without ever getting wet. One by one they return to the rocky ledge and bathe in the sun.

"This is the most fun I have had in a long time. I understand why you enjoy this kind of life," says Gus. Bird smiles slyly and points to the sky, and with euphoria they scramble to see who can take to the air first and fly the fastest. They are happy and filled with anticipation as they return to their quest.

When the sun begins to sink, Bird descends to the tree tops. He scans the landscape looking for just the right place to spend the night. He gently turns to the right and sails toward a cliff with an opening in its face. The group fills with excitement as they approach the interesting looking cave. The dragons land in the entrance.

"Wait out here while I take a quick look inside," says Bird. The blue dragons meander around in the entrance studying the rocks laying around. The rocks are jagged and look as if they had been blown apart when the cave was formed.

Bird emerges from the darkness into the sunlit entrance. "There is plenty of room in here." Everyone smiles, and they move deeper inside.

"We're lucky to find a place like this to shelter us from the weather, and no predators will be coming in this entrance way up here," says Nom.

Leon is captivated by what appears to be little paths zigzagging through the rocks on the floor. Curious, he disappears into darkness wandering down one of the paths. The cave turns colder the further he goes. The only light is behind him, and he can still see the others standing in the entrance. He spews a little stream of fire to see if anything interesting lies ahead. Instantly, thousands of *chirps* erupt and the rustling sound of a host of tiny feet scampering about fills the cave. Thousands of little bronze colored eyes reflect his fire, and they turn into streaks as the creatures scatter in all directions. Leon gasps and stumbles backwards in the darkness. He regains his balance and dashes in horror toward the entrance.

The path through the rocks is too winding for a large dragon to maneuver at such speed, causing him to trip and crash to the floor. He covers his head as bats dart in his face. He swats and they zigzag at great speed, avoiding his wing. Glowing orange red spit fire appears in their mouths as they dive at him. Several drops of fire zap his neck. He jumps to his feet, and runs faster. The fire on his neck is sticky and burns painfully; causing him to charge toward his friends. The swarm seems endless.

Bird runs toward him screaming. "Fall to the floor!"

As soon as Leon is down, Bird releases a powerful burst of blue and orange fire into the path of the oncoming bats. Then he unleashes another blast in the direction they came from. The pungent smell of burnt flesh and the sight of the burning creatures falling to the floor horrify the surprised blue dragons. Leon drags himself to his feet. Bird stares into the cave and slowly steps back.

There is an eerie quietness, but the slowly growing sound of thousands of wings fluttering sends chills down their spines. The intruders sprint toward the light at the entrance, dive out, and take flight. They fly far away and circle to catch their breath. Leon is burnt and bruised from the ordeal but keeps up with the others. Bird flies higher and searches for another place to spend the night. A grassy meadow looks inviting and they land.

"What kind of bats were those?" asks Leon as he cleans his wounds.

"They are little dragons. They are intelligent and have kings that they are loyal to. They look a lot like bats and can hang from walls and ceilings like bats, but they walk on two strong legs. When they are threatened, they take to the air in swarms like they did to you. My den calls them fire bats. They don't usually bother other dragons, but you triggered their survival instinct. They were only protecting themselves from our intrusion."

Bird gathers firewood, and the others search for fish. After a quiet meal they settle close to each other and drift off to sleep.

The next morning Leon groans when he moves, but he is able and eager to begin the trip again.

"One more night out here and tomorrow, we will sleep in the amazing dragon city," announces Bird.

"I'm looking forward to seeing this city. I hope it's not just a lily bulb illusion you experienced at an earlier time in your life," says Nom; looking Bird in the eye.

"You will apologize for that statement two days from now," assures Bird with a twinkle in his eye.

They fly until dusk. Bird turns toward a large river and leads the others to its shore. They land and everyone drinks their fill.

A meadow filled with waving stalks of golden-brown grass is visible above the flood plain beaconing the tired dragons to mash it into a warm comfortable mat. They amble toward the meadow.

"This is a perfect place to rest tonight, and tomorrow we can return to this river and catch our breakfast," says Gus.

Leon looks around cautiously. "I hope we don't see any fire bats tonight."

"I doubt we will, but you will see more tomorrow when we walk through the market at Dragonthal," says Bird.

"Will we have to be careful not to upset them?" asks Leon.

"No. They are locked in cages to be sold. Fire bats live all around Dragonthal. Hunting parties capture them as they fly out of their caverns to feed. Trolls weave nets of grass and reeds. They and the dragons work together and catch some every day. They bring them back and sell them to the trolls, who consider fire bats a delicacy."

Gus frowns. "I think I'm going to feel out of place when we get there."

"You will have no trouble fitting in and talking to the dragons, but it will take some time to understand what the trolls are saying," replies Bird.

The next morning the sky is cloudless, and the broom grass rustles in the breeze creating a soothing sound. The dragons look over the golden meadow where they slept. Like a windblown lake, waves of grass bow as they move across the meadow.

Bird takes a deep breath and savors the pleasant aroma of ripe grass before they lift into the sky.

At midday, they pass close to a lone silver and yellow dragon flying in the opposite direction. He doesn't slow down, but nods slightly. They nod back.

In the distance a mountain range peaks and stretches from east to west for as far as they can see. The terrain below is mountainous and grows taller with every mile they travel.

Bird looks back at the group. "We will be on the ground soon. Then the adventure will really begin."

The air grows cooler as they continue. The mountains below turn greenish grey, and the hue of the mountain on the horizon softens to a bluish purple. Slowly a shiny blue spot begins to appear at the base of the mountains.

"I see the lake at Dragonthal," says Bird.

He veers slightly changing their course so they will pass over the center of the lake. Several dragons come into view far ahead. Moving toward them with purpose and concentrating on their journey, they close in quickly and zip past bird's group paying them no attention. In the distance, a dozen or more dragons are in the air.

"There are more dragons flying over this lake than we have in our entire den," says Nom. Moments later it becomes obvious that two dragons are approaching, and they are not in a hurry.

Bird looks back. "Guard dragons," he says. "Just act natural. Pretend you do this all the time, and they will pass by." When the dragons are closer, the blue dragons are intrigued to see short, stubby trolls riding on their backs. Gus, Nom, and Bird act as if they are calm, but Lear and Leon are nervous and can't resist looking them over. The trolls are wearing leather vests and loin cloths. Their arms and legs are bare, and they are holding spears in their right hands. The spears point upward, and the blunt ends rest in pockets attached to a collar wrapped around the base of the dragons' necks. Their bows and quivers are attached to the collars also. Saddlebags are held in place by straps that circle the dragons' stomachs behind where the trolls sit. They bounce gently as the dragons flap their wings. Bird slows and nods. The dragons return the gesture, but the trolls turn their heads and study them as they pass.

Leon swallows with a *gulp*. "This is a different world."

"You will feel comfortable in a day or two," replies Bird.

As they approach the shore next to Dragonthal, they see boats with trolls paddling and dropping nets into the water. A dock is bustling as boats are unloaded. Just past the docks, a bluish-green meadow lies at the base of the majestic mountain range. The meadow is well-groomed and there are several rock paths running through it headed in all directions. A bubbling spring sparkles as it churns in the middle of the meadow. The paths all join at a wide area paved with stones that circles the spring. On the mountain side of the paved area, a rock-paved road leads toward a large opening in the mountain.

"That opening leads to a large cavern, and the king's courts are deep inside the mountain," says Bird. The blue dragons are busy looking at a world that they could never have imagined. "We will head toward the market so we don't draw too much attention to ourselves. I want to rest soon and find a place to spend the night."

They fly over the market and see two rows of rock buildings with a road running between them. Dragons and trolls are milling about. Some amble along slowly, while others are in a hurry moving from shop to shop.

The huts are made of various shapes and sizes of rock stacked neatly. The roofs are covered with grass, and most of them have one door and two openings for windows. There are large huts and small huts scattered around the knolls on both sides of the market. A path connects them for miles in both directions. Mixed in with the huts are gardens and orchards.

They land softly in a grassy area behind the market.

"Is it going to be a problem that we are blue and the rest of the dragons are silver and yellow?" asks Nom with a wrinkled brow.

"Don't worry, not all dragons here are silver and yellow. Dragons from caverns all around come here to visit and trade. Let's stroll around the market. When we feel a little more confident, we can talk with some vendors."

Bird takes the lead, smiles and walks confidently into the market. Occasionally a passerby takes a second glance at them. The market is lined with shops trading chickens, nets, baskets, fish, and much more. They approach a shop where a small female dragon is trading grass rope and wool blankets. She notices Leon and trying to be polite she doesn't stare. But after several glances, Leon smiles and nods respectfully to her.

"I have never seen a blue dragon," she says in a gentle voice. "We just arrived from far away. This is a whole new world to us," he responds.

She smiles again, "Then you should come and visit with me and my friend at our hut. My name is Bell. We can tell you all about Dragonthal, and you can rest for a while."

Leon introduces himself and his friends. Bell pleasantly nods to them. "All of you are welcome." Leon looks to Bird for approval.

Bird smiles, "We are very lucky," he replies

She gathers a few things and leads them out of the market. As they follow her she notices that they are quiet when they are near the guards, even though most of the guards nod as they pass.

"Don't worry about the guards. They are soldiers from the king's army. They're just here to show that he is in control and keep the peace," says Bell.

Leon raises his eyebrows, "This is so different for us. Our den doesn't even have one soldier."

Not far from the market the rock road narrows to a path that meanders past rows of rock huts. She leads them to her dwelling and opens the door. They are immediately greeted by a crippled troll. She introduces him as her mate, Deago. He smiles and appears to welcome them, but they can't understand what he says. He seems interested in her new friends. Bell sometimes tells him what their conversation is about, and he smiles.

Bird is all smiles as they talk. "We want to spend some time here and one day talk to the king," he explains

Bell looks at Deago and they both wrinkle their foreheads. Bell looks at them with a solemn face. "You may want to learn more about our king before you meet him. Guargin rules with an iron fist. He's afraid he might lose control of his kingdom. He has taken most of our freedom away. He commands a small army that is always ready to fight. He treats them so well that everyone wants to be a soldier, and all of them are very loyal. Those of us who are not in his government or army have to work very hard and be careful about what we say. If he finds out there is talk about some of us being unhappy, he will not be interested in hearing our excuses."

"Then we will have to spend some time here to be safe," replies Bird. He looks around at his new friend's hut. The floor is covered with smooth rocks and is swept clean. There are grass mats on the floor in one corner like most dragons sleep on. But unlike a dragon's special place, there are shelves made of wood around the room. Bell has items to trade at the market neatly stacked on them.

"Your hut is beautiful," says Bird.

Bell smiles, "If you are going to stay in Dragonthal long, you will need to find something to trade in the market so you can fit in. You will also have to find your own hut. There are huts around where you can stay if you give their owners things they can trade in the market."

Bird smiles from ear to ear, "I can bring lily bulbs!" he laughs. Bell looks puzzled until he explains.

"That sounds like a good thing to me," she says. She goes to her shelves and returns with several saddlebags with long ties. "This is how city dragons carry things like lily bulbs. Hang them around your neck."

"Can we spend the night in your yard? We will leave in the morning," says Bird.

She smiles, "Of course."

Chapter 10

Mason works relentlessly to design better equipment. Sometimes when he is consumed in his work, time slips away and darkness surrounds the barn. Deeper and deeper he sinks into his work and doesn't realize everyone has left. When he realizes it's dark and he is alone, a lurid spell sweeps across the barn and strange sounds whisper through the barn doors. Barely distinguishable, the muffled clomp of horse hooves and squeaking wagon wheels combine in sorcery. Mason is sure that the spirits of the horses and men from the hunting party are returning to the barn. He creeps toward the doors and strains to hear distant, ghostly voices. A chill runs up his spine and he shivers. His trembling hands reach for the latch on one of the doors. Carefully and slowly he pushes it open. The hinges squeak, giving him away, and he quickly flings it open.

A pungent breeze whips across his face ruffling his hair and blowing the spell away. Heartbroken he stumbles back inside. Sobbing, he finds his chair, places his fingers across his closed eyes, and cries.

<>

Within a month Jim has finished building the equipment needed to return to the wilderness in search of the dragons. It is all stored in the barn behind the tents, wagons and cages belonging to Mason's exotic creature show.

On a cool morning when there is nothing that needs to be repaired for the show, Mason makes a trip to the barn. The hunting party is on his mind. Jim is building a fire in one of the forges just to warm the building. Mason smiles and walks close to warm his hands.

"Jim, I can't get the lost hunting party off my mind. I have been reluctant to do anything, but it is time go back to the burial site. I would like to learn more about what happened."

Jim wrinkles his forehead, "I know it is time, but frankly, I'm afraid to go out there again. Those men were the best hunters I have ever known."

Mason sighs, and lowers his head looking into the growing fire. "I will be willing to pay Dee, Sul, Cur, and Mo plus four more men to go with you. You will have the new wagons that can withstand the falling rocks, and a better crossbow."

Jim doesn't take his eyes off the fire. "I don't think I'll ever get the images of the battle site out of my mind. Just thinking about how those men died gives me the creeps."

"This time we will not try to capture any of the dragons. This trip is just to see what is out there," says Mason.

Jim shakes his head with a half-smile. "The dragons won't know that.

Mason pats Jim on the shoulder and leaves.

The next day at the barn, Jim and the men who traveled to the ghost camp are talking outside. Mason nods and passes. He wants them to continue talking, just in case they are considering his proposal to Jim the day before. He ties his horse and goes into the barn.

Sul comes in first and heads toward Mason. The others trail behind him. "I would be willing to ride out there with plenty of men and weapons if we have cages to keep us safe at night. I intend to follow the trail that's already there. I'm not willing to delve into the wilderness, crawling through underbrush hunting for trouble."

"If that is all that is expected of us, you can count me in as long as we take a couple dogs with us," interjects Dee. Cur and Mo nod in agreement.

Jim is wide-eyed. He walks away from the group nervously rubbing his chin. Everyone looks at him. "I need more time to think about this," he replies.

A week passes and Jim still hasn't made up his mind. The four men return to the barn. Each brings a friend who is anxious to go on an adventure.

Jim looks at Sul and the group. "Do your friends know how dangerous this trip will be?"

Sul takes a deep breath. "We have talked and they know what we found out there."

Jim grits his teeth shaking his head lightly. "Part of me wants to go and part of me is scared to death. He looks at the group of men, and they seem undaunted. "I can muster enough courage to go as long as everyone understands that I'm going to be very careful and turn back if we begin to have the least doubt about our safety."

Mason smiles and looks Jim in the eyes. "Jim, that sounds fair to me. I don't want anyone else to get hurt out there."

Jim's face lifts. "I have eight men willing to go with me and I intend to bring eight back."

Mason sighs. "I will make sure you all eat well and are comfortable. You can ask me for anything."

Two weeks later, Jim is ready to leave for the wilderness with two cage wagons and a crossbow. This time, the cages are fitted with doors that can be raised and latched on each side giving them more protection than just bars. Five horses are loaded with provisions, and the wagons have plenty of tarps and blankets. Mason brings out two hunting dogs that the men have been trained to control.

With little fanfare the group pulls out of the barn. The four new men are wearing clothing that looks like new, and their bows don't have any scratches on them. Jim smiles to himself and thinks, "this is an eager bunch and full of energy." He listens to their stories about hunting trips and unbelievable legends. A twinge of adventure brightens his face as he listens to them. They all step lively as the journey begins, and every step takes them closer to the wilderness. Late in the evening they are tired, but still enthusiastic as the Murray farm comes into view.

Miles, Uncle Matt, and Jackson are sitting on the porch enjoying the evening. Hearing the party approaching, they walk out to the trail.

Jim is a friendly man and tips his hat. "Good evening. Would you mind if we water our horses at your trough? We're passing through. Headed north to spend some time in the wilderness."

Miles looks frankly at Jim. "You are welcome to water your horses here anytime. I hope you find what you're looking for, and you return safely."

Jim tips his hat. "Thank you, my friend. I hope to talk to you again soon."

<>

The rebellious young dragons are back at Bird's place clawing around lilies and throwing dirt to the side as they enthusiastically unearth the plants. They tuck them in the saddle bags that Bell gave them and head for Bird's cave. Bird watches as they carry the bags in. "The bulbs need to stay moist until we leave for Dragonthal," he instructs.

In less than a day they have filled all the bags. "This should be enough to last a year! Tomorrow we will load up and start back," says Bird.

Lear looks at Bird with creased lips. "I want to visit our den before we go back."

"Fuzzy and your father will only try to talk you into staying if you go," warns Nom.

"I don't care. I'm not mad at anyone. I just think they gave up too easily. I am going to see them tomorrow."

Gus rolls his eyes and looks at Nom. He shakes his head and moans.

Leon stands. "I don't think it's a good idea for Lear to go alone. I will go with him."

Gus and Nom cut their eyes toward Leon. "We know you want to go too," groans Gus.

"Bird laughs and lays out a lily bulb. "Let them go. They need to get this out of their systems. They will see that it's going to be much more exciting returning to Dragonthal to meet the king than to hang around a damp cavern."

Leon and Lear head for the den's new cavern the next day.

Liz is outside watching the sun set. She smiles broadly when they land. "Leon, Lear, what a pleasant surprise. Are Gus and Nom with you?"

Lear smiles politely "No, they chose not to come. We're planning to return to the dragon city in a couple days, but we wanted to spend the night here with the den and see how everything is going." He looks around. The cavern is quiet and most of the den has settled in their special places. "I'm going to go to my parent's special place and spend the night with them."

"We miss all of you. Leon, are you going to see your parents tonight?" He gently nods.

Liz smiles and walks past them as she continues to the ledge where she can savor nature's artwork of red, orange and silver in the western sky. "What a beautiful ending to a beautiful day," she thinks.

Leon and Lear amble into the cavern. "I miss being with our den, but deep inside I still want to fight back against civilization. You, Bird, Gus, and Nom are the only ones who seem to feel the same way," confesses Leon.

"I am more interested in the adventure Dragothal has to offer. I sometimes feel angry at mankind, but now I'm more interested in discovering new things," replies Lear.

They part and head for their families. Lester smiles quietly when he sees Lear. He is careful not to spoil his good fortune. Sada smiles but can't resist wrapping her wings around her son and laying her head on his shoulder. After she releases him, she treats him no differently than she would if he normally spends the night with them.

As the sun rises, the den gathers as usual to fly to the lake where they catch fish for breakfast. Fuzzy, Lester, and Tee are content to sit on the beach and watch the younger dragons happily splash around. When everyone at the lake has eaten their fill and gathered enough fish for those who didn't come, they race back to the cavern.

The den is in a good mood and they gather around to talk. Lester calls for them to quiet.

"I want to know what Dragonthal is like!" shouts Victor, a young male.

Lear smiles. "We only visited a short while, but we learned a lot. The city is so large that they have outgrown a huge cavern deep in a beautiful mountain as tall as this plateau. They had to start building rock huts, and now they stretch along the mountain range. The city is occupied by dragons and trolls that work together, and some of them even live together. There are so many dragons and trolls there that I can't even guess the number."

Leon speaks up. "We still have a lot to learn, but Dragonthal is a fascinating world of its own. Most of the dragons are silver and yellow, and the trolls all look alike. There are guards all around the city. Some are dragons and some are trolls. The trolls carry spears and bows. Everywhere you go you feel like a guard is watching you."

Lear joins in. "We hope to see the king once we are comfortable there. We have been told he is half-dragon and half-troll, and a fierce ruler. He has an army made up of dragons and trolls. Most of the trolls carry bows and arrows as they ride on top of the dragons, they are trained and lethal. His army could be here in three days if they wanted too. Nom and Gus intend to tell him about the men who attacked our den. They plan to join his army in hopes of fighting civilization one day."

Fuzzy drops his head but doesn't respond. He whispers to Lester. "We have a lot to talk about when our guests leave. There is no use trying to influence them with our opinions."

No more is said about the dragon city and at midday Lear and Leo say goodbye.

Fuzzy and Lester talk quietly that evening. "I can't stop thinking about the story Bird told about dragons and trolls wiping out mankind once before," says Lester.

Fuzzy sighs. "It is my duty to warn Cap and Jackson like they did for us. Neither the silver and yellow dragons nor the trolls will care that the Murays and Brittains helped save our den."

<>

Gus and Nom watch as Leon and Lear land near Bird's cave. Bird smiles.

Nom looks at Gus. "I wonder if their families changed their minds?" says Nom.

"I think they will be going with us to the city for the adventure. I don't think they will join the king's army though," replies Gus. "Either way I'm glad to have them with us."

Lear and Leon approach, smiling. "Are we ready to leave for the city?" asks Leon.

"We will leave in the morning if you two are still going with us," replies Gus.

Bird is still smiling; he doesn't want any part of this discussion.

"Nothing has changed. We're excited about getting back to Dragonthal," replies Leon.

That night, Gus and Nom are pleased when they hear that all is well at the new cavern. They pause for a moment.

Gus stares at Bird's fire and his smile fades. "We still have a lot to figure out. It may take several days before anyone trades for a lily bulb, so it will be a while before we have anything to trade for shelter."

"We will have to make the best of sleeping in Bell and Deago's yard if they will let us." suggests Nom.

Bird smiles, "I assure you it will not take long for us to get more than we need."

<>

When the dragons show up at Bell's place, she's not surprised.

Bird slips the baskets off everyone's necks and sets them next to her hut.

"We have filled all our saddlebags with lily bulbs." He picks a bulb up and hands it to her. She wrinkles her nose and sniffs.

"I hope you know what you are doing," she sighs.

Bird takes it back and tosses it into the basket. "You will thank us later. If you agree to trade them in your shop, we will give you half of what you take in trade."

Bell smiles. "I do enjoy trading at the market. You are welcome to stay here a couple days."

Every day, more and more customers come to Bell wanting lily bulbs. Deago begins cutting them into smaller pieces and they still get just as much for them. Bird is delighted and shares the traded goods with the four blue dragons. They find a small hut and move in. The next day they trade for grass mats to place on its rock floor. They begin enjoying pleasant nights in the dry and begin trading at the market. They mostly trade for fish, but Lear is spellbound when he sees a shop filled with cages of fire bats. The shop owner is a dragon, and they have no problem communicating.

"Why would anyone want a fire bat?" Lear asks.

The owner cocks his head and studies Lear. "You look different. How long have you been around here?"

"My den's cavern lies far from here. We never knew this place existed until recently."

The merchant looks satisfied and is ready to make a sale. "I'm glad you came by my shop. The trolls love to eat them, but I have never heard of a dragon eating one. They are little dragons, you know.

"I may keep them for pets," replies Lear.

The merchant shrugs. "Build a fire and roast them or make pets out of them, I don't care. Trade me some of your rope and pick one."

Lear looks into a cage with two bats inside. The little creatures sense his presence and tremble. Their wings are tied together and with little grass baskets pulled over their heads they are helpless. When he touches their cage they frantically stumble about.

"I will take these two," he says.

"Wise choice my friend. Hold them by the legs and pop their heads against a rock before you remove the basket from their head.

Otherwise you will get burned. The burn will be unbearable if you don't wash it off quickly."

"Thank you, but I'm going to make pets out of these two."

The merchant shakes his head. "You're going to get burnt."

"Thank you for the advice. I may see you again soon."

Lear looks guilty as he walks with the two fire bats dangling from his claws. He picks up his pace as he nears the hut he and his friends have acquired. Several trolls pass by, carrying bats. They smile as they pass. He forces a smile, then rolls his eyes and wonders if he looked as ridiculous as he feels. As he walks along, he tries to figure out how to free the little creatures without getting burned. Before he ducks behind the hut, he looks around to see if anyone is watching him. When he is ready to take a chance, he pulls the basket off one of the bats. The little dragon blinks and struggles to focus in the blinding light. While it squints and tries to see what is happening, Lear removes the basket from the other, and they huddle close to each other. Their eyes follow his every move, trying to decide what to do. Lear knows it's a long shot, but he tries to communicate with them.

They're too afraid to respond. They squirm and make a trembling chirping sound. He reaches over to one of them and begins to untie the rope that holds its wings. The other little dragon panics, chirps loudly and sucks in a gasp of air preparing to spit fire. Lear squints, preparing to be burnt at any moment. As the rope slips gently off the first little fellow's wings they flutter and the glare in his eyes soften. He cocks his head as if in thought. The expression on his face begins to brighten. Lear notices that they exchange a different sounding chirp, and then the other little dragon relaxes turns and holds its wings out so untying them will be easier.

Once they're both free Lear bows. "You are free, take off and return to your den. The two little creatures spring into the air and fly a short piece. When Lear turns to walk away they sail back toward him. He shudders to think he's going to get burned for doing his good deed. They land in front of him, eyes bright and a smile is evident.

They face Lear and are no longer fearful. Their dragon sense of communication begins to work. "What is your name blue dragon?" one of them asks.

Lear's heart is warmed. "My name is Lear. I am pleased that we can understand each other."

"Thank you, kind dragon. We will remember what you have done for us." They disappear into the sky.

Lear has a peaceful feeling as he walks to the front of the hut.

"Where have you been?" asks Bird, not really wanting an answer. "We have to return to my cave and gather more bulbs, but it's getting late. We take to the air first thing in the morning."

<>

Fuzzy, Lester and several other dragons lay bathing in the sun, their eyes are closed, but they are not asleep. All are peacefully obeying their reptilian need to fill themselves with warmth. Except Fuzzy. Memories of Cap and Jackson risking their lives, trudging into the wilderness to warn his den of the hunting party; is grinding at his nerves. He groans and repositions himself several times.

"What is troubling you?" asks Tee.

"I have a duty I must honor. The dragon and troll army that Bird told us about sounds more dangerous now that Leon and Lear described them. As soon as their king finds out about the towns near our old cavern, they will pay our friends a visit. A large city of dragons and trolls will be able to assemble a great army. I feel they will be powerful enough to wipe out mankind." He sits, sighs, and his face grows longer. "I must warn our friends. Their red ribbons will do them no good this time, and because they live so close to the wilderness, they will be the first men this army will attack."

"I would like to go with you," says Tee. Lester wrinkles his brow and looks at Fuzzy. Fuzzy replies calmly, "I know you would like to go with me to warn our old friends, but even though it's a long trip, Tee and I will be fine. I will give Cap and Jackson your regards." Fuzzy then turns to Tee. "We will leave in the morning.

A blustery morning with clouds chasing one another across the sky greets Fuzzy and Tee as they step out of the cavern with Liz and Bee by their sides. They walk to the ledge, hug their mates, then take to the air.

Flying with determination, they make good time and by midday they're ready to rest and find water. A waterfall with its white misty tail gleaming among a sea of wilderness green comes into view. The majesty and sound make their mouths water as they approach. They land on the waters edge where the mist drifts past them.

"This is a jewel hidden between our new and old den. Even the beach surrounding the pool sparkles," says Tee looking at the fine white sand.

Fuzzy smiles. "We will stop here again," he says. They return to their journey, and as dusk approaches they see the river and cliffs where they weathered the stormy night on the migration. Fuzzy looks over at Tee and nods. They land there, find the little cave, and spend the night.

They wake early, and anxious to see the old cavern again they take to the air. By early evening they see the high spot that is the plateau on the horizon. "I have a funny feeling being this close to our old cavern. Something inside me feels happy and right," says Tee.

"I feel it too. There is something tranquil about returning to where you were born." A tear slides down his eye and the wind plucks it away. Memories float around them. Soon they land on the ledge near the sealed entrance. They are tired and the warmth of the sunny ledge relaxes them. They can't resist the urge to lay back and rest for a while.

Softly the sound of a horse whinny drifts across the plateau. Tee freezes and looks at Fuzzy.

Fuzzy's eyes pop open. "We're in danger. Be still. It isn't long until dark. We will sneak away when the sun goes down." As they wait, they hear laughing, chopping and an occasional yell.

Tee has a sly look on his face. "We should wait until the men are asleep and their fire has burned out. Then we sail down and stomp on the top of their wagons. We can shake them a couple times and then disappear into the woods. They will never see a thing."

Fuzzy wrinkles his lips. He doesn't like the idea.

Tee looks him in the eye. "I don't want them climbing up here and digging the entrance to our cavern out. They will be excited about what they find and go back for more men, and soon men will be crawling all over our home. If we scare them, they will be afraid to come back."

Fuzzy quietly thinks. He wipes a tear. "This place is very dear to our den. I know we can never stop men from discovering the cavern's beauty someday, but I think a good scare will stop them for a while," he sighs. "I don't want them to know what did this, and I don't want anyone hurt."

After the sun sets, they look over the ledge and there in the dark a campfire flickers. They wait until the men are quiet and the fire is only a red glow.

"Are you ready to scare the daylights out of those men?" asks Fuzzy.

They jump from the ledge and dart toward the wagons. The dogs bark and the horses go into a frenzy when they sense the dragons. Fuzzy and Tee each hit a cage wagon at the same time. They latch on with their claws, shake and stomp two times. Then with a mighty sweep of their wings they lift into the air and fly in the direction of the Murray farm. The sound of the dogs barking fades away quickly as they distance themselves from the men.

<>

Mayhem erupts in the cage wagons the moment the jolting thud hits. The men are helpless as the creaking wagons sway and bounce. In total darkness, they trip over each other, bump heads and struggle to stand as they desperately search for their bows. The dogs go wild, darting, barking, and hopping back and forth. Men on the floor ball up to avoid their sharp teeth. When some men manage to stand, screams of agony add to the roar as legs, hands, and bows are stomped.

The shaking stops, but the panic continues. In the midst of the squirming mass of men, leaves and dirt begin to churn in the air as huge wings flapping briskly are heard. The men's eyes fill with painful shards of sand and dirt, and they struggle to catch their breath.

"What's happening?' yells Jim, holding on to one of the dog's collars. Dee and Cur cower in corners of Jim's wagon. The other two men bite their lips and rub their wounds as they slowly stand.

With wild eyes Jim yells to the other wagon. "Mo! Are you and your men all right?"

"Something huge just tried to crush us?" cries Mo, breathing rapidly.

"I'm afraid it's not finished with us, and we didn't see a thing. Did you get a look at it?" asks Jim

"No! And if that thing comes back, we're finished!" rants Mo, looking fearfully into total darkness. "I can hardly see you." Mo looks around his wagon and helps his men to their feet. He squints trying to see Jim's men. "That thing almost turned us over, and some of us are still searching for weapons. One man tried to set an arrow, but fell and now it's stuck in my friend's leg. Whatever that thing was, it shook this wagon like a toy. What could be that powerful?"

"I shiver just thinking that whatever did this is still out there waiting for us to come out. Don't open your door and try to quieten your dog. All I can hear is him barking. If something is still out there, we will never hear it," says Jim pulling his dog close. It stops barking, but continues panting wildly while looking into the woods with bulging eyes.

No one sleeps for the rest of the night.

As light creeps into the foggy forest, men with red eyes look through the cage bars, searching for clues. They rub their weary eyes, leaning their heads tiredly against the bars, and wait for Jim to suggest what to do.

"Mo, I'm going to unlatch our door and step out. Have two of your men set arrows and be ready to defend me if I call, otherwise stay locked inside." He looks at the anxious men in his wagon. One of you come with me. The rest of you shut the door behind us and be ready to shoot through the bars.

He reaches for the latch and notices his hand is trembling. His mind is racing as he remembers his gut feeling that told him not to come out here. He takes a deep breath. "I must be strong for these men," he thinks to himself.

He pulls the latch and it flips to the side with a *snap*. He steps out and gazes all around before moving away from the wagon. He sees that the horses are still tied where they were left. He peeks under the wagon and sees nothing. He stops and thinks. His dog is wagging its tail and decides that is a good sign. He reaches inside and unlatches the door and lets it hop out behind him. The demeanor of the dog puts his mind at ease, and his men step out, but they all have arrows set.

Jim shakes his head, then looks at Mo. "Everything looks just like we left it last evening. I think it is safe to come out now. Two of you build a fire and let's get some breakfast started. Dee, hop up on the crossbow and be ready to shoot in an instant. The rest of you watch the woods and the sky and be ready for anything."

Warmth from the crackling fire gives a sense of security as a pot of root tea simmers, and Jim stands quietly studying the campsite. "Cur, climb on top of the wagon and see if there is any clue as to what happened last night," he says

Pulling and tugging, Cur muscles his way to the top and looks around. "I don't see a thing."

Jim moans, "I'm not surprised. The large logs up there won't scratch easily. Until last night I was beginning to feel pretty safe out here, even though I can't rest when I think about what happened to the hunting party."

Cur is still standing on the roof looking down on Jim and the others. He frowns, "I have to wonder if the hunting party didn't get a warning like we did last night, and they ignored it. Now they're lying out here under that pile of rocks for eternity." All the men turn and look up at him.

Jim turns back to the fire and warms his hands as Cur climbs down.

"I remember my promise to return if I had doubts about our safety. Load up. But keep the crossbow manned. We have probably found all we are going to anyway, so we're heading back to Water Town as fast as we can."

Smiles spread across tired faces, and soon they are ready to pull out. Jim looks at everyone nervously waiting to start. "Keep arrows set and guard the crossbow. Move out."

Chapter 11

Fuzzy and Tee sit crouched under a small tree whose limbs drape around the top like a giant mushroom; forming a canopy over their heads. The limbs are covered with tiny greenish-yellow leaves. Larger trees soar all around them, but their chosen spot is cozy. There is a slight dip under the tree that is filled with dry leaves which helped keep them warm during the night. They are surrounded by forest and underbrush and are completely hidden from anyone milling around the Murray farm, yet they can see the cabin through the limbs. Roosters crow before the sun rises and birds flutter and hop about above their heads. Smoke begins to swirl from the chimney, and Jackson walks out on the porch. He stretches and savors the freshness of the morning air. Tee moves slightly and nudges Fuzzy. Fuzzy gently shakes his head.

"We don't want to scare our friends. When they come out to start their work we will walk out in the open, staying far enough away that they won't be alarmed but can still see us. When we have their attention, we will bow and wait until they are sure it is us."

"This is a curious world," says Tee, peering at rail fences, barns, and animals contently feeding in the fields.

The front door swings open and Miles, Matt, and Jackson step out to start the day.

Jackson has a broad smile on his face. "It's going to be a good day today, Renay slept all night. I feel like a different man this morning."

The men all smile and head toward the barn. Fuzzy and Tee make their way to the clearing and step onto the green grass that covers the fields surrounding the farm. Miles catches sight of Fuzzy and Tee and stops in his tracks.

"Something is going on," he says energetically as he points toward Fuzzy and Tee.

Jackson cranes his neck and Matt stops to look. Fuzzy stops and slowly bows. Jackson understands the gesture. "Everything will be fine. We should all return the gesture." After the men bow, they walk toward their guest.

Fuzzy is smiling, and Tee stands quietly by his side.

"This appears to be a friendly visit," says Jackson, smiling as broadly as Fuzzy.

Fuzzy speaks first. "Hello my old friend. This is Tee."

" Jackson looks at Tee and nods. "Tee, you are welcome here anytime."

Fuzzy sighs and his smile fades. "I wish this was a social visit. I'm glad to see all of you are doing well, but my heart is troubled. I have news to share with you and your family. It is my duty to warn you of a serious situation developing.

The men gasp as their smiles disappear. "Surely it can't be as bad as the situation we have already been through," says Jackson. Visions of the battle in the wilderness flash through his mind.

"It may be much worse. Sit and I will tell you what I know. I am here as a friend, just like you were when you warned my den of imminent danger. Four of our younger dragons are filled with bitterness toward mankind and have discovered a dragon city that has existed for many centuries. They visited this city and were told that these dragons, along with dumpy, hairy, little men called 'trolls,' destroyed human civilization long ago. They have no idea that man has risen again and civilization is spreading, but it will not be long until our rebellious dragons tell them. These dragons are silver and yellow, and they have a tyrant for a king. He has an army that could be here in three days if he finds out about you. He knows nothing about your family and will think nothing of killing all of you."

The men are dumbfounded and speechless. As Fuzzy's words sink in they shiver. Chills travels down their spines, tearing at their hearts, and churning their stomachs. Jackson's face sags in sorrow. Sweat beads on his pale face as panic stronger than he has ever felt makes him tremble. Thoughts of his daughter are all consuming in his mind. She has just begun to live, and every ounce of him is determined to see that she lives as long as nature had intended. In a daze, he's haunted as he remembers Sandra saying how she hoped they could live a normal life when he returned from battling the hunters. A painful lump throbs in his throat and a tear slides down his cheek. He looks at Fuzzy but can only shake his head.

Fuzzy senses his pain and tries to think of something to say that can give him hope, but tears of sorrow fill his eyes and he loses his self-control. His thoughts flow like a river and Jackson hears all of Fuzzy's fears.

"These men will have nowhere to run, and no chance of surviving a fight. Even if they hide, the dragons and trolls will search them out." Fuzzy drops his head in anger at himself when he sees Jackson's mind is drowning in a sea of hopelessness. He turns and walks away. He returns and bows, "I'm sorry, old friend."

Jackson wipes his tears and takes a deep breath. "Take me to the Brittains. I must be with you when you tell Cap and his family this story."

Jackson climbs onto Fuzzy's back. There is no excitement as they fly this time. He pries into the corners of his mind, trying to find a little hope or something he can do, but no idea comes. His eyes are open, but he doesn't see any of the landscape below. He snaps out of deep thought when he feels Fuzzy lean to one side, preparing to land. His eyes focus, and the Brittain farm lies below. Cap is outside and watches as they settle to the ground.

Fighting to hold his emotions, Jackson slides to the ground. "We have a grave situation facing us. Gather everyone and listen as Fuzzy explains."

Cap walks toward the house thinking, "Surely this won't be as bad as last time." But when he returns, he feels great anxiety coming from Fuzzy, Tee, and Jackson who nervously wait to share their story.

The Brittains bow. Buck is smiling until he looks into Fuzzy's eyes. Jackson looks at the ground wiping tears as Fuzzy retells the story. The women sob and Janice holds Ren tightly. Jackson moves over next to Cap, and they are quiet.

When Fuzzy is finished, everyone stands spellbound. Buck tries to be strong and speaks first.

"Thank you Fuzzy." He closes his eyes in thought for a second. "Do you think there is a chance we could go to this city and talk to the leaders, and prevent this?"

"I have no suggestion. I actually fear for my den's lives too. This king is powerful, and the stories I have heard make him sound evil." Fuzzy and Tee are quiet and wait patiently.

Buck reaches for Flavie's hand and they sit on edge of the porch looking at the ground. Buck has his arm around her shoulder and is crying with her. Cap takes Renay in his arms and ushers Janice in the house. He comes out in a few moments and stands wiping tears as he looks around aimlessly. He shakes his head in disbelief. "Thank you," He manages to utter as he turns toward his brother and the dragons.

Jackson realizes that Cap and Buck will need some time to calm down. He turns to Fuzzy. "Thank you for traveling so far to warn us. Please take me home." As he climbs on Fuzzy's back, he looks with a blank face at the Brittians. "Load up and come to our house in the morning, and we will talk. I'm sorry to have brought such bad news. I love you all."

Fuzzy and Tee take flight, and sail away with Jackson.

Moments later Jackson slides to the ground at the Murray farm.

"Thank you, old friend, I know you have taken a chance by coming here to warn us. Your debt is paid. Do not do anything that would offend the king by trying to help us."

Tears fill Fuzzy's eyes. He opens his wings and hugs Jackson. Tee is amazed by their friendship. In a moment they release, and Jackson steps back. He looks earnestly toward Fuzzy and Tee. "Leave before the silver and yellow dragons see you here."

Reluctantly Fuzzy turns and takes to the air and is out of sight in minutes.

Jackson has a heavy heart as he opens the front door. Everyone is quiet and still in shock trying to make sense of what they have heard. No one doubts what Fuzzy has said.

"We must go on as best we can. We will figure something out, and we will soon be determined to fight and survive whatever comes our way," says Inez.

Jackson wipes his nose. "Cap and the Brittains will be here early tomorrow. We will start planning and as our mother says, 'We will fight and survive.'" He smiles, trying to be strong for Sandra.

<>

Longing to be safely home, Jim and his men travel at a pace that makes the horses sweat. Tired of fear and trudging along from sun up until sunset the men are numb to the surrounding beauty of the wilderness. Everyone is quiet. They all lose focus of the trail from time to time as lack of sleep causes them to doze. Slumping in their seats, horrid dreams flash by, planting the seeds of fear for the night that lies ahead. Bobbing along, they remain upright only from instinct until suddenly a horse's misstep causes them to jerk and sit up straight. If the daydream is allowed to last too long, they drift back to the cage as it is violently shaking. They grab for something to hold on to, but when nothing is there, they almost fall from their seats.

Jim is quiet and constantly studying their surroundings, He's too concerned for his men's safety to let a daydream steal him away.

That night, as they're lying in the wagons, one of the men frowns as he studies Jim's demeanor. "Jim, I'd feel better if you were a little more talkative. Aren't you glad we're almost home?"

Jim closes his eyes and rubs his forehead. "I have a bad feeling about what has been awoken out there. We don't live very far from whatever warned us that it is powerful, especially if it can fly and doesn't like us."

Everyone's jaw drops. "You just had to ask, didn't you?" says the man beside him. Worry races through their minds, and the men are quiet as they stare blankly at the cage's ceiling. The guard in each wagon sits beside a dog, carefully observing the sights and sounds in the forest as it grows ever darker. Occasionally they glance at men wrestling to find sleep.

As dawn breaks, the men begin to talk again as they build a fire. They soak in its warmth to comfort their spirits, and then return to their journey. At mid-morning they see the Murray's barn and head for the watering trough. Jim sees several men on the porch talking. He waves slightly when they look in his direction. When the horses have quenched their thirst, they pull the wagons over near the porch.

"Good morning men," says Jim.

Uncle Matt is restless. "It's not a good morning at all. A very evil situation is developing deep in the wilderness," he says.

Miles scowls. "Matt, don't start this, I'm in no mood to talk to strangers about this."

Jim looks at them with cold eyes. "We have been in the wilderness for almost a month, and after what we have experienced, you don't have to explain a thing to us. I will never be going back to see what that powerful thing is."

"You won't have to go back out there to see it," says Matt. Jim nods in agreement. "I wish all of you well and thank you for your advice." He tips his hat and the party returns to the trail.

Jackson hops off the porch calling to Jim. "Wait! I think we may want to talk again, and I am interested in where you got that crossbow."

Jim stops to look back. "We built them. When you're ready to talk, come to Water Town and look for the big barn on Main Street. Ask anyone in town where to find Mason Smith."

"Thank you. I hope your trip home is a safe one."

Jim waves a simple goodbye and nudges his horse.

Two hours later, Blade Town comes into view. Jim stops and turns to his men. "We're not wasting anymore time out here, and I don't intend to stop at any of the villages on the way back. Everyone we see will want to talk about our crossbow anyway."

They enter Water Town shortly after midnight, and the moon is shining bright enough for the people that are awake to watch as the wagons and crossbow squeak by. The tired men move slowly as they unhook the horses, and the horses move slowly as they drag their hooves into the barn. Mason is at home, and the men decide to bed down in the barn. Jim throws out his blanket too.

"I'm glad we're all spending the night in here. We need to talk with Mason in the morning."

It's dark, warm and safe in the barn. After they settle and turn quiet, Jim's mind wanders as he ponders whether they really are safer than they were on the trail. His thoughts ramble, and he recalls the demeanor of the family on the fringe of the wilderness. The moment is stuck in his mind.

"I could see fear and anxiety in the eyes of those poor folks on the fringe of the wilderness," he says out loud. Mo is beside him and replies moanfully.

"I just hope those things didn't follow us home,"

Jim gasps. "I think we need to be quiet; we're causing ourselves grief talking about this at bedtime."

Everyone is so tired that slumber soon takes them away from their worries.

Mason arrives early and is excited to see the wagons parked outside the barn. He throws open the door startling everyone sleeping in the dark barn.

Jim and several men scramble to grab bows, and arrows are almost set when they recognize Mason's silhouette dimly visible from the light streaming through the open door.

"Mason, you almost got shot, bursting in here like this," says Jim.

"The sun has been up an hour. I've been worried about you, and I can't wait to hear what you found."

Jim rubs his eyes, and several men throw their blankets aside. "We scoured the woods around the campsite and didn't find any sign of dragons or any other predators. We found crossbow arrows in the woods all around. They were stuck in trees and half buried in the ground."

Frowning, Mason interrupts. "Whatever killed our men must have moved on."

Jim's eyes glare. "Far from it. I wish you could have been there when, in total darkness, our dogs went crazy and the horses almost tore lose to get away from our wagon seconds before we were hit with a *thud*. Something large and powerful landed on both roofs and started shaking us as if they were boxes filled with rag dolls. I'm surprised the wagon's wheels didn't fall off. The instant the shaking stopped, we heard powerful wings flapping, and they whipped up a gust of wind so furious that dirt and leaves blinded us as they blew through the cage bars. The gust was so strong that half of our blankets blew out of the cage. We were sure it was about to finish us off, but then it was gone. We continued to stumble over each other, and it took quite a while to catch our breath enough to calm the dogs. They were barking out of their minds."

"You didn't get a glimpse to see if it was a dragon?" interrupts Mason.

"Are you kidding? We were terrified! Whatever shook our wagons could have killed us in seconds. It was toying with us."

Mason's eyes grow wide, "I know none of you will be willing to go back, but we need to figure out where they are hiding."

Mo's face turns red and with wild eyes he lunges at Mason, pushing him to the floor. Masons mouth drops open.

Jim pulls Mo back and looks sternly at Mason. Almost hysterical, his voice is angry and loud. "You better shut up and think about what I just said! There's no doubt in my mind that you won't have to hunt for them much longer. Next time, they will be hunting you, and I hate to think what it will do to Water Town."

The men all glare at Mason.

Mason is dumbfounded as he absorbs the look on everyone's face, and a sickening reality claws into his gut. His head spins in panic as a vision sweeps him away, and he sees through the eyes of a dragon in pursuit of his wife and children. They are helpless as they run with horror on their faces, and then with almost no struggle they are ripped to pieces. He stumbles and props against a wagon.

He gasps, then speaks softly. "Jim, you don't really think that, do you?"

"Not only do I think so, but I'm going to get ready to fight for my life as fast as I can, and you better do the same."

Mason's face grows pale. "You men need to go on home. Jim, I want to see you, Sul, Cur, and Mo tomorrow. I'm going home." He leaves without shutting the door.

Chapter 12

Mason opens the door to his house and enters. His nine-year-old daughter, Alma, smiles. She runs over and hugs him. "I'm glad you came back. Will you stay with us awhile?"

A smile grows on his face as he nods. Ella is in the kitchen and hears them talking.

"What brings you back so soon?"

"Where is Al?" asks Mason.

"He's in his room."

"We are going to have some fun today. Let's all go to the shops."

Ella raises her eyebrows and looks him in the eye. "That sounds wonderful, but why today?"

"Why not? Get dressed and let's go."

At the shops Mason takes a little more time than usual to talk to friends as they stroll around town. He listens to his children talking about ideas and things they like that he hadn't had time to realize before. Their conversation is different than when they were smaller. They speak kindler to each other now, and it's obvious that they're growing up fast. Ella walks close and takes his hand.

"We should spend more days like this," she says softly. He chokes back a tear realizing he has always been too busy chasing dreams, and he is growing older just like his children. In the back of his mind, Jim's warning causes him to worry. Mason struggles to appear as if he is enjoying the rest of a rare and wonderful day with his family. By the evening his worry has tuned into anxiety that gnaws at his soul, and his body fills with fatigue.

That night in their bedroom Mason takes Ella's hand. She can feel his sincerity as he explains how much he loves her and how important his children are to him. She worries. She knows his sudden change means something bad, but she patiently waits until he is ready to explain. When he tells her about the danger of dragons in the wilderness attacking the villages, she drops her eyebrows, and tightens her lip.

"I am not sure dragons even exist. You have gotten so worked up about them. It's making you worry about nothing."

Mason's lips tremble "I hope you are right, but I love you too much to sit here and be caught off guard. I have the means to prepare to survive an attack. I'm going to start building a place in the barn where we can defend ourselves. I will ask Jim and his men to join me, and we will build enough rooms for their families to take refuge too."

Ella gently shakes her head. "I will need more proof before I am willing to leave our home to hide in the bottom of your barn."

"I don't blame you. And I hope we never have to go there, but it has to be finished in case I'm right." Ella hugs Mason. She lies back on her pillow looking at the ceiling. She wants to believe he is wrong, but many times his ideas and hunches have been right. He has a way of knowing what is to come and knowing that will keep her awake.

The next morning Mason gathers Jim and his men. He looks in their eyes and talks calmly. "I have decided to prepare for whatever is out there. It may never leave the wilderness, but I want our families, if you choose to join me, to be safe if they come after us."

Jim and the men nod as they smile. Jim has been troubled about this and releases his tension by spilling his ideas.

"First thing to do is dig a well here in the barn. The walls of the basement are rock, and we will make them even thicker and add columns and beams to hold up logs covered with dirt piled on the floor above. The dragons can burn down the top part of the barn, but it won't affect us in the basement."

Mason smiles. "Okay Jim, show us what to do."

They begin working that day, and Mason heads to the shops to buy food to be dried, smoked and preserved for use later. Every day their shelter becomes more complete. Jim and his smiths begin building weapons, and Mason soon is confronted with the need for more room, and the barn grows to twice its original size.

<>

The first meeting between the Murrays and Brittains accomplishes little. Remorse captures the moment, and they spend most of their time trying to cope with the reality that their lives are about to drastically change. They decide to work their farms for a week, search their souls, and then meet again.

Several days later as dusk approaches, Cap and Janice are relaxing on the porch with Buck and Flavie. Cap is lovingly holding Janice's hand, but his face is filled with worry. Renay is busy playing with a toy that Buck whittled out of a stick. They both quietly watch the child they cherish. Cap squeezes her hand.

"I'm determined to make sure you and Renay will be safe during the coming war. I don't know how I'm going to do it, but you can rest assured that I will figure something out. Knowing that this homestead that our family has worked so hard to build will probably be burnt to the ground is trying my soul." He stops and sighs. "I can't make myself work on things around here, and there are things that must be done. I just want to stay close to you and Renay."

Buck is close and hears him. He walks to the porch.

"Don't give up Cap. I'll help you figure something out, and don't underestimate the power of our united families in a cause that can awaken our inner strengths and creativity. When our two families meet again, I will tell Miles that I am prepared to abandon this homestead and unite with him." He looks at Renay and wipes a tear, turns and goes back inside.

Cap takes a deep breath and adrenalin seeps into his veins. "When I wake tomorrow, I will be a new man. I vow to still be kind and loving to our family, but my heart will harden so that I will have the will to be triumphant over this evil."

Janice leans her head on his shoulder and tears drizzle from her eyes.

The week drags on and early Saturday morning they are in the Murray's yard before the sun has risen. Miles opens the door before they can knock.

"It has been a trying week around here. Come eat breakfast with us, and then we will make plans," he says.

After the dishes are put away, the families sit around the kitchen table. Janice and Sandra take the toddlers outside. Miles speaks first.

"I feel hope seeing all of us here ready to unite. I once wondered if we were taking Fuzzy too seriously, but when I saw the powerful crossbow and fear in the eyes of the man that built it, I realized that if dragons that hate men ever come, we will need to be ready." Cap looks at Jackson. "Those men probably had an encounter with Fuzzy and Tee. They have no idea that hundreds of dragons and trolls are what they will be up against, and we can never tell them all we know."

With a guilty look, Jackson nods in agreement.

Cap looks around the table. His eyes brighten, and he stands with purpose.

"It's time to dig up the silver. We will have to build a shelter underground large enough to hold all of us and many weapons. It will have to be as strong as a cavern and have a good source of water. We will use the silver for the good of everyone. It will pay for the help we will need to dig it out, and gather hundreds of loads of rocks, not to mention all the other things we will need to store while we can still go to Blade Town."

Mile's face lifts and he closes his eyes in thought. "We must break this tremendous undertaking down into parts. Everyone must take the part that they can best handle."

Buck pops up. "I will take a little ore to my shop, melt it into pure silver and beat it into coins. I can make them look just like the ones made in Water Town. Then as soon as I can, I will take them to Blade Town. If I don't have any problems trading them, we are all set to go."

"Somebody has to keep all of us fed, care for the livestock, and figure out how to take care of farm animals when they're put in underground stables. Matt and I will do that," says Miles.

Inez speaks up. "Flavie and I will start tomorrow smoking and curing meat. As soon as crops are ready, we will dry them and put them away."

Flavie smiles. "Janice and Sandra can help us as much as they can while caring for Ren and Renay."

Cap takes control again. "Let's concentrate on making silver coins first."

Matt stands, shaking his head. "We can't hope to defend ourselves hiding in a cave. This thing you call a cavern will need a fortress above it to help keep it dry below. It needs a thick stone wall all the way around and an open area like a courtyard in the middle. The only way to get into the courtyard will be to pass through a thick, heavy gate that we will keep locked."

Cap smiles broadly. "Matt, I think you have the right idea, but that may be more than we can do." Everyone is quietly thinking.

"We just need to go dig up some more silver, and then we can build whatever we want. I didn't mention we need a tower at each corner with a crossbow on each one," replies Matt.

"He's right, and I'm ready to go back to the old mine. How about you, Miles?" asks Buck. Miles nods in agreement. "I want our family to have every chance of surviving."

Cap raises his hand. "I agree, except you are the only one that can make our silver coins, and we must have them as soon as possible. We need a crossbow from Mason Smith right now."

Buck sighs and agrees. "Matt and I will stay here. He can keep the livestock fed, and I will forge the coins."

After the meeting, the men put bows and tarps across two wagons and pack what Miles, Cap, and Jackson will need for their trip.

<>

Sitting around Bird's fire pit, enthralled in conversation, Bird and his blue dragon friends make plans as the fire dances in front of them. Saddlebags stuffed with lily bulbs lay close by waiting to be slid around their necks in the morning.

Gus, with a smile on his face, seizes a quiet moment. "I love my new life and trading lily bulbs for interesting things in Dragonthal, but my plans won't be complete until I see the king. I think I may join his army too. I want to be there when the villages that the hunters came from suffer like we did."

Nom nods in agreement. Lear and Leon look at each other and remain emotionless.

"I will be glad to go with you to see the king, but you will never see Bird in any army," says Bird. He smiles and thinks to himself about how he plans to return to his old life at the cave when being with his new friends is no longer an adventure.

Gus's eyes light up. "I think we are ready to open our own shop."

Bird wrinkles his lips. "Let Bell sell the bulbs and give us half. Why worry with a shop?"

Lear quietly mulls over their suggestions and thinks to himself, "I plan to use my share to buy fire bats and set them free. I know the others would wonder why, so I will keep it a secret, I'm kind of like old Fuzzy." A smile comes to his face.

Two days later at dusk they land at Bell's hut.

"I'm glad to see all of you again. I see your saddlebags are full of bulbs. I look forward to seeing how well they trade," says Bell.

Bird smiles slyly. "In that case we'll not open our own shop. If you don't mind, take these and trade them at your shop. We would like to have half of whatever you get."

"That sounds fair to me. If you will dig them up, I will sell them," she smiles. "I know all of you are tired. I traded for several fish today and you are welcome to stay here and eat with us."

Deago calls her inside where they talk earnestly. Moments later Bell and Deago step out. "We want to introduce our son. He is not going to look like anyone you have ever seen. He is a gift from the wilderness to me and Deago. Nature brought us together. What started out as a convenient relationship turned into affection, and we fell in love. As only nature can do, we now have a son we love."

She opens the door and an amazing young creature stands before the dragons. "This is Bago. He is half-dragon and half-troll.

The young creature quietly steps out. Bell places her hand on his shoulder, and he looks up at her. She beams as they marvel. He is three feet tall. His legs look like that of a man, but his feet are dragon. He is cloaked in shiny silver and yellow scales. The skin on his face is like that of a man. His wings are like dragons, but in front of them he has arms and hands with five fingers and a thumb. His finger nails are claws that would be lethal in a fight. His nose and ears resemble the trolls. His eyes are beautiful bronze-colored dragon eyes. His head is covered with thick brown hair like the troll's, and horns are beginning to project above his forehead. He has no tail and stands like a man. He is young and uneasy in the presence of dragons that are blue. He clings to Bell while Deago beams with pride.

"What a wonder to behold," says Lear in awe.

Bell hugs her son. "You can imagine how hard life is for him. I only know of two more young ones like him in all of Dragonthal."

Bird and his friends are speechless but bow in respect. Bago smiles. He senses that their respect is sincere. Bell brings the fish outside and everyone enjoys being together. Bell watches them interact with her son and is convinced they will be kind to him. Bago eats quietly and doesn't say much, even though Bird tries several times to trick him into talking. After a short time, he goes back inside, but he leaves smiling.

The next morning Bell heads for the market, and Bird and his friends go exploring. Everywhere they go, they see dragons and trolls hard at work. They feel uneasy because everyone they see is working at something.

For several weeks, Bell has a steadily flow of customers wanting lily bulbs. There are plenty of things for Bird and his friends to use in trading for whatever they please.

Lear and Leon begin staying close to each other and soon Lear tells Leon how he feels about the fire bats being sold for food. Leon doesn't give it much thought until he happens to be with Lear when he trades for a couple at the market. After buying them, they head to the orchard and pull the baskets off the little dragons' heads.

"They really look like bats," says Leon. He has hardly finished speaking when one of them blurts excitedly.

"You are a blue dragon!"

Lear and Leon are surprised.

"Our den has been told about you. Your kindness is known throughout our kingdom. Many of our families have been overjoyed when they discover their loved ones have returned unharmed. We are all very grateful because this never happened until you came along."

Leon feels the respect and admiration of the little creatures, whose dragon dialect he can understand, and his heart is touched. "You may be small, and look a lot like bats, but inside you are dragons. I will help you from now on, just as Lear has done," states Leon.

The fire bats bow and fly away.

That night Bell goes to the blue dragons' hut. She has traded the last of the bulbs.

They decide to leave at daybreak and find more.

<>

Cap, Jackson and Miles are packed and ready to leave for the mine. Inez has ham, eggs, and bread on the table and the kitchen is warm, and filled with their wonderful aroma. The three adventurers are filled with energy and their faces are all smiles. They talk as they finish up and stuff ham into bread for later. Buck and Matt are too quiet.

"What's bothering you two?" asks Miles.

Buck creases his lips. "I keep thinking about the night cat that attacked us last time. You need at least four men to help keep watch at night."

Inez's head pops up from her work. "Matt, get your things together and go with them. I can take care of the farm for a while."

Matt glances at Miles, who is smiling.

"Come on Matt, we will hook up the horses while you hurry and get ready."

Matt beams. "I can't wait!" He hugs Inez before hurrying to his room.

Cap smiles broadly. "More help will get us home sooner, and I will feel a lot safer."

Two horses are hooked to each wagon in anticipation of bringing home a heavy load. Two more horses are saddled and saddlebags are strapped on them. Soon they're on their way.

With Jackson sitting beside him, Cap searches his memory trying to recall how much ore they left lying in the entrance. "I hope we can find enough ore to need two wagons. We won't have time to dig much."

"We can dig for a couple days. If we don't find a good vein, then it just wasn't meant to be," replies Jackson.

Four days later they see the white rocks they left as a beacon along the trail.

"This is it," yells Cap. They stop and unhook the horses and strap saddlebags across their backs and head into the woods. As Jackson ties his horse, he notices a mound not too far from the entrance. Neither he nor Cap noticed it before. He tramps through the brush to take a closer look. The mound is covered with a thick growth of vines. Dropping to his knees he pulls at roots and scratches around. A haunting feeling sweeps over him.

"This could be a burial mound," he thinks to himself. Cautiously he tugs at the rope-like vines. A thick layer of black mulch lies under them. He uses both hands to pull it out of the way exposing lose gravel. Smiling, he breathes a sigh of relief that it is not a grave. He walks with purpose to the entrance and helps the others tie horses and begin digging.

After digging half the day, an opening large enough for a man to squeeze through welcomes them to spend the night in safety. They slide inside, settle back, and before long they are enjoying supper. A small blue and yellow fire sways back and forth as it warms a pot of tea and lights the cool, damp mine. Jackson wraps up in his blanket as he watches the fire.

"I found a curious-looking mound where the miners dumped some of their rock waste."

"Did you look at the rocks to make sure they aren't ore?" asked Cap.

"I didn't look too closely. I was just relieved it wasn't a burial mound."

After eating, Matt and Miles lean back and rest, but Cap and Jackson are restless, they have regained their energy.

"Let's go take a look at that pile of rocks," says Cap. Jackson hops up and they stroll over to the mound. Jackson pulls at another vine as Cap scratches several stones loose with a stick. He holds several gravels in his hand and pours water from his pouch over them, and even in the dim evening light they sparkle.

Cap hollers, and Jackson looks at him sternly. "Don't worry. No one is out here. You have found where they were stockpiling their ore."

Jackson grabs a handful of stones and runs to the hole and slides inside. He can hardly catch his breath as he shows Miles and Uncle Matt.

Rain begins to fall and he crawls out and runs back out to help Cap cover the horses with tarps. They are so happy they hardly feel the cold rain splashing on their heads. Once they are back in the mine, they hover over the fire until they warm up.

As the sun rises, Uncle Matt rekindles the fire and prepares breakfast. Miles and the brothers shovel ore into saddle bags. They trudge back and forth several times, leading the horses to the wagons and dumping their bags of ore. Matt beckons them to stop and eat, but they are too excited to stop. At midday the wagons can hold no more, and they rest. Cap catches his breath and realizes how hungry he is.

"I'll race you to the camp fire and food!" he says. Jackson takes off, and Miles shakes his head, slowly turns and walks back. They are so hungry they don't care who won the race. They eat without talking at first, but soon, having eaten too much, they relax and talk.

"We have a lot more silver than last time. Our wagons aren't very full, but they are almost too heavy," says Miles.

"Surely we have enough silver to build what we need," says Jackson.

Matt creases his lips. "I hope you're right. It will take a lot to build a fortress strong enough to survive a war like Fuzzy has warned us about."

Cap sits with his elbows on his knees and his hands under his chin. A distant look is on his face. "I can't believe we're talking about how wonderful it is to have all this silver. Jackson and I decided long ago it would only cause bad things to happen. Now, if we didn't have it, we wouldn't stand a chance of surviving."

"It can still cause bad things to happen," says Miles. Everyone is quiet and looks at him. "We should bury this load in several places so if someone finds it, they will only find a little. Once we have a lot of men helping build this place, some of them will have only one thing on their minds---taking our silver."

They pack their saddlebags, cover the mine opening, and then hook the horses to the wagons for the journey home. The horses pull the heavy wagons slowly over the bumpy trail ,and everyone worries that the wheels will come apart. The horses move slower each day, suffering as they tug and pull. It takes several more days to return than it did last time.

When Inez and Flavie see them returning, they ring the bell. The men are so exhausted they barely smile. The women bounce out of the house with happy energy, and the men slowly slip to the ground and hug them.

"I hope no one is here except our family. We have a fortune in these wagons," says Miles.

After hugging Sandra and regaining his energy, Cap opens the barn doors and they pull the wagons inside. Everyone helps top off the wagons with straw to be sure no one stumbles across them. They decide to leave the first load where it is hidden, but the rest will be buried in small amounts around the farm. They'll draw a map to help them find it later.

That night at supper, Buck lays a handful of the coins that he had made on the table.

Cap picks one up. "They look just like the ones being used in Water Town." He flips one to Jackson, who smiles and keeps chewing.

"I don't think we will have any trouble trading these," says Miles reaching into his pocket, pulling out an old coin and placing it next to Buck's.

"We will have to be careful about where we buy things. We need to take turns going to the hardware store. It will be important that none of us spends too much money at one time. We are going to need a lot of tools and supplies to get started," says Buck.

The next morning, Buck and Cap each tuck five silver coins into their pockets and head for Blade Town. Buck visits the hardware store first and buys a pan that could be pulled behind a horse to scoop up soft dirt. They can move a lot of dirt long distances with it. He still has enough silver to buy several picks and shovels. Next, they head to a shop selling dried goods, ham, and jerky. It takes three coins, but the food can be easily stored for a long time. They return to the hardware store, and this time Cap goes in and buys ropes, hammers and other hand tools. The store has a sack of beans at a good price and Cap sets it on the counter. There will be a lot of mouths to feed before long.

Buck is pleased when he returns with several leftover coins. "With all the digging we are going to do, I think we should use these last coins to pay some men to come help us," says Buck. Cap's eyes brighten and he nods in agreement.

The wagon squeaks under the burden of its heavy load, and they don't talk much until they see two young men with packs headed toward town. Buck greets them as they pass. He likes their friendly smile. Their clothing is worn, but clean, and their horses are well-groomed. He turns in his seat and calls out to them.

"Are you fellows headed into town hunting for work?"

One of them turns and calls back. "Do you have any silver?" The other rider stops and looks on.

"If you don't mind digging, we will pay you with silver," replies Buck. The men smile and trot back to their side.

"Show us what you have in mind. We live near here and don't mind working," he points to his friend. "This is Loy and you can call me Mic." Loy tips his hat and nods. "Loy doesn't talk much until you get to know him," says Mic.

Mic is full of energy and asks more than a few questions as they ride, but Buck and Cap enjoy his conversation. He talks about his chickens. He has several that lay large brown eggs, and they taste so good that he gave some to his neighbors. He wanted to share his good luck with them. He continues to talk about interesting things, and there is an air of honesty about him. When they arrive at the Murray farm, Homer runs out barking. Mic slides out of his saddle, places a knee on the ground and holds out his hand. Homer sniffs it, then wags his tail playfully.

Jackson comes up and introduces himself to Loy and Mic.

Buck smiles. "Looks like Homer approves of the two helpers we brought back. Jackson, show these men where they can sleep tonight."

Jackson smiles and they walk toward the barn. Several chickens are pecking around and hop out of the way as they pass. Jackson politely listens to Mic talk about all the chickens he has at his farm. Upon entering the barn, Jackson points to an empty stall filled with straw.

"You should be comfortable in here. If you like, you're welcome to come to our house for supper."

The men smile pleasantly. "Thank you. We will take you up on that," says Mic.

Buck and Cap head home. Flavie and Janice are waiting on the porch when they ride up.

"Everyone gladly took our coins," says Buck. Cap hugs Janice and they go inside.

Buck stays on the porch and sits next to Flavie. They rock gently.

"We found two men to help us. I like them. They seem honest, but we will need to only make coins while they are hard at work. They must never know our secret and I don't want to tempt them."

Ren and Renay burst out of the front door and run across the porch. Cap is right behind them and soon he grabs Renay, picks her up, and hugs her. Ren hops off the side and scampers around the house.

Flavie smiles and looks at Buck. "Renay and Ren have been playing together today, and I told Sandra she could spend the night with us."

That night Buck lies awake.

Flavie looks at him with kind eyes. "What is keeping you awake?"

He reaches for her hand. "I know we just built this beautiful cabin, and I love the fact that Cap and Sandra are in their addition, but we must move to the fortress. As soon as the basement is ready, we must start building our rooms in it, and that will be our new home for a long time."

"I knew that was what the fortress was meant to be, but hearing you say it..." she stops and wipes tears. "I will start loading our wagon, and we can build a lean-to next to it. I am ready to get on with our new life. I will feel better when our children are in a safer home under the fortress."

"I will tell Cap and Janice tomorrow," says Buck.

The next morning, Buck and Cap leave early to work at the Murray farm. Miles, Matt, Jackson, Mic, and Loy are walking toward the fields when they ride up. Miles motions for them to come with them. When they are all together, Miles stops.

"Cap, if you and Jackson don't mind, I think we should choose a low place to dig out for the lower level so we won't have to dig too deep."

Cap looks at Jackson and they smile. "We know you have figured out the right place. Lead the way."

Miles walks to the middle of a large cleared field and stops at a dip where rain has washed the soil away. Everyone nods in agreement and work begins.

Mic and Loy are hard workers, and with help from the older men, Cap. and Jackson the basement is dug out in a few months. Soon after, several loads of stone are dumped where the walls will be raised.

Buck and Flavie finish building a lean-to, and after several wagonloads of their possessions they move to the work site.

Two weeks later, Cap and Janice finish their lean-to and tie their wagon next to it. They choose to stay close to Buck and Flavie.

Buck and Miles quickly build a temporary shed for the blacksmith shop. It will not be used very long because the forge and tools will be one of the first things they move into the basement.

Ed and Mary haven't seen Sandra in weeks and come unexpectedly to visit. When they find the Brittain cabin abandoned, they anxiously head for the Murray farm. They are shocked to see all the work going on. Sandra runs out to meet them.

She hugs them for a long time. "I am so glad you are here. We need to talk. There is so much you need to know about why we're building a fortress."

Ed gazes toward the building site. "Why would anyone need a fortress?" He hears a loud bang and looks back to see men rolling logs over a bank. "Everyone is so busy," he shakes his head in disbelief.

"I'm going to get Jackson. He will be glad to see you, and we can sit on the porch and have a long talk," says Sandra.

Jackson smiles when he sees Sandra approaching. "My parents are here, and it is time to explain to them what is happening."

Jackson rubs his forehead. "I will be glad to see them and happy to rest, but I dread trying to make them understand. Many times, I have been tempted to tell them about Fuzzy and the relationship Cap and I have with his den, but they have no reason to believe in dragons." He takes a deep breath and reaches for Sandra's hand.

He and Sandra go to the kitchen first. "Flavie, will you and Inez stop what you are doing for a few minutes and come with us to the porch? I am going to explain to Ed and Mary why we are building the fortress."

Flavie takes a deep breath and thinks for a moment.

"Let me talk to them first. They need to hear about dragons from me." She and Inez go out with Jackson and Sandra. Ed and Mary hug everyone.

"Have a seat and just listen for a while," says Flavie. Ed and Mary wrinkle their brows and peer at her as they sit.

Jackson and Sandra quietly hold hands and watch as Flavie talks about seeing Fuzzy. She speaks as calmly as she would if she were telling them how to milk a cow. She explains that Cap and Jackson helped defend Fuzzy's den from the hunters. Ed and Mary look toward Inez occasionally, and Inez always nods in agreement. Jackson is pleased when she tells of Fuzzy's recent visit to warn the Brittain and Murray families of the coming dragon war. Jackson squeezes Sandra's hand from time to time; he understands how they must feel,

"They will worry for days," he thinks to himself.

Flavie speaks to Mary as Inez stands. "Come with us. We need your help in the kitchen. You will feel better working with us while this settles in." They return to the kitchen. Sandra stays with Jackson and he continues to hold her hand as he waits for the ladies to go inside.

Then Jackson speaks kindly to Ed. "I was going to come see you in a few days. All of your family must join us. You will perish if you try to defend yourselves."

Ed rocks with nervous energy. He hasn't smiled since Flavie began her story. He sets has his jaw to one side almost in anger and one eye squints as if trying to pry into Jackson's mind.

"You have to understand, this is such a shock, I need time to think about this before I decide what to do. This sounds crazy. I'm sorry, but surely you understand."

Jackson closes his eyes and nods understandingly. "Ed, please come with me and let me show you what we are doing. You will understand why you should stand with us in this fight."

Ed is quiet as they walk around. He is troubled and impressed. Worry for his children's safety begins to consume his thoughts. His face is drawn and he is tentative. Jackson is compelled to explain that silver to buy building material and weapons will not be a problem. Ed nods but doesn't smile. He appears to be in deep thought more than distress after Jackson's reassurance.

"I hope you are beginning to have faith that our families can survive here. We will need all the blacksmithing help we can get to repair and build weapons," says Jackson.

A day later, while riding home, Ed and Mary sit close and talk about how wonderful the life and love they have shared has been. Ed tears up and can hardly speak as Mary reminisces about the spirit of their village.

"Special times shared with special neighbors," she says and then she is quiet. Ed wipes his eyes and they ride quietly, listening to the horse hooves clopping and the wagon squeaking as it bounces along. They hold hands the rest of the way home.

Several days later, Fred and Ed Junior arrive at the Murray house. They tie their horses and knock on the door. Inez comes out.

"I am glad to see you. Did Ed and Mary come back with you?"

Ed Junior smiles slightly. "No. Fred and I need to see what our father is trying to explain. He is worried sick and, frankly, we are too."

Inez solemnly looks at the two men. "I will take you to see Cap and Jackson."

" We are sorry to cause you trouble, but we can't help being skeptical," apologizes Ed Junior. Inez smiles a little. "I am thankful you are here."

Jackson sees Inez coming with Ed Junior and Fred and runs out to meet them.

"Thank you for coming, I know what we are up against is so hard to believe. Let me show you around and explain what we are doing."

Cap joins them after they have walked through the site, and they return to the porch to talk. He brings his piece of hatching stone to show them. They look at it as Cap explains how as children, they met Fuzzy and a lifelong friendship grew. Jackson tells of the dragons' battle with the hunters and how he felt like a member of their den when death looked imminent for him and Cap.

"After seeing what you are doing and hearing your story, I have no doubt that you are sure a great war is coming. But our families have lived in our village for generations and moving will be a serious task. We must be sure it is the right decision. How can you be so sure this war will ever come?" asks Ed Junior.

"None of us have any doubt. Fuzzy came a long way just to warn us. I know you will have trouble grasping this story. We will talk more tonight after supper. Janice and Sandra will be glad to tell you of an unbelievable ride on the backs of dragons that they experienced when it was time for us to help them understand. We need your help if we are going to survive, and whether you believe us or not, your families' lives depend on us convincing you to join us."

That night after supper, Ed Junior and Fred hear their uncle Buck, Flavie and their sister tell unwavering stories about the dragons Cap and Jackson have befriended.

Cap stands and ends the stories. "We can go on all night, but before you make up your minds you need to go to Water Town. The hunters that passed by here frantically fleeing the wilderness had a magnificent crossbow. We asked them where they got a crossbow so large that it takes a wagon to haul it around, and they told us to ask for a man named Mason Smith. Why don't you pay him a visit and tell him we will be coming to purchase some crossbows? Listen to his story and make up your own minds."

After breakfast the next morning, Janice hugs them goodbye, and they assure their Uncle Buck that they will find Mason Smith, and let him know the Murray brothers are coming to buy a crossbow.

<>

One week later, Ed and his sons ride to Water Town. When they reach the public watering trough, they ask a man where to find Mason Smith.

"You are close. Go further down this trail. When you cross the bridge, his place is the big barn on the right with a blacksmith shop attached. He's a strange one, though. He is turning his barn into an underground fortress. Everyone thinks he has gone nuts, but he's interesting to talk to."

When the Brittains arrive they see logs, piles of dirt and men working all around the large barn. Ed dismounts and walks over to one of the men; his clothes are worn, dirty, and damp from sweat. The man turns to him.

"I'm looking for Mason Smith," says Ed. The man looks Ed over. "Wait here, I will find him for you."

Mason comes out of the barn squinting in the sunlight as he walks up to the three strangers. "I am Mason Smith. What is your business here?"

Ed smiles, but his voice is strong and clear. "I hear you're building a fortress."

Mason looks him in the eye. "You are right. Why do you ask?"

Ed feels more at ease. "My brother and his family are also building a fortress; they say it is to survive a coming war."

Mason rubs his chin and discerns Ed is sincere. "You and I must talk inside. I need to know all about this."

As they follow Mason into the barn, they see the crossbows that Jackson told them about. The barn is smaller than the fortress the Murray's are building. Several men are busy working nearby. Mason points toward them. "These men are building rooms for their families to live in."

Ed studies the ceiling as they walk by. It is made of log after log touching each other. Mason sees his interest.

"These logs separate the basement from the barn above and on top of all those logs a foot of dirt has been spread across the floor making it fire proof. The top half of this barn can burn and not harm the bottom."

Ed loses the last of his smile as he surveys the surroundings and the concept. "This fortress has too much in common with the Murrays for this to be a coincidence. How can you be so sure something is going to happen that will cause you to need such a shelter?" asks Ed.

"I have already lost eleven friends to dragons hidden in the wilderness. I have no doubt that they will soon pay us a deadly visit." Mason's eyes are sincere as he digs the large claw out of his pocket. "They are armed with claws like this and if they don't grab you with one of these, they will cook you in seconds with fire that explodes from their mouths." He hands the claw to Ed.

Ed rubs it and hands it back.

"I need to visit your brother," says Mason.

Ed turns pale and looks at his sons, and they are speechless. Ed's forehead is filled with wrinkles. "My brother told me to let you know he will be coming to buy several of the wagon-mounted crossbows from you."

"Does he have silver to pay for such a weapon?"

Ed thinks for a moment. "How much will it take?"

"400 silver coins for one."

"I will tell him to come see you. If he brings the silver will you sell him a weapon that he can pull back to his farm the same day?"

"I will sell one, and then we will talk. I can build more, but I'm not going to stop construction on my shelter just yet."

Ed shakes Mason's hand and the bone-chilling look of anguish in their eyes assures each other that both parties are sincere. Ed sighs and turns to leave. He and his sons are quiet until they reach their horses.

"Mason is as sure dragons will attack us as the Murrays," says Ed.

Two weeks later, Ed Junior and Fred arrive at the Murray farm with a load of blacksmith equipment. Cap and Jackson see them and call Buck and Miles. The four of them dash energetically to the wagon.

"We struggled to decide what to do, but we have agreed to join you. We will help you build and fight," says Ed Junior. The men embrace tightly as a bond stronger than family joins their hearts and minds together. They all smile.

Cap feels his confidence surge "With all the knowledge and equipment your family has to share with us, there will be nothing we can't build," he says.

Ed Junior smiles. "We talked to Mason and he assured us he will sell one of his wagon-mounted crossbows to you for 400 silver coins. He is anxious to talk with you. He is building a fortress under his barn, and I'm sure he will have ideas that will help us."

Jackson's eyes lift. "Come let us show you around, I think you will be impressed with what we have already done," he says.

The next morning, Buck, Miles and his sons ride back to Ed's blacksmith shop with Fred and Ed Junior. When they reach the shop, the Brittain brothers say goodbye.

"When you return, stop with your prize. We would like to see it shoot a couple times," says Fred. Buck and the Murrays assure them they will be glad to show it off. They turn and trot toward Water Town.

Jim recognizes the Murrays as they ride up and calls to them "Come over this way. Mason has been anticipating your arrival." He quickly walks into the barn. They hardly have their horses tied when a man steps out full of energy.

"I am Mason Smith; I am glad to meet you."

Miles faces him and tips his hat. "I am Miles Murray and these two young men are my sons, Cap and Jackson."

Mason looks at Buck.

Miles continues. "This is Buck Brittain, he is family too." Mason motions for them to enter and proceeds to show them all he is doing to protect his family and friends.

"I only agreed to sell you one of my beautiful crossbows because with all the other things I must do to be ready for an attack, I hardly have time to replace it."

Nearby, Jim calls out to everyone, "It's time to stop and prepare for the evening meal."

Men and women lay down their tools and begin talking to each other. Jim looks toward Miles. "It's too late for you to start home. You are welcome to spend the night here in the barn with the families that have already moved in."

Mason smiles and looks at Miles "Spend the night here if you like and we will deal in the morning."

Miles accepts the invitation, and Mason heads for home.

After the meal everyone gathers around a fire pit in the barn. It has a chimney over it so they can cook inside if they are under siege.

As the flames dance, Cap and Jackson struggle to show little emotion as Jim tells about what he saw at the ghost camp. Buck and Miles wrinkle their brows and listen as do others of the group. By the time Jim tells about his encounter in the middle of the night, the brothers are calm and listen earnestly.

Mason arrives early the next morning and counts the pieces of silver, then sighs.

"Good luck to all of you. I hope you and I can convince others to prepare for what is coming."

Miles frowns and shakes his head. "Few will believe us."

Mason throws six arrows on the crossbow wagon floor. "I hope you can make a lot more of these."

Buck looks at them and smiles. "I can take care of that."

Mason and Jim watch them pull the crossbow out of the barn and disappear up the trail.

"I'm surprised you let one of our crossbows leave," says Jim.

Mason rubs his chin in thought. "I figure it's in our best interest to have someone else who thinks like us armed and ready to fight. Every dragon they kill will be one less we will have to deal with."

Just after lunchtime, the crossbow is sitting at Ed's house. Ed and his sons walk around it, admiring the workmanship. Cap climbs up and slides into the seat. Memories of the horror he saw the weapon inflict zip through his mind, but the excitement of manning the weapon overwhelms his emotions. He spins around and aims at several boards stacked against a rail fence. Everyone is speechless when the arrow zips across the yard faster than their eyes can follow. The arrow slams into one of the boards, tearing it to pieces and continues sailing into the woods."

Ed flinches and his mouth pops open. His heart is pounding, "I never imagined a man could build such a horrific weapon. I'm glad we discovered this thing before the dragons descend on us. I guess you know I can't wait to make arrows, and soon I'm going to build another crossbow just like it." He walks over and rubs his hand across parts of the weapon; his mind is at work taking it all in.

Miles, Buck and the brothers say farewell and head to the fortress.

When Ed opens his shop the next day, he begins to tell his customers that he is closing and many of them ask why. Reluctantly he shares the story Mason told him. When he describes the large claw he was shown, they leave troubled. Everyone in the village has known and respected the Brittains for a long time.

By the time Ed moves the last of his forges and tools, many of the villagers have visited the fortress, and they decide to join them. The extra help makes construction progress quickly. The basement walls are built. Being made of rocks and mud, they are strong. They are thick enough to keep the ground water out of the living areas. The basement ceiling is comprised of log after log, laid side-by-side across the walls and on large wooden beams lying on rock columns. After seeing Mason's floors covered with dirt to prevent them from burning, they do the same. A thatched roof is temporally built over the dirt floor to keep the basement dry until the thick rock wall is tall enough to form stables and rooms above. These rooms will have roofs made of logs covered with dirt, making them fireproof and strong enough to be used as walkways. Only a few rooms will open into a courtyard, but every room is connected by a hallway inside the walls of the fortress that goes all the way around.

A plentiful well has been dug in the basement. It is close to the kitchen and is ready to furnish water for the entire fortress. The defenders will have water whenever they need it, without having to go outside.

Half of the rooms are finished and several families have moved in. Everyone works from sun up until sun down. Cap and Jackson work hard, but they spend a lot of time coordinating the workers. The women work together, and some of them take wagons to Blade Town every day. Others go to Water Town. It takes two days and they must camp one night so they only make this trip once a week. Mary, Inez, and Flavie store the goods where they will lay in wait until the fighting begins.

A big kitchen is built in the center of the basement. Its chimney penetrates the floor above and stands taller than the highest wall. It is being used even though the women keep coming up with new ideas that keep the builders busy changing things. The builders don't mind because this is all a new experience for everyone, and every change makes the kitchen work better.

Mic and Loy are like family now and many more men have been carefully chosen to work with them. All the workers are dedicated to the fortress residents and a camaraderie has formed between the trades. The Murrays and Brittains are pleased to welcome many families to move into the basement. Even though everyone is squeezed into a small living area, they are so grateful to be part of a community dedicated to defending each other, and they all live peaceably. They help all they can and build their rooms when they find time. The rooms are tiny, but a chance for their children to survive the coming war is all that matters to them.

Chapter 13

Gathering lily bulbs isn't easy this time. Bird and the blue dragons search for months. They even have to find more lakes to dig around.

Finally, their saddlebags are full and they are sitting around Birds firepit.

"When we get back to Dragonthal, we will have to cut these bulbs into small pieces so we can make them last longer. We have dug up so many plants that it's going to take a longtime for them to grow back," says Gus.

Bird walks toward one of the saddlebags and reaches for a bulb. "We have worked hard and done without one of these too long. It's time to roast a couple, sit back and enjoy flying without leaving the ground," he says.

"Are you kidding? I don't want to feel bad all morning as we fly back to Dragonthal, and these were too hard to find to just waste," says Gus.

Bird puckers his lips and stomps around for a moment. "So, none of you want to enjoy a lily bulb tonight? I'm beginning to wonder if this adventure is going to be fun much longer."

"Sure, it will. We just prefer to have fun doing things in Dragonthal. We can't stay there if we don't have anything to trade," says Nom.

In the morning everyone is happy, even Bird. He realizes that he feels better than he would have, and he is full of energy. He doesn't wait long until he starts rushing everyone to begin the return trip.

When they land at Bell's place, Deago hurries out and tells them not to go to the market. He rushes them inside and tells them to wait there while he goes for Bell.

Moments later she walks in. "I don't want anyone to see you are back with lily bulbs. Trolls and dragons are causing trouble at my shop. They want your lily bulbs and are not satisfied when I tell them they will have to wait until I get more. I have had to call the guards several times to escort unruly customers away."

"What should we do?" asks Bird.

"Stay here tonight, and tomorrow I will take several pieces of the bulbs to the market. Hopefully I can sell a little to the ones that are causing trouble, and make some promises. With a little luck, things will return to normal."

The next morning at the market, guards are close by and when she lays out the merchandise. Several of them approach.

"Are the dragons that bring you these bulbs in town?" asks the leader.

Bell is surprised. She thinks for a moment and realizes they will watch her every move and she sighs. "They are at my hut today," she replies.

"We want to talk with them. These bulbs have become very valuable, and we want to know where they are finding them. The king is interested. and He has told us to bring the blue dragons to his court to talk with him."

He gestures for Bell to lead the way to her hut.

Escorted by seven guards, four of which are trolls, Bell approaches her hut. Gus, Nom, Lear, and Leon are lying in the sun when they walk up. Bird is inside and comes out when he hears them talking. The trolls have bows, and the dragons have spears. They do not act aggressively, but the looks on their faces assures Bird they intend to obey their orders.

Bird saunters out, "Are we in some kind of trouble?"

"Not yet, but your lily bulbs are of interest to the king. He has issued a decree for any guard that sees you to escort you to his court. He just wants to talk to you and these blue dragons," replies the leader.

Bell looks nervously toward the guards. "I'm not in any trouble, am I?"

"We have no need for you," replies the guard.

Bird walks along confidently as the guards escort them into the cavern. They soon turn to the left and stand in front of a large gate.

"This is the entrance gate to the area where you will wait until the king calls for you," says the leader.

The guard behind the gate comes forward.

"What is your business?" he asks.

The leader answers. "The king is interested in these blue dragons."

Bird studies the surroundings as he thinks.

The guard behind the gate turns and disappears into the cavern. Bird raises an eyebrow when he returns with four more guards marching behind him. They stop and stand quietly, with spears in hand, looking at the group as the gate guard opens the gate.

"You may enter the waiting area."

Bird and the blue dragons look at each other with curious eyes as the gate guard and four more guards march in with them. They enter a well-lit chamber. Bird and the others gaze in amazement as they take in the splendor of the waiting area. The floor has been chipped level and rubbed with stones creating a smooth finish.

The guard that led them from Bell's house notices the blue dragons are spellbound and speaks to them.

"Draganthal has been ruled by many kings. The trolls and dragons have labored in here for centuries, always making things look better."

Bird is taking it all in, too. Holes have been hewn into the walls allowing light to fill the chamber. Wooden furniture and benches are neatly placed around the room.

The guard from behind the gate motions for Bird and the blue dragons to sit. The rest of the guards seem unconcerned and sit chattering with each other. They are obviously pleased that the king will see they are doing his bidding.

Bird studies the room and the guards. He has a pleasant look on his face, but the blue dragons are quiet and fidgety.

Bird tries to imagine what awaits them behind the large and heavy wooden double door that is close to them. The doors are thick and reinforced with shiny copper straps which are fastened with pins from top to bottom. A polished copper handle waits to be turned to open them. Bird ponders, "Are these doors strong to keep intruders out or to keep prisoners locked in?"

He glances at the jittery blue dragons and realizes their imaginations are running wild. They jump when the latch releases with a snap. Two dragon guards push the doors open and hold them. Two trolls stand several feet away facing them with arrows set, ready to protect the inner chamber. Bird and his friend's raise their eyebrows. The chamber before them is bright and the floor is slick and shiny. Many faces are staring at them. Dragons and trolls are everywhere. The dragons holding the doors motion for them to enter. The original seven escort guards march up beside them. The dragons have their claws extended and the four trolls set arrows. Bird swallows hard.

The place is beautiful, yet intimidating. Arrows are aimed at them ready to shoot on command. In front of them a huge throne sets empty. On its right sit ten dragons on carved stone seats with open backs for their tails to pass through. The dragons are spotless and even their claws look shiny. There is a superior demeanor about them as they whisper to each other while examining the group. On the left side of the throne sits ten trolls who are obviously well-fed and well-cloaked. They are ornately dressed with purple vests that are adorned with red lapels and sleeves. They have inquisitive looks on their faces. After a few moments they begin to point and whisper too. Bird sweats and looks at the blues. They are trembling.

Behind the dragons and trolls sit members of Dragonthal society. They act reserved and hold their heads and noses high. Each row of seats is a head higher than the one in front and is rising to the back. An aisle of steps runs up the middle of the gallery terminating at the highest level. A row of lamps setting neatly in hewn out pockets are flickering across the back of the room. A large shirtless troll comes through a door on the left side. He walks without expression to a brass gong, picks up a mallet with a long handle, waits a second, and then spins around striking the center of the disc. The sound is unnerving as it resonates back and forth in the chamber. He then turns toward the gallery, takes a deep breath and melodically announces,

"King Guargin has arrived."

The dragons and trolls sit quietly as a large door, adorned like the entrance doors, swings open. A troll and a dragon step out. They each hold spears that have shiny brass balls where there would normally be points. The dragon and troll step forward several steps and tilt the strange-looking spears down to the side. The balls slide off revealing frightfully long sharp points. They then step forward as a large silhouette appears in the doorway. The room is in total silence. Dim light fills the doorway from behind and a figure standing on two legs becomes visible.

He is as tall as most dragons, and his horns appear to be the same as most dragons, but while standing in the doorway they look ominous. He steps into the brightly-lit room. Bird and the blue dragons stand in awe.

The king looks like Bago, only larger. He is carrying a large scepter that reaches from the floor to slightly above his head. It is ornately carved and has a brass ball with diamond patterns covering it. His robe is purple with yellow trim running around its perimeter. It covers his back and drapes over his shoulders to his knees. It is held together in front with two small woven ropes that tie to the robe. His forearms are protected with ornate leather covers that are laced together underneath his arm. His loincloth is made of many strips of different colored leather sewn together. The dragons and trolls stand and bow. The king proceeds down the aisle to his throne and sits. He looks at the escort guards and bumps the floor two times with his scepter. The guards all bow quietly and the five frightened dragons do the same.

Guargin cocks his head slightly and looks into the eyes of the five dragons in front of him.

"It has come to my attention that you are selling some kind of magic or medicine in our marketplace. Our citizens are quite fond of what everyone is calling mushy lily bulbs. I have never seen such an effect on our residents. We usually don't ask for a portion of what our subjects trade in the market, but in your case, we need half of the bulbs you bring here. You are taking business from our merchants and sometimes our guards have to keep your customers from causing trouble. This is all an expense to our city." He quiets and looks into the scared dragons' eyes. They all squirm and solemnly look toward Gus. Realizing he must speak; he confidently faces the king.

"We don't question you and will gladly comply. But we are running out of bulbs and will not have more for some time. When we do, we will come here and give you your share." Gus humbly bows. Guargin cocks his head and smirks.

A troll stands and Guargin nods for him to speak. "What is it about these bulbs that makes them so irresistible?" he asks.

Bird clears his throat and Gus steps aside. "These plants are few in number and only grow in the wilderness, in a place I discovered. When you are lucky enough to get one, you lay it close to a fire until it's soft. Then take a little bite, relax, and all your worries disappear. There is no magic."

The troll ponders for a second and then sits. Guargin looks toward them again.

"Who is the leader of your group?"

Gus bows. "I speak for us. We left our den and are interested in learning about Dragonthal."

"Where is the den you have left?"

"Two days from here," replies Gus.

"You will go with our guards, and they will escort the den's leaders here to speak with us. All the dens under our protection must come before us in this court and ask to be accepted."

Lear slowly looks to Leon who sighs.

"Why have you migrated here?" asks Guargin.

Nom smiles as he answers. "We were attacked by men. They are similar to trolls but are much taller and thinner."

"Ugly savage scoundrels!" yells one of the trolls. Guargin bumps the floor with his scepter and court is calm, but there is still movement and whispers behind him. He bumps the floor harder and silence returns. He has a grave look on his face.

With piercing eyes Guargin looks at the five. "It is legend that centuries ago a two-legged creature like this migrated here causing harm to dragons and trolls. We had to unite and eradicate him. This legend has been passed down from generation to generation. It is sacred to our historians. We can never forget what happened, so we will have the resolve to do what our forefathers did to protect our kingdom."

Gus and Nom reserve their smile, but are glad that Guargin now knows what they had come here to tell. Lear and Leon are worried about Lester and Fuzzy.

Guargin stands. "You will sleep here as our guests tonight. Tomorrow my guards will go with two of you to your den. We will bring your leaders back to stand before us."

Guargin bumps the floor and looks at the seven guards that escorted Bird and his friends to the cavern. They stand at attention. Their leader bumps the floor with his spear and they move quickly surrounding Bird and the blue dragons.

"Come with us," says the leader.

Bird and his friends look at each other with puzzled eyes. The large double doors open. They pass through and continue out into the main cavern entrance. They turn toward a darker part of the cavern that is not ornate and the floor is no longer smooth. Ahead, a room closed in with iron bars and a gate comes into view. The escort stops. The blue dragons' hearts tremble at the sight. Bird tries to smile at the escort, but they have frozen expressions on their faces. The leader comes forward and unlocks the gate.

"Don't worry, you will be comfortable in here, and your evening meal will come soon."

He motions for them to move inside, and when they are out of the way, he locks the gate. The blue dragons look at Bird. He rolls his eyes and leans against the wall.

<>

Mason approaches Jim who is finishing another crossbow.

"I'm eager to see what the Murray farm is doing. We need more people like them preparing for the battle ahead. They have had time to build enough for me to see if they will be of any help to us. I wonder if their place even looks like a fortress."

Jim glances at him and returns to his work. "I hope so. They looked convinced when they left." Jim stops for a moment. "If you don't mind, I would like to go with you tomorrow. We should take this crossbow with us and try to convince others to prepare for what is coming." Mason nods in agreement.

By mid-morning they are on their way. The pins have been pulled so the crossbow lies on the floor of the wagon. It doesn't look quite so ominous, but as they pass travelers, most of them can't resist stopping Mason to ask questions. At the watering trough in Blade Town, people take a lot of their time. Mason talks to them in a sincere manner and warns every one of the dragon attacks that will come. People smile and shake their heads soon after they hear the word "dragons." Some even laugh.

One man sitting on his wagon next to his wife cocks his head and looks Mason in the eyes. "That's an interesting story mister, but I don't have enough silver to buy a crossbow like that, even if I thought you may be right."

Mason looks at Jim. "All I can do is warn them."

A family beside them overhears their conversation and with doubtful faces they look away and head up the trail. Jim and Mason catch up with them after a while, and Mason's eyes tear up as a little girl looks out of the back of their wagon and waves.

Mason follows them until a couple wagons traveling together stop him.

"Show us how that thing works," says the driver in front.

Mason is happy to raise it and explain how to operate it. They are impressed until he begins to tell of dragons with intentions of war.

"That's quite a weapon mister, but I'm not buying your dragon story." Mason shows them the dragon claws he found at the ghost camp.

The man's wife is fidgeting and whispering for him to move on.

"Thanks, mister. We need to be moving on," he says.

Mason creases his eyes and drops the claws into his pocket.

"Let me see the dragon claws again!" yells one of the young boys.

"We have heard enough son. That thing isn't real," says his father.

Mason flips the reins and looks at Jim. "It breaks my heart knowing everybody we have talked to will be unprepared to survive what is coming." They ride on quietly and don't stop to talk anymore.

As he approaches the Murray farm, he is astonished to see a walled-in area large enough to set up his traveling show tent inside. He dismounts and walks around examining the massive structure still being constructed. Towers are starting to rise at each corner. He peeks in the tower door that opens into the courtyard. There a set of sturdy wooden steps going down to the basement and another going up into the tower cause him to gaze in awe.

Cap and Jackson notice the crossbow setting near the farmhouse and go in search of Mason. They find him heading for the basement.

"Mason!" yells Cap. Mason and Jim turn brimming with smiles.

"I am absolutely amazed at what you have been able to accomplish."

"We have all of our families here to fight with us, and many others have joined too. When their families come to see what they are working on they usually want to stay, and then we have more help," says Cap.

"I hunger to understand what is coming. I'm curious as to why you seem to be even more confident than us that an attack is eminent," says Mason.

"It is a long story, but we have discovered that there is a dragon city many miles north of here and it has been there for centuries. They wiped out civilization once before, and they intend to do it again. We think the attack will come soon."

Jackson nods in agreement.

Mason looks at Jim. Jim has a long face and shakes his head slightly. Mason turns back to Cap. "I would like to hear the whole story sometime. Show me around your fortress."

They walk through the basement and continue to one of the towers and climb its steps to ground level. They step out into the courtyard. Cap points to the surrounding wall. "There is a four-foot wide hall inside that wall. It runs all the way around the courtyard, and it has slots in it every four feet where arrows can be shot into the courtyard and out into the field around the fortress. The top of the wall is a walkway made of rock and dirt, so it can't burn."

Mason and Jim walk along in the hall with Cap and Jackson, and their footsteps echo as they move along. He stops when he sees the first crossbow that they bought from him.

Cap smiles. "We hid your crossbow in this wall. In front of it there is a large slot with a door hiding it. We can open the door and aim anywhere in the courtyard."

Mason studies how well the crossbow is protected. There are slots where archers can shoot into the courtyard close by. Cap points toward the top of the tower beside them. "If you will sell us the crossbow you brought today, we will disassemble it and build it back on top of that tower. Once the crossbow is finished, we will build a heavy log roof that can be slid away when we need to shoot overhead."

Mason squints. "Why would you have such a strong roof?"

"Several reasons. Dragons may drop rocks or land on top of it, and we don't want it to crash in on top of our crossbow. If the bowman is overwhelmed, he can jump through a trap door in the floor beside it to avoid a blast of fire. We will have buckets of water sitting around that can be dashed on the crossbow if the dragons set it on fire.

"So, you know about dragons dropping rocks?" asks Mason.

"Yes," replies Cap.

Mason holds his chin in thought as he looks into Cap's eyes.

"I will leave this crossbow with you, but I need 600 pieces of silver."

Cap nods to Buck and he leaves.

"Thank you. Buck will be back with the silver in a minute. You have helped us by doing this," says Cap. "I wish all of you the best of luck. It looks like you will need three more crossbows, but I can't promise you anything," says Mason.

Cap and Jackson smile. "We are grateful for what you have already done."

Mason looks around taking it all in and sighs, "I am going to prepare even more seriously after seeing what you are doing. I hope when this is all over, we will be able to meet again and celebrate victory."

"We are doing this for our children," says Jackson, looking toward a group of children playing in part of the finished courtyard.

"I am too," replies Mason.

<>

Lear and Leon sleep very little. They are standing near the gate waiting until finally they hear footsteps coming their way. Gus and Nom are still lying on small piles of grass. Bird is standing in the back of the room smiling. The closer the footsteps come, the antsier Lear and Leon become.

"The King lied. I didn't sleep here last night. I pictured a nice open room with a feast for supper, when he spoke to us in the chamber," says Lear.

Leon cringes. "Don't say that where anyone else can hear you. This is a world we know nothing about, you could get us killed.

"Why are we prisoners?" Lear sneers.

Leon gestures for him to calm down.

Bird comes up beside them, still smiling. "Both of you need to smile. They will treat us better if we act unconcerned." He cocks his head with a calm smile on his face.

"Good morning," says the guard as he unlocks the door and enters.

Gus comes forward. "We are ready to lead you to our den."

"King Guargin will call for you soon. The rest of you are free to go, but I suggest you stay in the city. We will want you back here when your leaders arrive."

Lear, Leon and Bird walk toward the entrance and soon they are standing in sunlight soaking in its warmth."

"Let's head for Bell's hut," says Bird.

Bell hugs them at her door. "Are you in trouble?"

"I don't think so, but I worry about what might happen after the king talks to Fuzzy and Lester," replies Lear, with heavy eyes.

Bird is not concerned. He is confident that he isn't in any trouble.

Bell leads them to a room filled with their share of goods she has taken in trade for lily bulbs. "I have been asking a lot more in trade but everyone keeps coming back."

Lear and Leon take some of their share and head for the market. They trade for ten fire bats and take them to the orchard to set free. The fire bats relax as soon as their baskets are removed and they see blue dragons.

"We owe you for our lives blue dragons and we are thankful that you have saved us. Your kindness is known throughout our kingdom. You are welcome to take shelter in any of our caverns and ask of us anything you desire," says one of the little dragons. They all bow and flutter away.

The next evening Gus, Nom, and four guards land at Fuzzy and Lester's cavern.

"Ureeeeee" summons Nom.

Fuzzy and Lester move quickly to the entrance to see why someone has summonsed the den. Fuzzy is in front and sees Gus and Nom. His smile fades when he realizes they are not alone. Two strange-looking silver dragons and two hairy, dumpy-looking trolls that look alike, just like Lear and Leon said they would, are at the entrance. Lester is by his side as Fuzzy addresses the visitors.

"Welcome to our cavern."

"Are you the leader of this den?" asks the guard with the most ornate spear.

Fuzzy steps beside Lester. "We speak for our den."

The guard stares at Fuzzy for a moment. "I have to tell you that I am amazed at the distinguished look you have."

Fuzzy is at a loss for words.

The guard looks around, and then back to Fuzzy. "King Guargin will be intrigued when you appear before him."

"Why have you come to visit us?" asks Fuzzy.

"We understand that you have recently moved into this cavern, and you probably don't realize how lucky you are to be under the protection of King Gargin, ruler of Dragonthal. You must stand before his court and swear allegiance to him. There are certain responsibilities that you must accept."

Fuzzy and Lester bow and offer them the best place in the cavern to spend the night.

"Lester and I will leave with you in the morning."

After the sun sets Fuzzy and Liz go to Lester and Sada's special place and they talk. Fuzzy paces as he thinks. "From the way these guards are acting, I fear we will lose most of our freedom. Even though this is a dragon kingdom, an eccentric king could have rules that will make our lives miserable."

Liz looks at them with a calm demeanor. "Don't judge what you have not seen. Be open minded until you understand what is required," she says.

Lee has been quietly listening.

Fuzzy looks at him, "Watch after our den while we are gone, but don't do anything that will let the guards know you are chosen to do so."

In the morning, several young dragons leave early and catch fish to feed the den and their guests.

After everyone has eaten, Fuzzy and Lester look around at their guests. Gus and Nom seem happy and have no worry about what may be required of their den.

Lester speaks to the den. "Fellow dragons, Fuzzy and I are glad the Dragonthal king has chosen to speak with us. I am sure we will all be safer once we know what is expected of us, and we can start doing our part to be accepted into the larger family of dragons and trolls. We will return soon."

All eight dragons depart, and the trip to Dragonthal begins. The guards are respectful, and their conversation is mostly about what a wonderful surprise lays in store.

Two days later Fuzzy and Lester land near what they are told is the main gate of the king's court. Their minds are racing, and they don't speak to each other. The entrance guard greets them and goes inside. When he returns, he has an announcement.

"The king will see you in the morning. You are to spend the night here as our guests. Gus and Nom are free to leave but they must return in the morning."

The guards escort Fuzzy and Lester to the dungeon and lock the door behind them.

There are several grass mats on the floor. Fuzzy chooses one that appears to be fresh, and Lester picks one beside him. Lying there, looking at the stalactite-studded ceiling, they are quiet for a minute.

"All these guards carrying weapons troubles me," says Fuzzy. "This is not a place where we will ever have any freedom. I never dreamed we would be locked up," replies Lester.

"I hope they don't throw someone else in here with us," says Fuzzy shuffling to a comfortable spot on his mat.

Gus and Nom find Lear and Leon at their hut.

"Lester and Fuzzy are here spending the night as guests of the king," says Gus.

Leon looks at Lear who has cut his eyes toward Gus.

"Are they staying in the same room we did?" Leon asks.

Gus doesn't answer.

"I'm anxious to hear what the king talks about tomorrow. You should go with us," says Nom.

Neither Lear nor Leon answer.

<>

Fuzzy and Lester have been awake for a while. They quietly mope around the dark, damp room. Lester sighs loudly and lies back down on his mat.

"I hear the guards coming," says Fuzzy, standing ready to get out of the cage.

The door swings open and a guard comes in. "Follow me," he says before turning and walking out of the gate where three more guards join them. They all quietly walk to the court entrance where the guard is waiting for them and opens the gate. He leads them through the waiting area, and they stand before the large wooden doors. With hearts pounding, they wait. They flinch when suddenly the latch snaps open and the doors swing aside. Fuzzy and Lester cringe at the sight that greets them. Two troll guards with arrows set ready to shoot are in their faces. Two more guards hold the doors and wait for them to enter. They're shocked to see such a beautiful place with dragons and trolls all around. They study the trolls. They are dressed so differently than the ones they have seen.

A shirtless troll strikes the gong and announces. "King Guargin has arrived!"

The unnerving clang of the gong adds to their uneasiness. Fuzzy feels his stomach twist into knots. The dragons and trolls turn and watch as the large door behind them opens. A dragon and a troll step out with spears in-hand. King Guargin appears with his scepter.

Everyone stands and bows. The king proceeds to his throne and sits. He looks at the escort guards, bumps his scepter two times on the floor, and the guards bow. Fuzzy and Lester follow suit, bowing slightly.

While bowed, Fuzzy whispers to Lester. "What is that thing?"

Lester closes his eyes and doesn't reply.

"Welcome, blue dragons. Why have you chosen to migrate into my kingdom?"

Fuzzy is nervous and catches a glimpse of Gus, Nom, bird, Lear, and Leon seated to one side. Fuzzy pauses and takes a deep breath.

"Thank you for honoring us by inviting us to your court."

Guargin studies him.

Fuzzy is surprised that he does not reply and continues.

"We were threatened by men---creatures that look similar to the men sitting to your left, but taller and thinner."

One of the trolls jumps to his feet. His face is red with anger. "We are not men! We are trolls! What you are describing is a scoundrel."

Fuzzy bows humbly. "I am sorry. The scoundrels discovered our cavern and came hunting us with intentions of causing us harm. After a brief battle with them, we decided to leave our beloved cavern so we could be free to live like dragons."

"Did you kill the scoundrels?" asks Guargin.

"Yes. We had no choice," replies Fuzzy. The trolls and dragons sitting behind Guargin clap and nod happily.

Guargin smiles. "We have heard from your den members that the population of scoundrels is on the rise again. Our legends tell us they are a curse upon us. You have done us all a favor by killing those that attacked you."

Fuzzy pauses and calms himself. "It is not that simple. We would have never survived without the help of two wonderful and kind men who warned us of the danger and even helped us fight the hunters. We have included in our legend that not all men are evil, and we can't harm those who helped us."

The dragons and trolls boo. Guargin bumps the floor loudly.

"Nonsense, blue dragon. I'm sure these scoundrels gained something from helping you. These creatures live at the expense of everything around them. Once you pledge allegiance to us, we will fight your battles and we won't have emotional ties to any of our enemies."

Fuzzy's eyes glare and his words are loud. "We have given our word to protect the men who helped us!"

Guargin slams his scepter hard on the floor. "Stop! It is forbidden to speak of anything that is not consistent with our legend! These 'men' are to be called scoundrels, and none of them are to be spared. They will rise again unless we eradicate their species."

Fuzzy hangs his head and worry squeezes the knots in his stomach.

Guargin squints, half smiling. "You have a lot to learn about our kingdom. Every dragon den that lives within our protection must pay for the privilege. Whatever you choose to produce, you are required to bring here to our marketplace and trade. You must give a quarter of whatever you receive in trade as tax to the king."

Fuzzy looks blank and turns to Lester, whose mouth is slightly open. They look bewildered as they look back toward Guargin. "We only produce what we need to live."

"Then you will have to give me some of your young dragons to fight in my army. They will fight for us all, and you will never have a problem with scoundrels again."

"I will let you think about what you have just learned, blue dragon. You may return to your cavern and my guards will visit you soon."

Guargin looks at Bird and the four blue dragons. "Guards, seize those five and take them to be trained for our army."

Fuzzy and Lester's faces fill with horror, but they are so overwhelmed that they do not resist. Tears fall from their eyes as the guards raise their spears and surround the five and escort them out of the court. The guards' faces show no emotion. Gus and Nom are smiling and talking to them. Lear and Leon are quiet for a moment.

"This may not be so bad. We are young and this may be exciting," says Leon. Lear looks him in the eye. "I don't want to hear that. I'm trying to smile like Bird said, but surely you realize we have lost our freedom."

Bird looks slyly happy and unconcerned. He talks to a guard in front of them.

They approach a dimly lit chamber with a locked gate. A guard inside unlocks it and stands aside as they walk in. When the lock clicks and the gate is secure, Bird is nowhere to be found. The escort guards reopen the gate and search frantically outside. With snarled lips they turn and run back inside angrily screaming at the four blue dragons.

"Where is the silver dragon!"

"How could we know?" replies Leon. One of the escort guards breaks his spear handle across Leon's shoulder and pushes him to the floor. Lear steps between him and the guard and bows.

"We are sorry and will help you. Please don't strike Leon again."

The guard grunts, looks at his companions, and they stomp out of the gate. He glares at the blue dragons and snorts in disgust as he slams the gate.

<>

Breathing heavily and looking over his shoulder, Bird knocks at Bell and Deago's door.

Bell opens the door and raises her eyebrows. "Where are the others?"

"I can't take time to tell you much right now. I must leave quickly. They have been locked up, and I must flee. Will you give me some of my lily bulbs?"

"Of course;" replies Bell. "I'm sorry to hear of your trouble. I hope Deago and I are not in trouble."

"I don't think there will be a problem for either of you. Thank you for your help. I hope to see you again someday." He hugs Bell and nods to Deago, then quickly walks out the door. When he is a few feet from their house, his wings dig into the air and he ascends frantically. In seconds, he is out of sight. Bell and Deago hold each other for a while.

That night they console each other and feel better, but very early in the morning there is a knock at the hut door. Guards with spears are impatiently waiting. Bell opens the door and they barge in. Bell tries to speak to them, but they ransack the hut and discover Bago.

"Why have you not told us you have a dragoll child?" growls the lead guard.

Bell runs to Bago and clings dearly. "We love him too much to part with him, he is our joy in life," she pleads.

The lead guard puckers his lips and sighs. "You know dragolls are required to be sent to the palace where they are trained and disciplined to take their place in the king's army." The guard grits his teeth and with a long face, seizes Bago and pulls him from his mother.

Bell falls to the floor and sobs as Deago hangs his head and gasps for air.

Chapter 14

With long faces, Fuzzy and Lester walk out into the green grassy area in front of the king's cavern. They sadly look at each other, raise their wings and laboriously take to the air. They have no desire to look around Dragonthal.

They fly quietly until they find a current that lifts them high, and they drift.

"My heart is so heavy I can hardly fly. After all we have been through the only thing we have accomplished is escaping from civilization. It breaks my heart to tell the den about the world we have stumbled into---a world ruled by Guargin, a dragoll king. Because of him we will never be free," says Fuzzy.

Lester doesn't reply and they continue to put distance between them and Dragonthal. Hours later, Fuzzy is in deep thought. "We must try to explain what we know to the younger dragons. Lee and Kim may want to search for another place if they want to be free of taxes and the whims of Guargin, not to mention the possibility of having to give up their children to fight in his army," he sighs.

<>

Not far behind them, Bird is flying as fast as he can. He has a hideout he prepared long ago. Things he might need are stored there, so he can disappear for a while. It is a cave far to the east of Dragonthal and it is well hidden. No one will ever find it. Bird is savoring the sweet feeling of freedom and smiles every time he thinks about how he outwitted the guards and slipped out of the king's cavern undetected.

"You can't catch Bird," he thinks to himself. His first stop will be at his old cave where he will throw a few things into a saddle bag that Bell gave him. He pulls a lily bulb and takes to the air, headed for his hideaway. The excitement gives him energy.

<>

Fuzzy and Lester land and are unable to muster a smile as they greet several members of their den at the cavern entrance. Word that they are back travels through the cavern and everyone knows things didn't go well. They normally wouldn't wait to summons the den.

Once they catch their breath and think about what to say, Lester calls for the den to gather. Quietly the den assembles around him.

"Fuzzy and I are relieved to be home. Our trip to Dragonthal, the city of dragons and trolls, has been trying for us. The city looks amazing and it is large. The dragons and trolls work together, but it is not a friendly place. And now, because we live close to the city, we are all indebted to his kingdom. His name is Guargin, and his army controls everyone in the city and for miles around. Fuzzy and I were helpless while in his presence. His guards were all around us and holding spears. The king looked at us with an arrogant smile and told us we would have to send some of our strongest and brightest dragons to fight in his army. We were shocked and complained, so he callously seized our four young dragons and Bird. Fuzzy and I are heartbroken. The guards will come and make demands of us, and there is little we can do about it. After all we have gone through, we are far from being free."

Lee steps forward. "The dragons that left with Bird wanted to join the king's army anyway. Hopefully they will satisfy his demands of our den for a long time."

Lester looks at him and slowly shakes his head. "King Guargin is building an army to attack mankind. The dragons and trolls of the city hate men, they call them scoundrels. He made it very clear that he didn't owe our friends any favors. To him, Cap and Jackson's families are nothing more than scoundrels."

The den is quiet and looks to Fuzzy.

"I gave Cap and Jackson a promise, and I am a dragon of honor. I will help defend their family. Lester and I have a lot of thinking to do. Our world has just changed again, and we must make decisions wisely. Lester and I want you to know that unlike the Dragonthal king's subjects, you are free to make up your own minds."

<>

Two weeks later, King Guargin calls his court into session. After the gong has been rung, he walks to his throne with squinted eyes and a long face. He studies the room for a moment, letting anticipation set the mood for what he is going to say.

"You have heard the legends about scoundrels. You know how they invaded our world. They slowly migrated into our midst, and when they were firmly established, they began killing trolls and dragons." The members of the court have their eyes glued on Guargin. His stern face is reflected on their faces, and he pauses for a moment.

"Our ancestors waited too long to unite and declare war on them. The scoundrels had weakened them, making the war long and hard. We must not wait until they begin showing up in our forest; we must finish what our ancestors started." He scans the room looking at the members of the court with piercing eyes.

One by one they join in a chant.

"Fight! Fight! Fight!"

Guargin raises his scepter quieting them before they get out of hand. "Thank you, I'm glad there is nothing to debate. We are a large and strong kingdom now and we will eradicate them. This very day, I will call on Commander Slash to prepare for war, and soon we will invade the scoundrels."

The chant starts again and continues until Guargin leaves.

Surrounded by guards, Guargin walks briskly toward Slash's quarters. Slash recognizes the three loud thumps on his door as the king's scepter, and quickly proceeds to pull it open. He bows when their eyes make contact.

"I am honored by your presence," he says.

Guargin bows slightly. "The royal court has met, and I have decided to declare war on the scoundrels and their civilization far south of us. The blue dragons can show you where they are. I want you to put our army into motion and begin this campaign. A successful war of this nature will serve your political ambitions well. We dragolls must look after each other."

Slash smiles slyly. "I am honored beyond words. My scouts will leave tomorrow. I will assemble an adequate number of soldiers based on their report. We will engage the scoundrels while their numbers are few."

The next day, Byron, the leader of the scouting party meets with Gus and Nom. They tell him how to find the plateau that holds their old cavern, and that the scoundrels have built a town south of it.

Feeling confident, Byron commands three trolls to strap saddles and harnesses designed to hold spears, arrows, and bows onto three dragons and by midday they are flying south. Several days later they are hovering over the plateau. The scouts land and Byron studies the landscape. He motions for the scouts to follow as he heads for an opening in the wilderness canopy. They all smile when they discover a small town built by scoundrels sits in a large grassy meadow there. They stay out of sight of the village and notice a blue lake shimmers to their west. Byron heads toward its banks. They are spellbound by the beauty of the beaches and the island rising in the middle.

Byron motions for them to land. "This place will be perfect to set up camp. The lake will furnish our food and water, and our enemy is close enough for us to easily keep watch over them. Build some shelters and we will rest here until tomorrow."

<>

The Brittains and the Murrays are the leaders of the fortress, and they meet often with different groups of its growing population to make decisions about everyone's needs and ideas. But today, the discussion is of a financial nature, and they are meeting alone. Cap leads the discussion.

"Construction is progressing well. I am amazed by how fast things are moving along, but with everyone working on the walls and buildings, we won't have enough food and supplies stored to sustain ourselves if we are locked inside these walls for a long time."

Jackson stands. "We must make more trips to Blade Town and Water Town to buy dried food, clothing and a lot more."

"We still have enough silver to finish the construction, but buying these things made outside the fortress will cost more than we have," replies Cap.

Buck interrupts. "We need every arrow we can get our hands on, and we don't have time to make them either. If the battle lasts a long time, they will be our biggest concern."

Jackson, still standing, smiles. "We left half of the silver we found at the mine last time we were there. It's still in a pile outside. We wouldn't even have to open the mine to load another wagon. That should be more than enough to buy what you are talking about."

The family agrees to let Cap, Jackson, and Uncle Matt make a run back to the mine for more silver. Three days later they are next to the pile of stones.

"It's such a beautiful day. I think we should ride to the lake that we never got to tell Uncle Matt about," says Jackson.

I would like to see it too, but I'm not sure we have the luxury of time for that," replies Cap.

Jackson sulks. "The path we took when we went to the lake wasn't bad. With the horses we can easily be at the lake in an hour."

Matt looks curiously at them. "A lot is riding on this trip. I don't think we should take any chances."

"Don't worry, you will thank me when you see this jewel hidden in the wilderness," says Jackson. "We will be back before dark and load up in the morning."

Once they head for the lake, Cap is happy to go and Jackson is filled with excitement. They weave through the trees following a path marked by limbs they cut on their adventure.

In an hour, Cap points ahead, "There's the hill where we first looked out over the lake."

This had better be something special," says Matt.

"Trust me you will be surprised," says Jackson.

As they top the hill and prepare to show Uncle Matt the beautiful lake, they stop suddenly and cringe. They motion for Matt to be quiet. There on the beaches are dragons and trolls.

Cap swallows hard and his heart races. He motions for Jackson and Uncle Matt to quietly head back to the mine. They ride slowly, trying to be as quiet as they can until they are halfway back. Then they pick up their pace.

"Those dragons were silver and those men were so short they waddled when they walked," says Uncle Matt.

Cap rubs his wrinkled forehead. That is how Fuzzy described our enemy from the dragon city.

"I want to load up now and head back as fast as we can," says Jackson.

Cap is sweating. "We can't build anymore fires, and we can't let our guard down until we are in the fortress."

They load less than they had planned, and head home before dark. The wagon is heavy enough to slow them down, but they are home in three days. When they pass through the gate, Cap looks up to one of the towers and calls out loudly.

"Ring the bell!"

Everyone stops working and gathers around the wagon. Cap stands and raises his hand to quiet them.

"I have grave news. We have seen what we believe is a scouting party of silver dragons and trolls. They are three days from here, but in flight they can be here in an hour. It is time to finish anything that must be done to defend ourselves."

Everyone moves closer to the ones they love.

Jackson speaks up. "Everyone needs to decide where they are going to fight, man the crossbows, and fill their quivers. Go right now and take your weapons with you, then practice what you are going to do. Those who will be in the basement need to take their places, especially those who will care for the wounded. In one hour, Cap and I will walk through and make final decisions as to who does what."

<>

The trolls climb on top of the dragons and sail over the lake, rising high in the sky. Soon they see the fortress and they head toward it. Standing tall in the middle of a cleared field and with flags waving in the wind atop the roofs of the towers, it spurs their curiosity as they approach. Byron motions for the scouts to separate. Some go to the left and the others go to the right, while he lands in the cover of the forest on the north side. They spend their first day safely hidden in the forest watching smoke curling from the fortress's chimneys and scoundrels walking around the walls. The next day they move from place to place, being cautious, so as not to be seen. They don't fly too close, so they don't see all the work going on in the courtyard.

That evening when darkness falls, they sail closer, but the dogs bark and they decide to return to the lake. After discussing what they have seen, they decide the fortress is built to protect the men from predators living in the forest. Unable to get a close look, they don't know about the powerful crossbow hidden in the wall of the courtyard or the one under the roof of one tower.

Two days later the scouts are in the woods near Blade Town. Scoundrels there are busy and bustling about, much like the dragons and trolls in the market at Dragonthal. It is obvious that they have no guards, and few scoundrels are carrying weapons. The leader gathers the scouts, and before they leave, he picks a troll to sneak over to a shed built near the woods. None of the scoundrels are nearby, and the leader wants to know more about the buildings. The troll is cautious as he approaches. He takes only a second to look it over, and then hurries back to the safety of the woods.

"This village will be easy to destroy. Everything is made of wood," he says laughing. They are happy as they head back into the forest where they can take to the air unnoticed and head south. When they pass over Sandra's village the sun is going down. It is so small that they continue following the trail until they reach Water Town. Even in the dark they are intrigued by what they see. They quietly hide in the woods and spend the night.

Just before the sun rises, the scouts hear roosters crowing around town. A horse clomps slowly along the road. When the sun is above the horizon, they hear more horses, but now they are moving at a trot. By midmorning the roads are abuzz with wagons rumbling back and forth. The town is a mass of motion.

"This village is as busy as Dragonthal. We will need to spend several days watching for weaknesses and seeing how the scoundrels protect it," says Byron.

They spend several days hidden in the woods, and one evening they take a chance. Two of the trolls steal coats and blankets from clotheslines behind one of the buildings. They put the coats on and grab a wagon. Then they wrap up in the blankets, sit up straight and ride down some of the side streets. Everyone is too busy to notice that they look different. The trolls study the scoundrels moving about carrying baskets and sacks in and out of shops. Some are talking and laughing, but they never glance at the wagon.

The trolls are smiling and bursting with excitement when they report to Byron.

"The scoundrels are too busy to pay us any attention and we got a good look at them. They don't appear to be as strong as we are and few of them are carrying weapons. None of them look like soldiers or guards."

Byron breathes a sigh of relief.

"Before we head back to Dragonthal let's fly further south. I want to see how many villages there may be."

They leave early and the trail is easy to follow, but the further they travel the fewer riders and wagons they see. The trail narrows until it disappears into the wilderness.

That night, hidden in the underbrush far from Water Town and convinced that he knows enough to report to Slash, Byron tells his scouts that it's time to return to Dragonthal.

Several days later, he walks into Slash's quarters with a smile on his face. "The scoundrels and their civilization are an easy target.

A small army will have no trouble destroying everything." Slash smiles with confidence.

He begins preparing a group of soldiers made up of trolls and dragons. He spends as much time filling their minds with evil stories about scoundrels as he does training them to fight. They practice with spears and bows until they are powerful and determined killers. He listens to their conversations and watches them drill. When he sees they are tired of doing the same thing over and over, they will be yearning to spill scoundrel blood. Then he will gather them, praise their accomplishments, and send them to invade civilization.

<>

After several days of surprising men and women with test alarms, he is pleased how sincere they practice running quickly to their post. Cap addresses the fortress. He clangs a bell two times and stands on top of one of the towers. His face lifts when he sees the courtyard filled with men and women eager to listen.

"Our drills are improving. Everyone was ready to fight moments after I rang the tower bell today. I have watched you practice shooting at targets from your posts, and I have noticed that you are turning into soldiers. I believe we are as ready for an attack as we can hope to be.

Our stored food and supplies grow every day, and we will continue to make trips to Blade Town and Water Town until we can store no more, or the war begins. I hope you are as confident as I am. We are ready to fight, and every day we make improvements. The longer it is until arrows fly in battle, the stronger we will be"

He stops and paces in thought. He focuses on the crowd. "Now that I have told you how well we are prepared, I must warn you. Do not become complacent. We still need to care for our crops. Our cattle will depend on grain and hay we store now, and we can use all the dried beans and grain we can get. Look around at the men and women standing beside you and all the others inside these walls. Every one of us is a member of your fighting family. Let our determination to destroy our enemy bond us and strengthen our resolve to save each other.

"Jackson and I will go to Water Town tomorrow to buy another crossbow and all the arrows we can find. Keep in mind the enemy could attack while we are gone. Keep your eyes and ears open and be ready."

That night, the Murrays and the Brittains, who live in six little rooms in the basement, come together out in the courtyard to talk. They sit around several tables while Ren, Renay, and several other children run and play. Janice smiles as she watches them.

"Look at our children. They have no idea what is happening. The bliss of childhood, I wish I didn't know either."

Sandra shakes her head. "I hope they never see what is happening out here once the battle starts. Their lives will never be the same if they see war at its worst; they may never act like children again."

Inez speaks up, "Flavie and I will keep the children out of harm's way. We will figure out how to entertain them far away from the sights and sounds of battle.

After settling in for the night, Cap and Janice lay side-by-side. They gently hold on to each other.

"We will never have a chance to live a normal life like our parents," says Janice.

Cap squeezes her hand, rolls over and hugs her. "As long as we are together, you and I will make the best of whatever this world throws at us. Life will be harder for us, and I can accept that as long as I see that our children will be able to live in a world like we grew up in."

Janice sobs.

Before the sun rises, Cap and Jackson are on their way to see Mason. In the city, they feel strange when they see everyone going about their business as if nothing is wrong.

"These people are living in a different world than us," says Cap. "Too soon they will be slammed into a war, and it will be horrible."

A family crosses the road. They are laughing and having fun. The children wave. Cap smiles haphazardly and waves back. His heart aches as he turns to Jackson, his eyes filled with sadness. He closes them and rubs tears away.

Mason is working on his barn fortress and catches a glimpse of Cap and Jackson in the distance. He drops his load of rocks and walks briskly out to meet them.

"Do you have news?" he asks.

"Yes, we stumbled across a scouting party out in the wilderness and were lucky to escape without them seeing us. Mason gasps. Jim steps close.

"Then we are running out of time!" exclaims Mason.

"I agree," says Cap. They were camped out in the open on the beach of a nearby lake. They had bows, spears, and other gear. They're probably all around, spying on us,"

"Do you have a crossbow ready?" asks Cap.

Mason is slow to answer. He's mulling over the news he just heard. "I have one crossbow I can sell. After what you just told me and all that is yet to be done, I can't part with more. I know I promised to make a wagon load of arrows for you, but I need all that I can make. There are plenty of arrows in the hardware store. Buy all you can and return to spend the night here with us. I want to hear more about the scouting party."

When they return, the barn is a happy place. Families that have bonded together are laughing and lost in conversation. Several men and women smile and toil as they huddle around open fires near the barn. The smell of roasting meat and flavorful steam from boiling pots drift among the members of Mason's fortress barn residents.

Ella, Al, and Alma are hovering near Mason. He stands when Cap and Jackson dismount. He calls the gathering to quiet.

"I want to introduce two men who have news that will help you understand why we are turning this barn into a fortress." Cap and Jackson blush and bow politely." Their families are building an unbelievable fortress north of Blade Town. They are here to purchase another crossbow from us, and their silver will help us buy more supplies that we must have to survive."

Mason motions for them to come forward. Cap steps over and takes a deep breath. The people grow quiet and apprehensive. Their eyes are glued on his every move.

"Several days ago, my brother Jackson and I stumbled across what we think is a scouting party. The group was made up of shiny silver dragons with yellow bellies, and trolls that look like dumpy little men. All are armed with bows and spears. They are from a dragon city far north of Blade Town. The trolls ride on the backs of the dragons, and they work together in battle. They are camped on the banks of a large lake many miles from here, but as a dragon fly, it is not far."

The group moans and gasps at his description.

"The dragons are as large as six men and adorned with long black horns, and long sharp claws. I am sure all of you have heard from legends about the flames they are capable of unleashing. Jackson and I are convinced they are scouts that have been sent here to learn all they can about us before they attack."

Jackson sees that everyone is horrified and is moved to speak. "I see the looks on your faces. Take heart! Don't feel helpless. We are now brothers in arms, and when I see all the work you have done on your fortress, I have no doubt that you will be ready. I see determination here, and I'm sure you will win the coming battle."

Mason stands. "Cheer up everyone. These men have given us good news. We know more about our enemy and that our new brothers in arms will be nearby helping us kill them. It's time to eat, drink, and enjoy their company before they leave."

The next morning, Cap and Jackson hook their horses to the crossbow and load the arrows they bought at the hardware store on its floorboard.

Mason smiles as Cap counts out the silver.

"This silver will help us finish preparing for the war," says Mason.

Cap shakes his hand. "Even though we are far apart, we are in this together, and we will help you with anything we can. Remember that."

He and Jackson climb up on the seat of the crossbow and head toward their fortress. As soon as they arrive, Buck and several men begin disassembling the weapon and in three days it is perched on top of the tower diagonally across from the first tower crossbow.

<>

A wave of animosity floods the barn fortress as Cap and Jackson's words settle in. Mason realizes the war will be worse than he first imagined. Everyone sees it on his face. Jim catches Mason alone in his office.

"Mason, you have got to believe in me and yourself. There is nothing we and these fine people can't do if we all work together. Call on your inner strength and help me get ready to kill these evil creatures. We can do it!" He pounds Mason's desk with his fist.

Mason's eyes brighten. "You have never talked to me like this. You actually believe we can do this."

Jim looks him in the eyes. "We will destroy them. But we need your leadership."

Mason fills with energy welling from his deep conviction to protect his family. He joins the workers and works hard. When he grows tired, he hugs his children and his inspiration returns. At night he is kinder to Ella. He reassures her that he has thought everything out and they will be safe, but she must stay close to their children. It is imperative that they never venture far from the barn any more.

Jim becomes the force that keeps everyone in the fortress barn bonded like family. He is kind and respected, and under his guidance they prepare and practice their duties for when the battle comes.

<>

Bird can't rest in his hideout. Every evening when he tries to relax on his grass mat, his thoughts are of Lear and Leon's plight. He knows they want to be free like him. Even lily bulbs won't calm his mind and he decides to return to Dragonthal.

The moment Bell sees him, she runs to him and falls to her knees in agony. Bird can hardly control his emotions as he listens to her plea.

"They took our precious son," she sobs over and over.

Bird's demeanor crashes as he blames himself. He helps her stand. "I had no idea that would happen," he replies with tears flowing from his eyes. He walks toward Deago with his mouth half open, searching for words.

Deago turns away and limps several steps. "I know you had no way of knowing. All dragolls must be sent to the king's court so they can be trained to assume positions of leadership, and possibly become the next king. We don't blame you. It's just that seeing you revives painful memories."

Bell wipes her cheeks and looks at Bird. "Stay here tonight. Tomorrow we will feel better."

In the morning Bell, Deago, and Bird share breakfast and talk.

"Why have you returned? You can't show your face around here. The guards are watching for you," says Bell.

"I must try to help Leon and Lear. My poor judgment cost them their freedom. I intend to find them and help them escape. Do you know where the army is training?"

Bell looks at Deago. He nods and speaks softly, "I know they are training in a valley nearby. Talk in the market place tells of a valley north of here where soldiers spend their nights out in the weather. They are not allowed to take shelter from the wind or rain. Part of their training is to become accustomed to hardship."

Bird squints and his mind wanders in thought. He shivers to think of the rain and cold his friends are enduring.

"Thank you," he says. He turns and starts toward the door, and stops and looks back. "Forgive me for the pain I have caused you."

He takes to the air and flies north until he sees the army training. He cautiously hides where he can watch from a distance. The blue dragons are easy to spot. He studies their surroundings and everyone's routine for several days. He ponders and watches. A sparkle appears in his eyes when he realizes the most predictable thing they do. Lear and Leon always head into the woods to relieve themselves before they lay down for the night. Their leaders and guards are further away at that moment than at any other time.

The next evening when Leon and Lear head to the woods, they are shocked to hear a voice coming from behind a tree nearby.

"Are you two enjoying spending the night here as guest of the king?"

"Bird, is that you?" whispers Lear.

"Don't look like you are talking to me. Just do your business and listen," states Bird. "Tomorrow you must convince everyone that you have seen the light and that you want nothing more than to be in the king's army. Do as I say for a week. With a little luck, when I meet you here in seven days, no one will be watching you and we can slip into the woods and fly away. Now go back to where you bed down, think about it, and don't tell Gus or Nom. Do as I say and I will come back for you."

The next morning Leon and Lear smile and obey every command just like Gus and Nom.

"What has happened to you two?" asks Gus. Several other soldiers are close and Leon replies loud enough for them to hear.

"I have been watching the residents of Dragonthal and everyone in the army lives better than most of them. I am beginning to think we have fallen into good luck."

Lear smiles and nods.

Gus beams. "I hadn't thought about it, but you are right."

Seven days pass and Bird is waiting where he promised. When Lear and Leon enter the woods, Bird steals a peek and smiles. No one is watching. When they are close, he pivots out from behind a tree. "Follow me."

They run through the forest, not stopping as they enter the meadow that Bird had planned to use. They unfurl their wings and fly. Nervous energy hastens their ascent, and soon they are high in the sky with darkness closing in. Heading south, Lear and Leon continually look back to reassure themselves that no one is following. Even though Bird looks happy, he too, is struggling with fear. After several hours their tensions ease and a zestful feeling of freedom courses through their veins.

Bird zigzags for a moment, making Leon and Lear smile for the first time. Then he darts toward the ground, landing in a meadow so dark that only a dragon could have found it. They pull tall grass, bundle three piles, mash them flat, drop on their bellies, and quickly fall asleep.

Lear and Leon wake feeling a joy that only new-found freedom can bring, and they are ready for adventure.

"On the way home I want to stop at the fire bat cave we found on our way to Dragonthal. They have invited us to stop and meet the den several times, and their cave is on the way." says Lear.

"Why would you do such a thing?" asks Bird.

"In their world Leon and I are highly respected."

Bird happily rolls his eyes. Lear takes the lead as they head for the cave, but when they see the entrance, they are shocked to see trolls outside waving grass nets. The nets are tied to long sticks and they are trying to catch bats as they fly out to feed. A large net is rolled up and propped above the entrance. Once the fire bat den tries to swarm, the trolls will drop it across the entrance. The trolls will be gone with their captives by the time the den burns the net away.

Lear looks at Leon and snarls. Anger fills his eyes, and without thought he dives faster and faster toward the trolls. The trolls are startled, and in panic two of them lose their balance and stumble. They fling their nets over their heads and, in desperation, grab the netting over the entrance. It rips loose and pulls across the other two trolls, tangling them all in a web of netting. In chaos, the mass of net and troll tumbles over the ledge.

The dragons below shriek when ear-shattering screams cause them to jerk their heads upward. They scatter as the blob of trolls wiggles and squirms in the mangled netting twirling toward them. It slams to the rocky ground with a juicy thud. Trolls splatter like watermelons. The dragons flap their wings so furiously that they slap each other in the face. One of them smashes into the mountain as he rises and careens to the ground. He lands upside down, striking his head with a loud pop. He twitches in death before releasing a blast of flames. The remaining three terrified dragons pick up speed and flutter away without looking back

Bird, Lear, and Leon flap furiously to stop their dive and land on the ledge where the trolls had been. They stare at the burning mass below. Suddenly they are startled when hundreds of fire bats fly out of the cave and peer over the ledge. Even more hover above the dragons' heads in swarms. They start to flee in fear, but stop when the fire bats begin to chant.

"Blue dragons! Blue dragons! Blue dragons!" the chant grows louder as more and more fire bats realize what has happened.

Bird's mouth falls open as he realizes how many fire bats are at the entrance praising his friends. Lear bows in respect. Leon and Bird follow suit. The den begins to quiet and step aside as their king approaches the ledge. He bows for a moment, then raises his head and smiles.

"I have heard many stories of your kindness and how honorable the blue dragons are. Please come inside to meet the rest of the den."

Bird is hesitant to go in. Lear turns to the king.

"This silver dragon is not from Dragonthal. He is our friend. He saved our lives."

The King bows to Bird and turns to the den. "This silver dragon has no yellow breast. He is to be treated as a blue dragon."

The dragons follow him inside as thousands of eyes look upon them. The fire bat king stops beside a large flat rock and flutters atop. "Welcome blue dragons. I am King Earl. This is my den. There are many fire bat dens scattered across Venosta. They all have their own king, but we help each other in times of need. You are known to them and will be welcome at any of their dens."

King Earl motions for several fire bats to spit flames into pockets around the chamber and light begins to fill the space. King Earl stands proud and turns in a full circle to see everyone and then faces the blue dragons. These blue dragons and their friend, though they look different, are now part of our den."

The multitude chirps in unison three times and bow.

The dragons are humbled and return the bow.

Lear raises his head first. "We are honored and will be your friends as long as we live."

Bird still feels uneasy, but he can smile in the face of danger. He beams like he knows he should. He turns to his friends, and while still smiling he talks through his teeth. "We really should be on our way."

Lear, filled with joy, speaks loudly. "We must be on our way, but never forget that blue dragons and fire bats will be friends forever!"

He turns and leads Leon and Bird to the entrance as the den chirps in unison. It evolves into a pleasant melody.

Once outside, Bird looks over the ledge and sees a small pile of ashes and black streaks on the side of the mountain where the trolls and dragon burned. His stomach churns. "Guargin will be furious at us. The dragons that fled this mess are telling him their story right now, and he will not be interested in hearing how it was an accident."

"You're wasting your breath. We just deserted his army, and if he ever catches us, he will kill us anyway," says Lear. They look over the ledge one last time and then quickly take to the air.

The next day they land at their den's cavern. Bird stays back out of the way. Lear is behind Leon as they approach Fuzzy and Lester. Fuzzy smiles and many of the den members are assembling around them. Lear drops his head while Leon takes a breath and tells everyone what has happened.

Fuzzy loses his smile and squats to the floor. He is overwhelmed and breathless. Lester just shakes his head.

Fuzzy's heart aches as he feels anger welling. He and Lester warned them about rushing off to a strange place. He glares at Bird, who turns and moves further away. Fuzzy waits until he begins to calm down.

"Even though the troll deaths were an accident and the den had nothing to do with Lear and Leon's escaping, Guargin will come to punish us."

Lester sees how devastated the fugitives feel, and steps beside Fuzzy. "Leon and Lear are victims of circumstance. I forgive them and ask you to do the same."

The den is quiet but they all bow respectfully.

Lear is in tears. "We care deeply for all of you, and we are truly sorry for what we have brought upon our den. We will hide in the wilderness. Hopefully Guargin will believe you when you explain that you had nothing to do with our actions."

As soon as they are out of sight Fuzzy turns to Lester.

"We have no choice but to return to our old cavern."

Lester smirks and squats to think. His face is wrinkled and he rubs his eyes. He stands. "There is no other choice, so I agree." He turns to the den. They are dumbfounded and quiet, but slowly one of them bows and the rest follow.

Fuzzy raises his wings. "We will leave in a few moments. All of us are healthy, and in three days we should be home. War is coming for mankind and his civilization will be devastated. Hunters will not be coming into the wilderness for a long time."

He bows and heads to his special place. Lester is solemnly walking behind him.

"Fuzzy, I know this is even harder on you than you shared with the den. You can rest assured that I remember our promise to the Brittains and Murrays."

<>

Three days later, the den is hard at work removing stones from the old cavern entrance.

Bird, Lear, and Leon are on their way to his hideout. With little joy to share, they labor in their flight. Bird's heart grows heavier when he hears Lear's lament.

"Our poor judgment has threatened our den's very existence. Every ounce of my heart aches to rejoin them. I long to wake with my family and work to make their lives better, and to see approval in Fuzzy and Lester's eyes, but we are going to be stuck out here alone in the wilderness."

<>

The Dragonthal dragons who witnessed the deaths of the trolls at the fire bat cave tell King Guargin of a vicious, intentional attack. They describe the killers as two blue and one silver dragon with no yellow on his breast. They become emotional as they explain how frightened they were as they fled for their lives.

"This sounds like the work of the two blue dragons that deserted my army and their silver friend. These dragons will soon realize that when they moved into our kingdom, they assumed responsibility for their actions, and they can't just do as they please. This is not the wilderness they are used to. When I'm done, not one of them will ever dream of disobeying my commands or harming any of my subjects again." His eyes are piercing as he looks at the lead guard.

"Go quickly to Slash and tell him to give you his best fighting group. Take shackles to subdue the prisoners. Leave tonight and bring back the deserters and the two leaders." The guard bows, turns and sprints out of the court.

When Byron sees the blue dragon's cavern, he motions for the troll on his back to raise the white flag, which means prepare to land. In minutes they are creeping into the entrance and the trolls set arrows. The dragons pull spears from the sheaths. They search the cavern and find no one.

Byron grits his teeth, "Load up, soldiers. We aren't going to find them here. They know they are in trouble, but they have only made things worse for themselves. Raise the green flag and let's move out."

Fearing Guargin's anger keeps the soldiers quiet until they return to his court. Byron does his best, but Guargin is furious. He leans within inches of his nose and screams.

"Get out of here and drag Gus and Nom back!"

As the guards escort Gus and Nom to King Guargin, the glare on his face eats at them. They tremble as they bow as low as possible.

"A humble bow is a waste of my time. Stand and talk. You and your den are about to become a pile of blue hides and broken bones rotting in the sun. Tell me where your den is hiding. If I like what you tell me, I may only beat you."

Gus stands first and looks into Guargin's eyes. "Nom and I are loyal to you and this court. We have no ties to the other blue dragons. We only wish to fight with you against the scoundrels. We are as loyal to you and your army as any other dragon or troll under the command of Slash." He bows and waits.

King Guargin shakes his head slowly in thought, then grunts and looks at the court. Several of them nod in approval of the blue dragon's words.

One dragon stands. "I sense honesty in these two."

Guargin turns back, his face is wrinkled as he studies the two dragons, who are standing humbly with their claws folded and resting under their chin. He slowly takes a deep breath and smiles slyly.

"I, too, detect sincerity in what you have said. If I find out you have tricked me, you will die a very painful death."

Gus and Nom raise their eyes and relax slightly.

"Guards, take these soldiers back to Slash and tell him to keep an eye on them."

<>

Lee and Kim, like the other young dragons can hardly wait to visit places near the old cavern where they played while growing up. They dream of happier times as they wade in streams they once splashed in, and taste the fruit from the nearby trees. Memories made at a time of carefree playing fills a place in their souls that the new cavern could never fill. Familiar places, smells, and sounds deep in the cavern spur their youthful, happy energy. They begin to spend more time socializing with each other. They are so glad to be back in their old cavern that they are working harder than ever, and they don't even notice it. They want things to return to the old normal.

Fuzzy and Lester's pride grows as they watch the future of their den blossoming. They are wise enough to know that their time and energy is shorter than it once was. They are still the leaders, but Lee and Kim's opinions are respected by their peers, and often they are asked to speak for the younger dragons.

<>

Deep in the wilderness, far from Dragonthal, tucked away in his hideout, Bird is happily living a life of exile with his lily bulbs. Lear and Leon enjoy Bird's company and they are safe and have plenty to eat, but there is nothing there that can fill the hole in their souls that begs to be satisfied.

One evening while sitting with Bird, Lear stares silently into their fire.

"What is on your mind?" questions Bird.

Lear sighs and stands. He paces in thought.

"I appreciate you helping us escape, and I will always be your friend," he says.

"But this is not the life I want to live. My heart feels the call of my den, and I must obey."

Bird fixes his eyes on the flames as they dance, but he doesn't appear to see it.

"Do you feel this way?" he asks Leon.

Leon waits a second and sighs. "I feel the same way. But I hate to leave you out here alone. Come with us."

Bird shakes his head, "No." A tear on his face glistens in the firelight.

The next morning Lear and Leon begin their journey home. They fly for a while and see what looks like other dragons on the horizon. When they realize the dragons are approaching, they gasp.

"Can you tell what color those dragons are?" calls Lear, his heart racing.

"They look silver to me. We better drop quickly and hide. This could be Guargin's guards looking for us."

They land in a meadow and scramble into the thick of the surrounding forest. Briars, covered in rows of thorns sharp as flint knives dig into their scaly bodies as they claw into a thicket. They lay motionless and quiet. Drops of blood ooze from their wounds. They hold their breath. The sound of flapping dragon wings breaks the silence as a battle group lands in the meadow. Lear sees them through a slit in the vegetation. He closes his eyes as fear sweeps through his body. Ten silver dragons and trolls scatter across the meadow, poking and pulling at the fringe of the underbrush.

"All right, move into the thicker brush and flush them out," yells the leader.

One of the silvers heads straight for Lear and Leon. They hold their breath. The silver dragon clenches his teeth and looks at his legs. He moves again and grimaces as he tries to push his way into the thorny thicket.

"There are too many briars out here. They didn't come this way," he blurts.

"I don't care how many briars are out there, just find them," yells the leader.

The soldier shakes his head in disgust. He slowly takes a couple steps, and the sound of rasping can be heard by those close to him.

He wipes a tear and takes a deep breath. Seeing that the battle group leader isn't looking, he moves over a little where there are fewer briars to push through. He passes a few feet from the hidden dragons.

The group searches until sunset. The group battle leader is furious.

"Somehow you fools let them escape into the wilderness! I will have a talk with Slash tonight. I hope he beats every one of you."

They fly away as the forest turns black.

Lear whispers to Leon. "We need to go."

Leon touches his wing and points to their left. "The guard showed us where there are fewer briars."

Lear smiles for the first time. They quietly make their way to the clearing and fly away. They decide to fly all night and hide while they sleep during the day. It takes longer, but two weeks later they land at their old cavern in the dark of night. They find a resting place above the entrance and wait until daylight.

As the sun rises, they see Lee leaving the cavern. They hop down to the ledge in front of the entrance and bow.

They land so close to Lee that he stumbles back. "What are you doing here?" he asks.

Lear's eyes squint. "We are alone and we made sure no one followed us. Are you not glad to see us?"

Lee tries to calm himself. "I am glad you are back, but I need to talk to the den. It would be best for you to hide in the cavern next to the cremation pit until I talk to them. No matter how sure you are that you have not been followed, the den will worry that Guargin's army is behind you."

Lear and Leon leave with aching hearts.
Shortly after dark the next day Lee sails from the ledge and glides toward the small cavern. With only the light of the evening moon he lands. He pauses quietly for a moment and then pokes his head into the cavern entrance.

"Lear, Leon," he calls.

Hearing movement, he waits outside.

Lear comes out followed by Leon. They are quiet and look unhappy.

"Hello, Lee. We thought living with Bird hidden in the wilderness was lonely, but this is unbearable," says Lear.

"I know, but this situation is even harder on your fathers. They fear for your lives and miss you beyond words. The den has agreed to let them visit you at this time every evening and bring you fish. Try to be strong and hide a little longer. I will come and get you the moment the den feels it is safe for you to return."

<>

King Guargin calls for Slash to come to his court. Moments later, Slash stands proudly as Guargin makes his way to his throne. He bows humbly as Guargin sits. Slash stands confidently after Guargin bumps the floor two times. Guargin looks him in the eye.

"Are you prepared to wipe out the scoundrels, leaving no young ones to grow up and rise again?"

Slash smiles. "I have assembled an army of dedicated soldiers longing for a fight. We can leave any time you wish."

"I wish for you to leave tomorrow morning."

Slash nods, smartly turns and leaves. Every ounce of his body energized and determined to win the conquest quickly.

Chapter 15

Above the Murray fortress, puffy white clouds float in a deep blue sky. Several months have passed since the brothers saw the scouting party in the wilderness. Everyone is busy enjoying a pleasant work day. With no signs of trouble for some time, the lookouts are relaxing as they watch children play in the courtyard.

One of the men in the fields looks up to wipe his sweaty brow and catches a glimpse of what looks like a flock of birds approaching from the north. He turns to others working beside him.

"Hey, look at all those birds," he says. Others are curious and stop to look.

Cap is not far from them and stops working to see what everyone is looking at.

The moment he looks up he screams.

"Ring the bells! Ring the bells!" he runs toward the entrance. He is two minutes from the gates. Running as fast as he can, he continues yelling. The bells begin ringing. Women in the courtyard grab children and lead them deep into the basement. Men in the basement drop their work tools and grab their bows. They dash into the courtyard. Some run up the tower steps and to the top of the wall while others continue toward the entrance gate and prepare to fight.

Guargin's army is only minutes away by the time Cap makes it through the main gate. Every ounce of his survival instinct begs him to slam the gate shut, but he trembles and holds it open for those who are still outside running toward him. Arrows sing *zip, zip, zip,* around him as they hit the fortress walls in waves. He catches a glimpse of an imminent impact, but before he can scream a warning, it pierces a man's leg. His teeth clench as the arrow point disappears in flesh. The man screams and tumbles. Another man grabs him and pulls the wounded man along. They fall to the ground just inside the gate, and Cap slams it shut. He slides the lock into place as archers beside him drop their bows and grab logs lying next to the gate. The logs have been waiting for the day when they would be used as reinforcement locks across the gates. Two men open tiny doors in the gate that cover slots where they can shoot out. The men set arrows and wait.

Jackson runs up the tower steps and dives into the seat of his crossbow. He loads, cocks, and aims an arrow at the group of dragons heading straight for them. Ed Junior is seated in the other crossbow and is ready. Arrows zip through the air and *ping* when they hit rock walls. They sound like hammers striking stone. Others plunk into the dirt floor of the courtyard and look as if they are standing at attention. Soon the yard is peppered with arrows, with their colorful feathers waving.

Everyone who is not shooting, hides under roofs, behind walls, or anywhere that is out of the volley of arrows. Two archers scream and cry out in pain. Their eyes stream tears and their hands tremble, but they pick their bows back up and refuse to leave their posts. Wracked with pain, they fumble as they set arrows and wait for a target. The two towers with no crossbow are each manned by two archers. They pop up and down, shooting at the diving dragons. If any of the dragons get too close, they quickly dive through the trap door in the floor.

The crossbow hidden in the wall is manned and waits to surprise any dragon or troll that lands in the courtyard. Ed Junior lets a crossbow arrow fly. It zips into the thick of the attacking army and slices a dragon's legs in half. The creature screams and flips upside down dropping its troll rider. The troll tries to land on his feet, but bounces to a stop and never stands. The dragon slams to the ground head first. Its body explodes blasting chunks of meat and limbs into the air. The arrow continues, and curving slightly it sinks into the chest of a dragon in the distance. The beast screams and gushes fire over nearby dragons. The hot red cloud of flame flashes back across his troll rider. The dead dragon and blinded troll hit the ground with a *splat*.

Jackson aims his crossbow to the left, pulls the trigger and the arrow becomes a blur, singing only a second before it rips into the boney edge of a dragon's wing. The wing buckles and the dragon's body swerves ramming into the dragon behind. The trolls are flung into the air. Their legs flail, making them look like they are running. They scream until impact. The dragon with the broken wing slams to the ground and crawls a few feet before flames gush from its mouth.

Ed Junior has taken down two more dragons. He turns in surprise when dragons land in the court yard. One of the troll riders shoots an arrow at him. He dodges at the last second. When he looks again, the archers atop the wall release a hail of arrows, killing the trolls.

The hidden courtyard crossbowman pops open the door in front of his slot. He releases an arrow that slices through a dragon so close he can almost touch it. He slams the door shut seconds before fire bursts from the dead dragon's mouth. As soon as the fire subsides, the man pops the door open again and launches an arrow toward another dragon. He slams the door shut and waits to hear its blast of flames. When he opens the door again, the last dragon in the courtyard is lying on the ground with dozens of arrows in its sides. The crossbowman shuts the door, peers through his peephole and waits.

Jackson continues to shoot as he watches arrows fly from the slots in the exterior walls. They zip through the air from all directions. By the time he realizes there are more dragons and trolls in the courtyard, they are already dead. Two men fighting beside Jackson scream and fall to the floor. Women reach through the trapdoor to pull them through. They hurry down the stairs and move quickly to the basement. In seconds, two more men pop through the door and begin shooting.

Jackson glances for the first time at the ground outside the fortress walls. Dozens of dragons lie in the fields. Scattered among their corpses lie dead trolls twisted and flung in every position imaginable. Their hair waves in the wind, but nothing else moves. Arrows are peppered all around.

Suddenly a dragon drops from above, landing hard by Jackson's side. It lets out a mighty roar that rattles the fortress walls. The creature is too close, and he dives through the trapdoor. An archer follows him. Another Archer runs across the top of the wall and jumps into the courtyard. The dragon releases a relentless flow of flames across the weapon. His troll rider slips off the dragon's back and shoots at an archer on a nearby wall. His arrow slices into the archer's arm and he falls to his knees. This draws attention to the troll and four arrows pop into its chest instantly. The harry thing wilts to the floor. Then the archers take aim at the dragon. *Thunk, thunk, thunk,* arrows sink into its back and the flames stop. It leans toward the courtyard and tumbles over the wall.

Jackson peeks through the door. He almost cries when he sees the crossbow smoking. He raises the door, and flinches as an arrow lunges into it, inches from his hand. Another troll riding on top of a dragon is diving toward him. The troll is traveling so fast that Jackson's only chance is to duck back through the door. Before he can slam it shut, the troll crashes into him and is knocked to one side. It tumbles to the bottom of the stairs. Jackson grabs his knife and dives down the steps. The troll tries to stand. Its eyes fill with fear as he grabs for his blade. Jackson, with uncontrollable instinct and strength, thrusts his knife at the troll tearing into its chest. The troll's blade clangs to the floor, and his dead weight pulls Jackson over before he can yank his knife loose.

Even though he has killed many trolls that day his heart is sickened. Touching the man-like creature and seeing the look in its eyes tears at his soul. He leans against the wall and tries to regain his strength to kill again.

Suddenly his remorse disappears when the troll's dragon shrieks above him. It is almost at the door, and the sound rattles down the hallway. Jackson grabs a long blade and runs up the steps, but when he opens the trap door, he sees the dragon staggering. One of Ed's crossbow arrows is half-way through its neck. The sound of strangling and sight of spastic convulsions as blood pours into the dragon's lungs throws Jackson back into sorrow. He can't take his eyes off the creature as it melts over the wall, dropping to the courtyard floor. Seconds later its death-flames explode.

The rising cloud of white-hot flames is close and Jackson quickly covers his eyes, then grabs a bucket of water and dashes it over the crossbow. Out of the corner of his eye he sees a dragon rising beside the outside wall. It is too close for him to escape. He dives into the steaming crossbow seat, and it scorches his legs. He fumbles but manages to set an arrow just in time to shoot the creature as it tops the wall. The troll on its back hops off as the dragon falls back over the wall. It is only a few feet away and releases an arrow that tears across Jackson's shoulder. Jackson grabs the painful wound as an archer beside him pushes him out of the way. The archer shoots the troll, but the arrow only grazes it. The troll screams as it lunges its blade toward Jackson. Jackson kicks him in the face, but the troll spins around and attacks again. A second archer shoots without aiming sending an arrow into the troll's forehead. It drops like a rock.

Cap is peeking through the trap door and sees the encounter. He climbs out when he realizes Jackson is wounded.

"Get to the clinic! I'll take over this crossbow."

With blood dripping from his shoulder, Jackson limps to the trap door and descends to the hallway. The troll he stabbed is lying on the floor in a pool of blood. The short, hairy rough-skinned creature's eyes seem to follow Jackson as he walks by. A chill sweeps across his body and he shivers.

Cap is flooded with adrenaline as he looks for a good shot while fearfully watching out for himself and the archers next to him. Even though he has been busy helping archers in the hallways below, he has kept a close eye on Jackson and Ed. They have killed dozens of dragons and trolls. He grits his teeth knowing that the crossbows are the main targets for their enemy.

Cap glances at Ed and screams. "Behind you!"

Ed careens through the trap door, tumbling down the steps. Cap cringes as the dragon grabs an archer standing beside the crossbow. The archer releases his arrow as the dragon's teeth dig into his body. The archer's head drops and his bow tumbles to the floor, but his arrow is slicing through the creature's throat. It drops the bleeding man and staggers back, gasping. Blood squirts everywhere as the dying dragon stumbles haphazardly and collapses. The dragon's head is pointed toward the crossbow when it collapses, and its death flames scorch the weapon.

Ed and an archer peep through the door amidst the flames and see a troll running down the wall toward other men. They flip the door open and have no choice but to stand in the dying flames. Ignoring the pain, they shoot arrows into the troll's back and it collapses before it reaches the unsuspecting men.

With nothing more than a quick glimpse of a dragon, Cap spins around and aims toward a tower that has no crossbow but is manned by four archers. They gasp as they see Cap appear to aim at them. They hit the floor trembling and watch the large arrow pass over their roof. A dragon standing on their tower's roof is split in half. Its troll rider hops over the edge landing on the floor next to the archers. One of them pushes him off the outside wall before he can gain his footing. The archers cringe when blood from the mutilated dragon lying on their roof drips like rain around them, splattering on the floor.

The battle has been furious and many dragons are dead. The bodies of trolls are scattered everywhere. The dragon major raises the orange flag. The assault ends and the wounded army disappears into the woods.

<>

Byron, the dragon major, lands in a nearby meadow and waits for Slash to appear. Slash lands near him with an evil squint on his face. He paces back and forth and looks at Byron.

"I can't say you're not doing your job. This is unbelievable!" He paces more and looks at wounded dragons and trolls lying around, they are out of breath, and many are dripping blood.

"How did these scoundrels know to be ready for us?"

Byron's face is wrinkled as he bows and remains quiet.

"You can raise your head and not fear me. I see what you are up against. We will see if these scoundrels are ready for a different kind of battle. They can't see as well as we can in the dark. Gather the group leaders. We will attack again late at night."

Byron relaxes and calls his group leaders.

<>

The archers are so nervous that they are reluctant to leave their posts. Slowly, one at a time, they leave to help with the wounded. The guards on top of the towers are antsy. They feel the burden of warning everyone if another attack comes, and they don't dare move from the alarm bells.

The courtyard is noisy as men and women begin the gruesome task of gathering arrows. At first, dozens of volunteers pull arrows from the dead, but wading in puddles of blood and the smell becomes too much for most of them. Only the strongest volunteers can pull hard enough to tear arrows free of some of the corpses.

Soon only a handful of them remain. They dump the arrows on the floor near the basement entrance. Women and older children put them in baskets and carry them to Ed and his sons where they are cleaned or repaired. Then they are taken to the archers who are refilling their quivers for the next encounter.

Once the arrows are retrieved, men use horses and ropes to drag the dragon corpses outside the fortress gate. They don't drag them far because the enemy could charge again.

In the kitchen, Mary is hard at work boiling beans and baking bread. Everyone is starving after the battle. Sandra and Janice work tirelessly beside her as candles flicker from their holders attached to the grey rock walls. The smell of the food gives the fortress families a feeling of security that they all need badly. Mary rings the bell and only a few at a time come to eat.

Near the kitchen, Inez and Flavie boil water and wrap wounds. It is a hard day in the little clinic. The odor of blood and burned flesh blend with the smell of medicines creating a morbid atmosphere. Many of the older men help, but when patients have arrows sunk deep into their bodies, they have to move out of the way. Strong, younger men are needed to hold the wounded down while the women cut the arrows out. Tears are in everyone's eyes as a line of wounded and bleeding fighters parade through the little room. Screaming is not limited to the clinic. Many of the badly wounded are taken to a room further down the hall, but the heart-wrenching screams still grind at everyone's nerves.

The basement is a-buzz for hours after the battle stops. Aloe, oil, boiled cloth and splints are continuously carried into the clinic. The caregiver's job doesn't end when the sun goes down. The wounded men cry out in the night as their pain increases. Everyone will be called on to take turns comforting them. The wicked hours of early morning take the lives of those who surrender to their wounds. Those who live through the night will continue to suffer for days, taking precious time from the caregivers who are already deprived of sleep.

<>

At midnight, Byron nods to the battle group leader who has planned the surprise attack.

"It's time to avenge our dead brothers. Have no mercy, and good luck."

The dragons and trolls bump their spears on the ground in unison. Two at a time, they lift and circle higher and higher before sailing quietly toward the fortress.

Candles glow in each tower and occasionally one is visible on the walls. The group leader smiles and silently thanks the scoundrels for lighting the target.

The air is cool, and the lookouts are tired from the first battle. Many of them are relaxing. Homer sits close to Jackson who occasionally rubs his head while sitting in his crossbow seat. Jackson takes notice when Homer's ears perk up and he turns his head toward the woods. Jackson reaches for a candle. He hears a strange muffled sound in the courtyard. The dogs all scramble and howl. Jackson lights a pile of rosin-soaked straw next to him. Instantly, arrows fill the air zipping by him. The straw is blazing and he pushes it over the wall where it falls into a larger pile in the courtyard. A hail of arrows forces him to duck behind the crossbow.

With the light from the burning straw, the other crossbow spins around and sinks an arrow into an approaching dragon's chest.

One of the archers beside him furiously clangs his bell and the slots in the courtyard walls come alive. Arrows zing into the air, and several trolls fall to the ground. The door covering the slot in front of the hidden crossbow opens and its arrow flies through the flickering firelight and plunges into an unsuspecting dragon. Blood squirts from between its eyes before it explodes, throwing flesh and fire across the courtyard. A split second later, another dragon crashes to the ground and releases its death flames. The stench of burning flesh fills the courtyard as fire consumes trolls and dragons.

Burning straw lights up the courtyard. The remaining attackers are in plain sight. The hidden crossbow is cocked and the crossbowman opens the door in front of him. He jerks in surprise to see a dragon among the flames looking directly into the slot. He instantly pulls the trigger and the arrow rips through the dragon's body before it or the troll rider can react. As the dying dragon wilts to the courtyard floor, Jackson jumps up in his seat and aims down as far he can. A dragon is hiding in the shadows next to the wall below. He slowly squeezes the trigger. The arrow scrapes the top of the wall, ripping its feathers off, but it continues and zips through a troll on its way to the dragon's back, where it sinks deeply.

The last dragon, dodging flames and running in panic, flaps its wings furiously attempting to flee. Ed tracks him with lead and gently squeezes his trigger. In midair the arrow disappears into its left side and hardly slows as it rips out the other side. The dragon explodes falling into the courtyard in chunks. Three trolls dash toward the basement door only to be met with a shower of arrows from the slots in the door. With no movement for a few minutes, the men turn their attention to calming their dogs.

The fires slowly languish and, in a while, only the candles on the towers are burning.

Not one dragon or troll returns to Byron. He waits and watches until the sun begins to rise.

<>

At first light, Slash lands in the meadow where he and Byron met the day before. Byron looks at the ground and swallows hard as he comes forward. Slash cocks his head and glues his eyes on him and the soldiers watch

"I can tell by your demeanor that last night was a disaster."

Byron trembles. "I watched at a distance. Our soldiers fought courageously and the battle raged. Fires lit the sky and when it was over, not one soldier returned." Slash looks into the eyes of the soldiers standing around. He sees that they don't blame the major and turns back to him.

"I will deal with you later. You have managed to lose a third of Guargin's army. I am giving you your last chance. I want the scoundrel's town south of here destroyed before the sun sets. They will not have a defense like the fortress."

Byron raises his eyes and looks at Slash for the first time. Slash focuses on his pupils, looking deep inside the dragon. "Try to kill some scoundrels this time, or I assure you that you won't see the sun set."

"I will lead the troops and kill the first scoundrel myself." He turns with renewed resolve and looks over the troops. With a commanding voice that demands respect he quiets them all. "We are heading for the villages! You are to show no mercy as we attack. If I see any of you hesitate to follow this command, I will make sure you are bound and incinerated in front of this army."

Everyone flinches and stands straight; not one dares move.

When Byron has walked away, Gus looks at Nom.

"Finally, our battle group will be called on to fight. Tomorrow will be our day. The major will call on everyone to attack this time. He has to make a good showing or he is a dead dragon," says Nom.

Gus wrinkles his lips. "He better. We have endured a lot of training and come a long way not to have a little satisfaction,"

<>

The fortress slowly comes to life as the sun rises. Few men have slept, and several wounded heroes suffer no more. Cap sadly looks toward the heavens as if he can see their souls ascending and says goodbye to them. He realizes how beautiful the day is high above all their problems, but the smell of death drifts by. He takes a deep breath and looks into the courtyard.

The sight is more dreadful than he expected. Many of the enemy soldiers are burned badly and others are lying in puddles of blood. Flies and bugs prey on them as he watches. He turns and walks to one of the bells. He taps it gently two times. Few people dare venture into the courtyard, but he addresses the ones who climb to the top of the wall.

"We need volunteers to relieve the crossbowmen so they can take a break. Everyone else round up your friends and come to the basement for a meeting."

He quietly descends to the basement and waits for everyone to gather. Tired, wounded, young, and restless men and women look at him with eager eyes.

"I am proud to be with a group of men and women who are strong and willing to fight without regard for their own safety. We will win this war in time; we have determination! As long as we all work hard, and are kind to each other, we will fight as one. We will cry when one of us is hurt and we will rejoice when good things happen. We are one big family now."

An old man, who helps in the clinic and is known for his compassion, stands. "We need to anoint you as our leader; will you carry the burden for us?"

Cap is speechless and tears moisten his eyes. "I am no different than any of you. I am honored, but have no desire to be anointed."

Mary stands with a determined look on her face. "You have no choice; you are the kindest man here and that is what we want."

Miles stands. "Son, what we and this man want is for you to let the rest of us shoot the arrows and fight while you look out for everyone. You must have the authority to keep peace among us and to move anyone of us where we will be of the most value in this war. Your job will be to have the last word. We are all soldiers now and you need to take command."

Other men and women stand in approval. Cap wipes his eyes and stands tall. "I will do my best." The group cheers. Cap raises his hand.

"We must clear the courtyard and bury our dead. We can only do that by opening the gate. All who agree raise your hand." Several of the dead men's families sob. All hands slowly rise.

Uncle Matt speaks. "I volunteer to help dig." Several other men raise their hands to join him.

Cap nods." As you work, we will watch and be ready for an attack. Our enemy could be waiting for us to drop our guard."

Soon, the first heroes of the fortress lay in peace near the fortress walls, and a stone lies atop their graves. Cap taps the tower bell again.

"We need volunteers to drag the corpses of our enemy out of the courtyard and as far away as we can. I know this will be dangerous, but it has to be done soon."

A handful of men shout their intent to take on the duty. They bring horses and start dragging dragon and troll bodies to the woods. By mid-evening the courtyard is clear, but time is all that can wipe away the smell of death.

<>

In the dark of night, while the residents of Blade Town sleep, Guargin's army assembles in the woods near the village. Slash calls for Byron before daybreak.

"I fully expect this army to kill these scoundrels and burn their wood shelters to the ground with few Dragonthal casualties." He looks directly into the major's eyes. "You are to lead this attack if I remember your statement yesterday."

Byron snaps straight and nods quickly. "Yes. I will prove myself today. We will win this battle."

He orders every battle group to take to the air and follow him.

Gus and Nom feel jolts of adrenaline as they taste the essence of long-awaited vengeance. The sight of silver dragons flying into formation sends a surge of energy through them and they fly to their positions.

The entire army quickly wings along close to the treetops. At mid-morning they pop out over the rooftops of Blade Town. At first the people are so surprised that no one runs. But then the trolls unleash a hail of arrows, killing men, women, and children in the streets. Their horses run loose or lie squirming in agony. Screams, crying, and panic erupt and chaos sweeps from one end of the village to the other. People run for the cover of the buildings. Only a few people have their bows with them, and almost no weapons are to be found in the buildings. In moments, the people who ran into the hardware store are shooting through the windows. Several trolls fall to the ground, and the sound of wounded dragons shrieking echoes in the streets.

Byron leads a line of dragons and commands them to target the hardware store and spew fire as they pass. When their gas bladders are empty, he motions for another group of dragons to drop their trolls and follow him. The second line of dragons finishes covering the store with flames and they head for other buildings. Gus and Nom are soon out of fire, but they chase the men and women who are fleeing. The stench of burning flesh rises to the sky mixing with soot and floating embers as the hardware store crackles in flame.

A woman, out of her mind with grief from the loss of her child, crashes through the hardware store door. Flames leap out the door behind her as she attacks a troll standing with an arrow aimed at her. She has a pitchfork in her hands and her back is blazing. She doesn't flinch as his arrow slices her shoulder. Another troll aims at her and shoots an arrow into her thigh. She leaps onto the astonished troll while thrusting her pitchfork through its neck. They both crash to the ground in flames.

Screams from inside the hardware store fade, and the only remaining sound is crashing, popping, and crackling from burning timbers. The rest of the village is on fire, and people are scattering. They run with all their might for the cover of the forest.

Gus and Nom grab several people before they can disappear in the brush. Once the rest of the buildings are smoldering heaps, the dragons sail over the trees while trolls run into the woods in search of scoundrels. Screams echo from the forest for hours, but many trolls pull back limbs and brush to be met with blades, rocks and arrows. After several hours, patches of the forest are blazing.

Only the men and women who ran deep into the wilderness survive, but they have no food and no hope of returning to their village.

Byron raises the white flag. It flaps in the wind as he circles among the soldiers and the troops assemble in the streets. Slash is standing in the street smiling and bows to the major.

"You did as you promised, but you also lost several troops. I expect you to improve as this campaign continues."

Byron bows humbly.

Slash turns to the troops. "I am proud of you. Return to the lake and enjoy your victory. Come back here before dark. If you see scoundrels as you travel, kill them. We will spend the night here in the streets where no scoundrel will ever walk again."

The troops chant, Yaheee, Yaheee, Yaheee! and take to the air.

<>

In the wilderness north of Blade Town, small groups of frightened and hungry survivors find each other. Several are wounded and groan as they struggle through the underbrush searching for the trail that will lead them north. They have heard of a fortress there and have no other hope. They stumble upon a wagon with a frightened family hiding close to the trail. The family is scared out of their wits until they hear about the fortress and gladly help the wounded on board. The group walks briskly with the wagon and horses behind them. Before sunrise they arrive at the fortress gate where they are welcomed to enter.

A larger number of survivors come together south of Blade Town and they manage to find several horses. In the dark of night, they reach the trail and head toward Water Town. On their way, they discover families camped along the trail who are planning to go to Blade Town at first light. They refuse to believe the story they are being told until they see burned and wounded men. Some of the poor souls still have arrows sticking out of their sides.

Filled with fear and compassion, the families share water and room for riders in their wagons, and then quietly travel south in the dark. When the refugees reach Sandra's village, they find that most of the families have left. The few that remain are warned of the coming army. They ring their bells, light torches, load what they can, and disappear into the woods.

The refugees hear roosters crowing as they ride into Water Town. They are cold and hungry. The first houses they pass are dark, and they continue until they see a man coming out of his house. He turns to look at them and several horsemen call out.

"Help us wake the town and warn everyone! An army of dragons and trolls have killed everyone in Blade Town. The village is in ashes, and they may be right behind us."

The man freezes and his mouth drops open. He is in disbelief until one of the women hops from a wagon and runs to him. "Please could we have some water?"

We have been hiding in the woods all night, and we have not had anything to eat or drink since yesterday morning."

He runs to his porch, grabs a mallet and strikes his bell over and over. A neighbor next door peeks out his window and sees the commotion. He dresses quickly and runs over.

The first person he meets looks at him with weary eyes. "Ring your bell and don't stop until you wake everyone. An army of dragons and trolls has burned Blade Town to the ground and killed everyone."

The neighbor stumbles backward in disbelief as famished people beg for water and food. A frantic woman approaches driving a wagon. When he sees her husband lying behind her on the wagon floor with arrows in his back, he screams for his wife to come help them. He takes one of the refugee's horses and gallops to the center of town. He hops off and quickly rings the bell there wildly, and people run out to see what is happening.

"What is wrong with you?" asks the first man there.

"The dragon war Mason has been telling us about is real! Blade Town has been burned to the ground!"

Several people look at each other in disbelief, but when they hear more and more bells ringing in the distance. They dash back to their houses. Groups of people begin to panic and run in the streets.

Mason is outside nostalgically looking at the cages that once were part of his traveling show. Longing to return to his former life of excitement and silver, he has been awake for some time. He freezes when he hears the first bell ring. He walks over to get a better look and more bells begin to ring. Wagons and dozens of men on horses are trotting toward the barn. The men on horses have bows and quivers within easy reach. Those in the wagons have desperation on their faces and many look around anxiously.

Jim and several men in the barn pop out and gaze at the town which is coming coming alive. "I don't see any fire, what is happening?" asks Jim.

Mason turns to them. "Listen up. I think the war is starting. Grab your bows and stand behind me. If I'm right, we will have to fight these people to keep our barn."

Jim and the men quickly return and stand between Mason and the barn door.

Mason speaks with his traveling show voice.

"Calm down everyone. You in the red shirt, tell me what's going on."

"I ran for my life as dragons and ugly fat men riding on their backs unleashed a storm of arrows and flames all around. Men and women were screaming and several arrows zipped past my head," says the man nervously pointing north. "I am one of the few that made it to the woods before a line of dragons sailing close to the ground incinerated everyone behind me. The heat and fear were unbearable. I ran for hours through the brush. In the dark I began walking toward Water Town. I would not be here yet if my fellow survivors hadn't pulled me aboard their wagon. Blade Town is in ashes, and a dragon and what some are calling trolls are to blame. They are probably on their way here right now!"

Mason turns to Jim. He slowly shakes his head, "There are too many people in the barn already. We have no room." Mason turns back to the noisy crowd. "Go to the hardware store and get what you can. Head back into the woods. These buildings in town will soon be burnt to the ground. Go as far as you can and hide.

Stay silent and don't build any fires. Hopefully you can return when the battle ends. Good luck."

The people gather and talk among themselves. Mason walks through the barn door and locks it. He trembles in sadness. When he looks outside again, the group is gone.

He turns and sees the crossbows he built for the Murray's fortress. Jim is close and stops beside him.

"Jim, I hate to see these weapons setting in here taking up space, but if we roll them out where they can be used, the bowmen will surely die."

Jim thinks. "Push them outside and place them close to the small door. We can open the small door and offer a brave soul a chance to earn the right to shelter with us if they are willing to man a crossbow. Hopefully they will kill several dragons before they have to run. We will do our best to cover them and get them in the door. It's a gamble, but some will make it inside," says Jim.

An hour passes and six young men approach the barn. One of them yells to the archers standing in their slots. "Good luck to all of you! I wish I had a barn like this to hide in."

Jim opens the door. "Are you willing to fight for the right?"

The men stop. "Tell us what we would have to do," replies another man.

Jim hastily shares the proposition and shows them how to use the crossbows. The men calmly look at each other and nod in earnest.

"We will prove our worth," says the talkative one.

Jim grows fond of them instantly. "I will do everything I can to get all of you inside."

Several more men have walked up and are standing around listening.

"We will stand with these men and protect them with our bows for a chance to come inside too," says one.

Jim looks at Mason. "We will make room," he says. "Good luck men." says Jim. He turns and goes into the barn leaving the door open.

Inside, Jim surveys the four crossbows to be sure they are ready. They are hidden in small rooms made of thick rock walls. The two on the upper level protrude into the yard and have a slot on each side for an archer to defend them. The two in the basement only stick out slightly, but they all have thick timber roofs that can be slid back to shoot skyward.

Jim then addresses the archers and their families. "I wish you luck. We have no idea when or if the battle will come, so stay close to your position."

<>

Slash scans the troops as he approaches Byron, who is quietly following Slash with his eyes.

"It is a beautiful day for a battle, don't you think?" ask Slash.

Byron smiles. "It is, and we learned a lot yesterday."

"Lead our troops to victory and I will congratulate you as the next village burns."

Slash raises an eyebrow and ponders as he watches buzzards hoping around pulling flesh from corpses in what was once a busy street.

"War is not a pretty sight, and when we return to Dragonthal, you will experience more horror that this war has created, even in victory. You will see it in the eyes and hear it in the shrieks of grief from the families of our fallen soldiers. They will study our demeanor and listen to every story that is told. We will be judged by them when we return. I expect you to think about that and keep our losses to a minimum."

Byron swallows hard and snaps to attention. He sets the green flag ordering the army to move out. The troops lift into the air and line up in battle groups ready to head south.

When they arrive at Sandra's village, they find no scoundrels. Slash kindles the first flames, and soon fires rage burning houses to the ground and sending swirls of ash and flames high into the sky. The troops circle the rising smoke columns watching for a scoundrel to make a move in the woods, but the men are hidden far away in the wilderness.

Slash sails over to Byron. "By hiding, they have chosen to die slowly. Have your soldiers kill all the livestock. Nothing the scoundrels can use will be left alive. Burn the sheds and tear down the fences."

When the troops head toward the animals, Gus disappears. Nom searches and finds him in the forest. He looks guilty as Nom approaches.

"What's wrong?"

"I have never killed innocent creatures, and I can't watch our army mindlessly killing everything in sight." he shakes his head looking at the ground. "If Slash and the major wouldn't punish you, I would fly away," says Gus.

"Sounds like you need time to become accustomed to what we must do. Don't give up. I will fight hard enough for both of us today."

At midday, the army heads for Water Town, and in no time, its roofs stand out as the endless canopy gives way to civilization.

Byron drops low, and dragons begin burning buildings. The trolls set arrows, but few scoundrels show themselves.

Byron raises the white flag and they retreat to a field of grass and boulders where he can look over his troops.

"This village has been warned. The scoundrels are hiding. I am sure many of them are deep in the wilderness by now. There are too many empty buildings for us to waste our flames on. When we find a building full of scoundrels, we will incinerate it. I want the trolls to search the buildings."

He raises the green flag and the dragons head for the center of town. The trolls slide off the dragons and creep around town searching for signs of life, but none are found. The dragons wait and follow the trolls. They all are puzzled by the empty buildings and drop their guard.

Suddenly they are pelted by arrows, bringing trolls to the ground and dragons shriek as arrows slice through their scales.

When they discover which house the arrows are coming from, dozens of trolls charge the structure. Byron cringes as scoundrel's arrows mow the trolls down at first. He sweats as he weighs his options. Dragons can expel a limited amount of flames. The possibility of targets ahead, that only dragon flames can bring down, causes him to restrain the dragons.

One scoundrel after another falls to the floor, and in time, the trolls move inside. They begin dragging wounded scoundrels out into the street and quiet returns. More carefully the trolls move from building to building knowing an ambush could be waiting.

They find a large group of scoundrels hiding behind logs and fortified doors. They fight fiercely. Too many trolls die trying to overwhelm them. Byron signals the dragons to take to the air. The trolls back away, and the scoundrels cheer until dragons surround the structure and unleash a fiery attack. The men wound several dragons until the heat overwhelms them, and they run out only to be shot by trolls or grappled by dragons.

Mason covers his ears, as do most of the people in the barn. Mothers hold their hands over their children's ears and refuse to let them peek out.

Tears stream from Mason's eyes. "As soon as this cruel army is close enough, shoot every last one of them," he says.

The north side of the barn sets arrows and every slot is manned, but they can only watch for what seems like an eternity. They can't possibly hit any of the enemy until they move closer. Mason's fighters tremble in anger as they wait.

Several dragons sail toward the barn. One of the crossbowmen who can wait no longer shoots his arrow. Every eye on the north side of the barn watches as it sails toward the unsuspecting creature. Half of the barn roars in excitement as the dragon is impaled and spins to the ground while flinging the troll rider to his death.

Gus and Nom's battle group leader looks at the barn and motions for them to follow him there. He is at top speed and diving toward the barn when a crossbow arrow slices his head open and his body explodes. Pieces of dragon splatter to the ground.

Nom screams, "Follow me, these scoundrels must die!"

He sails over the barn to the south side and leads the battle group down. The south side has been waiting for a chance to fight, and these are the first enemy they have seen. All arrows are waiting for the battle group as they attack. A wall of arrows flies bringing down three dragons and half a dozen trolls. Nom jerks as arrows slice into his chest and sides. He hits the ground hard. Blood oozes from his wounds and out of his mouth. Gus is untouched, but drops like a rock to his side.

"Nom!" he screams.

Nom turns his glassy eyes toward him. "Good bye, old friend. Why couldn't we have been born a hundred years sooner and lived like happy dragons at our old den?" He chokes and begins sucking air.

Gus jerks away and hops into the air flapping with all his might to escape Nom's final burst of flames. Tears drip from his eyes as he ascends. He cringes every time an arrow zips by. In a daze, he meanders aimlessly among the other attackers. His entire battle group is dead, and his will to fight is gone.

Byron raises the orange flag and the remaining battle groups retreat to conjure a plan.

"We have to burn this structure to the ground. I want twenty dragons on each side of the building to attack at the same time. Unleash all the fire in your bellies and then get out of there. We will stand back and watch flames end this."

He raises his green flag and four battle groups sail toward the barn. The young men manning the crossbows in the yard duck as arrows zip all around them. They and the archers standing beside them bring down several dragons. But soon there are too many dragons and trolls to handle. The archers and crossbowman dash for the open door. Flames gush toward them as arrows sail through the bright orange and yellow fire. Several of the men in the back scream and hit the floor rolling as defenders cover them with blankets. The door slams shut and arrows pepper it. All but four of them make it inside.

The crossbows and archers in the barn continue their barrage, and half of the dragons lay dead in the yard before the rest of the attacking dragons unleash their flames. The sod roof blazes with furry as the wind whips the fire across the roof, but when the fire wanes the dragons notice a layer of dirt and logs remain. The barn still has enough cover to protect the men inside the upper level, and the crossbows in the small rooms are untouched.

Byron is furious and sends another wave with orders to land on the log roof and tear holes in it. The crossbows and bowmen unleash another hail of arrows, bringing down more dragons and trolls. But several dragons succeed in tearing holes in the roof, where they take turns spewing flames inside the upper level. Many defenders are killed, but some dash to the stairwells and descend to the basement. Mason wisely built the stairwells out of stone, and they extend all the way from the basement floor to ceiling of the upper floor.

Byron and his troops comfort their wounded and wait while the barn smolders.

When the ruins cool, a battle group returns to be sure there are no survivors. All is quiet and Byron sends more battle groups to look around and celebrate their victory.

Mason and most of his defenders are waiting in the untouched basement and stairwells. Word is whispered down the stairwells and Mason is told that enemy soldiers are on the floor above. He peeks through a basement slot and sees more soldiers milling around the basement door.

"Shoot!" he yells.

The crossbowmen open the cover over their weapons and kill several more dragons in seconds. The bowmen in the basement unleash a hail of arrows from their slots, and the men hiding in the stairwells jump to their slots with arrows pulled back. The trolls and dragons on the floor above are caught in crossfire, and their blood drenches the floor. Panicked, the remaining army races to the empty streets of Water Town.

Slash is seething as he approaches Byron.

"What have you let happen to our army?!"

Byron trembles as he stands beside his drooping orange flag.

Mason pulls the top over his crossbow back as far as he can and peers at the soldiers gathered on the main road. He settles back, takes a deep breath, and aims at the dragon with the flag by his side. It's a long shot, and his heart beats wildly at the thought of picking him off. He takes his time and squeezes the trigger. The arrow sails away, growing smaller as it travels far from the barn. The dragon's head drops to the street. The men cheer and set arrows. They are sure the soldiers that are left will return wanting revenge.

Slash gasps, and takes several steps backward, turns and runs while furiously flapping his wings. The soldiers look at each other in shock, then take to the air and follow.

Gus flies with them. His heart is filled with grief, his body aches, and his mind is torn by thoughts of anger while his soul demands that he kills no more.

<>

Fuzzy's den is once again living in harmony with nature in their ancestral cavern where things feel right. There is a congenital peace among the den members. Fuzzy strolls to the entrance to soak in the sun. He closes his eyes, takes a deep breath, and relaxes. He and Lester are the only ones at the den. It is a beautiful day for gathering fruit and nuts, and the younger den members are in the forest working together.

Lester meanders to Fuzzy's side and looks to the southern horizon. He stands still and Fuzzy opens one eye to see what has caught his attention.

"Something is headed this way," says Lester. They watch for a while and when it is obvious that they are silver dragons, and the smiles on their faces fade. Fuzzy drops his head and sighs.

"This is a group of the king's soldiers. I see trolls on some of their backs."

Lester rubs his chin. "I hope they are not hunting our cavern. I fear Gus and Nom have told them about this place."

"I'm concerned that they attacked the fortress and are headed back to Dragonthal," says Fuzzy. He continues to watch for a moment. "I hope none of our den is in the air where they will be seen. I hate to think what would happen if they follow them here."

The group fades out of sight. The two friends are relieved, but neither smiles again.

"Tee and I need to visit the Murray brothers to see if they're all right," says Fuzzy.

Lester looks at Fuzzy with wrinkles on his forehead. "Things seem so normal now that we are back here. Sometimes I forget that our world is still in turmoil."

In the morning, Fuzzy and Tee sail from the ledge and head toward the Murray farm. While they are still far away, they see the fortress and look at each other in amazement.

"Their shelter is almost all rock. Cap and Jackson have built an aboveground cavern," gasps Fuzzy.

"Things look different now. We need to be very careful. The manmade cavern looks large enough to hold many men. Only Cap, Jackson and a few men know that we are friendly. If Guargin's army attacked them, we will just look like more dragons."

Bells begin ringing frantically at the fortress. The sound causes Fuzzy's heart to speed up. Men dash from the towers and take their places on the walls. The scene sends chills down Fuzzy's back.

"I hope our friends are still alive. Follow me." He turns toward an open place in the field that surrounds the fortress, and lands far from its walls. He bows and waits. Tee isn't sure, but does the same.

The men anxiously await with crossbows cocked.

"Something strange is going on," yells one of the men from the tower.

Cap leans against the wall looking at the two dragons. He rubs his forehead.

"This could be a trick. Keep an eye on the other direction." He studies the situation. These dragons are not silver, they look darker and they appear to be bowing.

"Get me a horse. I'm riding out to see what this means."

Moments later, he takes a deep breath as the gate shuts behind him. A rush of energy mingles with fear chilling his blood. The horse walks slowly as Cap strains to see. He dares to smile as the darker color turns blue and then the red head is obvious.

"Fuzzy!" he yells and bumps the horse to a trot. The men in the fortress hold their breath and are more confused when they see Cap bow.

"My old friend, I am glad to see you! You must forgive our caution. We have just endured an attack by silver and yellow dragons. Many men died, and everyone is antsy. I will ride back and talk to all our residents to ensure your safety." He turns and trots back toward the gate.

The fortress doors open and Cap enters the courtyard. He is smiling as he speaks loudly.

"Ring the bell one time and call everyone to the courtyard except for lookouts in the towers. These dragons are our friends."

A bell rings loudly one time. The men and women file out of the basement and gather. Cap remains on his horse so everyone can see and hear.

"Two dragons stand in the clearing near the woods. They are our friends. They are not to be hurt. These are the dragons that Jackson and I have told many tales about. They warned my family of the war we are now fighting, and that is why we built this fortress. The friendship shared by my family and this den of dragons is why we are still alive. Unload the crossbows and put the arrows back in their quivers. Keep an eye out for the silver dragons, but respect our friends. Please bow when they enter, and they will return your courtesy. We need to know why they have come".

Cap rides out to Fuzzy and Tee and they walk back slowly. Everyone watches in amazement as Fuzzy comes closer, his beauty and demeanor cast the spell he is famous for. At first only a few men can understand what he is telling the brothers, but soon most everyone feels his trustworthiness, and understands his thoughts. A deeper respect for the Murray brothers sweeps through the members of the fortress, and they realize that some dragons are not thoughtless killers.

As Cap dismounts, Jackson steps beside him and bows to Fuzzy and Tee. They move to the center of the courtyard. Cap quiets everyone.

"These are our friends Fuzzy and Tee. You will never meet more honorable creatures. Open your minds and listen with your heart. If you trust them and are not afraid, you will hear their words and understand what they say."

Some people raise their eyebrows in doubt.

Fuzzy looks around at the anxious group. He can feel their allegiance and respect for the brothers. He speaks to Cap and Jackson.

"We are honored to be allowed to enter your fortress; I feel safe here. Our den has settled back into our old cavern. I planned to pay you a visit once our den was settled in, but when I saw King Guargin's army coming from this direction, I feared for your lives. I am pleased to see you survived their attack.

"We are close to you again because Guargin is a tyrant. When he realized we were in a cavern near his kingdom, he demanded things from us that we cannot give him. Infuriated by our response he seized five of our young dragons and forced them to join his army. Some of them escaped and in their attempt to flee, several trolls and a dragon were killed. Now he hates us. We had to flee in the night and our old cavern is the only place we have to hide."

Cap looks at Jackson and they smile. "We are pleased that your den is close again. I hope Guargin's army is through with us."

Fuzzy frowns. "The war has only begun. I am sure that when the survivors of this battle tell him of defeat, he will explode in anger. Dragonthal is very large and Guargin is very vane. The next battle will be ferocious. He will send an even bigger army next time. When he returns, he will probably attack us too. We will help you if we can."

"And we will help your den," replies Cap.

Fuzzy bows. "Our friendship still lives, friend. May you and everyone here be safe, but I must warn you that two of our young dragons have chosen to be loyal to Guargin's army."

Cap's face drops. "You are in danger. Those dragons know where your old cavern is. You are welcome to join us here. We can build you a place to stay."

"I will think about your offer. Be safe."

Fuzzy and Tee walk out the gate. They unfurl their wings, flap them briskly and lift into the sky. The children of the fortress watch in amazement. They can't take their eyes off the dragons until they are out of sight.

Chapter 16

The next morning, Jackson gathers a group of men to see if anything is left of Blade Town. As they approach, a stench lays heavy across the land, and there is no breeze. Birds squawk angrily in the woods, and the sun is hot. The men are quiet and their horses move cautiously. Sadness grows as they anticipate what lies ahead. The trail enters the clearing that surrounds what were once the buildings of Blade Town. The sight of ashes heaped in piles with chimneys towering above them like skeletons shock them, and they stare. With long faces, the men tremble.

Jackson stops and his heart turns cold as he laments. "After what we endured, we knew what the dragon and troll army was capable of doing, but seeing it..." He breaks into tears and weeps.

He rubs his sleeve across his face, takes a deep breath and motions for everyone to move on. "We must prepare for what we are going to witness up ahead."

He flips the reins and moves slowly as a field of devastation unfolds. They pull bandanas over their mouths and move on. The streets are speckled with bodies. Some look peaceful, but others are warped and twisted in horrible positions, dead before they were flung to the ground.

None of the men can handle the emotional jolt, and slowly they move away, trying to calm the panic raging inside. Several are overwhelmed by the stench lingering inside their nostrils. They heave until their stomachs erupt spewing their contents.

"Pull back and regroup in the woods where we can't see or smell this," says Jackson as he bumps his horse and quickly trots away.

In the woods, he dismounts and ties his horse. One by one, the others come to his side. Everyone is in a daze. Some wet their bandanas and wash their faces; trying to cool off. Others reach for their water pouches and take small sips. It takes time for them to regain their composure.

"These people didn't have a chance," says the first man to speak.

"So many bodies need to be buried, but who knows how many dragons could be in the woods watching," replies another.

"We have no choice but to leave the bodies of these poor souls to the mercy of the wilderness creatures. There are too many of them, and we must hurry to Water Town. We are too vulnerable out here like this," states Jackson.

Movement in the woods nearby causes everyone to scramble.

"Grab your bows!" yells someone. The men fumble to set arrows.

"Don't shoot!" A man's voice cries from the woods. Limbs push out of the woods and he steps out wearing tattered clothes. "Please put down your bows and help us," he says as he helps others step into the daylight.

Jackson counts the survivors. "Are you all that are left of Blade Town? There are so few of you."

The man nods. "Some of the others rode into the brush and disappeared into the wilderness. I hope they survived. We are starving. We searched around the ruins and found very little."

Jackson takes jerky and bread out of his pack and hands it to hungry children. The other members of the search party open their saddlebags and share too. Jackson watches as the survivors share among themselves, and he knows he must escort them to the fortress.

"We have two wagons and some of you can ride double. Load up and we will take you where you will be safe."

As they load the wagons, a whimper comes from the woods on the other side of the street. Jackson walks toward the sound and steps into the woods. There he catches a glimpse of a little girl still hiding behind tree limbs. She is wearing a torn and dirty dress that once was pretty. She has dirt and ashes smeared across her face and tears have made streaks though them down to her chin. When he reaches out for her, he sees her father. The unconscious man is lying in a pile of leaves.

"Come pick this man up and put him and the girl in one of the wagons," says Jackson.

The little group begins their journey to the fortress. Tired and hungry, they sway back and forth as they bounce up the trail. When they first see the fortress, the survivors are speechless. Some smile for the first time since the attack.

When the gate opens, Cap runs out.

"How bad is it?"

Jackson swallows hard remembering the sight. "Nothing is left, only ashes and bodies strewn everywhere."

Cap gasps and steps back. "Our village is gone," he looks at the weary survivors. "At least we can help these people, and we will need their help when Guargin's army returns."

Jackson slides off his horse. "I am worried about Water Town after what we saw. I intend to leave early in the morning."

As the sun rises, Jackson and his search party wave to the tower guards.

"Good luck, brothers!" yells one of the tower guards. Jackson feels a surge of camaraderie and bond for the family of defenders that will anxiously wait for their return. The gate opens and their fearful journey begins.

As they get closer to Blade Town a heavy fog lies low to the ground in the forest, and they grow quiet. A feeling of wandering spirits and dampness hangs over the streets. They quietly trudge along. When Sandra's village comes into view, they don't stop.

Late in the evening, Water Town comes into view and many of the buildings are burned to the ground, but some buildings remain. There are fewer bodies lying in the streets. A horse whinnies, and the men can hear voices.

"Someone has survived," says Jackson and he bumps his horse and trots ahead.

There, in one of the streets sets several wagons. Men are loading bodies into them. Mason recognizes Jackson.

"Jackson! You survived!" he yells, running toward the men. Jackson barely has time to dismount before Mason grabs him. "You don't know how glad I am to see you are still alive. Were you attacked like this?"

Jackson steps back and looks around. "Yes, we were ambushed, but managed to man the crossbows before they hit us too hard. Our people fought courageously. Sadly, we lost some men, and many more are recovering, but we killed wagonloads of trolls and dragons. It was a fierce battle and we are lucky.

"The most amazing thing was when they attacked us again later that night. Our dogs warned us the moment they landed in our courtyard. Our archers slaughtered them all." Jackson's eyes tear up. "Blade Town no longer exists."

Mason drops his head. "I know, I'm glad I haven't seen it. Several of their people fled here during the night. I took in what I could, and they helped us fight. I had no choice but to send others into the woods to hide."

Jackson looks toward Mason's barn. He turns and gazes at the damage. "From the looks of your barn, I am surprised you survived."

"I have never been more frightened in my life," replies Mason.

"Did you lose many men?"

Mason sits. "We lost twenty-seven of our brave fighting family. Some were men, some women, and several children. It was horrible. But worse than that, we could only watch as dragons and trolls killed hundreds of people hiding in town. Watching that filled us with rage and when they came close enough for us to kill them, we did so with a vengeance.

"Then they swarmed over us. We wiped out many as they circled my barn. We hit them hard until their entire army turned their attention to us. They tore the roof off and burned everything on the top level, but with a foot of dirt covering its log floor, the flames didn't reach us in the basement. To the enemy it looked like our barn was burned to the ground.

"They dropped their guard and came close to gloat over their kill. We opened fire and wiped many of them out. They retreated to where they thought they would be safe, but I picked one of them off with a lucky shot. They took off and haven't been back. Now we can rebuild and start again." Mason smiles for the first time.

Jackson wrinkles his lips and slowly shakes his head. "This war has just begun. They will be back with even more soldiers."

Mason pauses. "Then our town will rebuild with stone and thick log roofs covered with earth. We will be prepared next time. I will start building crossbows tomorrow and give them to anyone in town that will help us fight," says Mason.

Jackson and his men bed down for the night next to Mason's barn. As the fire dances, Mason brings out pouches of apple wine, and hands cups to Jackson and his men.

"I wish we could fight side by side," Mason says, He reaches for Jackson's hand. They shake long and hard before filling their cups. Mason raises his.

"Good luck to you and everyone in your fortress. It will be too dangerous for us to travel and check on each other from now on. I hope peace will return one day." Jackson raises his cup and touches Mason's, and then they drink.

When the sun rises, Jackson and his men leave in a trot, longing for the safety of their fortress.

<>

Guargin is soaking in his bath, which is fed by a warm spring. Guards are near and servants tend to his whims. Everyone knows when he spends too much time relaxing in the warm waters, he is troubled. He climbs out and attendants dry him gently.

A guard appears in the chamber entrance and taps his spear on the floor.

"Please excuse my intrusion, but I thought you should know that several dragons are approaching from the southern horizon. Guargin moves quickly, and the attendants drape robes across his shoulders and fastens his loin cloth. He reaches for his scepter and heads to the field in front of the cavern. Guards rush to position themselves around him as he marches out to where Slash will land.

"This must be a group of wounded soldiers returning," he mutters as he looks into the sky. The guards cut their eyes toward each other.

As the soldiers land his face reddens, and the guards slowly back away. Slash marches toward Guargin.

"Forgive me, my king. This is all that remains of our army." He trembles as he speaks. Guargin clinches his scepter and slams it to the rock path. It clangs loudly. Slash tries to stand still, but Guargin's face wrinkles and his eyes glare red. Several guards set arrows, and Slash sinks to his knees. Guargin raises his hand.

"Don't shoot this dragoll. Escort him to the waiting area at my court." He motions for guards to take Slash away.

Guargin looks at the wounded and tired soldiers. "Eleven dragons and four trolls," he says shaking his head. He grunts and starts to leave but turns to face them. "Drangonthal is indebted to you, and you will be rewarded." He turns to the guards. "See that these soldiers feast tonight." He marches toward his court as guards scramble to keep up with him.

Slash sits hunched over and quiet as he waits outside the king's court. The heavy wooden doors swing open. Two trolls with arrows wait in the door to escort him in. The guards in the waiting area step up behind him and slowly approach the throne. The dragons stare at Slash with sullen faces. The trolls point and whisper to each other. The gong echoes, Slash flinches.

"King Guargin has arrived," announces the shirtless troll. The dragon and troll guards come to the throne and stand one on each side. Guargin walks to his throne looking at no one. He bumps the floor two times with his scepter and everyone bows. Slash bows deepest. Guargin stands with an arrogant posture.

"Members of this court, this is Slash our army commander. He has returned with only eleven dragons and four trolls. He left with a hundred of the finest dragons and a hundred of most dedicated trolls we have ever assembled. We will listen to his story and then we will discuss how we are going to punish him for this disgrace."

Slash trembles as his blood turns cold. His heart beats rapidly pumping it through his veins. He forces himself to muster his strength and he slowly stands proud. He knows he has only one chance to turn the opinion of the court in his favor. He breathes deeply and looks confidently into the eyes of Guargin and begins his story.

"I don't know how, but many of the scoundrels knew war was coming. The ones who knew built fortresses out of stone that can't be burned. The walls have slots on both sides that rain arrows high into the air, but that is nothing compared to the weapon setting on top of the towers. It kills with ease. It is unlike anything I have ever seen."

The court jeers in disbelief. Guargin bumps the floor; hushing them.

"Tell me about this weapon," he growls.

Slash begins to move about in front of the court. He gestures to emphasize the magnitude of the foe his army encountered. "The weapon fires arrows that weigh half as much as a troll. They zip through the sky so fast they cannot be dodged, and they can almost reach the clouds. Any dragon or troll that was hit by one of these arrows died instantly."

The court is quiet and he doesn't want to lose their attention so he tells about the village that fell easily. "We regained our confidence after the village fell and headed to the larger village that appeared to be the center of their civilization. We were very successful there until we came upon a large structure. The scoundrels there were savage in battle. We sacrificed many of our troops trying to burn it to the ground, but even after it was lying in ashes, it somehow came back to life." Slash bows and waits.

Guargin turns to face the court.

They debate for some time and Guargin's eyes cut back and forth, watching them. Slash breathes easier and a look of confidence grows on his face.

"We have weakened them, they lost many scoundrels," says one of the dragons.

A troll stands. "I think we should attack them with twice the soldiers."

Slash smiles for the first time, "I agree, but I want two hundred soldiers for the fortress and two hundred for the large village."

Guargin looks at Slash. "You want four hundred dragons and four hundred trolls?"

"These scoundrels are smart. They have learned from our attack. We must hit them hard before they build more weapons."

Guargin looks at his court waiting for their opinion. They all agree and bow in consent. Guargin looks at Slash with piercing eyes.

"I will give you your wish, but I will kill you myself if you come back with anything less than complete victory."

Slash swallows hard and bows.

<>

Jackson and the men of the search party bond like brothers in determination to protect each other. They scan the forest in fear after witnessing the horror scattered along the trail. A strangely warm feeling radiates across their skin raising the hairs on their arms as the silhouette of their fortress looms on the horizon. They look at each other and break into a gallop. The bells atop the towers ring lightly and the fortress residents rush to the top of the wall and cheer. Their families are waiting and emotions overflow. Cap lets them savor the love and security they all need so badly. He finds Jackson and wraps him with a bear hug.

After hugging his brother, Cap strolls to one of the towers and climbs the stairs. The sound of happy people in the courtyard is a welcome change, and he looks down and smiles. When the crowd's passion subsides, he rings the bell one time.

"Jackson, bring your brave men up here and tell us what you found."

Jackson speaks.

"I do not have great news. We did find some survivors, but death is scattered along the trail from here to Water Town. Our friend Mason has survived. His fortress barn is badly burnt, but he is full of fighting spirit and determined to build it back. The remaining people of Water Town thirst for revenge. Mason told us he is going to help them prepare for the next battle."

The man beside Jackson interrupts. "Water Town is in shambles. Mason won't be building us anymore crossbows."

Cap steps forward and calls to Ed. "How soon can you and your men build us a crossbow like Mason's?"

Ed smiles and yells back. "We won't have to put wheels on ours, so two weeks should be enough time to build one. Then we will start on another." The crowd cheers.

"We don't know how long we have until the next attack or how bad it will be so, everyone must start making arrows," says Cap

Another of Jackson's men steps forward and can hardly contain himself as his words paint a vivid picture of death and destruction. Many people have long faces and they are quiet.

Miles is moved to rekindle hope and steps up beside Cap. "My heart is broken to hear of the needless suffering and death outside our walls. I am proud of all of you and I feel a kinship building among us. With that kinship growing, I am more confident than ever that we can win this war. Let us resolve to work hard so we will have a future to give to our children. Many of you are still young, and you will live long lives, free of worry about dragons. Now is the time to fight for that dream."

Cap and Jackson look at each other and smile.

Cap taps the bell lightly. "Tomorrow morning, we need volunteers to take wagons and search through the ashes of Blade Town. You will be looking for iron, copper, and anything else the fortress can use. Come see me if you are willing to go. It will be heart wrenching and dangerous."

<>

Mason repairs the burnt crossbows while Jim starts building four new ones. He has found four families that live close to each other that will build small shelters and man the crossbows. With luck, they can draw the dragons and trolls into crossfire and protect each other. These shelters will allow the crossbow to shoot through slots around the wall, but if the need arises, they can shoot at high-flying dragons by opening a log-covered door in the roof.

Families that don't have crossbows are building mini-fortresses where several families can share in the work and in its defense. They will only have bows, spears, and knives to defend themselves. Women and children practice shooting when they can, but most of their time is spent gathering rocks, digging holes and helping build the shelter. Logs will be laid across their roofs with dirt covering them, so they won't burn easily. Many shelters are dug around wells, so the people inside will have water.

Some families flee, hoping to find a village far away or hide in the wilderness until the war is over.

<>

Lear and Leon are afraid to leave their small cavern during the day and are stuck in the never-ending chill of underground living. They relish the short period of time at midday when they can bake in the sun's rays that bathe the entrance floor.

Lying on grass mats at midday, they are drifting peacefully in blissful dreams soaking in the warmth when something touches their tails. They jump to their feet, swinging with claws extended and hearts pumping.

Lee jumps back and winces. Lester and Tee are behind him.

Lear's face is wrinkled and his lips are tight. "What is wrong with you? You scared the life out of us!" he growls.

"Calm down. I am here with news. Guargin's army is in a costly war with mankind. The den has decided that they will be too busy to bother us, so you can return." Lear's face brightens as he looks at Leon whose face is filling with a smile. Lee moves away and the fathers open their wings to hug their sons.

The group returns to the cavern. Lear and Leon beam as they land at the cavern that is their home. The den is waiting near the ledge. Lester walks to Sada's side and places his wing around her as she sheds happy tears. Fuzzy hugs one then the other, steps back and speaks to them.

"I am thankful for this day. Our den is a little more complete now that you are back where you belong."

Lear and Leon nod respectfully. Then Lear moves around the entrance speaking to everyone. He stops in front of his parents.

"I am ready to go to our special place and prepare a fresh grassy bed, if I am welcome."

"I have already done that. I hoped you would stay with us," says Sada.

Hearing them, Leon turns to his parents, Tee and Bee. They sigh and their faces glow as they nod for him to come with them. They walk side by side and disappear into the dark of the cavern.

In the distance, Vada, a pretty female, feels drawn to learn more about Leon. That night, she visits Leon's special place. Their attraction is magical.

The den is ready to grow and everyone has mates except Lear. Seeing Leon's happiness with Vada makes his heart ache for a loving companion. His instinct tortures him to find a mate, but there are none his age.

His only relief from frustration comes when all alone he sails from the ledge into the dark of night. The air blowing in his face and the freedom of weightlessness cleanses his spirit, and he is at peace.

One evening as he is flying over the wilderness south of the den, he sees a flame spew below. He is intrigued and slips through the canopy to get a closer look. The forest is dark and he stands still, listening for predators. He hears a sorrowful moan that sounds like a dragon. Pulling limbs out of the way, he spies a dragon propped against a tree lying on brush and weeds crushed to the ground, like a mat. He pauses.

"Please help me," the weak voice pleads. It is a sweet gentle voice that tempts Lear to take a chance. He moves closer and discovers it is an injured female.

"Water. I need water..." she whispers. His compassion overcomes his fear, and he rushes to her side. "Please bring me water," she pleads.

He knows where there is a nearby stream, so he scrambles into the air and sails to it. His only choice is to transport the water with his mouth. Returning, he moves close to her and spews it into her mouth. Desperate, she closes her eyes and sucks it down.

"Thank you, kind dragon." She closes her eyes and lays still for several minutes. "I was wounded in battle and unable to keep up with the fleeing army. They left me here to die."

Lear looks into her face, "are you one of Guargin's soldiers?"

She looks away, "My den didn't have any males old enough to serve in his army, so they took me. I'm sorry if that doesn't please you, kind dragon."

Lear's heart melts and his eyes soften. "What is your name?" he asks.

She softly replies, "Cloey."

Lear smiles, "I promise to return in a few minutes. Please believe me. I will get you out of here. He struggles to tear through the canopy and flies to the cavern. He dashes to his special place and convinces his mother and father to come back with him.

They sail in the dark back to the wounded soldier. They examine her wounds and Sada feels a bond growing for the gentle dragon.

She looks at Lear. "She should recover. I will stay with her."

"I will stay too, until she is strong enough to come to our cavern," replies Lear.

The silver dragon smiles for the first time.

Lester leaves to catch fish so she can begin gaining her strength. Several days later, though weak and thin, Cloey lands at the blue dragon's cavern. Sada and Lear help her to their special place.

<>

King Guargin relentlessly pushes Slash for two months. "We must hit the scoundrels again before they recover and build more weapons." His story is the same every day.

"I agree, but our solders need to be trained if they are going to survive."

"You have enough to sacrifice a few. Time is what we can't afford to give the enemy."

Slash stands his ground, but two weeks later Guargin stomps into his quarters.

"I expect this army to be in the air in two days."

Slash starts to object, but Guargin slams his scepter on the floor, abruptly stopping him. Slash bows.

"We will leave tomorrow. Half of the soldiers will go to the village and half will attack the fortress. That way, neither of our foes will be warned this time."

Guargin smiles. "Good luck, I expect you to return soon with total victory."

With tight lips, Slash bows and says nothing.

They fly south. On the evening of the fourth day, they see a blue dragon in flight and follow him.

<>

Tee swallows hard when he notices a mass of dragons turning in his direction. Soon he can vaguely see trolls on their backs and he knows he has little time to warn the den.

"Ureeeeee!" he screams before he lands.

Lester dashes to the entrance.

"Guargin's army is behind me and it is massive. Leon, Lear and Cloey must hide immediately." Gasps Tee.

Other den members run to the entrance to see why they were summoned. Leon, Lear and Cloey run frantically toward a passage high in the ceiling. A huge rock sits just inside the opening and when they roll into place, the passage is undetectable.

Just as they roll the rock in place and it seals with a thud, Slash lands and Lester meets him and bows politely. Slash looks at him and cocks his head slightly, creasing his lips.

"Why do you go to the trouble to bow? I know you are full of contempt."

"All we want is to live in peace and be free like our ancestors. We hoped that with the king's army at war with civilization we could return and be left alone," says Lester.

"You won't have to worry about hunters anymore, but we can never leave you completely alone, blue dragon. Two of your young dragons deserted our army, and they are accused of killing four trolls and a dragon. They will have to suffer the consequences. Where are they?"

"I have not seen them, but you are welcome to look around."

"My army and I will take shelter in here tonight, as we hunt for them." Slash motions for his solders to come in. "If I discover you are hiding them, you will receive the same punishment they are going to suffer."

Lester bows. Fuzzy and Lester carefully squeeze past Guargin's soldiers who are entering the cavern. They stand side-by-side on the ledge and look out on the landscape. Silver dragons and trolls are everywhere. Some of the trolls are gathering wood.

Two battle groups search the cavern for the fugitives. When they return empty- handed, Slash motions for Lester to come to him.

"If we weren't on a mission of greater importance, I would use methods at my disposal that would make you beg to show me where your hidden dragons are. You have some time to think about it. We will leave in the morning, but you will see me again soon."

Lester and Fuzzy just bow.

The fugitives sit quietly. Lear wraps a wing around Cloey. Leon smiles and misses Vada.

As the sun rises, Slash wakes everyone. The place is crawling with dragons and trolls tromping about. As the soldiers prepare to leave, Slash is at the base of the plateau, wandering about and studying the ruins left by the hunting party.

Fuzzy and Lester's hearts ache as they watch scores and scores of dragons with troll riders fill the sky. Fuzzy and Lester look at each other.

"I'm afraid Cap and Jackson don't have a chance this time," says Lester.

Fuzzy sighs and slowly walks back into the cavern. The den is quiet, and no one is in the mood to go about their daily activities.

Worried for the safety of the fugitives, they decide to leave them hidden for a while.

That night, Fuzzy approaches Lester. "I hope the brothers cripple Slash's army badly enough that they leave us alone on their return to Dragonthal. If they don't, Slash will probably stop and torture or kill as many of us as it takes to make us give him Lear and Leon."

Lester waits to reply. His brow is wrinkled as he speaks. "If the fortress survives, an even larger attack could come. Our only hope for a future is to join the brothers and help them end the Dragonthal tyranny."

Chapter 17

Slash savors the moment as he glides over the canopy leading his soldiers. Filled with confidence, but wishing he could have trained them longer, he feels the thrill of eminent battle and it gives him a rush of energy. His mind is free of worry as he opens his mouth to fill his lungs with fresh wilderness air. A meadow comes into view and he motions for the army to land. He calls Major Fidel, second in command to his side.

"Take half of these soldiers and finish off the large village. Be careful around the barn-fortress. I will wipe out the scoundrels at the rock fortress and wait for you. Together we will celebrate our victories."

Fidel bows. He energetically motions for his battle leader to raise the green flag, and they move out with all his soldiers chanting "Yaheee, yaheee, yaheee!"

Slash waits until they are out of sight, then turns to his group.

"I have seen these scoundrels fight. We must be cunning and surprise them. They are well-prepared to fight once they are in their positions. Our first priority will be to kill the scoundrels on the towers. We must not let them ring their bells or man the crossbows."

He marvels as he looks at his troops. They all stand quietly and obediently. Slash thinks to himself, "They did listen when I told them evil tales about these fierce scoundrels."

He feels renewed confidence, "From here we will fly just above the treetops. Watch for my signal to land. We will slip through the canopy to the forest floor. From there we will move quietly toward the fortress. If any of you makes a sound, I will kill you. We must circle the enemy and remain hidden. When it is dark, four groups of trolls and dragons will creep across the fields toward each tower. If we are successful, we will catch them by surprise and burn the crossbows before they know what is happening.

<>

Jackson is helping Ed lash down the last crossbow. Homer is anxious and keeps hopping up on the outside wall, looking toward the woods and whimpering. "Calm down boy," says Ed. "Jackson will be done in a little while."

Homer hops down and plops to the floor beside him. His ears twitch occasionally, and he is restless. He hops up on the wall again and barks.

Jackson stops and rubs his head. "Homer, we have got to finish this crossbow. No one knows when the enemy will return."

Cap walks by. "I feel better seeing that this last crossbow is almost ready."

"We would be finished if Homer would leave me alone."

Cap looks at Homer who hops up and puts his paws on the top of the wall and whines. Cap stares into the forest, then back at Homer.

"Grab this crossbow's quiver and stuff it full of arrows. I think Homer is trying to tell us something. All the crossbows need to be ready right now."

Jackson gazes toward the woods and shrugs slightly. "Maybe, we should be more careful the rest of the day" Jackson squats and rubs Homer, who loves it.

As the sun sets, Cap and Jackson stroll around the top of the wall with Homer by their side. One of the guards reaches out to pet him, and Homer acts uninterested.

"That's not like Homer," he says.

"Homer is anxious tonight," replies Jackson.

The man pulls a couple arrows and lays them close. "I want a dog up here next to me," he says. The other guards notice and soon several dogs are in the towers. They are restless too. The evening wears on with dogs whimpering.

Suddenly Homer starts barking and the rest of the dogs bark wildly. The men in the towers set arrows. They grow tense when they realize the dogs are all looking in different directions toward the wilderness.

The sun sets and with a moonless night, darkness is deep surrounding the fortress. Many men are relaxing when *slam*-- two dragons land hard next to Cap and Jackson. Homer tears into one of their legs stopping it from blowing fire long enough for arrows to fill its sides, but the other dragon aims for the crossbow. The crossbowman jumps from the seat and barely escapes its flames. Two archers to their left release arrows the instant the man is out of the way. With arrows in its neck, the dragon chokes on its flames and falls into the courtyard.

The trolls grab Cap. Jackson has his blade drawn and slices one of them across its neck. With eyes white it falls to the floor. Cap is straining with all his might to hold back the other troll's hand that is holding a blade inches from his neck. Jackson kicks it in the ear and with a grunt it flips to the side. Before the troll can stand, the archers fire arrows into its chest.

Chaos erupts in every tower. Cap throws water on the crossbow and jumps into its still very warm seat. The string is worthy and he quickly fires an arrow into the back of a dragon in the next tower. Its flames spew above the men.

Jackson manages to clang the bell as a troll's arrow sinks into his arm. Jackson grits his teeth in pain, but when he sees two more dragons are about to pounce on the floor next to him, he forgets it and screams. "Cap!"

Cap spins around with arrow ready. He releases it inches from the creature and the arrow disappears as it passes through its body, wounding the other dragon. Then he leaps on its troll rider.

Jackson tears the arrow out of his arm and screams as he stabs the other troll with it. The troll stumbles to the floor as Jackson hops into the crossbow seat and shoots the other dragon again. The men hurriedly push the dead dragons and trolls off the wall. Before Jackson returns to the crossbow seat, the dragons spew their death flames into the field outside the fortress.

Jackson spins around. Hay is burning in the courtyard. He can see well enough to shoot at the enemy on other towers. One tower is on fire and all the men are dead. Several crossbows turn their attention to that tower, and unleash a hail of arrows killing all the dragons and trolls.

Men charge up the steps to the tower with arrows flying around them. The light in the courtyard grows giving off plenty of light. Several more dragons with riders sail over the wall. Jackson, with blood dripping from his arm, follows one of them with his crossbow and squeezes the trigger. It jerks on impact and falls to the courtyard bursting into flames, giving more light. Arrows fly from slots in the courtyard walls. A dog hops up on the wall looking into the courtyard and goes into a barking frenzy. A dragon below aims a blast of fire at him, but he dashes out of the way. The flames wash over a dragon and troll trying to land in the courtyard. They are blinded. The troll screams and falls to the ground while the dragon's wings fall apart, and it slams into the courtyard skidding over trolls and crushing them.

Dragon flames and burning stacks of straw make the courtyard glow. With plenty of light and the dragons flying close, the crossbows bring them down. Soon so many dragons die outside the walls that the grass in the meadow around the fortress is blazing. There is enough light to see everything in the sky and on the ground.

The archer's arrows impale dragons and trolls in waves as they approach the fortress.

The courtyard quiets and the dragons stop coming. The eerie sound of moaning in the field and on the courtyard floor casts a somber mood. Many men head for the basement to escape the smell of burning flesh and blood-soaked soil.

Once they are below the walls, they realize there is no escape from the sickening smell of death. Everyone in the basement is in shock. The clinic is a frantic, sickening sight as men scream and women cry as men take their last breath. The dark of night drags on and on.

In the morning, Cap and Jackson are overwhelmed to see a mass of motionless dragons and trolls laying in the yard. Their bodies twisted and prickled with arrows. Flavie and Inez, seeking a break from heart wrenching surroundings, walk out next to Cap and Jackson. The sight makes them turn in disgust and return to the basement. Cap follows them as they head for the clinic.

In the hall, they pass a screaming man with burns so bad they are impossible to bandage. With the help of his family he is hobbling toward their living quarters. There, everyone will suffer and cry. They will try with all their might to save the life of the man they love. Cap's heart breaks and he convulses in grief trying to catch his breath. His tears flow, his head drops. Unable to see, he stops and rubs his eyes.

He regains control and breathes deeply for a moment. He walks through the door of the clinic and gasps. Blood is everywhere, and men moan as they suffer from burns. Some men have arrows sticking out of their bodies. Many more have long tears and gaping holes where arrows have been torn out. Others have been sliced by knives in hand-to-hand combat with trolls. The enemy's cruel flint blades slice thin lines, but they cut deeply. He passes into the room in the back of the clinic. As he enters, he sees several bodies covered with tarps. Cap raises one, then another. They look peaceful as if they are sleeping.

He is startled when a man screaming and fighting those who are trying to help him is rolled into the room and the door closes behind them. Those working on him are attempting to spare others in the clinic from his heart-wrenching bellows.

Flavie places her hand on Caps shoulder. "We just covered these men, but there are eighteen more we have already moved into the room next door. They are out of pain and in a better place."

Cap swallows hard. He knows if he looks at any of them, he will be haunted by memories of special things they had done. There wouldn't be one of them that he didn't dearly care for.

Cap climbs to the top of a tower and looks out over the fields where vultures are feasting. He rings the bell gently. Tired faces look at him.

"We need volunteers to pull carcasses out of the courtyard," he says weakly. Everyone else needs to stay close to your weapons in case there is another attack.

<>

Slash walks among the soldiers he has left. Their number is so small they can assemble in a little meadow. Most of them are in too much pain to care what he says. Many of the dragons moan and try to lie where the arrows sticking out of them won't touch anything. The trolls have pulled and carved out their arrows, but now they are aching from gaping wounds. Dried blood is caked over their bodies. Only a few have tied leather straps smeared with aloe over their wounds. Slash counts thirty dragons and thirteen trolls. His spirit surrenders and he rubs his forehead.

"Fellow soldiers, I have done my best. Please forgive me for the pain I know you are suffering. We can't wait for Fidel to return with his army. We must leave for Dragonthal so you can be cared for."

<>

As the fortress begins the dreadful task of dragging carcasses into the field, the battle in Water Town is starting. Fidel's troops are in the air as the sun rises. They arrive high above Water Town and dive quickly without warning. Cabins burn and trolls shoot everyone fleeing the flames. Few people with crude shelters built in their yards ever reach them. Slaughter is everywhere. The families that manage to take refuge in their shelters kill some dragons and trolls, but they are hopelessly out numbered.

When the houses and shelters are in flames, the army turns their efforts to the four small fortresses that have crossbows. The Dragonthal soldiers suffer many losses until they destroy one of the structures. With a burst of revelry, they swarm over the other three. The dragons tear them apart, as trolls fire endlessly at men, women and children trying to flee.

Mason and the defenders cover their ears and turn away. Not one of them can bear to witness the horrid sight in front of them. Anguish tears at their hearts, but their neighbors are too far away for their arrows to reach.

Late in the day the army attacks the barn. Mason and his defenders are filled with rage, and when they begin to kill dragons and trolls, they lose all human compassion. Their will and energy turns them into a super army. With their superior bows and magnificent crossbows, the dragons and trolls fall like flies around the barn.

Heavy losses and fatigue forces the enemy to end their attack. The army retreats and hides in the woods until morning. When the sun is high enough to warm the ground, they lay in meadows and the streets of Water Town soaking up the sun's energy for the fight. The green flag goes up, and they return to the barn to unleash a powerful assault, but they suffer heavy losses again. Fidel raises the orange flag, and those who are left retreat to the meadow. When they land and he walks among them, he is shocked. "We are too weak to attack the barn again. We will return to the fortress and rejoin Slash's army. Hopefully he has already won his battle." Fidel raises the green flag and they head for the fortress.

<>

Cap and the guards in the towers see a small group of dragons with troll riders approaching. Cap calls quickly to everyone.

"Don't ring the bells. Get out of sight. Make these soldiers think we are all dead. Send messengers to the basement and tell everyone to stay out of the courtyard and be still. When I give the word step in front of a slot in the wall and shoot all the trolls and dragons you can. Don't worry about the crossbows."

The first dragon lands on the wall and looks around. The others see nothing is happening and land around the wall. The first dragon hops into the courtyard and Cap yells for everyone to shoot. The archers release their arrows. The air fills with hideous projectiles streaking toward the enemy's hearts. Caught off guard, dragons topple into the courtyard and trolls slam to the ground. In moments they are lying lifeless in the yard.

Fidel is dead.

Cap dashes to the top of one of the towers and counts ten terrified souls fleeing for their lives.

Fuzzy and Lester watch from the cavern ledge as the retreating group comes out of the south, and passes; continuing their journey north. Fuzzy nods in thought.

"Too many of them have perished. There is a good chance that Cap and Jackson have survived."

<>

Wounded soldiers that returned with Slash spread stories about scoundrels with horrific weapons of war and a fortress as strong as a cavern, only above ground.

Slash is nowhere to be found and Guargin is furious. He paces around the grassy area in front of his cavern for days, refusing to accept that most of his army is not coming back.

A guard calls out, "Soldiers on the horizon."

Guargin rushes to a clear spot and gazes south. A pitiful sight comes into view, and his anger boils. There is no flag, no battle-leader, and no dragoll commander. He waits until they land and then forces his self to bow. Almost all of them are dreadfully wounded, but they respectfully bow.

Guargin's face grows long. "I am humbled by the sight of such pain and devotion. I am sorry for your pain. Go to your loved ones and let them treat your wounds."

He turns and gnashes his teeth. His face grows red as he stomps toward his court. As he enters the members cringe as they witnessing his seething fit. Guargin flings his scepter across the hall and screams, "Aahgeerraah!!"

Dragons and trolls alike tremble as he turns toward them with eyes glaring. "Find Commander Adrian! I want him in front of me right now. Guards scramble and return in minutes with a confident mannered dragoll behind them. He walks without fear and stops in front of Guargin, who is still red in the face. He bows humbly until Guargin speaks.

"Raise your head and listen." Adrian looks him in the eye. "Assemble every dragon and troll that can possibly fight. Take every able-bodied soul from every den. They are to serve in our army. Do it now. I want a massive army to inflict as much pain and agony as possible on these scoundrels, and then I want them all to die--ending civilization."

Adrian stands proudly. "I will do your will." Guargin looks him in the eyes, "I want this army ready in days."

With an air of confidence, Adrian looks Guargin in the eye. "It will take some time to assemble an army worthy to represent you, my King. I will search your kingdom and gather numbers so great that it will not matter what kind of weapons or fortresses these scoundrels have."

<>

Little blue dragons run back and forth on top of the plateau. It is a sunny day and most of the den are relaxing and soaking in the warmth. Fuzzy and Lester end up close together enjoying a time when the den is happy. They smile as they watch Liz and Sada trying to keep up with their grandchildren at play. After a while Fuzzy and Lester walk quietly back toward the cavern.

"It has been such a wonderful day. Little dragons are exploring and playing together, and an egg is lying in a nest inside the cavern, giving hope to all of us that a happy future lay ahead. This is the way things were in our younger days," says Lester. Fuzzy doesn't reply and Lester looks at him. "Why aren't you in a happier mood?"

"I am struggling with a thought."

They are close to the cavern entrance and Lester walks to the ledge. Fuzzy follows and they pause to look out over the countryside.

Fuzzy speaks softly. "The den is more content than they have been for some time. This cavern is where they belong. But after I watched the young ones playing today, and thought about the beautiful egg inside, a realization brought me to my knees in grief. Their future, that could be so wonderful here, is uncertain."

Lester looks over the countryside for a moment. "We must weigh our situation carefully. Civilization has been set back hundreds of years. Men and hunting parties will have no need to move into the wilderness until they have rebuilt what they have lost. We can live here in peace for a long time."

Fuzzy shakes his head and frowns. "I don't trust King Guargin. He will enjoy punishing us as soon as he is through with mankind. He may even decide to wipe us out too. Dragonthal must be set back the same way that civilization was. I trust Cap and Jackson's family. If we help them, they may defeat King Guargin."

Lester moans. "I will call the den together in the morning." He turns and slowly ambles toward his special place.

Fuzzy doesn't sleep that night. His wing is cupped around Liz when Lester calls. He is quiet as he walks to the entrance with Liz by his side.

With a straight face Lester speaks loudly and confidently.

"Beloved den our freedom and whether we can continue to enjoy this beautiful cavern will depend on the decision looming before us. If we get it right, some of us may die. If we get it wrong, we could become slaves or all die. King Guargin will never let us be as free as we once were. His soldiers may come at any time and take more of our family to replace Lear and Leon. They will come back and take whatever they want.

"I think we should visit our old friends Cap and Jackson and then decide whether they can defeat his kingdom if we help them. We must keep in mind that King Gargin will return with a massive army now that he has been humiliated. If we choose to join Cap and Jackson and they win this war, we will have no more problems with Dragonthal or civilization. If we join them and they lose, we will die by their side."

The den wilts in worry. Fuzzy moves to Lester's side.

"I, like all of you, am sickened that we have been in a world of turmoil for years. I long for happy times to return, but once again we must fight for our freedom."

Tee marches up and stands next to Fuzzy. "I am ready to fight with the men at the fortress. I saw mankind differently when Fuzzy and I were there." The young dragons gasp. Tee looks them in the eyes. "Will you go with me and allow yourself to feel their worthiness? Together we would be unstoppable."

Lee's face brightens. "I will meet with Cap and Jackson." Lear and Leon nod in agreement.

"We will leave for the fortress tomorrow," states Lester.

As the sun rises the next day, one by one the blue dragons assemble on the ledge. They quietly look over the forest below as they warm in its light. A feeling of peace is present.

Lester arrives last and greets them.

"Hopefully today will be the day we discover a way to overcome the tyranny of the king and win lasting respect and peace between us and mankind."

Fuzzy nods in agreement. With a gentle hop over the ledge, he unfurls his wings and dives slightly into the breeze where the rising current lifts him into flight. They soar effortlessly toward the Murray's fortress. Fuzzy sails in peaceful thought for only a moment.

The fortress begins to appear. It looks majestic rising above the forest canopy. The towers made of many stones look strong, and with colorful flags attached to short poles on top of them, they are captivating.

Fuzzy slows and they land in the field that surrounds the fortress. It is the same spot where he and Tee landed when they came to visit.

"Stay behind me and we will wait for Cap or Jackson to come out and escort us in. Don't be afraid, they are good men. They have been thrust into this conflict, against their will, like us. Some of the men with them do not know us and will be uneasy at first."

The tower bells begin ringing and crossbows swing around aiming in their direction.

Fuzzy bows and the others follow his lead.

The bells stop, and the crossbows turn away. The gates squeak as they open. Jackson and Cap's horses prance out and break into a trot. Fuzzy watches and cocks his head. The grass in the field is high enough that it appears that they are gliding toward them.

The brothers stop in front of the intrigued blue dragons.

"Welcome and peace to all of you," says Cap. He smiles and looks into Fuzzy's eyes. "I'm glad to see you, old friend. Why have you come?"

"I thought it would be a good idea to let our young dragons get to know you and the men in your fortress. We have talked about joining you, as you and Jackson did when we were in battle."

Cap looks at Jackson and they beam.

"We are honored that you have come. I will return to the fortress and tell every one of your intentions. I will tap the bell when everyone understands, and Jackson will escort you inside. You will be treated as our honored guests." Cap turns and gallops back.

Jackson moves close to Fuzzy. "I am glad to see you. We have been is mortal combat. Many times during the battle I thought about the heart-wrenching pain you suffered as you endured your battle." One tower bell rings one time and Jackson dismounts.

"Fuzzy, you and Tee walk beside me. I will lead my horse." The group heads for the gate.

Inside the fortress, everyone except the watchmen come forward to greet their dragon guests. Fuzzy and Lee are the center of attraction for the young children. Their glistening fuzz and red heads catch everyone's eyes. The other young dragons stand proud as their blue scales glisten in the sunlight. Even though they are uneasy, their demeanor is pleasant.

Cap and Jackson step forward and everyone is quiet. "Fuzzy and honored guests, we're pleased that you are here," says Cap.

Fuzzy bows. "Thank you," he responds.

Half of the residents of the fortress understands him and gasp. Fuzzy stands tall and stately as he surveys the people surrounding him. He contemplates their look; they have the same expression on their faces that his den members have when they await his words in times of distress. At that moment, he realizes these people are united the same as his den.

He continues, "Dragonthal must be defeated. They will never rest until they destroy all of us. We fled north to be free, only to find that a kingdom of dragons and trolls has seized control of the northern wilderness. There will be no freedom for our den as long as they rule. The dragons and trolls united long ago and wiped out civilization. Now the kingdom they formed has decided to do it again. We must unite and fight together, or you and our den will perish."

Fuzzy looks at the young dragons and they bow in agreement.

Cap speaks with joyful energy. "Men, I know of many reasons we should accept the offer of help from our dragon friends. Raise your hands if you agree that we should join together in this battle."

Most of the men and women feel the sincerity of the dragons and raise their hands in approval. Cap smiles and Fuzzy bows thankfully.

"We will leave for now so I can share the news with the rest of the den. Tee and I will return in two days to meet with Cap and Jackson. We will discuss the possibility of a man and dragon-made cavern being built next to this magnificent fortress."

Cap and Jackson bow, and the fortress defenders look pleased.

The dragons walk out of the gates spread their wings and rise into the sky. Most of the men and all the children watch as they disappear over the horizon.

Two days later, Fuzzy and Tee return to the fortress.

They move with purpose and bow once they are in the courtyard.

"I am very pleased to see you and Tee," says Cap. He introduces several men and then they all move where they can draw in the dirt. Cap hands every man a stick. When he looks at Fuzzy, they both smile.

"I draw with my claws." says Fuzzy, flipping one open. The men cut their eyes and study Fuzzy's claw for a second. Cap clears his throat and they look away and squat close to the ground.

The sound of children playing nearby is pleasant to the group as Cap draws an outline of the existing fortress. After an hour they come up with a plan to construct a cavern as an addition to the back of the fortress. It will be underground with a large passage into the basement and a second passage winding up into the courtyard that will be protected by a gate similar to the main gate. The gate will have a slot covered by a small door where a hidden crossbow can shoot into the courtyard.

Fuzzy feels the men's respect as they plan together and smiles fill the faces of both men and dragons. Decisions fall into place quickly and work can soon begin. Fuzzy and Cap's friendship is stronger than it has ever been.

Fuzzy speaks to the men. "I am honored that you are going to allow us to work with you. When the time comes, we will fight like one of your family, and we will make you proud of our den."

Chapter 18

Mason and his defenders wait fearfully for two days. Afraid to venture far from the barn, they sink into depression. Corpses are hidden from sight just outside the small door. Wounded men moan and cry out as their wounds fester and fevers rage. The smell of death and decay grows as every minute passes. Several men dare to run outside and dig shallow graves. Every time they slide one of the bodies into its resting place sorrowful wailing fills the barn.

Several survivors who have been hidden in the ruins of Water Town see them outside and walk cautiously toward the barn. Mason opens the door and they tremble and wipe tears as they walk in.

"We didn't know if anyone else was alive," remarks one.

Women bring them water and jerky, and they eat for the first time since the battle.

With no dragons or trolls to be seen, Mason decides to call everyone except the towers guards to meet in the basement. A quiet, dirty group gathers around him.

"Look around this barn at your fellow soldiers. We have fought with all our might, and it appears that we have given the dragons and trolls a painful defeat. It is time to search for anyone still alive and gather as many of our arrows as we can. But we must be cautious. I only want one small group to search the ruins at any given time."

The first group of men climbs and crawls through rubble. The sight of lifeless friends and neighbors is more than they can bear at first, but gathering arrows is too important for them to spend time with the bodies. They grit their teeth, tie bandanas over their noses and begin pulling out arrows.

The next day more men take horses and wagons to the streets. They search for the crossbows first and tear them apart. The pieces are loaded and brought back to the barn. Then they fill wagons with arrows. Most of the arrows have to be cut out of dead dragons and trolls. The stench and experience inflict a life-changing toll on the men.

At midday several loads of smelly, blood-drenched arrows cover the yard beside the barn.

That evening, horses and men drag bodies into piles and build fires with wood from buildings that were ripped apart. With weary eyes and long faces, they quietly head back to the safety of the barn.

From the slots in the towers, everyone watches the cremation fires burn into the night.

A week later, survivors are returning from the woods and the living conditions at the barn grow worse every day. There isn't enough food, and hunting parties struggle to provide enough game to feed everyone. Mason and his family are hungry most of the time and they can hardly find a place sleep. His wife and children try to smile and support him.

Ella looks at him with kind eyes. "Why don't you see if the fortress has survived. Maybe we can get help from them."

He holds her close as he considers the possibility.

In the morning, he wakes feeling confident and calls everyone together.

"We are fortunate to be alive, but we can't live like this. Time is short for us to decide how we will survive another attack, and we are out of food. We need a couple men to see if the fortress north of here is faring better than we are." He looks at his children and they try to smile. He swallows hard. "I hope for all of our sakes that they will allow us to join them."

A dozen men volunteer to leave for the fortress; but Mason says no, "We can only spare two of you. We may be attacked again and will need all the archers we can get. Cur, you and Mo get your gear and go to the fortress. Be careful, but hurry."

<>

Fuzzy and six eager dragons return to the fortress. Lester will remain at the cavern until it is safe for the den to take refuge in the man-made dragon lair.

The gate swings open. Cap and Jackson carry spades on their shoulders. A line of men follows them with tools and horses hooked to turning plows. Cap greets Fuzzy and nods to the other dragons.

"I look forward to our first day working together. Follow me and we will start digging."

The group walks energetically around to the back of the fortress. The men measure and mark a large area with four sticks stuck into the grass before plowing and loosening rows of dirt. Behind them another group of men scoop up the dirt and move it out of the area. The dragons, full of energy, become restless watching the men work. Lee speaks to Fuzzy.

"The dragons are eager to help, but have no idea what to do."

Jackson hears Lee's comment and approaches Fuzzy. "The most important part of this entire project needs to get started, and dragons are perfect for the task. Thousands of stones the size you gathered to close the cavern entrance will be needed to build the walls. You can pile them close by, then when the digging is finished we will all work together to set them."

The other dragons agree and take to the air. They are glad to be busy at last. After gathering stones for several days, the dragons have trouble finding stones nearby.

Two of them happen to fly over the ruins of Blade Town and discover lots of stones in chimneys, root cellar walls and foundations. They return with some of these stones and tell Fuzzy about their newfound place.

Fuzzy's mouth drops open. "Don't go back there until I speak with Cap," he says.

Cap listens to Fuzzy as he expresses concern about removing possessions of the dead men from Blade Town.

Cap bows. "You are still a very wise and kind dragon old friend. I assure you no man here will be offended; they all have a strong desire to protect their families. I will tell everyone tonight."

The next day, men are in motion digging and shoveling in continuous labor while dragons drop stones and the pile grows.

Fuzzy moves over to Lee, who is watching intently. "Men working with a purpose and discipline are an amazing thing to watch. Creativity and intelligence can do wonders, says Fuzzy" Lee's eyes brighten as Fuzzy motions for the other dragons to gather around.

"Fellow dragons, soon the men will be finished digging and I would like to have all the stones we need waiting for them. Let's carry two at a time when you can. Several of you pull the stones lose and have them ready so those who are flying back and forth can quickly grab them and return. Let's show these men what dragons can do."

He and Lee take off with the rest of the dragons, and they work until a very tired bunch of men and dragons trudge toward the gate for the evening meal.

The men gather around a wonderful supper the women have prepared. Fuzzy and the dragons take to the sky and soon with their stomachs filled with fish, they return to spend the night within the walls."

Before darkness closes in, two men appear from the south. They ride next to one of the towers. "What is your business?" yells one of the guards.

"We are survivors of Water Town and Mason Smith has sent us to talk with you."

The guard motions for the gate to be opened and the men ride in. Cap races to warn the visitors, but before he can reach them, their horses rear wildly when they see dragons huddled in the courtyard.

Cap yells. "Hold on to your horses. These dragons are our friends!"

The men gasp but manage to back their horses out of the gate. Cap and Jackson run to them and try to help. The men sweat with fear, and wrinkles appear on their faces.

"Everything will be all right. These dragons have been our friends for a long time. They are nothing like the dragons that have been attacking us. It is a long story.

Cap cocks his head. "I know you. You were with Jim when he came out of the wilderness and warned us that something powerful is in the wilderness."

Cur and Mo nod. "My name is Cur and this is Mo."

Cap smiles slightly. "My name is Cap and this is my brother Jackson. Come with me and I will find you something to eat."

The men try not to stare at the dragons, and they notice that everyone else is calmly going about their business. They walk cautiously following Cap to a small dining area inside the wall.

Cur and Mo look around in amazement. The walls and floor of the room are made of rock. The ceiling is constructed of log after log, laid side by side. Slots stand ready for archers to shoot into the courtyard or outside. Candles dance as they light up a table long enough for twenty men to sit.

Several men from the fortress come in to meet the visitors. Women bring water and food. The visitors are so hungry that they eat while Cap tells them about a lifetime of friendship with the blue dragons.

"Mason will think we have lost our minds when we return and tell him about this magnificent structure and dragons helping build it. I'm not sure that my friend and I aren't dreaming, either." says Cur.

"I assure you this is real," says Cap. "But even with this fortress and all we are doing to prepare; our efforts may be futile. The dragon and troll army will throw everything they can muster at us next time, and they come from a large kingdom."

Cur sighs. "Our fortress was nothing but a barn made with a lot of rock. Now it is destroyed to the point that we can hardly stay out of the weather. We are desperate to find a place to fight for our lives. Will you allow us to join you?"

Cap looks to Jackson and the rest of the men. Everyone raises their hand in agreement. "All of you are welcome here if you are willing to fight with us and befriend the blue dragons."

Mo's eyes fill with tears. "Thank you. We never expected to find such a wonderful possibility of surviving another attack, and that you would be so kind." Cur smiles and rubs his eyes too.

Before the sun rises the next day the two men fill saddlebags with food.

Cap walks out with them and introduces Fuzzy. "Make sure Mason and all the survivors of Water Town understand that these blue dragons are not to be harmed. They are working far from these walls gathering stones we need."

The men nod. "You have our word," says Cur.

They mount their horses. "We look forward to being friends with all of you--dragons and men," says Mo.

The gate opens and they gallop away.

<>

Cur and Mo are tired when they return to the rubble-strewn streets of Water Town. The sight of the two stairway towers rising above the burnt barn's ashes come into view.

Cur shakes his head. "I wonder how we survived," he sighs.

When they are close enough to see the yard next to the battered barn, they see smoke swirling above a fire and children running in play. Everyone looks raggedy and hungry.

The bell rings one time. Mason and his family watch the men ride up. Before they speak, the smile on their faces gives Mason a spark of hope.

"Welcome home, I hope I see good news in your smiles."

"We were received graciously by a group of men and women who are prepared to fight a dragon war. They are still building," says Cur.

Mo breaks in. "There is even a small den of dragons there.

They have joined forces with the men and are building a cavern beside the fortress."

Mason's eyes turn cold.

Mo, still excited to talk about the dragons continues. "We are to warn all of you not to harm any blue dragon because soon they will be our friends too."

Mason is silent. His mind is spinning.

"Why aren't you overjoyed?" asks Mo.

Mason shakes his head. "I have many questions and lots to think about. I can hardly wait to hear why these dragons are the Murrays' friends." He rubs his brow.

"Start loading wagons. We will leave as soon as possible."

People burst into cheers and hug each other.

"Listen up," booms Mason, quieting the celebration. "We are going to be more vulnerable than ever as we travel to the fortress. We must be armed and ready.

"Two of the crossbows must be made ready and manned as we travel to the fortress. Every bow and arrow we can find needs to be in someone's hand or in a wagon. Go now and search for any crossbow arrows we may have missed and load them in the wagons. Our lives may depend on them if there is a battle on our way to the fortress. The next thing is to load what food we have, and then families can load any possessions if they can find room."

He notices that all the families look frightened, and he softens his tone.

"We will help each other. Take heart, soon we will be safe inside the fortress. Understand that we will take as many belongings as we can." He pauses for only a moment.

"It's time to get to work; we leave at daybreak," he booms.

Mason wakes to the smell of ham and bread. Everyone is anxious, and a fire is burning.

Mason slips on his jacket and walks over to the fire as more people wake.

When the sky brightens, Mason assigns two archers to ride at the rear behind one of the crossbows. Four more are placed in the middle of the train. He trots to the front where two archers and the other crossbow is located.

With pride he looks at a raggedy group of people he loves as much as his own family. In his heart he yearns for them to one day return to the life they once enjoyed.

"Move out!" he bellows.

Chapter 19

Alone and bored, Bird looks around at the lonely space he occupies. One grass matt lays solitary up on a ledge, where there once were three. There are plenty of apples lying near the fire pit, but he never eats more than two a day and they are beginning to rot. He misses Lear and Leon. They are on his mind most evenings when it would be nice to share a lily bulb, laugh, and talk.

"I wonder if they ever think about me. Does anyone even know I exist?" he mutters sadly to himself. He stares at the bulbs next to the fire. "Lily bulbs can only numb the pain; they can't solve any problems," he mutters again.

He picks them up and flings them out into the night. Sad and a little afraid to be alone on this night, he promises himself to reconsider what is important, in what is left of his life. Chilly and lonely, he cuddles up listening to unnerving sounds drifting out of the wilderness. He shivers. He has never paid them any attention before.

After eating a big fish for breakfast, Bird thinks of things that would be fun to do. His thoughts turn to Dragonthal and Bell.

"It would be nice to visit again, and the excitement of evading the guards would be fun."

He turns on a whim and faces a gust of wind as it whooshes by. He raises his wings, leans into the breeze and lifts into the sky. Instant gratification fills his veins. He takes a deep breath that tastes like freedom.

Two days later, the lake at Dragonthal comes into his view. Halfway across the lake, he sees dragons with trolls on their backs flying in all direction. They are in a hurry. He flies lower, trying not be seen. He sees the fields where Lear and Leon once trained for Guargin's army. He is curious about all the excitement going on. Some dragons are sailing along with trolls on their back. The trolls have arrows aimed at targets shaped like men, and they are shooting at them as they pass by. Other dragons are a blur as they plunge toward the ground, stopping at the last second for the trolls to hop off and attack man-shaped targets, and then dash back to the dragon.

He lands and hides until it is too dark to be easily recognized. Then he calmly walks to Bell and Deago's hut. He taps on the door in a silly rhythm, and Deago knows it's Bird.

"Old friend, we have missed you but you are here at a dangerous time," says Deago as Bell walks to his side.

"I came to visit, but now I'm intrigued by all the activity in the army training fields."

Deago frowns. "Everyone is talking about a great battle that is to come. King Guargin intends to end scoundrel civilization once and for all. The market is abuzz with rumors that say he's lost so many soldiers in battle that he's seizing young dragons from their families. He's taking anyone old enough to fight, whether they're male or female. If the chosen ones resist or show disrespect, they are beaten." Deago sighs. "Word is spreading in Dragonthal that several of the dragons that were seized ran away, and the army killed their families. No one resists anymore; we are slaves to Guargin. He justifies his action saying it is for the greater good of Dragonthal. It is just as bad for the trolls. Their young are forced to join the army and work in shops making weapons and gear needed for war."

Bell breaks into tears. "Our sweet son Bago is held hostage by this monster king.

Bird's smile fades into sadness. A tear comes to his eye as Bell cries loudly. Deago smothers her in his arms and drops his head.

"My heart is broken. I am truly sorry." Bird doesn't know what else to say and hugs them both. "One day I will rescue him, but now I must leave to warn the blue dragons. Guargin already hates them, and my friends Lear and Leon are in more danger than ever."

In the dark, he leaves Dragonthal and heads south. Early in the morning he enters his friends' cold quiet cavern.

"Ureeeeee!" he calls loudly, but only echoes answer. Nothing indicates that a battle has occurred. He walks to the hatching stone wall and the stones are gone. He breathes a sigh of relief. He recalls stories Lear and Leon told of their ancestral home.

He walks to the entrance and gazes across the canopy and thinks. "If the plateau Lear and Leon talked about is as grand as they said, I can find it." He smiles, drops over the ledge, and sails away.

Two days later he sees an impressive plateau rising above the surrounding countryside. He circles for a few minutes before gliding gently to the entrance floor.

Lester is startled. Bird looks a lot like one of king's dragons. Bird stands facing him and bows in submission. Lester's tension melts when he realizes there is no yellow on this dragon and he recognizes his friend from the migration. He graciously returns the bow.

"I come in peace to share grave news and in hopes of visiting with my friends Lear and Leon," says Bird.

"I must summon our den and let them know you are here," replies Lester.

Bird eyes brighten.

"Ureeeeee," calls Lester. The den members approach with caution until they recognize Bird.

"Fellow den members, I feel it proper to let you know that our old friend Bird will be with us today." The younger dragons remember how alive and mischievous he is and watch with interest. Bird tells them of King Guargin's plans and what he has seen.

Lester's face is grim. This is something the people and dragons at the fortress need to know," he says.

The next day Lester, Bird, and a small party of dragons land in the field and waits for Fuzzy to escort them inside. One of the tower bells rings, and the guard calls out for Cap and Fuzzy. All work stops. Fuzzy flies to the tower and sees a silver dragon with his den mates.

"I think I know what is going on. I will fly to them. Don't drop your guard," he says.

Cap and Jackson stand at the gate and watch. They see Fuzzy bow and lead the dragons toward the gate. The crossbows follow the group. Cap and Jackson walk out to greet them. Fuzzy explains that Bird is the silver dragon that told them about Dragonthal.

"All is well," hails Cap loudly.
They all walk together and enter the courtyard. The residents of the fortress are gathering in the yard and on top of the walls.

Cap motions for Fuzzy to address them.

Fuzzy steps to his side.

"Friends and fellow dragons, we are fortunate to have a friendly silver dragon visiting with us. His name is Bird and his breast is not yellow like the king's soldiers. Our den knows him and he has proven his worth. He has just returned from Dragonthal where he watched Guargin's army gathering in unbelievable numbers. The city of Dragonthal and the surrounding kingdom is preparing to descend on us with a massive force."

With a solemn face, Cap steps to Fuzzy's side. "What we have just been told is scary, but hearing from someone that has seen what we will be up against will strengthen our resolve to overcome this evil army." Cap goes on, but Bird's mind drifts away.

He is overcome with the wonderful feeling of unity he senses between the men and the blue dragons. His soul longs to enjoy that feeling.

When Cap finishes, Lester and Fuzzy are close to Bird and feel his need; it is so obvious. Fuzzy places one wing around him and with his gift of gaining respect, he hails the fortress.

"My human den members, this is an honorable dragon and I hope you will treat him kindly. He has no den of his own, but our den is always pleased when he graces us with his presence."

Bird's heart is touched. "I will help you and my blue dragon brothers in any way I can during the war that is to come. I pledge my allegiance to all the members of this fortress."

The men cheer and all the dragons bow. Bird feels acceptance for the first time in his life. A wonderful warm feeling tingles in his veins.

When Lester and the visiting dragons leave, Bird goes with them. He stays close to Lester as they walk toward the cavern entrance. Lester sees a solemn, yet pleasant look on his face. Bird clears his throat.

"If you don't mind, I would like to stay here with the den for a few days," says Bird humbly.

Lester smiles, "Our den will be honored. Come spend the night in my special place and consider staying with us until the war is over."

<>

As the Water Town survivors begin their trip to the fortress, Mason is reminded of the hunting party and their train of wagons and weapons. The sounds are the same and the people are afraid, but excited. He fumbles in his pocket and pulls the dragon claw out, then drops it back. As they make their way down what was once a bustling trail, ghostly shells of buildings lay in smelly piles of ash.

Tears fall from many eyes as they remember friends and shop owners who are no longer alive.

The wagons squeak and bump over the trail. Most of the people keep an eye on the forest. They aren't looking at its beauty; they are watching for movement.

At midday, they eat dried meat and fruit as they bounce along. No one wants to stop, and they continue to move on.

At the ruins of Sandra's village, a wagon carrying a family with two children emerges from the woods and Mason stops.

The couple is dirty and the children whimper. "We have nowhere to go and are almost out of food. Can we join you?" cries the man with a look on his face that breaks Mason's heart. He motions for them to pull their wagon into the line. A man on horseback rides to them and hands them jerky. They thank him with tears in their eyes.

Mason calls for Cur and Mo to move ahead of the train and keep an eye out for trouble. They gallop out of sight, and Mason decides to move along at a faster pace. Blade Town appears and the refugees gasp. Dragons are in the air above the ruins. Cur looks at Mo and they gallop back.

"The blue dragons are gathering stones, just like Cap said. These are the dragons at the fortress."

Mason rubs his chin as he rides to the middle of the train. "I know the sight of dragons ahead is frightening, but our scouts say they are from the fortress. We will have to be brave. Crossbowmen, load your weapons, but do not cock the triggers." He looks at Cur and Mo. "One of you will have to ride up there and see if it is safe for the rest of us to pass."

"We will both go," says Mo. "Cap and Jackson said that bowing in respect to the dragons is important. Let's ride close and bow. I hope one of them will come to greet us in peace."

The dragons stop their work and watch as the men approach and bow. Lee gently glides in their direction, lands in front of them, and bows.

"I remember you from your trip to the fortress," he says.

Chills run down Mo and Cur's spines as they understand his thoughts.

"We remember you too. We are with the survivors from Water Town. We are on our way to join with you and the men of the fortress," says Cur.

"We are glad you have chosen to join us. You may pass in peace." Lee returns to the other dragons and they continue their work.

The scouts return smiling and explain how they understood what the dragon said and that it would be safe to pass.

"Please lower the crossbows," says Mo. The bowman in front raises his eyebrows in defiance. Mason nods for him to obey. He unlatches his weapons and lowers it to the floor. The bowman in the rear does the same.

Everyone holds their breath as the train makes its way forward, but soon they forget about the dragons when the horrid sight of ashes and debris overwhelm them. A wisp of death lingers in the air until the ruins are out of sight.

Two hours later, the fortress towers rise before them as they come closer. The refugees whisper to each other in awe. Emotionally overwhelmed, many of them wipe tears.

The tower bells begin ringing happily. Men, women, and children appear on the walkway atop the wall, cheering and waving to them.

The gate opens and the wagons enter the fortress. Cap and Jackson walk out to greet Mason.

"Welcome. We're glad to see you. I hope your blacksmiths have survived and are with you," says Cap.

"Jim and most of his men are with us, but it appears you can build whatever you need already."

"We are fortunate to have several fine blacksmiths and a wonderful group of people. We are also lucky to have the blue dragons working alongside us. They are like family and will be a great asset when the battle begins.

Mason looks Cap in the eyes and doesn't comment, then looks around at the courtyard. "We can't pull all of our wagons in here."

Cap pleasantly smiles. "Your wagons will have to remain outside until we finish the dragon's lair. They are sleeping here in the courtyard until then. Your people can bed down in the basement halls until we build rooms above their lair. Mason is quiet for a short time. Cap can tell that Mason is used to being in charge and is struggling to adjust. In a less commanding voice he speaks.

"Thank you for allowing us into the safety of this fortress. We will gladly do everything we can."

"Try to settle in as best you can. Please tell everyone we are expecting them to join us for supper," says Cap.

After supper is cleaned up and everyone is getting to know each other, Cap rings one of the tower bells. When they are quiet he comes down to address them.

"We are glad the brave people of Water Town have come to join us. Fighting together will make us stronger and, I hope, make the war shorter. There will be some problems at first, like finding enough room for everyone to be comfortable, but with every passing day we will add more space."

Cap sees Fuzzy has a suggestion and nods to him.

"The biggest problem I see arising from all the extra help is a need for more food. We dragons are better at fishing and can gather nuts, fruit and other foods and fly them back to the fortress quickly." Cap nods.

"I think everyone here agrees. That will give the men more time to finish the stonework and build weapons."

Mason quietly listens, but he still has the dragon claw from the ghost camp in his pocket and ponders troubling possibilities.

In a few months the walls and rooms above the dragon's lair are completed. The fortress looks like a large building with a small courtyard in the back and a large courtyard in front. The walls that extend from the main building travel the length equal to ten wagons. Then they turn toward each other and meet at a strong gate. The fortress now has six towers with crossbows atop them all. Mason's courtyard is smaller, but it has two crossbows hidden in its walls.

The dragon's lair is dry now that the roofs over Mason's rooms are thatched.

<>

Fuzzy and the dragons gather in the lair that they and the men have built.

"It is not as grand as one of nature's caverns, but it will do," says Lee.

Fuzzy motions for them to be quiet. "I am pleased with this space. It will serve its purpose. I hope this war ends soon and I can live long enough to see our den occupy a real cavern again. I would like to see my grandchildren play and grow up like dragons."

"Yaheee!" remarks one of the younger dragons.

Fuzzy smiles "It is good to hear some enthusiasm. It's time for us to return to the cavern and help our family move." He leads them to the courtyard. The sun is shining brightly and men are busy smoking jerky as children play. He wonders if these children will become friends with the young dragons."

Cap approaches. "Looks like you are ready to move the rest of the den into the lair."

'We will leave now and will return in a few days."

Cap bows. "Everyone is glad you are part of our fortress family. Be safe. We look forward to your return."

Lester is keeping watch at the cavern and sadness fills his heart when he sees the workers returning. He knows this is one more step closer to a battle that could wipe out his den.

Busy days pass quickly and they gather to depart. Fuzzy stands near the ledge in front of the entrance looking over the countryside. He soaks in the view that he will not have the opportunity to enjoy for some time.

Bird walks to his side. "I have a request if you have time to hear me," he says.

Fuzzy turns to him. Bird looks into his eyes.

"I'm tired of having no family and am very happy when I'm here with your den. I know I didn't help build the fortress, but I am asking if I can go with you and be part of your den."

Fuzzy's face lifts to a smile as Fuzzy looks at Bird. "If you do your share of work and fighting, you will be loved by my family and I will show you the same respect as I do any of them."

Bird starts to hug Fuzzy, but bows humbly instead.

Lester hears their conversation and smiles before taking off. Groups follow. They lean into the breeze and sail toward the fortress that is barely visible and looks tiny in the distance. Fuzzy is the last to leave with Liz by his side. They sail along, glad to be close together.

"My heart yearns to enjoy a peaceful life like our ancestors did," says Liz.

"You, my dear, are so worthy of a happy life, and I will do everything I can to make it happen," replies Fuzzy.

Liz nods lovingly. "No matter what happens, my love for you will never end."

Soon the den lands near the fortress gate. Cap and Jackson rush to greet them as it swings open. Families gather and cheer as they enter. Before they go into the lair, Lester raises his wings.

"Our hearts are warmed by this reception and we will make you proud of us!" He turns and leads the way as the den disappears into the new lair.

Once things have settled, Fuzzy asks Bird to join him and Liz in their special place for as long as he likes.

In no time, the sound of laughter fills the courtyard as young dragons play with the children and older dragons bring fish for the men to smoke and store away. The residents of the fortress become comfortable with each other—except Mason.

<>

Adrian is confident and shrewd. He gathers a small group of his best advisors and they discuss what the soldiers that survived Slash's attack have told them. He looks at the advisors.

"To encourage you to figure out how to win this battle without getting most of my soldiers killed, I intend to take you with me, and I will not hesitate to send you with a battle group. I will not end up like Slash."

The advisors grit their teeth.

Rye, his second in command, speaks. "Some of Slash's soldiers told us of a cavern near the fortress. Adrian smiles slyly. "We leave tomorrow."

When they arrive at the cavern, they are pleased to find it empty. Adrian looks over the countryside from the ledge and smiles. "I can't believe our good fortune. This place is perfect, and the blue dragons aren't here to get in the way."

The next day Adrian and the advisors circle far from the fortress and gaze upon the structure. The grassy field surrounding the fortress has been cleared far from its walls allowing no cover for them to hide. The towers stand tall and are intimidating with their little flags flapping in the wind. The building is large and, even though the dragons are far away, they can see men on the walls. Adrian smirks and shakes his head.

"This is going to be a costly battle. I need to study the towers and get a closer look at the weapons Slash talked about, but we can't take a chance of being seen."

Rye frowns. "The structure they have built implies a high level of intelligence. This enemy will be cunning. I want to explain this to Guargin."

Adrian sighs and ponders.

"One thing we can do is to study the activity around the fortress. I want to know everything about them, especially where their main food source is located. We may want to cut it off." he snarls.

"Leave now and tell Guargin what we have seen and that I want the scoundrels weak and hungry before we attack."

<>

Cap, Jackson, Fuzzy, Lee, Mason and several other men meet to discuss responsibilities and make plans for the battle. They all have solemn expressions on their faces. Everyone knows that time is growing short. Cap stands and everyone becomes quiet.

"I am pleased with our progress, but I have been troubled since Bird told us that the coming army will be massive. We must face reality. Many of us will die. We must decide who will assume our duties if one of us falls." The room is quiet.

"I will go first," says Cap. "I choose Jackson as my first replacement, then after him Miles, then Buck, then Mason, then Jim. Fuzzy will lead the dragons and will assign the line of descending leadership in his den. Every one of you are just as important. Crossbowmen, after the meeting go to the one you know who can take your place and have a long talk with them. He is to do the same and so on. All of you are leaders. Go have a talk with those who will replace you. Things must be run orderly so if one of us dies, the next in line will instantly take over." He looks around and no one has a question. He can feel the tension that fills the room.

"My next concern is our food supply. The women have built up a good supply, but now that construction is complete, we must produce and store all we can. We must continue to work as hard storing food as we did when we were building this place."

Fuzzy stands. "The dragons will continue bringing fish as the men smoke them."

Two men stand. "We will organize a group to hunt and dry meat. Jerky can be stored longer than dried fish."

Buck and Ed stand. "Arrows will need to be made continuously, and a lot of wood will be needed to fuel the cooking fires and make arrows."

Two men volunteer to assemble a crew of men to stock up the wood supply.

"Plants for medicine, spices, and teas need to be stored," says another, and several men agree to help him.

Mason stands. "The people of Water Town will cut grass and grain in the fields to feed the horses. We will store it under the walls where it will be safe from dragon flames."

Cap is pleased and confident that he and Jackson can find others to handle any other needs.

<>

Two weeks later, Rye returns. Adrian rises and bows when he enters the cavern.

"Guargin likes your suggestion of starving the scoundrels. He has sent a hundred dragons and a hundred trolls. He suggests hitting the scoundrels with a surprise attack doing as much damage as you can, and then cutting off their food supply until the rest of the army arrives."

Adrian smiles. "We will attack when the scoundrels are outside working. They will be sitting ducks.

In the morning while it is still dark, a lone silver dragon hides in the woods where he can see the gate. When it opens and several men and dragons come outside to work, he steals away where he can take to the air without being seen, and sails back to the plateau.

"Scoundrels are outside the walls," he screams.

Twenty dragons and trolls hustle to the ledge and take to the air. They fly low over the treetops and are upon the fortress before any bells ring.

Many men are hit before they see the enemy coming. Others drop their tools and run for their lives. They are run down and grappled, screaming until they are dropped to their death or cut down by the cruel arrows shot by the trolls. One of the blue dragons grabs a young man by his arms and quickly flies over the fortress wall, landing safely. They are the only two who make it back.

The gate stands open and men dash to shut it, but before they reach it they realize it doesn't matter. The attackers are too close. They rush for cover, leaving the gate open. Most of the soldiers fly to the open gate. The crossbows on the towers follow them while the one hidden in the dragon lair gate and in the back wall lay in wait.

The crossbowmen's hearts are filled with rage as they squeeze their triggers and five dragons slam to the ground. Most of them explode on impact and their riders roll like tumbleweeds, never to stand again. The rest of the silvers continue and before they are close enough for the trolls to unleash their arrows, five more silvers are split open by crossbow arrows. Half of the attackers are dead. The rest are killed by archers who unleash a hail of arrows so thick that they darken the sky.

<>

Watching the battle from nearby woods, Adrian stares as dragons explode or release aimless fire in death. The trolls lie lifeless on the ground. An eerie silence prevails until the fortress rings their bells. With his mouth open he stands in disbelief. He flexes his claws nervously as his face wrinkles. Hate and anger course through his veins, pumped furiously by his broken heart. He has never experienced such a devastating defeat. "So many wonderful warriors killed in minutes," he laments to the surrounding forest and the rest of his soldiers. Filled with anger, he tears through the canopy, his wings flapping furiously. He doesn't slow down until he lands at the cavern.

<>

As darkness settles over the fortress the number of guards is doubled. Cap walks around the top of the wall in deep thought. He stops at Jackson's crossbow. "Our enemy is trying new tactics. We will have to be ready for anything they dream up." Jackson nods understandingly.

Cap starts to walk away. Jackson calls to him. "You should console the families of the men who died in the field."

Cap sighs. "I intend too." He walks to the stairs and descends.

Cap sleeps little that night and rings the bell one time early the next morning. He stands on one of the towers looking out at the bodies lying in the field. The courtyard fills with men, women and dragons from the fortress lair.

"We lost good men yesterday. They deserve a decent burial, but they could be the bait the enemy is using to draw us outside again."

Fuzzy hails Cap. "The blue dragons will fly out and bring them back to the gate if that is acceptable to their loved ones.

Several families sob, but no one objects.

Soon the corpses lay peacefully at the open gate. Everyone helps the families bury their dead, and then the gate is closed.

Later that day, Cap calls the leaders together to discuss what they have learned from the battle. It is agreed that a small door should be cut into the wall so the gate can be closed most of the time. Fuzzy proposes that members of his den stand guard on the surrounding hills where they can see an approaching army long before the tower lookouts.

Everyone agrees when Jackson suggests that dogs be tied in each tower in case of a night attack. Buck stands and informs everyone that too many arrows are wasted when there is an attack. Cap nods.

"We will tell everyone to try to do better." Jackson stands.

"We should gather the trolls' arrows. They are crude, but we could use them if we run out? Everyone nods in agreement.

The meeting is about to end. Fuzzy stands.

"I suggest that the blue dragons gather rocks and pile them on top of the walls where they can be dropped on the enemy if the need arises."

Mason cuts his squinted and piercing eyes to Fuzzy upon hearing the suggestion.

As Mason walks away from the meeting, he calls Jim to a corner where they can talk. Mason is trembling.

"I had a feeling the moment I saw the blue dragon's claws that they were the dragons that killed my men."

Jim gasps and looks to see that no one is hearing this conversation. "You are probably right, but Fuzzy surely knows you are the one who came after his den and caused them much grief. Think about it. Let's fight the war at hand."

The dragons begin gathering stones and placing them around the walls. Bird is in the woods gathering stones when he hears a noise. Cautiously he creeps into the brush. Crunching sounds erupt as a large creature tries to flee. He catches a glimpse of a silver dragon. The trees are too thick to take to the air, so he dashes through the foliage in pursuit. He gains on the wounded silver and is ready to burn its wings off when he hears a feminine voice plea for mercy. He stops in his tracks. The silver stops and drops to its knees gasping for air. He is stunned to see that the dragon is a young female. She has lost a lot of blood and her eyes look weak, but she shows no aggression.

"I am at your mercy. I never wanted to be in this war, but my family's life depends on me obeying the king," she pleads. "Will you help me?"

Bird fills with compassion. He looks into her eyes and she looks down in shame.

"I trust you and I will help, but I must first go get help so we won't be shot as we try to enter the fortress."

Bird flies to the fortress and finds Fuzzy.

When he hears Bird's story, the kindness he is known for shines through. They return to the woods and together they help her into the open. Fuzzy flies to the gate and asks one of the men to bring a wagon.

As they pass through the gate, many men are quiet. With piercing eyes, they watch another silver dragon enter the fortress. Fuzzy walks to the center of the courtyard and bows. Cap taps the bell and asks them to listen. Fuzzy raises his head.

"I understand how everyone feels about silver dragons. This female is a victim of Guargin's cruelty. She is only here so he will not kill her family. She has no more loyalty to him than you or I."

Cap speaks "I respect Fuzzy's judgment and compassion. Please let the dragons give her the care she needs." The defenders talk among themselves and some shake their heads.

One of them yells, "Make these silver dragons that are our friends wear a blue scarf around their necks."

Bird gently guides her to Fuzzy's special place and helps her settle in his grassy bed.

What is your name?" he asks.

Her eyes brighten. "Robin."

Bird smiles.

Liz touches his shoulder. "It would be best if you leave for a while. Robin will want to be alone with me while I remove the arrows."

<>

Adrian is seething for a fight. He still has plenty of soldiers he can use to inflict pain on the fortress. He studies his options. He knows the lake in the wilderness is the fortress's main source of food, and he could ambush the blue dragons gathering fish. Another surprise attack on anyone outside the walls of the fortress is tantalizing too. Now he knows not to pursue them as they run toward the waiting crossbows.

Two days pass and none of the scoundrels leave the safety of the fortress.

Anxious, he summons his soldiers.

"It's time to use what we have learned against the fortress. Tomorrow I want four teams to ambush the blue dragons as they return from the lake," he orders.

The next day, six blues head for the lake with baskets strapped around their necks. After filling them with fish, they head back. Suddenly one of them screams in agony.

The others look back and see arrows sailing toward them. Another blue is wounded and flutters to the ground. The airborne blues dive into the forest, twisting and turning through trees, gaining speed and moving faster. The silvers pursue them with trolls holding on with all their might. One of the trolls tries to duck under a limb, but misjudges. He slams into it flipping him lifelessly to the ground.

The blues drop their baskets to improve their speed and maneuverability. Silvers flap their wings harder; expelling lots of energy. With trolls on their backs, they are less agile. A silver flinches, but it's too late to zigzag around the trees in front of him. He slams head-on into one of them. A *thunk* followed by an earthshaking *boom,* echoes through the forest as fire explodes around the tree. The silver behind him is blinded and slams into limbs. With a loud *crack,* bones break and limbs rip loose falling with him and his troll to the forest floor.

The blues look back and motion to each other to break up. The silvers follow the two that stay straight. The two circling blues are soon behind the silvers. One undetected blue slips up close, stretches his neck, and sinks his teeth into one of the silver's wings, tearing it to pieces. It spins to the ground and hits hard. When it explodes, the blue barely escapes the flames. The last silver has no troll on his back and has accelerated to great velocity. The two blues ahead of him turn suddenly and face him. The surprised silver can't stop in time to avoid their flames and they cover him with both their blasts. He falls, leaving a trail of smoke behind him as he crashes to the ground.

The four blues hurry back to find their den mates. One is dead and the other has two crude arrows stuck in its wings. He is in too much pain to fly, but he can limp. Two of the dragons help him start the long journey back to the fortress.

Fuzzy knows things aren't right when two blues land in the courtyard with no fish. He hurries to them.

"We were ambushed. One blue is dead and another is badly hurt. The other two are helping him hobble back."

Cap and Jackson rush out to the dragons. Cap tearfully places his hand on Fuzzy's shoulder. Several men stand solemnly and feel the dragon's sadness.

Dragons rush out of their lair. "Wiiiiii," echoes in the courtyard as dragon tears flow.

Chapter 20

Adrian waits. He becomes fidgety and looks out over the horizon again and again. Finally, he accepts that his soldiers are not coming back. Furious, he stomps around the cavern in a rage. He calls a messenger.

"Leave for Dragonthal. Say nothing about the defeats we have suffered. Tell Guargin and the court that I have studied our situation and we must stop fighting like our instinct tells us to. These scoundrels will outwit us. Luck is on their side. Our only hope is to descend on them with numbers too great for them to overcome. Send the largest army Dragonthal can muster. Every soldier must attack at once and force the defenders of the fortress to hide like rats under its walls. We will then tear the fortress down rock by rock and kill them one at a time as they try to scamper away."

When the messenger delivers Adrian's message, Guargin looks him in the eyes. "This sounds like Adrian has come to this realization the hard way. Has he lost many of the soldiers I sent him?"

The messenger closes his eyes and trembles. "Yes, my king. We have suffered a heavy loss."

Guargin's face reddens and his eyes squint almost shut. The messenger bows in submission.

"Raise your head dragon. Those who died did not die in vain. I intend to send Adrian his requested super army, but I don't intend to dump them all on the fortress at once. I will wear them down slowly. I may want to use the fortress as a summer palace, so I don't think we will tear it to pieces. Go back and tell Adrian he will have his army soon."

Guargin turns to the representatives in his court. He appoints a dragon named Aham and troll named Peato to travel with the army when they go to the battle site. They nod with respect.

"Aham, you will speak for the dragons. Peato, you will speak for the trolls. Neither of you will make military decisions. You are to inspire your soldiers to give their all in this war, and when it is over, you will personally console the families of the dead." Aham and Peato bow.

Guargin bumps the floor with his scepter. "I will be going to the battle site to command our forces. We leave in twenty days."

<>

When the day of departure arrives, Aham proudly stands in front of one thousand dragons. They have harnesses strapped around their necks to assist in carrying weapons. They all stand at attention.

A short distance away Peato stands proudly in front of one thousand trolls. They hold spears in their right hands with tips pointing up. Across their shoulders are quivers filled with arrows. They hold bows in their left hands.

King Guargin marches out with his court behind him. He stands and gazes across the sea of soldiers.

"I am honored to stand before such a great army. Together the united trolls and dragons will defeat the scoundrels. Our ancestors would be proud to see this fine army. Fight for what we believe in, and good luck."

He watches as the massive army takes to the air; darkening the sky.

Three days later, the wilderness around the plateau is crawling with dragons and trolls. King Guagin and his leaders land at the blue dragon's abandoned cavern where they are met by Adrian.

Adrian bows. Guargin returns the bow.

"I am glad to see you, Adrian. I have with me a thousand dragons and a thousand trolls. This should be enough force to crush the fortress." Peato is close and nods confidently.

Adrian gestures to the cavern. "We can shelter two hundred soldiers in here. My king, you and your advisors please pick your places, and then all that can find space will be allowed to settle in. All others should start searching for shelter," he says.

The next morning, Adrian and Guargin lead the army to the streets of Blade Town. It is the only cleared area that is large enough for the soldiers to gather and listen for their orders. Guargin comes forward and asks the leader of the trolls to address the army.

Peato steps forward. "Guardians of the world of trolls and dragons, scoundrels and their civilization are a threat to our very existence. We must suffer out here far from our families for a short while to preserve our way of life. If we fail, in time the decedents of this fortress will assemble armies of scoundrels to destroy us. It is our responsibility and honor to serve our families and generations of trolls and dragons to come. Fight hard and fight smart!"

He turns and bows to Guargin, who nods to the dragon's leader.

Aham steps up. "We are a team, and we are proud to fight with our troll brothers. I know we face a well-prepared, smart foe, and we will lose soldiers. We must not lose hope, even if our losses are great. We will destroy the scoundrels and the blue dragons that are helping them."

King Guargin raises his scepter and stands proud. "Fifty dragon and troll teams will attack within the hour. If they are repelled, a fresh wave of fifty teams will attack when they return. The rest of you are to gather food and build tarps to shelter wounded and provide cover from sun and rain for the troops waiting."

He motions for Adrian to come forward.

Adrian moves smartly, hoping it hides the disgust he feels for Guargin's decision to wear the fortress down slowly. He forces a smile, and bows.

"Choose the first one hundred soldiers," commands Guargin.

<>

It's midmorning at the fortress and the people are enjoying a beautiful day. Children and young dragons run around, burning energy better used up playing outside. They chase each other across the top of the walls and catch glimpses of the world beyond the rock walls. Women hang clothing out to dry and talk happily as if there isn't a care in the world.

In the basement kitchen, food is simmering. The blues have gathered a pile of fish to be smoked. Several men are unloading firewood that will be stored in the basement.

Cap, Jackson, Mason, and other leaders are discussing ideas. Cap appears to be daydreaming, catching the attention of several men.

"What is on your mind?" asks Mason.

"I was thinking about how to use our blue dragons in the war ahead. The more I think about sending them to battle silvers with troll riders, the more I feel we should not send them out to fight hand-to-hand. We only have a few blues. I don't want to see them die needlessly."

Mason glares at Cap.

Fuzzy feels turmoil bottled up inside Mason. He closes his other senses and lets Mason's thoughts drift into his mind. Fuzzy's face drops. Mason's heart is filled with hate and his anger is for the blue dragons. Something he carries with him keeps reinforcing his anger.

Lester sees Fuzzy appearing to be daydreaming and bumps him. Startled, but thinking fast, Fuzzy blurts, "We are not afraid of these silvers."

Lester squints his eyes.

The dogs begin barking and the blue guard dragons on the surrounding hills are shrieking, "Ureeeeee! Ureeeeee!" as they frantically fly toward the fortress. Then the tower bells ring wildly. The men rush to their assigned positions. Women scramble to herd the children into the basement, while others grab clothes and bedding off of clotheslines trying to save as much as they can.

Crossbows swing around and face south. A guard at each tower keeps an eye to the north for good reason. Approaching quickly, fifty attacking dragon and troll teams are an ominous sight. The trolls have their arrows nocked, but are out of range. When the closest crossbow shoots, it misses.

With trigger fingers trembling, the crossbowmen wait a second, then six large arrows streak toward the oncoming silvers. Two dragons in front dodge them, but several dragons behind them are impaled. Dragons and trolls fall from the sky, slamming to the ground. Fire bursts from dead dragon mouths, and some explode on impact. Trolls bounce, roll, and flop like rag dolls in the grass. The crossbows send another volley into the line of attackers before the trolls are close enough to shoot. More dragons and riders scream as they crash to the ground. Fires burn and smoke swirls amidst the attacking army.

Cap shoots frantically, but the silvers keep coming. Soon they are hovering around his tower. He ducks arrows and keeps shooting. Flames and arrows force the crossbowman beside him to leap through the tap door. He follows; tumbling down the stairs under the floor.

Arrows from the surrounding walls continue to bring down trolls and dragons. All Cap and the crossbowman can do is wait. Three crossbows in the courtyard are still fighting and continue shooting at dragons.

As the dragon numbers lessen, men behind the slots step left and right looking for a good shot, and when it comes, they unleash their arrows. Cap hears constant thuds as trolls fall to the ground.

A frantic bowman runs to Cap. "The crossbows are quiet and the dragons are turning their attack to the men on top of the wall!" he screams.

Cap moves to one of the slots and sees men running toward the trap doors. Trolls are in pursuit. Most of the men safely dive through the doors by the time arrows from the opposite side of the courtyard fill the trolls' backs. Seeing their riders die from arrows shot from slots in the courtyard walls, most of the dragons angrily dive toward the courtyard. They are caught in crossfire from the men on one side and women and children on the other. Hundreds of arrows fill the air. Fire bursts from the dead silvers impaled in the yard. The heat is unbearable, and archers hidden in the walls step to the side until the fires die down.

With only a few silvers in the sky, Cap takes a deep breath. He and a crossbowman push the door open. Extra archers protect him and the crossbowman as they restring the crossbow. Soon the crossbowman is following silvers as they streak by. In moments he and the extra archers clear the enemy from around another crossbow.

A surge of energy fills Cap when he hears their battle leader scream, "Sharee, Sharee, Sharee," The silvers retreat and head south. Many are wounded, and two of them fall to the ground before they disappear from sight.

The men cheer.

"We have lost several men, but at least the battle is won," says Cap.

Bird pokes his head out of the opening to the dragon's lair. As he comes out, Cap sees he has a blue rag tied around his horns and a blue blanket across his shoulders.

"What are you doing?" yells Cap from the tower.

"I fear for my life every time we're under attack because I look so much like the silvers.

"Then why are you out here?"

"I must warn you. This is only a handful of the troops I saw training. Another attack is imminent. Prepare quickly, there is no time for grieving."

"Thank you, Bird." Cap rings the tower bell and barks orders. "Get ready to start fighting again right now. Cool the crossbows and restring them. Gather as many arrows as you can and return them to the quivers. When you are done, fill buckets with water and set them next to the crossbows. Tower guards, do not drop your watch for even a second. Harness horses and drag the enemy's dead outside. Stay close, another attack could come at any moment."

The defenders barely finish putting the last crossbow together when the southern tower bell rings again and the men outside dash toward the gate. The horses are spooked and run through the gate with the men close behind. The gate slams shut as the men prepare to fight again. The crossbow cranks click away and arrows are ready to sail.

The men are shocked to see fifty more silvers and trolls approaching, and not one of them is wounded. The crossbowmen know when to shoot this time and they are deadly until they are overrun by fire-breathing silvers. The archers on the wall only shoot a few arrows before they rush down the stairs to a slot. They learned a lot from the previous battle, but they're tired.

Fuzzy, Lester and the dragons congregate in the dragon lair and part of the basement. They are ashamed, but they would be killed quickly if they take to the air.

A team of Guargin's soldiers drop to the courtyard. Trolls hop off and charge toward the basement entrance. The hidden crossbow in the thick gate shoots once, and then a silver kicks it open. The crossbow is smashed and the trolls run inside. Four young blues are in the hall and charge toward the trolls, dodging arrows until they are close enough to incinerate them. All the trolls smolder as the blues guard the entrance. Lear and Leon hear of the feat and rush to their side and join them until the attack is over.

Bird comes from inside the lair and walks with a solemn face to Fuzzy and Lester's side. They look puzzled.

"I'm going to follow these retreating soldiers back to their camp. We must know what we are up against." He places the blue cloth on his neck and pokes his head out and Calls to Cap. The enemy is in retreat and Cap comes down. When he sees Bird, he smirks.

"Bird, what are you doing?"

"I'm going to see how many soldiers are left. When I return, I will be flying high and drop a stone that will land harmlessly in the courtyard so you will know It's me about to land. Tell everyone not to shoot."

Cap bows respectfully. Bird flaps briskly, stirring up dirt, causing Cap to look away as he lifts into the air.

Bird watches the fortress grow smaller as he flies higher and higher. Soon, the clearing that once was Blade Town comes into view. The streets are visible and rows of ashes are piled along their sides. His heart sinks more and more as he grows closer. The streets are stirring with dragons and trolls. Some are marching while others are lying around. Everywhere he looks, there are soldiers. There are even places in the woods where soldiers are under tarps. He continues to fly high, trying to count them until several soldiers begin watching him. He quickly sails toward the woods where the tarps are hanging. He lands where soldiers are too busy talking to each other to notice that he has no yellow on his breast. He walks with purpose through the camp and disappears into the brush.

He stops once when he is well out of sight and catches his breath. When he is confident that no one is following him, he walks until he finds a meadow. He picks up a stone and takes to the air. His mind is racing, knowing everyone will be crushed if he tells them there is no hope. His stomach churns. He ponders running away, but deep inside he is displeased with the thought. That is what the old Bird would do. He takes a deep breath and tries to decide what to say.

Moments later, he is in the courtyard, and Cap is coming toward him. He looks down and sighs. Cap stops and senses Bird is filled with distress and swallows hard.

"I will gather everyone. Stay here." Cap hugs him and leaves.

Once he is surrounded with anxious members of his den and the families of the fortress, Bird begins his story. He can't bring himself to tell the group how bad it is. Feeling it is his duty to give them hope he tells them that there will be many more waves to come, but if everyone gives their all, the fortress can outlast the enemy. He never smiles or looks anyone in the eyes. Cap is at a loss for words. Everyone walks away knowing no more than they did, but they leave with hope."

<>

That night Bird is on his way to spend time with Robin when he comes face-to-face with Lear and Leon.

"We don't stand a chance, do we?" asks Lear.

Bird's eyes answer his question and they look at each other with cold eyes. They leave Bird, and with tense brows they make their way to Fuzzy's special place. They don't stop to talk to anyone as they walk with purpose. Fuzzy sees them and gestures for them to enter.

Fuzzy smiles. "I am pleased to hear that you helped guard the basement today. What can I do for you?"

Leon nods to Liz and looks Fuzzy in the eyes.

"Bird told us that Guargin has a massive army camped where Blade Town once stood. Guargin is toying with by us sending these waves of battle groups. When he tires of these little battles, he will unleash a massive attack."

Fuzzy takes a deep breath. "I can only hope you are wrong."

"We want your permission to find help. We will be gone for a few days."

Fuzzy squints. "Have you lost your minds? There is no one to ask."

"Lear and I have an idea; it is our only hope. Please give us your consent."

Fuzzy looks to Liz. She ponders a moment and gently gestures why not.

Fuzzy looks to Lester, and he nods.

"You have our permission," replies Fuzzy.

When they leave, Fuzzy looks at Liz and Lester. "I don't think these two are running out on us, but at least they may be the only blue dragons who survive this war."

Over the next two days, battle comes in three waves every day, always fifty silvers and their rider. There aren't enough men to take turns resting and fatigue is taking its toll.

On the third day, in the last wave, Cap spots a blue dragon with a troll on its back. Word reaches Fuzzy that one of the blue dragons has joined the silvers. He tears out of the basement and leaps to the top of the wall. A troll's arrow zips past his head as he gazes into the sky. He doesn't even flinch. His heart throbs to think that this could be Lear or Leon. An arrow nips Fuzzy's shoulder. He grabs the spot and grits his teeth, but he doesn't take his eyes off the blue.

The blue jerks as arrows pierce its side. It spins wildly, throwing the troll off before careening into the courtyard. Fuzzy hops to the yard screaming to Cap.

"Stop shooting at the fallen blue! I must see who it is!"

Cap hammers his tower bell one time and yells the command. Arrows strike near him and he has no more time to think about Fuzzy.

Fuzzy approaches the gasping blue. Blood is squirting from three wounds, and the ground grows red around him. In great pain, he looks up.

"Gus!" cries Fuzzy.

Gus chokes as blood drools from his mouth. "We never got to live like dragons. Please help me die like one. I regret that I let hate consume me. Tell me I am forgiven. I still love our den and could have never harmed any of you. Tell me I can soar in the heavens with our ancestors for eternity and that one day I will be with you and Lester again."

Fuzzy sobs as he speaks. "It is so. You did what you thought was right and I do not judge you. You are a real dragon and I will see you in eternity. We will fly together again."

Fuzzy's tears fall on Gus's face. A painful smile fills Gus's cheeks and then a blast of flames shoot harmlessly from his mouth. The blood stops oozing and Fuzzy lays his head on his fallen kin.

Behind Fuzzy, Bird has heard every word. He is emotionally destroyed. He drops to his knees beside him and sobs uncontrollably.

<>

Early the next morning, before the attacks begin, Bird approaches Fuzzy. "I have a plan and I need your blessing and help. I look like the silvers, and I am the only one that can fly over their camp without drawing their attention. With your permission, I am going to try to kill Guargin. We can't defeat his army. Our only hope is that without him his army will have no reason to continue fighting."

Fuzzy wrinkles his brow. "It may work. Come with me and we will talk with Cap. The men need to know what you are about to do, so they won't shoot you when you return."

Cap and several men look up as they enter the small dining room. Bird is by Fuzzy's side.

"Bird has a plan that could end this battle," says Fuzzy stepping aside.

"I have seen the enemy's forces, and we cannot defeat them. I am willing to take a chance that I can catch King Guargin outside," says Bird as everyman looks on intently. "It is a long shot. If I do, I'm going to try to crush him with a rock. With their king dead, the army may leave."

Cap looks at the other men.

Buck nods. "It may just work; Bird looks like the silvers and may be able to get close enough to do it. I'm worried that he will be shot by us when he returns."

Bird replies, "I will have a blue cloth hidden in a basket strapped around my neck. When I drop the rock, I will flee and pull it out. Tell everyone that I am the silver with the blue cloth."

The men all agree that this may be their only hope. Fuzzy bows and leaves with Bird.

Standing in the courtyard Fuzzy hugs him and steps back. "Good luck, Bird. Try not to get killed. We all care too much for you."

Bird hops up on the wall and picks up one of the watermelon-sized rocks piled there. He places it in the basket tied around his neck so it won't be noticeable. Then he flaps with purpose and rises into the sky. Energy fills his body as he sails south. He sees the first wave of silvers below heading toward the fortress. They notice him but continue on their way.

Once he is over Blade Town, he sees a Dragoll standing before a formation of troops. It is obvious that he is addressing them.

Bird pulls out the rock and flies calmly so he doesn't draw anyone's attention. He stops flapping and sails gently, drifting closer to the ground. He holds his breath and turns toward the assembled troops. He is on course to pass directly over Guargin. The troops see him, but are not alarmed.

Guargin is consumed with his own words and has no idea that Bird is coming. Bird holds his breath, then gently releases the stone.

The troops are captivated by Guargin's ranting and don't notice the rock crashing to the ground. Before they can react, the stone crushes his right side, knocking him off his podium where he slams to the ground. He doesn't move. Several healers rush over to Guargin's limp body and place it on a tarp. They are met by more healers and they quickly lift off the ground and fly toward the cavern in the plateau.

Overwhelmed with rage, the formation scrambles into the air. Their eyes fix on Bird, and Bird's heart explodes with energy. He flies with all his might toward the fortress. When he arrives, he sees it is still under siege and grabs the blue cloth. The towers are too busy fighting for their lives to be concerned about his defense. Luckily, several of the silvers that are almost in reach of him are brought to the ground by fortress arrows, but others are closing in.

Bird cringes as one of the fortress arrows slices across his back, and the pain flashes through his body. He swerves downward, diving to the courtyard. Almost on the ground, he clinches his teeth as an arrow penetrates his tail. Then one of the silver's digs a claw into his leg. He pulls loose and lands.

The fortress archers come to his defense, and with help from the crossbow hidden in the courtyard wall, the dragons close to Bird are shot to the ground. Flames leap by his sides as he painfully limps into the basement. Robin shrieks when she sees that he has gashes and an arrow protruding. He whispers for her to be calm. "None of these wounds are lethal. Grab the arrow and pull with all your might. Don't stop until it is out of my body. She gives the arrow a yank and Bird faints.

<>

The sound of battle grows to a roar as the first wave is joined by the second wave. Men are forced to abandon their crossbows and shoot through the opening in the tower floors trying to stop the dragons from destroying the weapons. Archers continue to shoot from the slots in the courtyard and outside walls as dragons come close.

Mason's side of the fortress has one last crossbow firing feverishly at the enemy. Four silvers dive from high above the tower at once, and all land with a thud, surrounding the men. The trap door is blocked by dead archers. Only one archer manages to jump to Mason's courtyard before the rest are incinerated. The trolls pull the dead archers off the door and open it. They are met with arrows from below. Many of them die, but more keep coming until a heap of bodies is piled up at the bottom of the stairs.

The trolls come relentlessly until finally they begin hopping to the floor and firing inside the wall; killing the men who were shooting from the wall slots. A battle of knives and spears erupts between trolls and men. The floor is soaked in slippery red blood and bodies are strewn about.

The silvers on top of Mason's unprotected tower tear apart the crossbow and, stone by stone, begin dismantling the tower. Fuzzy and six blue dragons rush to Mason's inner wall and incinerate the trolls in the hall. But the dragons on top continue to pull the tower apart. Blues, women, and men frantically carry stones to fill the bottom of the stairwell and stop the silvers from entering the fortress.

Mason and several of his men run into his courtyard and attempt to stop the destruction. Fuzzy watches through one of the slots as they kill the trolls in the yard. When the men begin slaying the dragons on top of the tower, they venture close enough for the dragons to toss stones at them. One of the stones cracks Mason in the head. He falls to the ground.

Fuzzy runs into the courtyard and fearlessly rushes into the falling stones to pull the wounded men to safety. He grabs Mason and drags him back into the hallway. The men, blue dragons, and women finish sealing the fallen tower passage except for a slit across the top where archers can defend the hall.

The attack ceases and the silvers retreat. The encounter is the costliest of the siege.

Fuzzy picks up Mason and carries him to the clinic. As he lays him down, Mason reaches up, holding the dragon claw he has kept since he visited the ghost camp.

"I know this belongs to your den. Please take it. Fighting by your side, I have grown to realize you were only protecting your family. I once intended to inflict great sorrow on all of you in revenge for the death of my hunting party, but your true nature is obvious. You and Lester are honorable creatures. I am sure it didn't take long for you to figure out that I was responsible for the sorrow caused to your den by my hunters. Please tell your den I am sorry for what I did."

Mason squints painfully and gasps. "Protect my wife and children and the survivors from Water Town," he whispers as his eyes glass over and his head tilts to one side.

A painful lump sticks in Cap's throat. "The fortress has lost a powerful fighting man," he says as his heart aches.

<>

Fuzzy and Lester return to their lair with long faces and teary eyes. Fuzzy hides the dragon claw before he enters. "It will be taken to the cremation pit later," he says.

Lester nods in agreement, then calls the den. When everyone is close, he speaks.

"We have lost Mason. He was a great fighter. He asks for our forgiveness for things he did in the past and we granted him that. He died an honorable man."

The den is quiet and ponders his words.

Fuzzy walks to Bird's side. He is lying on his grass matt with Robin by his side. Bird tries to smile, but groans in spite of himself. The den feels his emotions stirring.

"Lester and I wonder why you risked your life to do this."

"I wanted to make your den proud of me. I hoped they would accept me as a member. I need to know without any doubt that I will fly eternally in the heavens with you and your ancestors like Gus."

The den is deeply moved. They circle around Bird and Robin. They raise and touch wings in a circle around them and bow their heads. Fuzzy raises his head first.

"Bird, the members of this den did not ask me if you could become one of us. They came forward and did this out of love and respect for you. I can assure you that they are so fond of you that you didn't have to risk your life to be accepted."

Bird's eyes light up and he tries to stand so he can bow, but Robin stops him and bows in his behalf.

<>

Deeply troubled, Adrian flies to the cavern in the plateau. When he enters, the healers usher him to Guargin's side. Guargin's right horn is torn loose and his head is swollen. The healers have wrapped bandages across his shoulder. Adrian is quiet and listens to Guargin's shallow breathing.

He looks at the healers. "Will he recover?"

They hesitate. Adrian waits. He looks into one of the healer's eyes. "What do you think?!"

The healer shakes his head.

Adrian looks into the eyes of another, and the healer gestures the same, as do the rest as they are pressed to give an opinion.

Adrian wrinkles his lips and nods. Thank you. I hope he doesn't suffer long.

<>

As a new day dawns over what was once Blade Town, Adrian smiles. He is the next in line to be king of Dragonthal, and now he holds the scepter in his hand. He has no desire to make the fortress a summer palace. The scoundrels are all that is keeping him from returning to Dragonthal as king, where he intends to enjoy his good fortune.

He marches into the street and steps up on a makeshift throne that has been prepared for him. It is built of wood and stone and rises to where he can look down on his remaining army.

"Good morning soldiers. Would you like to finish off these scoundrels and go back to your happy life in Dragonthal?"

"Yaheee," the tired army cheers.

"I am now King of Dragonthal. We will end this today. No more attacks in waves. We are going to smother the fortress and tear it down stone by stone. We will kill the scoundrels one by one."

"Yaheee," rings out again.

When Adrian realizes they are cheering for him, he shivers with joy. A rush of euphoria courses through his veins. He is still soaking in the pleasure when he notices a dragon flying in from the north. The troll rider is holding up a green flag. A wave of joy sweeps over him again as three hundred fresh dragons and trolls land. His army dances and shouts, "Yaheee, Yaheee, Yaheee!"

King Adrian raises his scepter and they quiet. "Victory is meant for us today; this is a sign!"

Dagon major Rye walks before King Adrian and bows. "Raise your head Rye. You are now commander of this army and we will celebrate victory tonight. Lead this massive attack and end this madness."

Adrian raises his scepter and the attack begins.

<>

As morning breaks, the southern tower guard rings his bell and stands speechless. The approaching army darkens the sky. Cap swallows hard and tears stream as he slides into his crossbow seat.

His heart beats faster with every passing second, and his mind is wrapped around Ren and Janice. His arrow is set and he glances toward Jackson. He looks back at the mass of soldiers when he sees Jackson begin to aim at them. They will only have a minute to use their crossbows.

The sound of Jackson's arrow exploding into flight sparks even more energy and he releases his first shot. Dragons spin. Trolls scream. Ten attacking soldiers are dead before Cap dodges the first troll arrow. Arrows ping all around hitting stones and wood on the tower roof. It sounds like a hail storm, and Cap shoots two more times before dragons are close enough to blast their fire.

With no choice, he jumps down the stairs behind the archers that stood by his side. They latch the door and watch their crossbow being blast with endless flames. The archers shoot through the holes in the floor near what's left of the crossbow. Dragons pile up amidst the flames that surround it, and occasionally one of them explodes; throwing embers through the small slots in the floor. Archers cry as these embers burn their arms and faces, but they refuse to give up. Cap has moved to a slot in the wall where he can shoot any troll that tries to pry open the trap door that the archers are protecting. He sets an arrow and watches for a shot.

Every time he sees an enemy on top of the wall near the tower, he shoots. Dead trolls and dragons are lying along the top of the wall from tower to tower. The flames are out at the crossbows and the silvers begin rocking the weapon, without regard for arrows flying past them.

When one silver collapses, he is thrown over the wall and another continues to pull the weapon apart. They intend to tear the floor out from under the crossbows and open the tower stairwells so they can send trolls charging down the steps.

The men who were on top of the wall retreated before the first arrows flew. They are in the interior hallways, and every slot is manned. Every man, woman, and child old enough to fight has taken up arms. The only crossbows still working are the two that are hidden.

Dozens of silvers charge into the courtyard trying to stop the crossbow in the wall. With hundreds of arrows flying from the surrounding walls, a pile of troll and dragon bodies is too high for the crossbow to shoot. The crossbow behind the gate to the dragon lair is still hidden.

The tower weapons are ripped loose and thrown to the ground. Desperate men at the base of the stairwells take turns firing at invading trolls. The dragons are pulling stones from the towers to open the floors.

Sweat and blood streams from many frightened and injured men, women, and children. Some weep, seeing that the battle is hopeless.

Jackson takes bows and quivers to everyone in the kitchen. Then, hurrying to the clinic, he gives bows to the women frantically helping the wounded. Mothers holding their children cry, but gladly take spears and knives to defend their home to the end. They will be the last to fall.

Cap grabs his brother by the shoulder. "Let's try to take back one of the towers so we can see if the dragons are any less in number."

Several men grab spears, clubs, and knives. The brothers have hatchets in each of their hands. The men at the base of the stairwell fire quick volleys, move aside, and watch as the brave men stab and slice their way into the daylight.

Blood drips everywhere around the steps, and a trickle flows from one corner where the door was once hinged. The crossbowman in the courtyard sees what they are trying to do and aims up toward the tower. He swings the weapon to the left and shoots arrows that plunge into silvers around Cap and Jackson. Cap glances at the sky and gasps in desperation. Hundreds and hundreds of silvers are still swarming the fortress.

He glances toward the northern sky. A fast-moving grey cloud is approaching. Fighting and ducking behind what's left of the tower wall, he peeks again. Puzzled and risking his life, Cap sees two blues diving full speed toward the courtyard. He smacks the bell with his long knife and screams for everyone to help the two blue dragons land unharmed.

Fuzzy hears him screaming and dashes to the gates that protect the entrance to the dragon lair. Lear lands, spraying fire on dragons and trolls near the gate. Leon is behind him and grapples a troll aiming at Lear and flings him over the wall and sprays fire while he lands. Fuzzy pushes the gate open and they dash inside. Gasping to catch their breath, Lear screams.

"Get everyone into the depths of the basement! Abandon the slots and run!"

Men who hear Lear's warning dash to the halls running as fast as they can screaming as they run.

"Drop your weapons and run to the basement!"

Without regard for arrows or silver dragons, Fuzzy pushes the gate open and flies to the tower beside Cap. Arrows strike his wings and his legs, but he lands next to Cap.

"Get all your men under cover of stones. Everyone not under stone will die."

Cap shakes his head, dodges and arrow, but bangs on the bell and screams.

"Dive into the basement! Forget about the enemy!" Fuzzy sails toward the basement entrance, slams it shut and drops the log lock into place, then dashes deep into the dragon lair.

Cap continues screaming the warning as he runs to the basement! Men throw down their weapons and dash to the depths of the fortress.

The enemy soldiers look at each other in dismay.

Then, high above them shrieking erupts.

The grey cloud turns black and thousands of fire bats are above them. Their flocks are so thick that they block the sun. A few bright red-orange glowing streaks hurl toward the earth far to the south and then from the north. The Dragnothal army is caught in the middle. Soon streaks of flame reach the fortress and They whistle as they zip toward the ground. Enemy soldiers jerk their heads skyward and scream. Dragons consumed in flames are twirling helplessly, and blazing trolls drop like shooting stars with a trail of smoke following their decent.

Suddenly the heavens burst into light brighter than any sunny day, and globs of glowing fire bat saliva falls like rain on the fortress and far out into the forest. Chaos sweeps across the army and many try to dash away, but they all scream and shriek as they crash to the ground where they squirm and melt in blue and yellow flames. Many dragons burst into small mushroom clouds as they explode, and the sound is deafening.

Deep in the fortress everyone shivers in fear. Muffled sobs come from huddled groups holding to each other as the sound of agony and explosions outside increase. They cling to each other in the darkness and flinch at the sound of every explosion. The air around them begins to smell of brimstone and burnt flesh. It grows so warm that they are sweating.

Cap uses his knife to pick mortar out of a spot in the wall above the ground. He peeks out. Not one of Dragonthal's soldiers is left alive. Flames leap and dance as wooden objects and flesh is incinerated. The fire spit oozes down the walls, reaching the ground. The courtyard is white hot, melting away the pile of bodies. He fills the hole with dirt and tamps it back. All they can do is wait for the inferno to burn out. Many worry when the smoke grows unbearable and forces them to move toward the kitchen. Families find each other by candlelight, and many fear the roof will collapse or drip sticky drops of fire on them.

Leon speaks strongly and confidently. His words echo in the confined area. Frightened men and dragons listen intently.

"My fellow family and den members, take heart! The fire bats are on our side! We will survive. When the fires burn out, you will have no reason to be fearful. Many friendships came together to build this fortress and our friendship with the fire bats will help us win this war, and I believe it is over."

Many faces brighten in hopes that he is right.

<>

The fires languish. At midevening, the men and dragons emerge into the sunlight. The wooden gates are gone and the courtyard is black. Only a few chalky bones remain where piles of trolls and dragons once lay.

As time passes, Fuzzy and his den help clean up and repair the stones that the silvers tore loose. They enjoy being with the residents of the fortress and everyone's mood brightens. The blues bring fresh fish for everyone from time to time. Jim and the Murray blacksmiths have one crossbow repaired and another is almost ready to assemble.

Several weeks after the fire, Fuzzy meets with Cap and Jackson.

"My den is anxious to return to their cavern. Thank you for everything. None of us would be alive had it not been for the friendship we forged as children." Jackson tears up and Fuzzy opens his wings and they hug. Cap steps to Fuzzy after Jackson steps back.

"If this war is not finished, we must join forces again," says Cap.

The dragons are in the courtyard ready to leave. The men cheer from the walls. The dragons bow and then take to the air. They fly peacefully toward their cavern. The younger ones are far ahead.

Suddenly Fuzzy sees smoke coming from the cavern entrance. Many of the younger dragons are fleeing in panic. Some have arrows in their bodies.

Anger boils in Fuzzy's veins as he charges toward the cavern. Before he can reach the ledge, a group of silvers sail head-on into the returning den. He opens his claws and slams into one. The troll flips off. Fuzzy's claws tear the silver from front to rear. It shrieks and plunges. The dragon behind it is caught off guard when Fuzzy appears from nowhere and with claws still extended, he rips it open too. Fuzzy lands on the ledge and roars when he sees several young blues lying on the floor.

An arrow zips past his head. Before the troll can re-nock, Fuzzy charges and rips him apart. Fuzzy glances toward his den fighting for their lives. He sees Bird turn up as his silver scales help him escape but he only flies higher so he can dive back, knocking trolls off as he grapples unsuspecting silvers. His claws rip in rage and silvers spin lifeless all around him.

A sound in the cavern grabs Fuzzy's attention and he enters, then stops. He senses someone. A troll charges with a spear. Fuzzy flaps his wings wildly blowing leaves and dirt into the troll's eyes, blinding it. Fuzzy grabs the troll with his front claws and slams him to the floor.

Movement deeper in the cavern beckons Fuzzy to move further in. Suddenly a large creature flies toward the ledge. Fuzzy ducks.

When the light of day hits the creature, Fuzzy sees that it is Guargin.

Fuzzy's anger explodes and he tears after him. Guargin lands suddenly, side steps, and with his dragon-like claws he shreads one of Fuzzy's wings. Fuzzy hits the floor, spinning toward the cliff's ledge. His claws grab and scratch at the floor. Unable to latch onto a stone, he drops over the side.

His claws are all that is holding him on the edge. With a wing that is useless he has little hope as he dangles high above the base of the plateau. Guargin smiles and walks toward him. Guargin stomps Fuzzy's claws and laughs. He hops into the air to stomp them harder.

The moment he is off the ground, Fuzzy blasts fire into his face. Guargin grabs his eyes and lands next to Fuzzy's claws. In a burst of energy, Fuzzy pulls with all his might and grapples one of Guargin's legs. He sinks his claws in as deeply as he possibly can.

Guargin tumbles backward, pulling Fuzzy up over the ledge. Guargin curses as he tears Fuzzy's claws loose and stands. With red eyes and rage boiling in his veins, he leaps for Fuzzy, who locks his teeth into one of Guargin's wings. He jerks and twist wildly ripping it to pieces as he pushes Guargin toward the cliff. Guargin tumbles to the edge but manages to stand teetering on the rim. He wobbles back and forth for a second, then growls with pain as he tries to flap his useless wings. He curses as he slowly tilts over, shrieking until he hits the ground far below.

<>

Weeks later, little dragons are scampering across the plateau in play, and the den is ready to grow again.

<>

Many of the fortress families leave.

Cap, Jackson, and their families choose to stay at the fortress. They dream of the possibility of finding time to enjoy their lives, be in love, and have more children. They plan to help them happily grow up while taking care of their aging parents who once had that same dream.

About The Author

Fred J. Hoyle was born in 1947 in Lawndale NC a little town nestled in the foothills of the South Mountains. With few neighbors close by, he explored the woods and creeks surrounding his family's farm. Energetic imagination provided adventure as he played in his own little wilderness. A love and respect for the beauty and reality of nature evolved. At age eleven his family moved to Shelby where he attended Shelby High School and Gardner Webb College. While in college he discovered that Business administration was a gateway to a different kind of adventure. Fred fell in love with a wonderful woman and they raised three amazing children.

Working as a team with his father and two brothers he enjoyed the plumbing industry and has been president of the family's business for thirty years. Now with more free time, he has discovered that with pen in hand he can once again use his imagination to venture into natures beautiful woods. Endless dangers and triumphs wait to be savored. He is the author of *Dragons of Venosta*, and *Notions In Rhyme*. They are available at Amazon books.